Damaged
and the
Beast

Bijou Hunter

ERICA,
Happy reading!
Bijou Hunter
xoxo

Dedication

To Freckles, Tigger, Pooh, Roo, and Owl

To Aunt Sherry – Jodi's inspiration

To Eusebia, Wanda, Jennifer, Katelyn, Arnie,
and the rest of the awesome Denny's crew

Damaged Series

Damaged and the Knight (July 2013)

Damaged and the Cobra (Sept 2013)

Damaged and the Outlaw (Nov 2013)

Damaged and the Dragon (Winter 2014)

Chapter One

Standing at the bus station, I put on a brave face. As Dad fished around in the back of the car for the suitcase, my younger sister Tawny didn't even pretend to be brave. Crying her eyes out in the backseat, she had said goodbye to me already and I didn't think she could do it again. Finally, Dad handed me the suitcase he stole from tourists in Florida.

"Mom is waiting for you," he said quickly. "She'll pick you up."

"I know."

Glancing around, Dad was nervous about being seen. People with guns were looking for him and only some of them carried badges. He planned to run like always, but this time I wasn't coming. After five years as his copilot, I was on my own. Tawny wasn't so lucky.

"Be careful," Dad said, hugging me. "Be smart and safe. Don't take risks. Don't trust people. Just keep your head down and get that education and become a teacher. Be the good kid so I can drop off Tawny with you when she's eighteen. I want my girls to have everything, but you've got to want it too."

"I do," I said, nuzzling my face against his jacket. The smell of leather comforting in its familiarity.

"Your grandma says Mom is doing better. Aunt Tess says it too and Aunt Tess lies like crap. If your mom was still messed up, we'd know. You'll be okay."

"What if Mom stops doing better?"

Dad released me then took my face in his rough hands. "You ditch the bitch. Take care of you and only you. Get what you need out of that place and don't worry about anyone else."

"Okay."

Stepping back, Dad looked around again, his brown eyes surveying the bus station. Tawny and I got our eye color from Dad. Our brown hair too, though Tawny's was lighter and nearly blonde in the summer. Just thinking about my sister sobbing behind her hair nearly brought me to tears. Dad gave me a half smile and stepped back again.

"You're ready for this, Farah. You've been ready for a while, but now is the time for you to make a great life for yourself."

I made no attempt to wax poetic about how great my life had been with him. He wouldn't buy the lie and I didn't think I could sell it anyway. Tired after the drive and crying in the backseat with Tawny, I wanted to say goodbye and yank off that Band-Aid.

"I love you, Dad."

"Right back at you," he said, heading to the car.

As the urge to cry rushed up inside me, I said nothing. My lips trembled and my eyes felt hot, but I angrily blinked away the tears. In a few minutes, I would be on the bus with strangers. A girl alone crying like a fool, I had victim written all over me. In the past, I'd taken advantage of girls like that and I had no intention of allowing it to happen to me.

Carrying my suitcase and backpack towards the bus, I heard the engine of the compact start. I considered looking back and maybe waving goodbye to my sister and best friend. My dad might give me one last confident grin. Instead, I refused to look as they drove away.

Soon, my suitcase was in the cargo bay and I was in my seat. I gave my "screw you" face to anyone who dared make eye contact. Spotting a few possible threats, I sat against the window with my feet on the second seat, knees in the air, and a blade waiting for anyone who thought to mess with me.

The next few hours moved slowly as I hid under my long hair, allowing me to watch for trouble. I wore a jacket even in the heat because my body had a weird way of looking sexier than it was. With my fat lips and small C-cup sized breasts, I endured a lot of leering from the wrong kind of men. Yet, those few possible criminal-types on the bus got the message that I wasn't someone to approach. Ignoring me, they eyed a middle-aged woman closer to the front. My mind was so focused on avoiding danger that I never let myself worry over what happened when the bus reached my destination.

I was moving to a college town where I would find a job, go to school, and hopefully make friends. I didn't think about any of this until the bus pulled into a station one town over from Ellsberg.

Having not seen my mother in five years, I only spoke to her a few times over the last two. I didn't know how she felt about me moving in with her. I wasn't really consulted about the school and its reputation. One day, I was told if I wanted to attend college that my grandma would help me go to New Hampton College in Ellsberg, Kentucky. While it was never actually stated I couldn't go anywhere else, it was implied. I wanted to go to college so badly I didn't care where the school was or its merits.

Dad didn't want me to leave. Knowing he didn't trust my mother, I also suspected he feared without him around I would get into trouble. Yet mostly, he would miss the money I brought in from my waitressing jobs. My dad loved me, but he wasn't the kind of man to let sentimentality get in the way of paying his debts. Dad had a lot of debts.

The bus finally arrived at my stop and I collected my suitcase then looked around for Mom. I saw a few women talking, but they weren't waiting for anyone. Had Mom forgotten? Did she have second thoughts about me staying with her?

When a woman waved at someone behind me, I glanced around, but saw no one. Was she waving at me? Had my mom sent a friend in her place? Walking towards her cautiously, I was nearly on top of the woman before realizing she was my mother.

Still pretty in a rough way, Amy Jones Smith had bleached blonde hair and mossy green eyes. She looked worn down in a way I didn't remember and I was surprised by how small she appeared. I had last seen her when I was thirteen, not really a child any longer. Yet, this woman looked like a tiny older version of the woman I never said goodbye to.

Based on her expression, I hurt her feelings by not recognizing her.

"I wasn't sure because of the glare from the sun."

Amy nodded, but I doubted she was convinced. Even if I was an above decent liar, my mom spent most of her life as a grifter and had a talent for seeing through people's bullshit.

"Do you have everything?" she asked.

I had chosen that exact moment to lean in for a hug. An awkward few seconds passed while we embraced. Pulling away, I gave her a smile. "I have everything. Thanks."

Nodding, she turned away and walked towards her car. It was an older sedan, but in good shape. I knew from my grandma how Amy worked in an office. She was clean now too. Living a respectable life was how Grandma Delta put it. I'd heard a hint of mockery in her tone, but was never sure why.

My grandma looked the role of a church-going, God-fearing, tax-paying citizen. In reality, I knew she spent most of her twenties running cons until scoring a mark that paid off big enough for her to retire. Now, she looked the part of anyone's grandma, but she had the devil in her heart. She told me this last part during a visit when I smiled at her for too long.

Amy asked if I was hungry and I said yes. These were the only words we exchanged between the bus station and the restaurant near her apartment complex. Our apartment complex, I reminded myself. It had been a long time since I lived in a real home and I was excited to see my room. First, we sat in a small Mexican restaurant and avoided talking.

"How do you like your job?" I finally asked.

"Boss is a nag. Otherwise, it's fine."

"My interview for the job at Denny's is scheduled for tomorrow."

Amy nodded. "Don't expect much tipping around here. College kids are cheap."

For the next few minutes, I picked at my food while growing irritated by how Amy hadn't asked about Tawny. She didn't ask about me either, but I felt worse for Tawny. My sister was stuck with Dad who was hiding from criminals again. She didn't know where they would sleep, when they would eat, and how long before they were running somewhere else.

"Tawny's gotten tall," I said when Amy remained silent through the whole meal.

"Brian is tall."

Nodding, I waited for her to take the hint and ask about her daughter. Why didn't she show any interest in the child she hadn't seen in five years? Instead, my mother fell silent and never spoke again until we were at the apartment.

The dark brown apartment complex was spread out over a large area. There were two stories with our apartment on the bottom floor. Once inside, I found a small living room opened up to an even smaller kitchen. Down a little hallway were two bedrooms and one bath. One of the bedrooms was mine, holding a sparsely covered bed and a white dresser.

"I bought you a bed with the money your grandma sent. It's used, but clean. I also got you a dresser. That's new. Your grandma sent fifty dollars for you to use for school or clothes."

Smiling at my mom, I suspected Grandma sent more than fifty. Likely a hundred with the assumption Amy would steal half of it. Grandma was good at sending money for school, holidays, and birthdays. As a grandmother, it was her job to do certain things and she took these responsibilities seriously. If we visited and someone commented on our ratty clothes, she would spend money to buy us new ones. Yet, if we were homeless and living in a car, it didn't fall on her list of responsibilities so she wouldn't even pay for a motel room. My grandma was weird that way.

"I go to work at eight and come home around four. I have my meetings and friends I spend time with. I won't be around a lot. I can't chauffeur you around, but there's a bus stop down the street. I got you a bus schedule and you can make it to school with two busses. Three for work. The schedule is on your dresser."

"Thanks, Mom."

We shared another awkward embrace then she sighed. "I'll need your rent by the first of next month. Your grandma told me you would pay half, so I moved into a bigger apartment."

"I'll have it by then. I'm sure I'll get the job. If not that one, I'll find another one."

Amy stepped back, wanting to leave. "Get settled in."

Once she disappeared into the kitchen, I shut the door and looked over my room. It wasn't tiny, but it was tight. Yet, it was all mine.

I'd never had my own room before and it felt amazing standing there knowing I didn't have to share. Grinning while I unpacked, I couldn't believe I was finally on my way to becoming the new Farah. An educated woman, instead of simply the daughter of losers. I loved my parents, but they made bad choices. I intended to do the opposite for the next four years so I could get my dream job and build the life I had always wanted.

As the sun set and I ate a bag of chips because there wasn't much food in the refrigerator, my excitement faded a little. As much promise as this move brought, I was scared. I'd never slept in a room on my own, let alone been away from Tawny for so long. Mostly, I had never been normal, no matter how much I pretended. Here I could be anyone, but I wasn't sure if I was strong or smart enough to fool anyone.

Chapter Two

I started the next day by acing my interview and landing the Denny's job. Next, I visited the local bank to make sure I could access my nest egg. Three years of tips were saved for school and I'd need them to pay for school supplies. Waitressing would pay for the every day stuff and I was thrilled how everything was falling into place so easily.

After a bus ride from the bank, I reached New Hampton College. It was prettier than in the online pictures. Very green with large old trees lining the pathways. It felt fancy even if it was a small college providing mostly for the local kids. I nearly hyperventilated a few times out of sheer excitement. In third grade, I vowed to go to college and become a teacher. Now, I was on my way.

I handed in all of my paperwork, spoke with a counselor, and checked over my schedule. Ready to start on Monday, I explored the campus. Even though I was alone in this place, I felt a sense of true accomplishment. The thrill was so great that I didn't let myself get bothered by how most students were with family and friends. They all had support systems and I had Amy who barely acknowledged me that morning.

Locating my classes so I wouldn't get lost on Monday, I sized up the other girls and how they were dressed. I wanted to fit in and was happy to see how casual everyone appeared. Most girls wore their hair down even on the hot late summer day, so I planned to do the same. My dream was to disappear into the crowd and never stand out.

The final stop was to pick up food at a grocery store near the apartment. My mom's tastes were particular and she claimed to eat at work a lot. Buying as much food as I could carry back to the apartment, I settled in with a sandwich in front of the television.

When my mom arrived, she stared at me. "Did you get the job?"

Realizing she was nervous about paying for the apartment by herself, I nodded quickly.

Amy smiled with relief. "It was nice to upgrade to this place. Your grandma paid for the deposit and first month, but a two bedroom is pricey on my salary."

"The Denny's manager has me working evenings Monday through Thursday. I'll probably pick up extra shifts too. I can get you the money for next month's rent."

My mom gave me the first genuine smile since I arrived. While I wanted to think she was proud of me or happy I was there, I suspected she just liked having a nicer apartment. After fiddling around in the kitchen and making approving noises about how I'd bought my own food, she disappeared into her bedroom. A half hour later, she reappeared, ready to go out.

Aunt Tess swore Mom was clean. She also claimed Mom didn't date. While I didn't think my mom was heading to a date in the outfit she was wearing, Amy was definitely going somewhere nicer than McDonalds.

I didn't ask though. I was afraid to know too much and realize my mom and I would never be close. I really hoped with enough time we could slowly rebuild our relationship. Even doubting this hope would come true, I still held onto it.

Mom stared at me for a minute. When I finally met her gaze, she smiled awkwardly. "You're not one to hold grudges, right?"

"No, Mom."

This was the closest we would come to discussing the reason she hadn't been my mother for five years. That was how it worked in my family. We didn't discuss things. We didn't hash them out. A pretty impressive fact for two families filled with drunks and addicts.

My mother's side of the family was known as sullen drunks. Moody, broody, silent. We didn't talk about ugly things. We swept them under the rug where they could fester. On my dad's side, we were known as violent, yet incoherent drunks. We screamed about football teams or who voted for what crappy president. We never discussed ugly stuff even while screaming over the most minor infractions.

When Cousin Jesse got caught touching a little boy, we didn't talk about it. When Cousin Jesse disappeared, we acted like he'd taken off for a job. We all knew the little boy's family disappeared him, but there was no reason to hash out such ugliness.

When Cousin Pauline killed herself, we pretended she accidentally took too much pain medicine. Could happen to anyone. Nothing to see there. Move on.

When bad things happened like five years ago, no one talked about it. No therapy, no discussion, no hashing out the ugly. We ignored the problem and it went away. My dad took us away from our mom and ditched her in a shithole in Oklahoma because they just didn't click anymore. Nothing more to the story.

I knew my mom was thinking about the ugly thing from five years ago, but she didn't say anything and neither did I. Even if I wanted to shrug off the Smith/Jones ways, I wasn't sharing with my mom. What the hell could she say anyway besides sorry? Then, she'd turn it around and claim I attacked her for merely mentioning how fucked up she had once been.

"Have a good night," Amy muttered, no longer nervous.

After she left, I dug my phone out of my backpack. While Dad had given me a cell phone, my grandma was the one who put more minutes on the account. I hoped to make enough money soon so I could call Tawny all the time. For now, I was just happy to hear her voice.

Tawny answered on the second ring. Her voice was quiet and I suspected she was scared.

"Are you alright?" I asked immediately.

"Yes. I'm alone in a motel though. I'm not used to being alone."

"Where's Dad?"

"I don't know."

We said nothing for a few seconds then my sister spoke. "I miss you."

"I miss you too."

What's it like there?"

"It's pretty. Lots of trees."

"Is Mom's apartment small?"

"It's okay."

"Do you have your own room?"

"Yeah."

"Is it really small?"

Realizing what Tawny was asking, I said, "We can share a bed. Do you want to come here?"

"I don't know. Dad says Mom can't handle having you and me there. He says she doesn't want a minor in the house."

"I've got a job already. Once I have enough money, you can live with me."

Tawny exhaled and I knew she was ready to cry. She and I had spent every day of her life together. When Mom and Dad had their drama, Tawny and I were together. When we didn't know where the family would sleep at night or if we'd eat dinner, Tawny and I were together. When that ugly thing happened five years ago, Tawny and I were the only ones who knew how ugly it really was because we'd been together. Always together, but not anymore.

"Soon, Tawny," I whispered, afraid to speak too loudly and jinx us. "I'll save as much money as I can and get my own place. It's pretty here and you'll like it."

"I miss you," she said again.

"I miss you too."

Silence lingered because without the ability to talk about the bad stuff, we really didn't have anything to talk about. Dad was likely tense with keeping himself hidden. Since Tawny hated school and had dropped out at sixteen, she was around a lot for him to dump crap on. She couldn't tell me about this though because talking about her loneliness and fear was ugly. Ugly meant silence, so we sat there for a while.

"We're in the same time zone so maybe we can watch TV together?" I suggested.

"It'll be expensive."

"I'll get a good phone plan and call you every night I'm not working."

"I miss you," she said, crying now. "I miss you."

Long after we cried ourselves into silence and hung up, I thought about those three words. I imagined Tawny in a dump of a motel in the middle of nowhere. Scared and alone, she had no one to talk to or trust.

Even though I was building something new in this place, nothing would be good until my sister was with me.

Chapter Three

The first day of classes was overwhelming. Though I tried making friends and people were nice, it was all superficial stuff. I noticed many of the students already knew each other. They had friends and didn't really need new ones. Before I started feeling too left out, I remembered it was the first day.

The classes at New Hampton tended to be small with desks like in high school. The more popular classes were held in large rooms. My English Lit class was in one of those big halls and I had trouble getting comfortable with so many people whispering around me. Most of my classes were smaller though and I knew with time I would get used to the crowded ones too.

I also liked how a majority of instructors preferred to be addressed by their first names. With such a relaxed atmosphere, I was finally getting the hang of things by the time I reached my final class.

Spanish was my elective for the semester. My plan was to become fluent and make myself a better job candidate for the many areas where non-English speakers lived. Plus, I had always wanted to learn another language. I'd started taking Spanish in high school, but we moved and it wasn't offered at the new school. This year with no unexpected moves, I would finally learn Spanish. Just one of the many things on my checklist for my new life.

Running late after taking a wrong turn, I entered the room to find it mostly full. The class was heavy on girls who appeared to be lifelong friends. I found a spot towards the front where only the nerds sat including a very cute guy to my right. Glancing casually towards him, I pretended I was looking around, just so I could check him out. Tall, lean, maybe a little on the underdeveloped side, I suspected he wasn't really done growing yet. His brown hair fell over his eyes and I caught him swiping it away a few times. I wasn't sure his eye color until he caught me looking and the green-eyed Sweetie Pie grinned. Giving him a quick smile, I hid behind my hair and pretended to look for a pen.

Behind me, the BFFs laughed and talked about their summer fun. I was used to being on the outs with the cliques. Most of the time, the girls had been friends since kindergarten. As the motel kid who wouldn't be around by the end of the year, no one wanted to be my best friend. In the end, it had always been just me and Tawny. The girls behind me were tanned, pretty, and confident. Pack mentality gave girls power and I wished to find a pack of my own in college.

The back of the class was the spot for the cool and/or indifferent people. One guy was already asleep while two chairs down was a stoner who kept looking behind him like someone was lurking. Three chairs down from the stoner was Hot Guy.

This was a guy who got what he wanted. When I pretended to tie my shoes, I noticed the girls grinning at him. He gave them a wink like he wasn't in the mood right then, but later he would allow one of them the privilege of servicing his needs. His dark blond hair was all kinds of messy like maybe he just came from being serviced and didn't have time to clean up afterwards. I couldn't see his eyes, but they were dark and menacing. Even when he winked and gave the girls a grin, Hot Guy looked ready to hit someone upside the head for blocking his view or simply breathing.

He was exactly the kind of guy that scared the shit out of me. Wide shouldered, muscular, casually scary, tattooed, and stunning, he made my stomach flip with both lust and terror. If he ever showed interest in me, I'd both shiver with excitement and likely wet my pants.

While Hot Guy was bad news, Sweetie Pie was more my style. He looked like the kind of guy I could marry. We would have a few kids, a dog, maybe a cat. We would spend our weekends fixing up the house and yard while the kids played. We'd have a routine of a family meal out on Saturdays or when kids ate free. Then, after the kids wore themselves out from a day of play, hubby and I would enjoy dull un-terrifying sex and fall asleep thinking about our taxes.

Anyone else would find this fantasy lame, but I always got myself a little hot and bothered imagining it. A safe calm life with a man who loved me in a safe calm way. Sweetie Pie would never gamble away our Christmas money. He would never forget my birthday, though he might need hinting to remember our anniversary. He was the kind of guy who wanted to buy himself lots of electronic toys, but wouldn't if the kids might lose out on getting something great from Santa.

Sweetie Pie was boring to some, but he was the kind of guy who wouldn't make me cry or fear his moods. He was the kind of guy I would enjoy in my life as a teacher, mom, and wife. I was a good person and deserved to have my simple dreams come true.

Once class began, the Spanish instructor Manuel kept smiling at me. He smiled at everyone in the front rows and pretty much ignored the rest of the class who likely wasn't paying attention anyway. The girls whispered about upcoming parties, stoner still thought someone lurked behind him, sleepy guy barely stirred during class, and Hot Guy looked bored whenever I casually glanced back at him.

No, Manuel knew his audience and he worked hard to make Sweetie Pie, me, and a dark skinned girl feel comfortable. He helped us try a few phrases and didn't get mad when I would only whisper my answers.

After class as I walked the half mile to the bus stop, I suspected Spanish would be my favorite class. The day went exactly how I imagined.

Feeling special to attend New Hampton, I smiled about how my future wasn't so unattainable anymore.

So many nights I cried in the dark and worried my dream was the stupid fantasy of a poor kid hoping for too much. Now, my dreams were coming true and I'd help them come true for Tawny too. Life wouldn't be a mess of dependency and violence like with my parents. Life would be safe, dull, and happy.

Still thinking about my future, I dressed in the Denny's uniform. I'd taken my first waitressing job when I was twelve. Using fake documents, I worked at an I-HOP in Colorado. Dad had trouble getting legit jobs after he served time for theft back in his early twenties. Mom had trouble getting legit jobs when she showed up for interviews stoned. I never minded working for the family in the summers, but spending six hours working at night on top of schoolwork made me resentful.

Having plenty of good references from the jobs I worked legally, I never found it difficult to get a shot from managers. They said I had an honest face. A lot of girls in my high schools didn't want to waitress. They frowned at the uniforms and thought it was cooler to work at the GAP or somewhere else in the mall. Discounts for overpriced clothes were useless to me. I wanted cash and made it with my tips. Without those tips, I wouldn't be in college now. That was the deal Dad made with me when I was fifteen and complained about being the only one working. His first solution was to get Tawny a job, but she looked her age and most places checked her documents too closely.

His second solution was to take my pay, but let me keep the tips for college. I opened an account in a bank and deposited my tips every day because keeping cash around a motel wasn't safe. At the very least, I had to worry about my dad's sticky fingers.

Unsure how a Denny's in a college town would rate when it came to tips, I made five dollars in two hours. Half was from college kids who tipped me in quarters. The other half was from an older regular who bossed me around a lot and was really particular. Smiling a lot, I gave him what he wanted and he tipped me well. Especially considering he only spent four dollars.

The other waitresses were broken down between the pros and the college brats. I overheard one of the pros tell another one how I was the newest nightshift brat. They made wagers on how lazy I'd be. The other nightshift brat was exactly what they were expecting. Piper frequently disappeared into the bathroom where I suspected she was texting. I kept an eye on her tables, cleaned whenever I wasn't working, and constantly checked the ketchup levels in the bottles.

Despite what my family thought, kissing ass wasn't shameful. While Dad's side of the family would especially disagree, most of them couldn't keep a job for more than a few months. In fact, they were often fired for texting in the bathroom.

At eight, while I was wiping the other brat's empty tables, Hot Guy from Spanish class showed up alone. He carried a bag and strolled to a corner table to plug in his laptop. The spot he chose was Piper's table, but I didn't know where she was so I decided to help out. I also wanted to talk to Hot Guy, but that was neither here nor there.

"Root beer," he said, without looking up.

Maybe it was best if he didn't look at me. Wearing a black shapeless shirt and slacks with ugly shoes, I barely wore makeup, having wiped off much of it when I sweated on the walk to work.

Even if I had looked good, I probably didn't want Hot Guy checking me out. He was the type of guy who didn't do white picket fences or potlucks. He probably didn't know who Paula Deen was and wouldn't want kids until he was too old to bang jailbait any longer. Not much older than me, he had a long way to go before settling down out of necessity and playing tattooed family man with his twenty year old biker babe wife named Bambi.

"Do you know what you'd like?" I asked, torn between wanting him to pay attention to me and hoping he never looked up.

The moment I leaned fully into hoping he wouldn't notice me, Hot Guy looked up. His brown eyes were such a rich color that I felt both drawn and repelled by their darkness. No matter the beauty of those eyes, his gaze possessed the kind of directness common with assholes. They didn't look at people, but through them. They knew extensive eye contact was viewed as a challenge and they didn't give a shit. They enjoyed making people uncomfortable and watching girls squirm.

"Spanish class," he said.

"Yes," was my super awesome response.

"Freshman."

"Yep."

Love match for sure. Nothing says romantic connection like grunting out a conversation.

"Do you know what you'd like?" I asked again.

"Yeah," he said, still staring at me like I was up to no good and he didn't dare look away. "The Slamburger with seasoned fries. I'll want dessert so don't bring the check yet."

"How do you want your egg?"

"Medium," he said then gestured behind me. "That girl is hating on you."

Turning, I saw Piper glaring at me. She twisted her lips and cracked her neck like she might throw a punch.

"That's my table," she muttered.

"You were on break and he wanted to sit here."

"Fine, well, I'm back."

Unsure if Piper wanted to look at Hot Guy or knew he was a good tipper, I stepped back when she grabbed my pad and glanced over the order.

"Medium?" she clarified, giving him a big pretty smile.

"Nope. I'm keeping this one," Hot Guy said, pointing to me. "We have Spanish together. Don't we, baby?"

"Yes, but…"

"No, but," he said, losing the hint of a smile. "If you want, I can talk to the manager and see if he gives a shit what this one here thinks?"

Piper and I stared at Hot Guy then she handed me the notepad and walked away.

"I'll put this in for you."

"I don't get a thank you?"

Nodding, I forced a smile. "Thank you."

"Ah, that's right. You don't know how well I tip hot girls from my Spanish class. Once you do, your thank you will sound more sincere."

"Sorry."

A smile lit up his face. "You look like you're gonna cry."

"You're being scary. I assumed you wanted me to cry."

Smile widening, he leaned back in the booth. "Please, don't go crying on my account."

"Let me put this in for you."

Hot Guy nodded and I felt him watching me until I disappeared into the kitchen. The urge to sneak into the restroom and fix up my appearance was unbelievably strong. Then, I reminded myself how I shouldn't flirt with tattoo boy. Even if I wanted to hook up with a guy who wouldn't acknowledge me as soon as he was finished, Hot Guy had already seen me looking like crap. No need to clean myself up and give away how I'd nicknamed him Hot Guy.

In the kitchen, Piper walked over and whispered, "Guys like him hit their girlfriends. Good luck with that."

Taking the food and a refill, I walked towards his table and noticed him typing. With his tight shirt riding up over his muscles, I could see what looked like an eagle tattoo on one arm and maybe an angel on the other. When I reached two tables away, his gaze locked onto me like a laser, heating my skin.

"I hope the egg is okay."

Grinning, he lifted the bun then shrugged. "I have a cousin named Farah," he said and I gave him a tight smile. "She's a bitch."

My smile turned weird. While I couldn't see it, I sensed the smile had gone wrong because he was creeping me out.

"I'll be back to check on you in a few minutes."

"Don't you want to know my name?" he asked, grabbing the ketchup bottle without taking his eyes off of me.

"Sure. What's your name?"

"You don't sound genuinely interested."

"I'm not begging if that's what you're waiting for."

Throwing his head back, he let out a deep rolling laugh before focusing his dark gaze on me again.

"I wouldn't mind seeing you beg," he said then added when I frowned, "Cooper."

"Anyone ever call you Coop the Poop or Poopy Coopy?" I asked, messing with him because his iron stare made me nervous.

"No," he muttered.

"Not to your face anyway."

A smile lifted the corner of his mouth and his gaze softened. "No, not to my face."

"I guess there are benefits to being scary."

Cooper gave me a half smile, but his eyes watched me in a weird way now. Like he was memorizing me for possible dissection later. Or maybe he just wanted to fuck me. Whatever his reasons, he was creeping me out again.

"I'll be back."

For the next twenty minutes, I checked on Cooper a few times, cleaned tables, and filled salt shakers. No matter where I went in the restaurant, I felt Cooper watching me. I told myself I was crazy, but then I'd glance over to find him watching me. Not even casually either. Leaning back in his booth, he ignored the laptop and his few remaining fries.

"Are you ready for dessert?" I finally asked.

"Where are you from?"

"I moved around a lot growing up."

"Family in the military?"

"No."

"Why New Hampton?"

"I'm a big fan of pork. Are you ready for dessert?"

Cooper smiled softly, but his gaze was dark. "Did you bring a boyfriend with you to town?"

"No," I said, stepping back. "I'm focused on school."

Nodding, Cooper gave me a little grin. "Message received," he muttered, taking the dessert menu and glancing at it. "For now anyway."

"I can come back."

"Nope. Bring me the brownie. Extra whip cream."

"I don't think that comes with whip cream."

"It does now. Extra whip cream in fact."

Walking to the kitchen, I prepared the brownie. Flirting with Cooper was a mistake. Based on his laptop and the big black Harley sitting in the parking lot, he had money. Based on his looks, he was tripping over girls. Based on the way he teased me, I was on his radar as a possible hookup. I'd already messed up. Yet, if I became cold, he might make things rough for me at work. I wasn't sure why, but I sensed he really would talk to the manager about a girl who pissed him off. I didn't want to be that girl.

"Here you go. Extra whipped cream."

Cooper shut off his laptop and closed it. "Do you do your schoolwork before your shift?"

"I'll get to it after I finish here."

Frowning, he glanced around. "You work every night?"

"Not weekends and most Fridays. The girls with seniority get those shifts." When his frown darkened, I continued, "Better tips."

Nodding, Cooper took his spoon and cut open the brownie. "You going to any parties this weekend?"

"Doubtful. I have schoolwork and I haven't finished unpacking."

"Where do you live?" he asked, mixing up the brownie and ice cream.

"With my mom."

Cooper glanced up from his food and squinted like I was messing with him. "Your mom moved here with you?"

"No, she lived here. It's why I came to New Hampton. Well, that and the pork thing."

"Yeah, the pork thing," he murmured, grinning. "You didn't live with your mom before?"

"No," I said quietly, hoping my tone shut him up.

"Why not?"

Sighing, I realized Cooper was either tone deaf or didn't care. I sensed it was the latter.

"My parents split up and I went with my dad."

"Is your mom fucked up or something?"

Stepping back, I frowned at him. "I should let you eat."

Cooper looked up from his brownie. "Don't be like that. I'm just curious. Most times when parents split up, the kids go with the mom. You didn't so I figured your mom must be messed up."

"No offense, but that's personal and I don't really know you."

"Do you want to know me?" he asked, his gaze too direct. "I can tell you whatever you want to know. Not here at work with your boss and that bitch watching, but this weekend I could show you around."

"That's nice, but I plan to stay in this weekend."

"Uh-huh," he said, twisting his lips in a grumpy way. "You can go check on ketchup bottles if you want, Farah. I'll eat my food silently and give you a break."

Standing awkwardly, I knew he was angry and I wasn't sure how to handle it. When he ignored me, I walked away. Though I considered checking the ketchup bottles, I stopped myself. Around nine, a drunk guy showed up and had me and Piper stand next to each other before choosing the waitress he wanted. Luckily for me, he picked Piper.

"Close one," Cooper said, standing up as I came for his plate.

"Tell me about it."

At six four, Cooper stood a solid foot over me, strong and intimidating. When I noticed a hint of whip cream on his chin, I wiped it away without thinking. His gaze locked onto mine and I could feel him breathing faster.

Cooper looked so dark, yet appealing as he stared down at me. I could imagine riding on the back of his motorcycle, my arms wrapped around his hard stomach, the air rushing through my hair as we had fun somewhere. Yes, I could imagine having fun with him and then walking away as he sexed up the next girl. College was about easy sexy fun and Cooper had easy sexy fun written all over his beautiful face.

"Sorry if I seemed cranky earlier," I said, aiming for casual. "Moving here has been stressful, but maybe when things settle, you might still want to show me around."

Cooper studied my face then ran his thumb across my bottom lip as if ridding me of a smudge of something. I wiped my mouth quickly.

"Did I have something on my face?" I asked, thinking I was such a dork to walk around with crap on me. Yeah, mirrors existed for a reason, dummy.

"No," he said, stepping back and surveying me. "I might sit next to you in class next week. If I do, try not to be a bitch about it."

Confident flirting officially over, I lowered my gaze and nodded. I'd never dated in high school and clearly had no idea what I was doing. Better to keep my head down, work hard, and forget about guys for a while. Well, Sweetie Pie might still be an option. I suspected he used the word bitch less frequently than Cooper.

Leaning forward, Cooper grinned. "I'm teasing you. Don't be so serious. Life is short and all that."

"Why next week and not tomorrow?" I asked before realizing I was an idiot to show more interest.

"I'm done with school for the week. I never attend Friday classes either."

"Good for you."

Still grinning, Cooper reached out and rubbed my bottom lip again. He held my gaze, almost daring me to complain.

"Thanks for the extra whip cream," he said, grabbing his bag and walking to the front with his check.

After watching him go, I realized he left me a twenty dollar tip. With anyone else, I might have thought it was an accident and taken the money to them. With Tattooed Moneybags, I figured he was showing off.

Slipping the twenty into my pocket, I figured Cooper could show off, tease, call me bitch, and whatever else he wanted as long as he kept leaving big tips.

Chapter Four

On Tuesday, I made my first friend. Her name was Skye Goldstein and she simply plopped down in the chair next to me in Government class. Suddenly, she was my friend and I nearly cried in relief because the negative part of my brain was convinced I would go four years without anyone to talk to.

Skye was pretty, but not so pretty that I felt ugly in her presence. She was one of those 50/50 girls. Fifty percent was pure luck in the genetic lottery. The other fifty was maintenance. Short, curvy, blonde, and tanned, she looked like a tiny Barbie doll. While Skye never said she came from money, she lived in the dorms and I knew that wasn't cheap. Plus, she mentioned having a single room and that really wasn't cheap.

The best thing about Skye was how she talked a lot. Like she sat down, started talking, and kept talking whenever the instructor wasn't speaking. I never had to say anything to keep her interested. Instead, I sat back and listened as she explained why she was at New Hampton.

"My parents know people here and they didn't want me going anywhere without someone spying on me," Skye said, giving me a wink.

After we left class, I planned to eat a P&J on the quad before my last classes. Skye frowned at the sandwich then shook her head.

"I might have a peanut allergy. I don't know for sure, but you shouldn't eat that around me." Frowning at my sandwich, I assumed I would eat alone like I planned. Skye brushed hair away from her sweaty neck and continued, "I'm really into tacos right now. There's a truck by the senior hall entrance. Let's pig out."

There were times in my life when I lost the ability to react. I froze in the moment, unable to respond. This moment was the first one since arriving in Ellsberg. I didn't have money to blow on a taco, let alone on however many tacos were necessary to pig out. While I wanted to have fun like everyone else, I also needed to save up enough money for Tawny to join me. If we were both working and careful, we could schedule pig out days. Yet, I sensed Skye didn't consider the prices of food.

"I didn't bring cash," I finally said after she stared at me, maybe realizing my brain was broken.

"Oh, I've got it."

Even wanting to say yes, I felt guilty for pretending. "I can't pay you back," I blurted out as she tugged me towards the senior hall. "I have a lot of expenses for school and my parents aren't helping me much."

Skye snorted. "Parents are so lame sometimes. Mine think I'm a virgin. They also think I'd never drink beer because I'm a calorie freak. No one is that much of a calorie freak."

Frowning as she yanked me along, I wondered about the calories in those tacos. Skye must have sensed my concerns because she snorted again.

"The freshman fifteen is expected. If we don't pack on a little weight, people will think we're full of ourselves. Those girls over there," she said, waving her hand in the direction of a bevy of pretty sorority girls. "They're obsessed with being hot. Unfortunately, while you can snag a man by being hot, you can't keep him. To keep them, you have to be confident and I am. I'm just confident enough to pack on a few pounds from eating tacos. I'm a keeper while those bitches are bang and hang girls."

"Bang and hang?"

"Guys bang them then hang up when the girl calls for a second date."

"So they're sluts?" I asked, not sure what the hell Skye was talking about anymore.

"Oh, we're all sluts. I'm liberated enough to cut me some notches on my bedpost, if you catch my drift? No, those girls are shallow. It's why they have to work in a flock. They can't go solo because their fragile egos can't handle the stress. I have no patience for weak girls."

As we neared the food truck, I worried I was weak. I worked hard and didn't take the easy path. Did this make me strong? Maybe, but I wasn't confident like Skye. I wasn't even as confident as the bang and hang girls.

"You seem down to earth," Skye announced, again just knowing what I was thinking. "I feel like you won't stab me in the back by stealing my guy or talking shit about me. You're solid and I need a solid friend in college. I visited here growing up, but I don't have a gang of girls who will be there when I need to work off my freshman fifteen. You think those bang and hang girls would say no to a hot guy I wanted? Hell no. They'd jump him in a minute. You wouldn't. You've got good character. I know about that stuff because of my mom. She's sort of a stuck-up bitch, but she knows how to see through people and tell who has good character. Like, you'd look at my mom and think she's a plastic ho who doesn't care about anything except appearances and showing off. She acts like those Housewives bitches, but my mom is solid inside. Her friends are too, but she had to work to find good friends because sometimes the outside isn't what's on the inside. See, I might seem shallow because I'm so well put together, but I just dress nice for guys. I don't do it so I can be better than you or those whores over there. I do it to attract my prey."

At first, I didn't understand Skye was kidding, but then she winked at me and I laughed.

"I like that you're quiet because I need someone who won't interrupt. I was an only child for most of my life and had two nannies at all times. Two. I'm used to being the center of the universe. I'm my daddy's angel and the pride of my mom's loins. I can't have people interrupting me because I take it personally."

Nodding, I looked over the menu, searching for the cheapest items.

"If you're a good friend to me, Farah," she said, suddenly serious, "I'll be a good friend to you. I'm loyal. I've been tight with my best friend in Memphis since second grade. Even when she got fat then slutty then went klepto, I supported her. Eventually, she settled down and got skinny, only slept with guys who respected her, and stopped stealing everyone's shit. She's solid now, but she decided not to go to college because she needs to find herself first. I sure hope that doesn't mean she'll become a fat slutty klepto again."

Like I said, Skye loved to talk. After she forced me to eat what she was eating, we sat at a picnic table. Skye then talked and talked even while stuffing her face. She never made a mess though. A lifetime of talking nonstop gave her mad skills.

Even though I barely spoke the whole time, I realized Skye was the perfect friend. She took all of the pressure off me. I didn't have to keep the conversation going. I didn't have to decide where we would eat or what I would order. I didn't need to worry over cost because she liked spending her parents' money. Skye claimed her parents expected her to waste their money and would be insulted if she didn't.

By the time we split up to head to our separate afternoon classes, Skye decided she would chauffeur me to and from work. She didn't like her new best friend taking busses at night. After all, what would people think? Besides, Skye hadn't finished telling me her life story. Apparently, it was very long so she needed the extra time to get me up to speed.

Chapter Five

Skye proved to be a reliable chauffeur until Friday when something mysterious happened to her car. That was how she phrased it. *Something mysterious.* She couldn't pick me up from work, so I would have to find another way home.

Cooper sat in the back booth, reading a book he clearly hated with a passion. Occasionally, he smacked the book onto the table then glared at it hatefully. Finally, he returned to reading. I had to admit he looked especially hot in the white tee clinging to his strong chest. The contrast of such bright white against his tanned flesh made it difficult not to stare, let alone drool.

While I considered asking Cooper for a ride, I immediately shot down the idea. I had successfully avoided him most of the week, seeing him only on Wednesday night when he came in for dinner. He did a lot of his intense staring and made a few comments squarely in the domain of inappropriate. He also left me another twenty dollar tip. We had created a nice relationship so far, but owing him anything was a mistake.

Cooper just wanted to fuck me. Though I wasn't wholly against the idea of sex with him, I sensed he would be rough and I'd cry. My tears would likely piss him off and he would find a way to punish me. Maybe I assumed too much, but I didn't want to take the chance of ruining my life in Ellsberg.

Giving up on asking him or anyone else, I walked outside towards the bus stop. As I hurried through the parking lot, I realized Cooper never left after paying his bill. When I glanced in the direction where he was talking on the phone, I found him staring at me. I turned away quickly, not needing any trouble. Hearing his motorcycle rev, I prayed he was heading to a party and would speed right past me.

"Need a ride?" Cooper asked, pulling over as I walked down the street. "Let me rephrase that. I know you need a ride, but are you desperate enough to take one from me?"

"Why desperate?"

"You tell me. You act like I'm a stalkey douche you can't shake loose."

Uh, I wasn't touching that statement.

"My ride cancelled and it'd be a pain to take three busses."

"Is that your way of saying you're desperate enough?"

Studying his grin and the rumbling hog, I figured the ride would take five minutes tops. As for owing him, maybe I could buy him dessert or take notes for him at school. You know, repay him with something besides my body.

"Yes, please," I said softly, hoping he didn't get mean or creepy during the ride.

"I don't know," Cooper said, scratching at his stubbled cheek. "I have somewhere I need to go first. Are you in a patient mood or will you give me crap?"

"I'll give you crap so you should take me home first."

"Nope."

Grinning, I tried to seem friendly, but not too friendly. "Will another please get me what I want?"

"No, not a please, but I can think of other things that'll make your case."

"Never mind," I said, walking away. "You're busy."

Cooper grunted. "Oh, lord, here we go. Now, I'm the one fucking begging. Just get on, will ya?"

"You'll take me home first before your thing?"

"Sure."

Walking over to him, I gingerly slid onto the back of the motorcycle. The feel of it between my legs returned my mind to the ugly incident never to be discussed.

"Hold on," he warned, glancing back at me. "If you fall off, it'll hurt like a muther."

Remembering nearly the same words said five years ago, I held on like my life depended on it. My first ride on a Harley had been terrifying, but I reminded myself I was safe this time. Cooper was a pain, but he was mostly bark and no bite. The rich ones usually were.

"I live at…"

"I know, but we're making a detour. I think I mentioned that."

"Wait…"

Glancing back at me, Cooper grinned then revved the engine on his Harley. Quickly into traffic, we headed away from my apartment complex. Irritated, I held on tightly and closed my eyes.

To avoid freaking out, I imagined myself home for the evening. After a hot shower, I could watch something relaxing on TV while catching up with schoolwork. Maybe my mom would join me. We wouldn't talk, but simply enjoy each others' company. If Mom wasn't available and she likely wouldn't be, I could call Tawny. All I had to do was get through Cooper's detour and his attempts to fuck me.

Without knowing the town well, I wasn't sure where we were when Cooper pulled over and parked his bike. I lifted my head from his back and removed my hands from the feel of his beating heart. Stumbling off the Harley, I wasn't selling cool and I didn't even want to know what my hair looked like. As for Cooper, he had the kind of windblown hair that made him hotter.

"What is this place?" I asked, hearing loud country music coming from a house with people flowing in and out of the front door. "A party?"

Turning to him with a look of horror, I felt stupid dressed in my Denny's uniform while all of the girls I could see wore shorts and skirts. Hell, I was barely wearing makeup after a long shift.

"Yeah, you've looked better," Cooper said, grinning as he flicked my loose hair out of my eyes. "A lot better."

"Thanks," I said embarrassed because I had hoped to make a good impression on people. I even wanted to find a boyfriend eventually and really embrace college life. Now, I would be that Denny's girl who showed up at a kegger wearing grandma shoes. Better yet, if they really wanted to mess with me, students could show up at the restaurant so I could serve them. Just wonderful.

Crossing my arms, I glared at Cooper. "I'll wait outside."

"Hell no. It's not safe," he said, completely full of shit. "Especially not with you dressed like you are. Too provocative. You'll need to stay close to me so I can protect you."

Ignoring his grin, I shrugged. "Whatever. I'm waiting here."

Cooper kept smiling like my embarrassment was the funniest shit ever. Then, he stepped closer and leaned over my shoulder to look at my hair. When I felt him messing with my ponytail, I considered complaining, but thought better of it. He pulled my ponytail loose then handed me the band.

"Much better. Shake it out and you'll look sexy as hell. That is unless anyone looks from the neck down."

"I'm waiting here."

"Don't be grouchy. It's not an attractive look on you," he said, stepping behind me and bumping me forward until we reached the front door.

Running my fingers through my hair, I tried to look my best as I entered my first college party.

"Much better," Cooper whispered in my ear as he passed me. "I've got to deal with Crazy Fuck Tuck. Don't wander off."

Standing in the packed living room, I watched Cooper join a blond guy who was pounding on a bathroom door and screaming for someone named Maddy. The man turned to Cooper and made his case in a very dramatic, slightly maudlin way.

"My brothers are idiots," a voice said from behind me.

Turning, I found Bailey Johansson from my Algebra class. The blonde, blue-eyed beauty wore a skimpy tank top and short shorts. Showing a lot of skin, Bailey had the lean tanned body to pull it off without looking desperate.

"Cooper is your brother?"

"I call him Crapface and the other one Fuckwad. They'll come to those names too, so feel free to give them a whirl," she said, laughing in a way that announced she was drunk. "Oh, no," she added, grabbing me. "Don't call them that. They'll freak out and you'll end up in a shallow grave and I'll feel guilty. I already feel bad enough for running over that possum yesterday."

"I won't say anything."

"Awesome. Hey, since you're cool and fucking my brother and everything, let's hang out after class on Monday, kay? I'm going to find me a cute boy and hump his leg before my brothers cock-block me. Distract Coop, will ya? He's a boob man so flash the girls to give me a head start."

Before I could respond, Bailey hurried off even though Cooper and Fuckwad weren't aware of her presence. They were busy talking heatedly, though mostly Fuckwad talked. Finally, Cooper opened the door to the bathroom and a blonde girl raced past them and out the front door. When Fuckwad yelled her name, Cooper pulled his brother into another room.

"Hey," a guy said, handing me a beer. When his friend whispered to him, the first guy shrugged. "Have a good night."

Suddenly, I enjoyed a wide berth as I took the beer to a couch and watched a football game with the sound down. My dad loved sports, mostly gambling on them. Tawny, Dad, and I would spend our Sundays watching games and cheering for whoever he bet on. If he lost too many games, he left and we wondered if he'd ever come back? If he won a lot of games, we went to dinner at Burger King.

"I'm Nick," said the guy taking up the spot next to me on the couch. "We have a few classes together."

Sweetie Pie had a name and a great smile he was focusing on me. I tried not to show how excited I was by this turn of events or how much I wished I was dressed better.

"Farah. We're in Spanish, English Lit, and Algebra together," I said, pretty much giving away how I was hot for him. Clearly, I was in one of my more brilliant moods.

Nick gave me a big ass smile announcing he was hot for me too so we were even.

"Are you from this area originally?" he asked.

"No."

"Me either. I grew up the state over, but my grandfather came here. Since he's the only one in my family to go to college, I figured I'd follow in his footsteps."

"I came here because my mom lives in town. I'm planning to be a teacher."

Nick's big green eyes lit up. "No way. Me too. Primary?"

"Yeah, I'd like the younger ones, but no kindergarten. They cry too easily. Or I might try high school math because they make better money. I haven't really decided."

Nick grinned. "I like fourth and fifth graders. You know, when the BO kicks in."

Laughing now, I realized this was what casual flirting felt like. I'd never really flirted, always shutting things down with guys out of fear and convenience. The thing I did with Cooper was about lust and paranoia. While I liked looking at him, I was also terrified he would get me fired if I didn't play nice.

23

"My friends told me not to talk to you," Nick said. "They said you came with Cooper Johansson and he's scary."

"He is scary, but he's just giving me a ride home."

"So you two aren't dating?"

"If I was on a date, would I be dressed like this?"

Studying my clothes, his gaze stopped at my shoes. Finally, he laughed. "No, probably not. Your hair looks pretty though."

Starting to thank Nick, I noticed Cooper out of the corner of my eye. He was staring at me and Nick in the dark overly focused way he sometimes watched me at the restaurant. The predator stalking his prey look was mostly focused on Nick.

Men like Cooper viewed girls as conquests and I was the newest one. Other males knew this and stayed out of the way. Nick hadn't, therefore he was a threat to be squashed.

"Cooper is watching us and he's acting weird," I said, without looking up. "I'll talk to you in class next week."

Nodding, Nick stood up and gave me a smile. "Nice to meet you, Farah."

Even with Cooper watching, I couldn't help grinning at Nick as he returned to his friends who looked ready to piss themselves.

Walking to Cooper, I asked, "Are you taking me home now?"

Cooper took the beer from my hand. "There's pizza in the kitchen. Are you hungry?"

"I'd like to go home."

"Maybe your boyfriend can take you," he said, glaring at Nick who ignored him.

"Is that your way of saying you won't take me?"

Cooper finally pulled his gaze away from Nick and focused it on me. "Who gave you this drink?"

"I don't know. Some guy."

"Your boyfriend?"

"No, some guy."

"Did you drink it?"

"I'm eighteen and it's illegal for me to drink alcohol."

Cooper laughed. "You're kidding, right?"

"No," I said, crossing my arms. "I take the law very seriously."

"Nerd."

Laughing, I tightened my arms and studied him. "Did someone mess with the drink? Like a roofie?"

"Maybe. These guys are idiots. Always fucking with stupid freshmen girls because you bitches don't know any better," Cooper said, his gaze locking onto someone behind me. I turned to find the guy who handed me the beer now standing near the door with his friends. "Should I drink this shit?" Cooper hollered at the guy. "Huh, asshole? What happens if I drink it?"

When Cooper lifted the beer to his lips, the guy looked ready to run. Only a second passed before the beer went flying and smashed against the guy's head. As he crumbled to the ground, the party fell silent except for the music.

"My sister is at this fucking party!" Cooper yelled, running at the guy's friends who ditched him and fled outside.

Standing very still, I wasn't sure what to do. I glanced around and noticed Nick watching me like he knew I was scared shitless. He gave me a tight sympathetic smile then his gaze flickered away. By the sound of fists against flesh, Cooper was beating the crap out of someone.

"You the Denny's chick?" Fuckwad asked, now standing next to me.

Glancing down at my uniform, I wondered if Fuckwad was drunk or simply stupid. "Yeah."

"He's going to fuck you. Try not to cry when he forgets your name afterwards."

With that comment, Fuckwad ran outside. Soon, the sounds of a fight intensified. Inside the house, everything returned to normal except for the guy puking on the ground from his head wound. As I walked past the asshole who tried to roofie me, I kicked him in the balls. Outside, Cooper stood next to his brother as they loomed over three bloodied guys.

"Denny's chick is getting restless," Fuckwad said.

"Shut up, Tucker," Cooper muttered while gesturing for me to follow him. "Watch Bailey and make sure these assholes didn't roofie her."

Arriving at his motorcycle, I avoided Cooper's angry glare.

"You need to be more careful," he said, studying me. "College is full of perverted shits."

"I was never going to drink it. You didn't save me from anything."

Cooper glared at me then snorted. "Denny's chick," he said, climbing on his bike. "My brother's a turd."

"No comment."

Glancing back at me as I settled on the Harley, Cooper sighed. "My sister dresses like a slut, but most of the girls at school dress that way. They act like whores, but they're not. They just like dressing up and playing sexy. These guys are losers and they come here with these ideas about the country girls being easy. When they aren't easy, they make them easy. They look down at local girls and poor chicks like you. Now that they know where you work, they'll come hanging around to make you dance like a monkey. If that happens, you tell me and I'll hunt them down and make them dance. Do you understand?"

I wrapped my arms around his waist. "We're going to my place now, right? I'm seriously tired and need to go home."

"When your makeup gets all wiped off, it's real obvious you're exhausted."

Unsure how to respond, I nodded. "Do you really know where I live?"

"I know everything. Hold on because it's getting windy."

Once the bike roared down the road, I hid my face against his back as my hands again felt his beating heart. It had been such a long week and I really needed to take a shower and veg out. In fact, I didn't even want to do schoolwork. TV time and sleep were all I craved. Maybe a little candy too.

Arriving at my apartment, Cooper not only parked, but turned off his bike. "Invite me in," he said softly while glancing around as if the place was beneath him.

"I'm not having sex with you," I said, getting off the Harley.

"Tonight? Oh, yeah, I know," he said, giving nearby voices a dark glare. "If you meant ever, we're not on the same page."

Sighing, I glanced at the walkway leading to my apartment. "My mom is probably home."

Cooper stood next to me and cracked his neck back and forth. "Don't let the tats fool you. I can do the choirboy routine. Real chivalrous crap moms love. Now, invite me in."

"How come?"

"Because I want to talk to you outside of school and Denny's."

"No sex."

Rolling his eyes, Cooper sighed. "You're so frigid. That's not healthy, you know?"

"Says who?" I asked, hitching my backpack tighter before walking towards my apartment.

"A very important doctor somewhere," Cooper said, following me. "Hell, I think there were studies that said fucking was good for your heart."

"Laughing is good for your heart too and there are no downsides to it. I think I'd rather watch a comedy."

"Fair enough, but you're missing out."

"Uh-huh. If you think you can get more attention from another girl, feel free to take off. Night's still young."

"No, I like where I'm at."

Certain he was checking out my butt, I spun around and glared at him. Cooper only smiled.

"Like I could see anything with those pants on," he said, shaking his head. "I'm not kidding either. Your ass could have fallen off on the ride over and I wouldn't be able to tell."

Staring up at Cooper, I soothed out the grumpy from my face and gave him my best Thumper eyes.

"You're so charming, Coop the Poop," I said in my sexy voice.

"I like when you do that with your eyes," he said, ignoring the rest. "The voice is hot too."

Turning around, I continued towards the apartment.

"You're welcome for the compliments, Farah. Please, stop thanking me. You're embarrassing yourself."

Sighing loudly, I realized I was screwed. Possibly in the literal sense because the lights were off in the apartment. Amy wasn't home and there would be no parental referee to keep Cooper from taking his charming compliments to fucking me in my brand new used bed.

"I don't think your mom is home," Cooper said as I unlocked the door.

"She likes to sleep in absolute darkness and silence. You should go."

"Bullshit," he said, pushing past me and finding a light. Once he lit up the room, Cooper flopped on the ugly brown couch. "Let's order a pizza."

"You just ate."

"I burned a lot of calories beating the shit out of those guys."

Standing over him, I crossed my arms and frowned. I couldn't think of a gentle way to tell him to go eat pizza at his own place.

"I don't have money for pizza. I don't know the number of a place. I need to take a shower."

Cooper glanced up at me and scowled. "Like I was going to make you pay. Take your shower and I'll get the pizza. Anything you don't like on it?"

"No."

"Anything you do like on it?"

"No."

Cooper sighed loudly like I was pissing him off. Taking my backpack into my room, I imagined him on the couch when Amy came home. I had no idea how that would play out.

After collecting suitable clothes for after my shower, I stopped in the living room and found Cooper watching bowling.

"You have shit for cable," he said, without looking at me.

"Could I please have ham on the pizza?"

Cooper glanced up at me with a soft expression. "You really like the other white meat, don't you, baby?"

Smiling, I nodded. "I'm going to clean up. If my mom comes home, please be gentle with her. She gets jumpy around new people."

"Best behavior."

Leaving Cooper to watch the crappy cable, I hid in the bathroom, locked the door, wished I could barricade it, and peeled off my work uniform. The hot water eased away a long day. After emerging from the shower looking like a drowned rat, I was ready for bed. The idea of pizza and whatever Cooper wanted didn't sound appealing, but I couldn't think of how to get him to leave.

After brushing my teeth, I stared in the mirror. Now looking like a sleepy drowned rat, I hoped he wouldn't stay long. In the living room, Cooper messed with his phone, but looked up when I entered. While I considered sitting as far from him as possible, I couldn't help admiring his full lips pursed in thought and how his dark eyes watched me. I also noticed how his muscles flexed while he shoved the phone into his pocket. Yet, he was a scary jerk who only wanted to add me to his list of hang and bang girls.

Even knowing all of that, I thought he was so beautiful. He actually looked warm and safe. Even my sleepy mind knew I was lying to myself, but I sat on the couch a few spots over from him.

"Thanks for the ride home."

Cooper leaned back a little then reached out and tugged at my size too large pink Minnie Mouse sweatshirt.

"You really wanted to put an exclamation mark on the no sex thing, huh?"

Balking, I smacked his hand. "Screw you. This is my sexiest outfit. It's frigging Minnie Mouse, Cooper. The chick exudes sex."

Grinning wider now, he played with my hair. "You can't know what I think about you."

"What does that mean? You're so mysterious that a mere mortal like me can't fathom your giant brain?"

"Sums it up pretty well," he said, twirling my hair around his fingers. "You get feisty after a shower. I'll have to remember that."

Crossing my arms over my chest, I was very aware of Bailey's comment about Cooper being a boob guy.

"So what are you studying at school?" I asked, watching the TV and not Cooper as he still played gently with a lock of my damp hair.

"Pre-law."

Glancing at him, I frowned then forced myself to stop. "You want to be a lawyer?"

"Nope. Hate lawyers. Hate laws. Hate it all, but I'm the only one of my siblings with an IQ over shitfaced so the burden is on me to be the lawyer."

"I don't get it. Tell your giant brain to dumb it down a little."

Grinning, Cooper leaned over and kissed the top of my head. "I like your shampoo."

"You're being weird."

"I'm just horny as hell. You were naked in the next room and I wanted you naked in here."

"I'm not having sex with you."

"Tonight," he said with an exasperated sigh. "You keep forgetting to end your declarations with the word 'tonight.'"

"Why do you need to be a lawyer?"

Shrugging, Cooper returned to messing with my hair. "Occasionally, people screw with my family. Why should we shell out money to shyster lawyers when we can keep the money in the family?"

While I considered asking why people would screw with his family, I decided against this line of questioning.

"How many years do you have left?"

"Huh, you haven't asked around about me at all?"

"No, why would I?"

"Really?" he asked, frowning darkly now. "I asked around about you. That's how I knew where you lived."

"I don't stalk every attractive guy I meet. Besides, I've been busy."

"What about your boyfriend from the party?" Cooper asked, his angry gaze scaring the hell out of me. "Did you stalk him?"

"He and I have a few classes together. I didn't know his name until tonight."

"You seemed pretty cozy. Maybe he's your guy and that's why you keep playing cold with me?"

"Why wouldn't I just say he was my guy?"

Cooper twisted his lips into nearly a snarl. "Maybe you like my tips too much and worry I'd ask for the bitch to be my waitress."

"You shouldn't call girls bitches."

"That chick is a bitch. I don't need to know her to know that much. The way she was looking at you the first night was like she wanted to kill you because you took her table. Who gets that pissed off about a fucking table?"

"She probably needs the tips."

"So you like everyone, huh? Is your nickname doormat?"

Crossing my arms again, I stared at the television and planned to ignore him. Except he was in my home, on my couch, and playing with my hair.

"Screw you," I said, smacking his hand away. "You're rich and people kiss your ass. Great for you, but I'm not rich and I have to get along with people. I have to take shit from people to keep my job and make enough money to go to school. So screw you for thinking I'm a doormat because I didn't punch Piper for giving me dirty looks."

Cooper very deliberately reached out and wrapped a lock of my hair around his fingers. All the while, he held my gaze, daring me to stop him.

"I get it," I said quietly. "What I want doesn't matter. I bow to your superiority. Should we just fuck now so you can forget my name like your brother said?"

"My brother is a turd. I told you that," Cooper said, taking one of my legs and resting it over his thighs. "Don't be so pissy. I just want you to admit you like me."

"Fine, I like you."

"Yeah, I know, but thanks for being honest."

Shaking my head, I grudgingly smiled. "Will the pizza be here soon?"

"Yes," he murmured, suddenly next to me. "You smell good."

Before I could speak, his lips were on mine for a brief touch. I froze for the seconds our lips met and remained a little frozen when he pulled away. As he leaned back, his lips curved into a gentle grin.

"Those lips of yours are fucking gorgeous."

Covering my mouth, I sighed. All of my life, I heard about my fat lips. As a kid, people would tease me about how my lips were big enough to eat my whole head. My grandma especially liked that one. When I got older, the comments were always sexual. I hated when people talked about my lips.

"You don't like them," he said as his fingers drifted along my calf. "Why?"

"I like them fine."

"Do guys want to do something with those lips?"

Resting my head back on the couch, I sighed. "I'm tired and you're making me feel dirty."

Cooper's hand stopped caressing my leg. When I looked at him, he stared back with an edgy expression.

"You take things too personally," he said, holding my gaze.

"When guys talk about using my mouth for stuff as if it's all I'm good for, why wouldn't I take that personally?"

"Not all you're good for, but you have sexy lips. Like when I threw the bottle, you did this thing with your lips and made a perfect little 'O' shape. It was frigging hot and I almost forgot I wanted to beat the shit out of those guys."

Nodding, I hoped he left me alone. Instead, he leaned forward and kissed me softly, licking at my lips without going any further. When he leaned back, his hand messed with the edge of my sweatpants down by the ankle.

"I'm glad you needed a ride tonight," he said, his gaze on the TV. "I'm glad I was around when you needed that ride. It worked out, but you look tired."

"I am."

Cooper ran his index finger along my face and under my chin. "I'm messing with you, but that's all it is. I'm just teasing. I know you're tired and nothing's going to happen tonight. You can rest your eyes until the pizza comes and I won't take advantage of that. I want you to want it too. Not to be an unwilling victim like with those assholes at the party. I don't take shit from girls. They offer it enthusiastically and I know you will too eventually, but you need to make me work for it first. I appreciate you keeping my seduction skills sharp."

Grinning, I rolled my eyes. "Life must be great with your giant brain and even bigger ego."

"Yeah, it's pretty amazing."

As he cupped my feet, I wished I had gotten a pedicure in the last... Well, I wished I'd thrown on a little polish. You know, just in case a pushy hot guy showed up and fondled my feet.

"Your sister is in my Algebra class," I said, resting my head against the couch again.

"Bailey's a cute kid, but don't show her up. She's insecure and turns mean when other girls get more attention. It's not personal. She's lost friends over the years for that shit, but she needs to be the center of attention. It's because she was the youngest for a long time until Sawyer came along. As the baby, Sawyer can't sneeze without my parents giggling like it's the cutest shit ever. Now, Bailey's super competitive. You should just be aware of her mental fuckups because you take things too personally."

When Cooper ran his thumb along the arch of my foot, I moaned. Smiling softly, he continued both the massage and talking about Bailey.

"Even with the competitive shit, she's a good friend. Loyal as long as she gets to be queen bee. She'll pick you up in the middle of the night, hold your hair while you puke, punch a guy for treating you bad. She's cool, but don't show up looking prettier than her or she'll claw out your eyes."

Sharing his smile, I felt my eyes drooping. "How many kids are in your family?"

"Four. Two boys then two girls. Sawyer's five and Daddy's princess. It's pretty lame how wrapped around her finger my pop is, but the kid is sharp and knows exactly how to get what she wants. She'd make a good lawyer, but likely she'll want to marry someone and spend her days wrapping her husband around her finger. She's got a talent."

Watching Cooper with my half closed eyes, I wasn't sure why I thought he was so scary? He seemed gentle and beautiful. Just the boy next door with a few tattoos. He was really a sweetheart and I read too much into his appearance.

"Do you have any siblings?" he asked, his voice sounding far away.

"A sister. Tawny. She's almost eighteen."

"Irish twins?"

Smiling, I nodded. "I miss her so much. She's my best friend, but she's gone."

One minute, I felt my eyes growing hot and wet from thinking about Tawny. The next minute, I heard knocking on the door and Cooper's voice low and distant. Opening my eyes, I realized I had fallen asleep. I checked for drool then watched him pay the delivery guy before locking the door.

When I started to stand, Cooper waved for me to stay put. "I'll get plates."

"Sorry about falling asleep."

"Yeah, you were halfway through a word then you were out. I've never seen a sober person crash like that."

"The last couple weeks have been stressful."

When Cooper returned from the kitchen, I noticed he strutted no matter what he was doing. It wasn't a showoff thing in front of guys, but the actual way he walked. Cooper set down two cans of soda then placed a slice of pizza on a plate and handed it to me.

"This one is heavy on the ham."

"Thank you," I said, taking a bite as my eyes fought to stay open. "I don't know why you want to hang out when I'm half asleep?"

Cooper leaned over and kissed me softly. His lips sucked at my bottom lip for a second before he pulled back and relaxed into the corner of the couch.

"You pout when you sleep."

"Huh?"

"Like an angry little pout," he said, demonstrating with his lips. "It's the hottest thing I've ever seen. I thought you might give me a real talking to like my old gym teacher. Man, did that bitch hate me."

"I'm sure she had her reasons."

Cooper snorted. "Of course, you'd take a stranger's side over the guy who's feeding you."

"Maybe you called her a bitch forty times."

"Yeah, there was that."

Forcing myself awake, I enjoyed the hot pizza. Never making a mess, Cooper ate three pieces without using a napkin. It was as if he willed the food into his mouth. He was the same way with his giant hamburgers. I'd never seen anything like it except with a man from Alabama who unlocked his jaws and shoved whole burgers in. Cooper didn't do anything so horrifying, but he managed to eat cleanly. One of his many skills, I assumed.

I ate a second piece as Cooper finished his fifth. When he offered me more and I declined, he took the box and shoved it into the refrigerator.

"Does your mom have a guy?" Cooper asked, returning to the couch.

"I don't think so."

"She didn't tell you?"

"We don't talk."

"Why?"

Wiping my mouth, I set the empty plate on the coffee table then glanced at him.

"Is your mom a bitch or something?" he asked when I didn't say anything.

"You think everyone is a bitch."

"Not my mom. She and I talk though. Why don't you and your mom talk?"

"We don't know each other well."

"Do you want to know her well?"

"Not really."

"Fair enough," he said, leaning over and pressing me back on the couch. "Don't panic. Kissing isn't sex. Besides, you'll be asleep in a few minutes so this is my last chance."

My first instinct was to panic. I didn't like tattooed guys lying on top of me. I also didn't want my mom walking in on us. Hell, I didn't want any of this, but I believed Cooper when he said we were only kissing. I believed he wouldn't hold me down and force me. I wasn't sure why I believed him, but I did.

His lips were soft on mine, maybe sensing my fear. He wrapped an arm under the pillow behind my head while his free hand caressed my hair and cheek. He felt warm and strong and I still believed he wouldn't take unless I offered. Yet, I was afraid to show enthusiasm and make him think I was offering. I wanted to kiss Cooper, maybe run my fingers through his hair and over his sharp jaw. I wanted to play a little, but not too much.

When I used both hands to stroke his face, he deepened the kiss. As his tongue tasted me in an agonizingly slow and thorough way, I felt the panic returning. I couldn't believe such a hungry kiss wouldn't lead to

32

sex. Would he pull his lips away and leave with the erection I felt pressed against my leg? Would I need to "help him out" first?

My hands found his strong shoulders and pressed gently, wanting him to stop. Instead, he tightened his hold and groaned as his groin nudged against me. I didn't want to freak out, but I wasn't sure how to make him stop without screaming and going feral. Before I acted, Cooper simply stopped. His kisses softened until he was tenderly pressing his lips against mine.

"The reason," he whispered, caressing my cheek and neck with his lips, "guys obsess over these lips is because they're so fucking sexy. Soft too. Little pink pillows that taste sweeter than candy." When he lifted his gaze and stared down at me, Cooper laughed. "You're pouting again."

Unsure what would happen next, I said nothing. Cooper spent another minute kissing my neck then he climbed off of me and fell back into the corner groove of the couch. Running his hands through his hair, he sighed. "You're still pouting."

"It's my lips. They always look like that."

"No, they don't," he said, grinning. "I want to see you this weekend."

"I told you I'm getting settled in and need to study."

"A quick lunch."

"You want more than lunch."

"Yeah, but you won't give me what I want so I'll settle for lunch. Think about it as a free meal, plus my wonderful company. We can take a drive and I'll show you fun places. Then, when you're settled in, we'll visit those places and I'll get what I want."

Glancing around the room as if looking for help from the walls, I didn't answer him.

"You're all alone here," he said, his voice softer now as his dark eyes studied me. "You and your mom don't get along. Your sister is gone. You're lonely and I like you. I can help make your new life easier. There's nothing wrong with having a little fun. Just working and going to school will burn you out. See how rational I am? Now, go to lunch with me."

"Just lunch."

"Yes."

"No detours."

"I promise nothing."

Shrugging, I sighed with frustration. "Okay, but not tomorrow. I have laundry to do. Sunday would be okay though."

"See how easy that was? I don't know why you fight my charms when we both know it'd be a hell of a lot easier if you just said yes to everything."

"I'll try to remember that," I told him, standing up.

"Oh, yeah, you need to sleep."

Cooper took my hand and had me walk with him the six steps to the door. Cupping my face, he kissed me softly like the sweet boy next door. Could his crap be all for show? No, only a certain kind of person could hurt another human being without blinking an eye. I didn't have it in me, but Cooper did. While those jerks at the party had a beating coming, it wasn't Nick or anyone else who pounded in their faces. I suspected by morning Cooper would struggle to even remember why his knuckles were tender. Hurting those guys had meant that little to him.

Cooper would never be the easygoing boy next door. He still kissed me gently and gave me a very warm smile like we were old friends saying goodnight. I watched him from the window as he disappeared into the night. After the motorcycle roared away, I looked around the apartment and realized everything still smelled of Cooper. The mix of sweat, soap, cologne, and pizza made me shiver.

Despite my intention to keep Cooper at arm's length, I could still feel him on my lips. Tasted him too so I didn't brush my teeth that night. I fell asleep pretending he was a nice guy who wouldn't use and discard me.

Chapter Six

Saturday was spent doing laundry and schoolwork while thinking about Cooper. By the time Sunday arrived, I fought the urge to bail on our date. Was it even a date? Should I tell him I was sick? Realizing he wouldn't believe me, I decided to roll with this new direction in my life.

Unsure what to wear for lunch, I wanted to look nice without looking too nice. Settling on jean shorts and a loose gray top, I figured any more effort might create the wrong impression. Or maybe it didn't matter. Likely, he would come around until I put out. Then, he would forget my name like his brother said.

As I waited for Cooper, Amy appeared in the living room and looked me over.

"I'm going out with a friend," I told her.

"Okay."

"I'll be back early."

"You're an adult. You don't need to tell me what you're doing."

"Oh."

Amy retrieved a coke from the refrigerator and grabbed a pack of smokes before disappearing into her room. Much like with Cooper, I didn't know what I wanted from my mother? Did I want space and freedom? Or did I want a caring woman who gave a shit if I ended up dead?

With Cooper, I found him sexy and interesting. I enjoyed his teasing, but also felt he was making fun of me. He possessed all of the power. The only control I had was the ability to say no to sex. Eventually, this power would fade and he'd move on.

It wasn't like I could decide he was great and keep him. Forever wasn't an option. Besides, he was the kind of guy who set off all of my alarms. When I saw his tattoos or those dark eyes dissecting me, I felt like I was back in the trailer during the ugly thing never to be discussed.

Logically, I knew Cooper never hurt me, but I also knew he had the power to do whatever he wanted. In this town, he apparently acted with impunity. Could beat up random guys, get me fired, and hunt down someone who messed with him or his surrogates. No fear of the law or any kind of punishment. He didn't even need to show up to class. Cooper's money and family meant Bailey's comment about dumping me in a shallow grave might happen and no one would care. My mom sure wouldn't.

Hearing Cooper's motorcycle arrive, I thought to go outside and wait, but didn't want to seem too excited. Pretending to be casual was lame too, so I grabbed my bag and opened the door to find him ready to knock.

Wearing a black tee and faded jeans clinging to his strong hips and thighs, Cooper looked hot. He also clearly skipped shaving since Friday and had thick growth, making him appear more menacing and honestly hotter.

His gaze rolled over my body before returning to my face. "You have really great legs."

"Thank you," I said, a little flustered. "Where are we going for lunch?"

Cooper waited for me to shut the door then he cupped the back of my head and leaned down to give me a soft kiss. His tongue explored my mouth for a second then he pulled back and smiled.

"You look sexy. Awake too."

"You look sexy too," I said like a dork.

Cooper laughed then stepped back and raised his arms. "What specifically do you like?"

My face had to be bright red because it was on fire as I lowered my gaze and smiled grudgingly.

"I like your shoes," I said, laughing. "That's what makes you stand out."

Laughing harder, Cooper rolled back on his heels and checked out his black boots. "Yeah, I can see that," he muttered, grinning at me. "Anything else?"

"Uh, that tattoo right there," I said, pointing to his forearm.

"The 'I shot a man in Reno just to watch him die' tattoo? Are you a big Cash fan or do you like murder?"

"Cash fan."

Cooper touched my chin then lifted my gaze to meet his. "You had no idea what it said, did you?"

"No, I just thought it was cute."

"Cute?" he said, kissing me quickly before sighing dramatically. "It's like pulling teeth with you."

Laughing behind my hand, I followed him out to his motorcycle. "I like to think I'm hot enough that I don't need to flirt well."

"Do you? Fortunately, I agree. In fact, this time when you walk in front of me and think I'm checking out your ass, it'll be true."

"Cooper, you have such a way with words. A real poet."

"Don't I know it," he said, sliding on his bike. "Hey, we're meeting my sister, brother, and his girl over at Whiskey Kirk's."

"Can I go into a bar if I'm underage?"

"Listen up, nerd," he said, glancing over his shoulder while I wrapped myself against his back. "Man, you feel good like that."

"Your huge brain is working at a wavelength I don't understand. Repeat what you just said in a dumb way so I'll understand what my being a nerd has to do with you liking this," I said, wiggling my hips against him before raking his back with my breasts.

After giving me a groan followed by a naughty grin, Cooper sighed. "I can't even remember what the hell we were talking about," he said, wrapping my arms tighter around him. "Oh, yeah, you being a nerd. So don't worry about getting carded. The Kirk in Whiskey Kirk's is my pop and he doesn't care if you get wasted. He doesn't believe in laws."

"I'm not drinking."

"Farah, you need to relax and enjoy life."

"I come from a long line of drunks and addicts, so I'm not relaxing and enjoying life if it means I become like my loser relatives."

Cooper glanced back at me and smiled. "Did you take a shower before I showed up because you're hella feisty?"

"Do they have good food at this bar?" I asked, ignoring his question.

"Burgers, hot wings, only the best bar food in Kentucky. You just keep holding on while I see if I can concentrate with your tits pushed up against me like that."

"I had them pushed up the other night and you concentrated fine."

"That's because you were wearing your uniform and I forgot you had tits. No forgetting today."

"If you ever want to be friends with them, you really need to stop calling them tits. They don't like that."

"Yes, mam," he said, laughing as he pushed off and drove away from the apartment.

Resting my cheek on his back, I really loved the feel of him. I felt happy too. Like maybe I wasn't a stranger in a new place, but a resident of this town. I wanted to be someone people recognized and waved at on the street. I'd never had that before, but I might enjoy it in Ellsberg.

Cooper pulled into the parking lot of Whiskey Kirk's and parked next to another Harley and a red SUV sporting the vanity plate, "PrncsBtch."

Once I was off the motorcycle, I fixed my hair. Cooper immediately messed it back up when he pulled me against him and glued our mouths together. His fingers slithered into my hair, caressing my scalp as his tongue and mine danced to the music playing in the parking lot. As Kid Rock serenaded us, one of Cooper's hands left my hair and cupped my butt.

"Hell, boy, you gunna fuck her right here in front of your little sis?" Tucker hollered, flicking away a cigarette. "Not that I blame you. I remember when I met Maddy and couldn't wait to get inside her."

Cooper let me go and blew upward so his hair fluttered out of his eyes. He gave me a smile then glanced at his brother.

"You're creeping out my girl," Cooper said.

"Your girl, huh?" Tucker gave me the once over. "She's sure hotter out of the Denny's getup."

"Fuck Tuck," Cooper growled. "Go leer at your girl."

"She's in the bathroom puking. Turns out that morning sickness thing is real."

I wasn't sure what my face did, but Cooper and Tucker looked at me and laughed.

"What?"

Cooper made an "O" with his lips then smiled. "You can't know how hot you look when you do that."

"His girlfriend is pregnant?"

Cooper finally removed his hand from my butt and got off the Harley. "Yep. Tucker screwed around with her pills and got her preggo so she'd stay with him."

"She was gonna stay with me anyway," Tucker announced really loudly like maybe he was deaf. "Besides, she was always saying she wanted to be a young mom so I did her a favor."

After rolling his eyes at his brother, Cooper glanced down at me and smiled. "I told you he was a turd."

"How old is she?" I asked as Cooper took my hand and walked towards the front doors.

"Nineteen. Same as Tucker. They'll be awful parents and my mom will end up raising the kid. Just a big old crash and burn waiting to happen."

"I get those shots," I said to him with my most serious expression.

Staring down at me, Cooper frowned. "I'm not planning to mess with your pills."

Smiling big, I bumped him with my hip. "Well, duh. If you won't remember my name after we do it, it's not like you'll want a kid out of it."

"Your name?"

"Yeah," Tucker said, coming up behind us. "You always forget their names."

"No, I don't. I just act like that so they'll go away."

"Much classier, bro."

No longer smiling, I kept my head down as we entered the bar. Cooper tapped my chin so I would look at him.

"That's not going to happen with you."

"Because I'm so special," I muttered, imagining how embarrassing it would be for a girl to hook up with Cooper then have him blow her off so coldly.

"Yeah, actually. I don't take girls to hang out with my family. The last girl I did that with was a chick I knew since I was a kid and my mom liked her more than I did. For me to hang with an out-of-towner at my pop's bar proves you're not like those girls."

"Did those girls know they were those girls?"

Cooper rolled his eyes slightly. "Don't get femifascist on me, okay? I'm a dick to girls, sure. I fuck them then blow them off and you know what they do next? Move on with their fucking lives and find someone else. It's not a big deal, so don't make it one."

Nodding, I gave him a little smile. "It would hurt my feelings if you did that to me, so I assumed it would hurt their feelings too. Maybe they really don't care though," I said then glanced around. "Can I have a soda?"

Cooper gave me a sweet grin. "It really would hurt your feelings, wouldn't it? Man, you're frigging adorable. Like I'm dating a little girl."

Losing my smile, I didn't respond immediately when he gave me a kiss. Soon, he wrapped me into his arms.

"You take things so damn personally. Chill out or you'll have a midlife crisis when you're twenty."

Reaching up on my tiptoes, I kissed him quickly. "I'll try, but I'm used to being high strung."

Cooper looked ready to say something then changed gears. "Do you know how to play pool?"

"I'm pretty good."

"How about cards? You good at them too?" he asked, gesturing towards a few tables where men and women played poker.

"I don't gamble."

"Of course you don't, nerd."

Stepping back, I glanced at where the card games took place. "I'm fairly sure my dad's love of cards was a reason I went to bed hungry some nights." When I looked at Cooper, he studied me in a weird way. "Can I have a burger?"

Cooper leaned down and kissed my lips so softly I barely felt him. "Baby, you can have whatever you want. Pig out to your heart's content."

"You're nicer than I thought you'd be," I said then covered my mouth in horror that I'd said the words out loud. "I'm sorry."

"What did you think I was like?"

"You seem scary. You knew that."

"Yeah," he muttered, shoving his hands into his pockets. "I'm surprised you're so weirded out by tats when you came from a less than prissy upbringing."

Saying nothing, I looked around and realized bikers, most of them over thirty, surrounded us. Freezing, I didn't know what I was waiting for, but suddenly I felt like I was in danger.

"They're just people, princess."

When I looked up at Cooper, I knew he was angry. There was no way to explain my fear without talking about things I was raised to never talk about.

"I really like you," I said weakly.

"Why?"

"Because you make me feel pretty and important and no one else does that. You also make me laugh and you're hot."

Shaking his head, Cooper sighed full of disappointment. "You're so shallow. I'm more than my natural good looks, you know? I'm smart and witty and shit too."

Laughing, I took his hand. "Don't be mad."

"I'm not. I just want you to smile and you stopped when you realized you were surrounded by my people."

"Your people?"

"Half of these guys are family to me. They ran with my pop when he was young and moved out here because he did. Some of these guys helped raise me, so I'm not cool with you thinking they're shit."

"I don't. That's not it."

"What is it then?"

Whatever my face showed Cooper, the tightness around his jaw eased and he squeezed my hand gently. Leaning down, he kissed my cheek then whispered, "You're pouting. You can't know how much I love when you do that."

"I didn't mean to offend you," I said then realized I owed him nothing. I even had enough cash to pay for my meal, though I'd need a ride home. Either way, I wouldn't fake anything just because Cooper was hot and a little scary. "I don't like bikers. They make me nervous and I won't pretend they don't."

"A little louder and we'll have bikers lining up to kick your ass. Just the lady bikers, but still."

"Won't pretend otherwise," I said, emphasizing each word.

"Fuck," he groaned, pulling me against him and stroking my hair. "Pouting along with your bitching is even hotter than the pouting alone. You can't know how horny I am right now."

Wiggling free, I walked to a pool table. When Cooper joined me, I squinted annoyed at him.

"Stop talking about your horny level. I'm not having sex with you."

"Today," he teased. "Damn, you never add the disclaimer."

"And I never will."

Leaning against the table, Cooper sighed as he stretched out his long legs. I placed my hand on his chest and his expression shifted. Those dark eyes found my face.

"I like you," I said softly. "Even if you scare me and hang out with bikers, I really like you."

Cooper didn't say anything, just watched me with a needy gaze. I was sure he was thinking about how horny he was and how pouty my lips were and a lot of other pervy things. Yet, I enjoyed when he watched me with such a gentle expression.

"Maddy might have puked her brains out," Bailey said, strolling over to us. Standing under a fan, she pulled at her bangs to keep them from floating around. "She likes Fuckwad so it's highly likely her brains didn't work anyway."

"True," Cooper said, still watching me. "Bailey, you know Farah."

"Yeah, kinda. You're in one of my classes, right?"

"Algebra."

"Yeah, I don't really plan to go to that one much. It's hard and none of the boys in class are cute."

Unsure how to respond, I just smiled and nodded. Bailey didn't seem to care. Glancing around in a grumpy way, she leaned against Cooper.

"I was supposed to meet someone here and he didn't show. Will ya kick his ass for me?"

"Sure. Now, get off me so I can play pool."

"With your girlfriend?" Bailey asked, making kissing noises while still leaning against her brother. "Tucker is ignoring me. He said I embarrass him. The name Fuckwad is a form of endearment."

"Bailey, if you don't get off me..."

"You'll what?" she asked, glaring up at him. "Whine to Mom? Poop your pants, Coop?"

"I'll tell Pop you got yourself roofied Friday night and he'll make you take a chaperone to parties."

Bailey pushed off of Cooper then looked at me. "Do you have brothers?"

"No."

"Lucky. Mine smell like feet."

With that comment, Bailey walked away and I fought the urge to laugh. Cooper watched me struggling against a grin. Sensing he was irritated, I figured having his little sister mock him on a date must be embarrassing.

"I don't think you smell like feet," I said, taking the pool stick.

Cooper grunted. "You give the best compliments. Award worthy really."

Leaning forward, I aimed the cue ball at the pyramid. Even with Cooper likely watching my ass stick out, I concentrated and hit the ball. The triangle scattered and a ball fell into a pocket.

"It's physics," I said, glancing at Cooper who grinned.

"Is your gambling dad a pool shark too?"

"No, my mom was," I muttered, turning towards him.

"And she taught you her hot moves, huh?" he said, trapping me against the table with his hips. "Bet you made a lot of grown men cry when you beat their asses. Not to mention the cash you won."

Losing my smile, I waited for Cooper to move so I could make my next shot.

"What's wrong now?"

"Nothing."

"Bad memories or you think I'm a dick?"

"I know you're a dick, but that's not why I'm grumpy. Let's not talk about my parents, okay? I shouldn't have mentioned my dad earlier."

"Why?" Cooper asked, crowding me physically and emotionally now. "Where is your dad now?"

"I don't know. He travels a lot."

"What does he do?"

"Odd jobs."

"Is he messed up like your mom?"

"Can I ask about your parents?"

"Sure. My pop is great. My mom is better than great. Anything else? No? Fine, now explain why you're pissed."

"I'm not pissed. I just don't want to talk about my parents."

"Or is it because you were a pool shark and took money from unsuspecting assholes and that makes the goody-two-shoes nerd inside you sad?"

Staring at Cooper, I realized he wouldn't back off until he heard details. "Yeah, I'm good at pool and I took money from unsuspecting assholes. Sometimes, they didn't like that. The goody-two-shoes nerd inside me doesn't want to think about the time one of those assholes cut off my ponytail and broke my nose. But if you'd like to discuss it instead of having fun, let's chat away."

Cooper stepped back. "Fuck. Your family is shit, Farah. Complete crap."

Setting the pool stick down, I glared at him. "I want to leave."

"No," he said, stepping forward and blocking me. "Hell, I figured you deserved to have a good time because you were the Denny's chick with the messed up mom. Now, I know you're the Denny's chick with two messed up parents and a reason for all of that high strung shit you pull."

Cooper leaned down and pressed his cheek against mine. "You're going to stay here and play pool. You'll eat lots of food and listen to my siblings act like idiots. I'll kiss all over you while wanting to do more than kiss. Then, I'll take you home with your stomach full and a smile on your beautiful face. That's what's going to happen here. If you can think of a reason you shouldn't have fun for the afternoon, I'm all ears."

Crossing my arms, I glanced around. "You push too hard and the way you talk makes me feel bad. I don't want to defend my parents, but you force me to by making fun of them."

"That's no excuse to lose out on a little fun with a hot guy who's got cash to pay for a big lunch."

"It's true that you're hot."

"I could flex my muscles if you need a little extra incentive."

Grinning, I glanced at his strong tanned arms. "Sure, why shouldn't I feel you up since you've got me pinned."

"Oh, don't play the victim, nerd. My crotch is right here in case you need to take a shot and make a run for it."

Laughing, I ran my fingers over the bicep he flexed for my inspection. His skin felt warm and inviting. As his body heat traveled into me, I rested my head on his chest and wrapped my arms around him.

"I know I'm doing this dating thing all wrong," I said as his arms draped me. "I should ask lots of questions and flirt, but I haven't dated a lot of guys and I don't really know how to flirt. I like you, but I'm scared you'll hurt me or make fun of me. I feel like I should get away from you except I don't really want away from you. I just don't know what I'm supposed to do or say. I'm doing everything wrong, but I'm not doing it to be mean."

Staring up at Cooper, I found the needy look from earlier and its intensity made me shiver. "I don't care if you're doing it wrong, just keep doing it. You're driving me nuts here."

Pressing his lips against mine, Cooper wrapped me tighter in his strong arms and I let myself enjoy his affections. Even with the loud music playing and bikers hanging around, I enjoyed the feel of Cooper against me. In his arms, I felt like someone new and better. After a long life of doing what I had to do to survive, I really needed to be someone new and better.

The kiss deepened to the point of sending hot waves of desire to parts of my body I really didn't want desiring anything. Soon, my nipples were tips of arousal pressed against his chest. Between my legs, I felt an unfamiliar sensation. Before I might think about what kissing Cooper like this in a public place could lead to, he eased his lips away.

"If that bastard who hurt you was here, I'd tear off his head and let my dogs eat him."

Smiling, I thought he was full of shit. "Going to jail over something that happened years ago doesn't make any sense. Even though, it's a hella sexy thing to say."

"I kill him around here and there's no jail."

"You're that special?"

Pressing his forehead against mine, Cooper smiled. "Yeah, I'm that fucking special."

"Good to know," I said, lowering my gaze.

"I'm not going to kill you," he whispered slowly like I was dumb or nuts.

"I hope not. Your sister did say you and Tucker would leave me in a shallow grave if I used her nicknames for you."

Cooper exhaled hard and glared at Bailey who sat on Tucker's lap while Maddy rested her head on the table.

"Let's play a game," he said, easing out of the embrace so only one arm hung loosely around my shoulders. "If you win, I'll give you a hundred bucks. If I win, we go back to your place and you lose the shirt and bra. Full second base action, but nothing more."

"Why would I agree to that?"

"Duh, so you could win a hundred bucks. That's like a week of tips from a twenty minute game."

Lowering my head, I thought about what he was offering. While I wouldn't mind getting closer to Cooper, I wasn't ready for such intimacy.

"Why do you assume you'll lose?" he asked, fixing the balls and setting them back in the middle of the table. "I'm good, but I'm not pool shark good. A hundred bucks is easy money and I'll just have to find another way under your shirt." Cooper inhaled and studied me as if thinking hard. "I can imagine a few ways to get that shirt off, but we'll leave them for later."

"Okay. I trust if you win you won't do more than second base. My pants remain on and you'll respect that. I trust you."

"If you say how you trust me a few more times, it'll sound like you really mean it."

Rolling my eyes, I took the stick. "Can I start?"

43

"Sure, baby. I'll just sit back here and watch you bend over."

"Making pervy comments won't distract my concentration. I'm accustomed to freaks cheating."

"Whatever you say, but I'm mostly interested in the view. A hundred bucks is shit to me."

"Must be nice," I said, caressing the stick as if it might be my buddy and help me win.

"Money makes life all kinds of nice. Oh, and the way you're fondling the stick is making me super horny here. I also suspect you're doing that on purpose. Now, who's cheating?"

Glancing back at him, I grinned. "You're in a constant state of heat. I'm not taking the blame for that."

Throwing his head back, Cooper laughed. "Fair enough."

For the next few minutes, I made great shots until a creepy biker guy stood too close and I missed. Cooper took the stick and studied the remaining balls.

"Don't cry when I beat your ass."

"Hell yeah," the biker said, laughing. "Some girls just love it rough."

Giving me a quick glance, Cooper glared at the guy. "Who the fuck are you?"

"I know your pop."

"Good for you, but if you don't back off and stop skeeving out my girl, my pop and I will be attending your funeral."

The biker opened his mouth to speak before changing his mind. Walking away, he cursed under his breath and I grinned at Cooper.

"I like when you call me your girl," I said, caressing his arm. "It makes me feel warm all over, but mainly in certain places."

"Fuck no," Cooper grumbled even while grinning big. "I'm not getting distracted."

"Big baby," I said, sitting down and crossing my arms over the prize. "Fine. I'll let you lose the old fashioned way. By sucking more than me."

Cooper made the next two shots perfectly like he was trained from birth to con idiots like me into playing against him.

"Tell ya what," he said, having missed the next shot. "Why don't we call it even and I'll give you the hundred and you give me second base?"

"So like you're paying me for sex?"

"Man, you're negative. No, Farah, it's a tie. We both get what we want."

"I want to win."

Cooper leaned down and glared at me eye-to-eye. "You just don't want me getting what I want. I think you only agreed because you figured it was a done deal that you'd win."

Standing up, I pushed past him, grabbed the pool stick, and aimed. If I missed this shot, I would likely lose and Cooper would win. I really didn't want him to win now. I didn't want him anywhere near me either. With him glaring at me, I wished I'd eaten before the game so I could ask to leave once I beat his ass.

"I want a burger," Cooper said loudly at the exact moment I hit the ball, startling me and throwing off my aim.

The final ball rolled towards the hole then stopped at the edge, having too little momentum to go inside. I'd lost! I'd fucking lost because he cheated and I never wanted him touching me. Anger rising up in my gut, I glared hard at the ball. I didn't care about the money. I just never wanted the asshole putting his hands on me.

Standing, Cooper hissed through his teeth. "So close."

Staring at the ball, I fought the tears and wiped angrily at my eyes when they fell anyway. Cooper stood next to the table and stared down at me.

"You're the prettiest girl I've ever seen and I've seen some hot chicks before," he said, crossing his arms before bumping the table with his hip. "There's just something about you that's special."

The bump was enough to knock the ball into the hole. I watched it fall then forced my wet gaze to him.

Grinning, Cooper gave me a defeated sigh. "I guess I'll have to find another way under your shirt."

"You're a jerk."

Uncrossing his arms, Cooper leaned down to kiss me. "I'm hungry. Let's order food."

As he turned towards where his siblings were seated, I grabbed his tee and pulled him to a stop.

"Thank you," I said, wishing Cooper knew how awful it would have been if he expected to touch me after he cheated. "I don't want the money."

"Screw that. You won fair and square. Besides, I don't want my girl going hungry."

Studying his face, I felt confused by how he bounced back and forth from asshole to gentle jerk. When he was sweet, I wanted him more than I'd ever wanted anything. When he was an asshole, he represented everything I hated in the world. Cooper was a complicated guy, but my feelings for him were a million times more complex.

Watching his brother and sister bicker, Cooper noticed my gaze on him. He focused his dark eyes on my face and stared hard like we were having a contest. I wasn't sure what he saw on my face this time, but he blinked and let me win.

"Are you hungry?" he asked softly. "We can go somewhere else if you don't like the food."

Breathing too fast, I wasn't sure what to do or say. He was being too sweet and I started wishing he truly wanted me to be his girl. I wanted to be close to someone so badly, but Cooper was scary. Even looking at me like he was, I saw the tension in his jaw as if waiting for someone to piss him off.

"A burger would be great," I said, sitting at the table where his brother, sister, and Maddy waited.

Cooper pulled a chair from the next table and sat an inch from me. He was watching me in the way he sometimes did at Denny's. Like he was dissecting me, breaking through all of my barriers, and soon would know my every thought. Hating being scrutinized, I avoided his gaze.

"I should give you your money," Cooper said after we ordered. "I have a feeling you might freak out soon and I don't want you storming off without your cash."

"Why would I freak out?" I whispered, hating to have everyone staring at me. "And I can't storm off when I don't know how to get home."

"I'd take you," Bailey announced. "But first, we could drop by a frat house and party." Cooper glared at his sister who grinned. "Find ourselves a few real men and get naked and..."

"Gross," Tucker muttered. "You naked is a real buzz kill. Now, Farah is someone I wouldn't mind getting naked for a little fun."

Cooper looked ready to hit his brother, but Maddy got there first. Elbowing Tucker in the jaw, she stood up and threw her drink at him.

"I'm carrying your baby and you're trying to fuck this whore!"

There were moments in my life when I wished I was invisible. Right then, I was having one of those moments.

"Baby," Tucker soothed, wiping his face, "you're so hormonal and shit."

"Don't blame this on hormones. You're a pig and I hate you for wanting to fuck someone else."

"Not fuck," Tucker said softly, hands out in a gesture of peace. "A blowjob at the most."

The next second everything exploded. Cooper punched Tucker then turned to punch another guy who did something I hadn't seen. Bailey yelled for Cooper to kill the guy then she yelled for Tucker to kill another guy. Maddy slapped Tucker on his way to the ground then she ran to the bathroom, screaming about a mother protecting her young. I didn't wait around to find out what happened next.

Bolting out of the bar, I ran without looking back. Once I reached the road, I guessed which way we'd come. Everything was so green and nondescript out by the bar, but my inner GPS screamed for me to head left. I ran up the road, ignoring honking cars speeding by.

I needed to get home behind a locked door so I would be safe. Growing up, how many fights had broken out with me and Tawny nearby? How many times had someone hit me trying to get to my parents? Tawny lost a tooth in such a fight. One minute, we were standing in a store. The next minute, Tawny took a punch to the face meant for our mom. I still thanked God we had dental insurance through the state. If not, my poor sister would be missing one of her front teeth. Like life wasn't hard enough with her teeth intact.

No more chaos of my childhood. No more madness. I needed free of my past. Free of danger and fear. The apartment I shared with my mother wasn't fancy or even all that welcoming, but it was nicer than most places

I'd lived in. It was as safe as I would find here and I hoped I was running in the right direction.

Past exhaustion with a bone dry throat, I whimpered when I heard the motorcycle. The rural highway had become residential and I believed I was close to my neighborhood. Even nearly safe, I couldn't outrun a Harley.

Cooper roared to a stop in front of me and let the bike idle. His gaze was angry and I noticed blood on his bottom lip. Standing there sweaty and thirsty, I felt glued to my spot much like I did when I got in trouble as a kid. My dad would tell me to come to him and I knew I would get the belt. Sometimes, I didn't care. The few times I turned bratty, I didn't mind a spanking because I hated our life. Those times when I hadn't really done anything wrong and my dad just wanted to punish someone, I did care about the spankings. I would stare at him and wait for someone to save me. I knew no one would, but I couldn't move towards my fate. Every time I panicked like that, Dad spanked me where I was glued to the floor.

Now, I waited for payback from a pissed Cooper. Breathing too fast and with a violent look in his eyes, he gestured with his finger for me to come closer. I didn't move though. I wasn't walking over to him so I could be punished. If he wanted to do it, he could come to me. It wasn't much of a stand, but I had learned to accept the small victories.

Cooper shut down his bike and climbed off. Watching him move towards me, I wanted to run. Just like when I was kid waiting for my spanking though, I had nowhere to go.

Before he reached me, Cooper lost the rage in his expression. His dark eyes softened and he sighed. "Why did you run?"

Shaking my head, I just wanted to go home and be safe. What if I said the wrong thing to Cooper and he hurt me? No one would care. No one would help me. He was rich and powerful. I was poor and nobody.

When I said nothing, Cooper frowned a little, looking more confused than pissed.

"Tuck needs to watch his mouth," Cooper finally said. "Pissing off his pregnant girlfriend is stupid. Like she doesn't have enough stress. Then, he's talking about you like you're a whore. Then, those fucks get in on it, making those gestures. I might not respect many chicks around here, but you and Maddy are solid," he said, stepping closer. "Why did you run?"

"I was afraid," I whispered.

"Why didn't you run into the bathroom like Maddy?"

The answer in my head wouldn't make him happy so I didn't say it. Cooper glanced around and flipped off a honking car. When his gaze returned to me, he let out a long sigh.

"Let's go eat."

"I want to go home," I whispered, terrified of his reaction.

"Why?" he muttered, no longer confused. He was just angry now.

"I'm scared and I want to go home."

"Why would you be safer at home than with me? No one fucks with me and walks away from that."

Willing myself not to cry, I looked at Cooper and he finally understood. Showing his unhappiness by saying "fuck" ten times, he glanced around like someone might help him out if he cussed enough.

"Screw this shit!" he yelled, walking back to his bike. "I don't need to chase an uptight bitch, just so she can turn around and think I'm an ass! Fuck you, Farah!"

I cried then. In the restaurant, I had really wanted Cooper to like me and had hoped much of his roughness was for show. It wasn't though and he was ditching me on the side of the road. Would he get me fired now?

"Get on," he barked, revving the engine. "Unless you want to throw another fit and walk yourself home?"

Exhausted, I needed to get home. Somehow, I was certain if I reached my apartment I would feel better. He offered me the fastest way to salvation so I climbed on behind him and wrapped my arms around his waist.

When I leaned into him, Cooper sighed in a weird way. Was he remembering how we teased each other when my arms were last wrapped around him? Was he wishing we could go back and change courses? I wished that too, even if I knew I'd still end up terrified while he hated me.

Crying the whole way home, I felt like the old Farah's bad luck had infected the new Farah's life. I still couldn't seem to find my way. I wished for the billionth time that Tawny was there with me. I would have someone to talk to. Someone who loved me. Someone I didn't have to pretend with. Someone who knew my dirty secrets.

When I got off the bike at my place, Cooper took my hand and stared at me. "I could pick you up later and take you out to dinner. Somewhere nice."

I wanted Cooper so badly. When he looked at me, I felt beautiful and special. I had never felt that way before and I craved it. Even unaccustomed to feeling special, I was familiar with fear. I desperately needed a life where I didn't worry constantly about my safety. With Cooper, I would always be one step away from danger or embarrassment though.

"I'll see you Monday in class," I said, sliding my hand slowly out of his.

Cooper's expression changed. For a painful moment, I saw regret and longing. For a painful moment, I saw the man I wished him to be. Then, his expression hardened and he exhaled loudly.

"One day, you'll be old and look back at how you pissed away fun shit. You'll wish you took chances when you were young. You'll be full of fucking regrets, but I won't."

Even as I nodded, I saw regret lurking behind his anger. He wished things had gone differently. He might have even wished to take me somewhere besides the bar. What Cooper hoped would show a sign of his genuine interest in me had turned into a clusterfuck.

"I had fun," I mumbled.

Rolling his eyes, Cooper shoved a wad of twenties into my hand. "Bullshit."

"No, some parts were really good."

Cooper held my gaze and the longing shoved aside the irritation. "I know a nice place we could have dinner. Quiet and the food is really good."

I think he knew how much I wanted to say yes, but I shook my head and stepped back. Cooper was beautiful and amazing in many ways, but he scared me and I needed to be safe. With him, I never would be.

Chapter Seven

Arriving at class before most students including Cooper, I found a seat in the front. I licked my lips and prayed there wasn't toothpaste in the corners. Just as I thought to run to the bathroom to check, Cooper appeared at the door. Clean shaven and wearing a white tee, he looked younger and softer than I remembered. He looked almost harmless, yet his dark eyes and tattoos reminded me how behind his beauty lived a raging beast who thought I was a bitch.

Cooper strutted to the seat next to mine, sat down, and pulled out a notepad. I smiled at him, but kept casual. Scribbling down the lesson on the board, I tried not to make a big deal out of Cooper joining me. Before I could speak, he leaned over and kissed my neck as if Sunday never happened and we were dating now.

"Want to copy my stellar notes?" Cooper asked, scooting his desk closer.

Glancing at his notes, I shrugged. "You do have very nice penmanship. Dainty even."

"Bitch."

"Jackass."

"Gorgeous."

"Stud."

"You have no idea."

Rolling my eyes, I noticed Nick and his friend enter. I smiled at the guys then glanced back at Cooper who watched them as if he was a lion about to snag baby gazelles.

"Do you want to sit with your boyfriend?" Cooper asked with his gaze on Nick even as his fingers caressed the nape of my neck.

"Maybe, but first I'll copy your stellar notes."

"Bitch."

"Asscrack."

"Nerd."

"Hotstuff."

"The devil disguised as an angel to trick me into losing my heart."

"That one was too long."

Cooper grinned. "Want to get something to eat after class?"

"I have to study then go to work."

"Blow off work and study with me then I can show you my stud moves," he said, wiggling his brows at me.

"I need my job."

"Not really."

"How do you know?"

"I know everything."

Rolling my eyes again, I wished the instructor would arrive. Instead, I was stuck with Cooper who focused more on Nick than anything else.

"I barely know him," I said.

"Good."

"I don't like possessive guys."

"Of course you do. After all, you like me and I'm possessive. If that guy touches you, I'm breaking his fingers."

"You're being a dick."

Cooper sighed loudly then shoved back into his chair, nearly snapping off the seat. "If you want the douche so bad, go sit over by him," he muttered, shoving my chair towards Nick.

"Fine," I said, embarrassed as I grabbed my backpack.

"No, not fine. Sit."

"You just said."

"Sit," he growled, glaring at me. "I will kick his ass if you sit by him."

"But you said," I pushed, just to annoy him since he was annoying me.

Expression shifting into horny stud, he tugged at the seam of my shirt. "I like this on you. Clingy."

Unsure what to do, I stood another few minutes. Cooper finally convinced me to sit by patting on the chair as if I was a dog he was training.

"So where do you want to eat after class?" Cooper whispered as Manuel entered.

"I'm not eating with you. I have to study and go to work."

"We can study together and you can call in sick."

"I'm ignoring you now."

Cooper spent the next forty five minutes glaring at me in the most obvious way. In fact, I was certain class ended a little early because Manuel wasn't comfortable with Cooper's behavior. Maybe he hoped to allow me to get away. Or maybe he knew who Cooper was and wanted to let the hotshot chase me.

Whatever the reason, class ended early and I walked out quickly. Cooper said nothing while walking next to me until I disappeared into a bathroom. When I exited, he was gone and I felt an odd mix of disappointment and relief.

Driving me home, Skye announced she met a guy named Tyler who was black and had shoulders like an ox. The ox thing made her giggle as if Tyler's beauty had sent Skye into heat.

As we arrived at my apartment complex, she sighed. "He's really into math. My dad is into math. A guy who is like my dad except super hot and with lips I could stare at forever. Tyler's perfect, but I think he's still into his old girlfriend at home."

"Give it time," I said, unsure about my advice skills. "It's our second week at school. Soon, he'll forget about her and only see you."

When Skye studied me, I knew my advice sucked. I had no experience giving dating suggestions and it showed. Then, Skye's brown eyes lit up and she smiled like a miracle occurred.

"Sometimes, I forget you can talk," Skye said. "Loyal and quiet, plus you give great advice. This year is turning out so perfect. First, a super awesome friend. Now, a super hot guy. College rocks."

Pleased with Skye's happiness, I said goodbye then hurried inside to study. A bag of chips later and only a part of my Spanish assignment complete, I rushed around to get in a shower before work.

Once at Denny's, I found quiet moments to work on assigned reading. I even hid in the bathroom, reading when I was supposed to be on the floor. Piper immediately mentioned my absence so I claimed diarrhea. Arnie told me about his last stomach bug and let it go. Knowing I was lying, Piper just grinned at seeing the goody-two-shoes slack off at work.

By the time Cooper arrived for his dinner, I was depressed and ready to call Tawny. I needed the friendly voice of someone who knew the real me.

"You pitching a fit about today?" Cooper asked, frowning up at me from his booth.

"What part of today? How you threatened Nick or when you embarrassed me?"

"He's really special to you, isn't he?" Cooper muttered full of hate.

"I've spoke to him twice and both times about school. I did more flirting with you the first night you came in than I've done with him, but fuck you."

Eyes widening, Cooper grinned. "Someone's in a shit mood."

"Do you know what you want?"

"You bent over the table would be a nice start." Staring at him, I didn't know how my face reacted, but his cocky swagger faded. "Fuck," Cooper grumbled under his breath. "How do you tie me in knots with a look? Is it witch magic or some shit?"

"If I was a witch, I'd figure out a way to get my schoolwork done, work, and sleep all in a twenty four hour period."

"Ditch work one night and catch up."

Frowning at him, I shook my head. "You really don't understand what it's like to be poor."

"How poor are we talking about? You don't look trailer trash, missing teeth, meth head level of poor. I'd peg you at working poor."

"It doesn't matter. What would you like and don't say anything gross please."

"I want you to go out with me again."

"Only as friends."

Cooper rolled his eyes and leaned back in the booth. "I'm not friends with girls. Why would I be?"

"So we're only good for sex?"

Cooper grinned. "When you say the word sex, your lips look so hot and I get a little horny."

"You can't stop yourself from being nasty, can you?"

"I haven't had sex in a week," he said, tugging at his sleeve just over the eagle tattoo. "It makes me weird and horny. Have I mentioned I'm horny, Farah?"

"You've hinted, yes."

Cooper's grin widened. "Let's go somewhere nice. No fighting, I promise."

"I don't want to date anyone. I wouldn't mind being your friend, but you don't have friends who are girls."

"Why my friend?"

"Why not?"

"Do you have a lot of male friends? Like Nick?" Cooper asked, hissing Nick's name like the guy was pure evil.

"No, but I like you."

"Then, go out to dinner with me," he muttered.

"I already said I don't want to date and you think girls aren't good enough to be your friends."

"I have nothing in common with most girls. What are we going to talk about? Bikes? Fights we've been in. Fucking chicks?" Cooper paused then snapped his fingers. "Hey, I do know this bull-dyke chick and we bullshit about that stuff. She's cool, so maybe I can only be friend with lesbos?"

"Then, I guess you and I can't be friends."

"Because you're hot for some other guy?"

"Why are you obsessed with Nick?"

"For the same reason you are."

"I'm not obsessed with him."

"I see the way you look at him. All wide-eyed horny schoolgirl. He's a loser and smells like cheap cologne. If that's what you're into, I can buy new cologne. I can also take you on discount dates and expect you to pay because I'm too poor to take care of my woman. Is that what you're looking for?"

Cooper was such an asshole. Whining like a spoiled little boy told he couldn't have a new bike from Santa, he figured he was right about everything. Never would he allow logic or sweet talk to change his mind. Something about his tone though caused me to laugh. Once I started, I couldn't stop.

"What?" he muttered.

"Hasn't a girl told you no before? Is that why you're acting like a nutball?"

"Nutball? That's insensitive, you bitch," he said, grinning. "And for your information, plenty of girls tell me no."

"Plenty?"

"Fine, a few have. There was the married one. The pregnant one who was trying to trap a guy into marriage so she was pretty booked for the next couple months. Finally, there was a girl who was afraid of tats and big cocks. I still don't know what her problem is."

"Well, now that I know you've gotten shot down left and right, I sorta pity you, Coop."

"Yeah, I'm a real charity case. You should go out with me as an act of kindness."

"I'm not ready to date anyone."

"Bullshit," he said, kicking the booth. "If Nicky asked you out, you'd fuck him on the first date. I can tell you've got it in you, but you have to make me suffer. Do I remind you of someone you need to punish?"

Yes.

"Never in a million years would I think not going out with you would be a punishment. There are a lot of new girls in school who would go out with you. They might make you work for it too. Why not chase them?"

"I want you," Cooper said in a way that made me shiver. "I've wanted you since the first day in Spanish class when you kept tying your shoes as an excuse to look back at me. I loved how you didn't just look. I also loved when you whispered your answers to Manuel. It was so hot. I want you and you'll give me a shot because you want me too. Hell, you need someone like me."

"Don't tell me what I need or want. You don't know me."

Cooper snorted angrily. "Nice move. You tell me nothing then accuse me of having no right to know you because I don't already know you."

Stepping back, I sighed. "I'll be your friend. One day when I'm settled in, I could be more. I can't right now though. Nagging won't change my mind."

"Nagging? That's cold. You make me sound like an old lady."

"If the shoe fits," I said, shrugging, "who am I to argue?"

Cooper opened his mouth to continue nagging then changed his mind. "A burger and fries will be fine, servant."

"I appreciate your order, jackass."

"As you should, beauty."

Our eyes met and I felt my skin warm from the way he said beauty. If only we could work, I might find such happiness with a guy like Cooper. Of course, a guy like Cooper didn't want my type of happiness. He wanted what he wanted and there were no picket fences in his future.

Even now when he gave up on nagging, Cooper hadn't given up on winning the argument. I had become more than a girl he wanted to bang. I was a challenge for someone so rarely challenged in life. Fortunately for me, I was accustomed to challenges and I knew how to do without in a way that Richie Rich didn't. As challenges went, I planned to crush this one.

Chapter Eight

On Friday when I had no work, Bailey joined Skye and me in the dorms. This was when I learned how the people Skye knew from the area were the Johanssons. In fact, Kirk and Skye's dad Randy were super tight. Somehow, I sensed Skye kept this information quiet on purpose.

Was Skye my friend because Cooper told her to be? Or was I full of myself to even consider such a thing? Yet, Skye talked constantly and never mentioned how the guy I had gone on a date with was her lifelong friend.

The way Bailey and Skye spoke to each another made clear how they'd been palling around since school started. I felt played and my feelings were hurt. I excused myself to the bathroom then dialed Tawny's burner phone. My sister answered immediately, sounding paranoid too.

"Are you okay?" I asked.

"Dad left two days ago and hasn't come back. I'm not sure how long I'm supposed to wait? What if he didn't pay enough for the room?"

"If someone shows up, tell them the truth and they'll call social services. The state will send you to Grandma's and I'll convince her to send you here. It'll be fine."

"What about Dad?"

"Maybe it's time for him to stop being in charge of you when he can barely be in charge of himself?"

Tawny exhaled. "You sound tense."

"I think my friend Skye was only pretending because that guy Cooper told her to."

"Is she mean now?"

"No."

"Is she still driving you around and paying for lunch?"

"Yes."

"So what's the problem? If she's faking it, you should enjoy the lie. What else can you do? Confront her and lose out on her fake friendship?"

"I just feel sad that she doesn't like me for real."

"Maybe she does like you. Just cause that guy told her to be your friend doesn't mean she didn't end up liking you. Everyone likes you, Farah. You're nice."

Smiling, I missed Tawny so much I nearly started crying. "I love you."

"I love you too."

"Don't be scared. Either Dad will come back or you'll be sent to Grandma's."

Tawny said nothing for a minute then blurted out, "I don't want to live with Mom."

"She's not messed up anymore."

"I don't care. I don't want to look at her face. I never want to see her again."

Shocked by Tawny's admission, I didn't reply right away.

"I'm sorry," she whispered. "I just don't want to pretend."

"I know and you shouldn't have to," I said, feeling guilty for not reassuring her more quickly. "If you come here, I'll find us a place. Just you and me."

"The place you're in is big, right? You'd be giving up all the space to live with me."

"Nothing I give up would compare to having you here. I miss you so much and I feel lost without you around."

"Me too," Tawny said, bursting into tears.

For the next few minutes, I reassured her while she sobbed. I could picture her twirling her golden hair in a tight knot around her fingers the way she did when the tension became too much. Finally, she calmed down and put her best face forward.

"I'll be eighteen soon then I can live anywhere."

"I'll send money. I'd send it now, but Dad or Mom might make a stink if you're a minor. I never know what they'll do."

"Soon then."

"Mere months away."

When Tawny sighed sadly, my heart hurt imagining her waiting in some dump for Dad to return. Then, I forced myself to picture her getting off the bus at the same station I arrived at weeks earlier. We would be together and no one could tear us apart again.

"Enjoy that friend," Tawny said. "Life isn't easy and you have to take what you can get sometimes. If she's just pretending, let her pretend. There's nothing to lose. Even if it hurts your feelings, it's still better than being alone."

"Soon, I'll never be alone."

"We'll die old maids together," Tawny teased.

"You and me living together with our cats."

"I'll learn to quilt."

"I'll pickle things we'll never eat."

Laughing, we pretended hundreds of miles didn't separate us.

"You better save the minutes on your phone," Tawny said.

"I'll call you soon. You call me if you need anything. Call me and I'll call you right back."

"Okay. Go enjoy your rich lying friend."

Smiling, I said goodbye then returned to where Bailey rested on Skye's bed.

"Where did Skye go?" I asked.

"Tyler works out at the gym right now so she ran over there to drool."

"She really likes him."

"I don't see why. He doesn't really like her."

Remembering what Cooper said about Bailey needing to be the center of attention, I shrugged. "Settling for one guy so early in the year might be a mistake."

"Exactly!" Bailey cried, sitting up. "I'm dating lots of guys because I don't need a husband. I need some manmeat. I need fun. I'm eighteen, not eighty. Skye's a loser to settle for the first guy who looks her way."

"She's not used to living here. This was always your home so you're more confident."

Bailey smiled at this. "I am confident. Sometimes, guys want me to be all meek and shy and shit. That's not me. I don't need their approval. I'm Bailey Fucking Johansson. I run the show, not some dick."

Nodding, I wasn't sure if I should leave now that Skye was gone.

"Are you passing Algebra?" Bailey asked, standing up.

"I guess. We haven't had any tests yet, so I don't know."

"I've been skipping classes because it's lame. I need to do this assignment though. Can you help me with it?"

Excited to show my worth as a friend, I assumed the work was in her bag, but Bailey headed for the door.

"I ditched school so my stuff is at home."

Part of me wanted to walk back my offer, but Bailey's expression left me little choice. I followed her out of the room and to the parking lot where her SUV waited.

Driving out to the Johansson house, I reminded myself that I'd seen Cooper in Spanish on Thursday. He played with my ponytail and told me my handwriting made him hard. I'd laughed before ignoring him for the rest of the class. He ignored me ignoring him and messed with my hair in a show of possession to Nick who likely didn't notice. That evening, he visited Denny's and flexed his muscles for me. Again, I giggled, but refused to go to dinner.

Convincing myself Cooper wouldn't be at the house, I enjoyed Bailey's company. Like Skye, she talked a lot. Unlike with Skye, Bailey needed constant head nodding and grunts of affirmation.

"My parents aren't home," Bailey said as we turned down a road off of the main highway. "They took my little sister to a spa so my mom could detox. Mom is very health conscious one day out of the week. The rest of the time, she drinks, smokes, and eats meat smothered with barbeque. Today is her health day."

"She sounds nice."

Bailey frowned at me. "My mom is the best person on the face of the planet. Nice doesn't cut it."

"Sorry."

"It's fine. You don't know her so you wouldn't know how she's the best."

Shadowing the road, tall trees lined both sides until we reached a clearing. A huge log-style house loomed to the left while a beautiful view of Kentucky spread out on the right. I couldn't imagine growing up with such beauty. Yet, like how Skye viewed money, maybe beauty would become mundane after awhile. Merely an expected element of life for people like the Johanssons.

"My brother Tuck lives in a condo in town with Maddy," Bailey explained as we exited her SUV. "Coop lives in the apartment over the garage. My room is in the house, but I'm not allowed to let strangers inside. Can you wait out here?"

Glancing around nervously, I nodded.

"We have a lot of big dogs. Don't freak if they run up to you," Bailey said, walking away. "Coop trains the monsters and they won't bite. They just like scaring people."

For the next few minutes, I stood in the large gravel driveway and waited. Hearing noises, I moved towards the house and saw those monster dogs running around. Rottweilers and a few Pit Bulls, they chased each other around except for one who only had eyes for Cooper.

I considered retreating and waiting in the car. My brain said to stay away, but my heart wanted to check out Cooper. He looked really sexy sitting shirtless and barefoot on the ground as he gave the dog a good hard rubbing. Wearing jeans, he seemed young and less intimidating. Whatever my reasoning, I walked to where he could see me and waited for him to notice.

When Cooper pressed his nose against the dog's, the giant animal licked him. Instead of being grossed out like I would have been, Cooper laughed. He was still grinning when he saw me. His eyes did the usual survey of me from head to toe, lingering an extra second on my breasts before he focused on my face.

"That's the girl making me crazy," Cooper told the dog that licked him again. "Yeah, I'd pay big money to get her to show me half as much love as you do, Plum."

Stepping closer, I focused on Plum. "Bailey says you train dogs."

"You talk about me a lot?" he asked, ignoring my question.

"Constantly. I'm a huge fan."

"Prove it."

"How?"

"Dinner tonight."

"Will you wash off the dog spit first?" I asked, giving into the idea of dinner with him. One dinner to answer my questions about us.

Cooper finally gave me a smile he saved for his dogs. An almost boyish grin hiding much of the menacing glare I normally focused on.

"Where do you want to eat?"

"I don't care."

"Why?" he asked, his smile gone. "Because you'll just go through the motions to get me off your back?"

"No, I've eaten a lot of crappy food lately and anywhere new would be a nice change."

Giving me a quick nod, Cooper smiled slightly. "Can you wear your hair down?"

Without thinking, I touched my ponytail. "Sure," I muttered, self-conscious now. "Should I wear any particular outfit?"

Cooper lost his smile again. "Whatever. I just like your hair down because you look less like my waitress and more like my date. I guess that makes me a dick."

Backing away, I felt nervous under his glare. Cooper gave the dog's head a good caress then left the animal and walked to me.

"It doesn't have to be this difficult. Why do you make it that way?"

"I have issues."

Cooper gave me a half smile. "Messed up chicks are hot."

"That explains why you're so into me. I'm super messed up."

Fully smiling now, he stepped a little closer. "Wear your hair any way you want." Nodding, I inched away from him and Cooper sighed. "Never in my life has it been this much work."

"I still think that's the real reason you're so hot for me. You want the chase."

"No, I want you."

Shivering at the need behind his words, I shrugged. "I think you'd lose interest if I gave you what you wanted."

Running a hand through his damp blond hair, Cooper looked over my head at the beautiful view then his gaze returned to me.

"Let me ask you this, Farah. If you want rid of me and I'll blow you off once I'm done fucking you, why don't you just let me fuck you? Is it that you think I might not go away and you'll be forced to admit something else is happening here?"

"No."

Grinning at my lie, Cooper moved closer. "Anything special you want me to wear tonight?"

I smiled despite my best efforts. "Don't get all dressed up on my account, Coop. I'd think you were plenty pretty even if you showed up in sweats."

Laughing in his deep way that I felt to my core, Cooper reached out to touch my face. I backed away because he was all kinds of bad news. While I planned to put his question to the test and get rid of him for good, I wasn't ready yet. Cooper sighed heavily when I dodged his affections.

"Don't cry," I said, giving him a grin. "I still like you. I just don't want the dog's sloppy seconds."

Smiling slightly, he studied my face. "I'm not giving up. If you keep running, I'll keep chasing. I know what I want and I'm not pissing it away because you have issues."

"Right because there'd be no logical reason to avoid getting involved with you."

"No, there wouldn't."

"You sleep around. You beat on people. You aren't exactly the warm and cuddly type."

Cooper shoved his hands into his pockets. "You don't know what type I am because you see what you want."

"Trust me that you're not nearly as mysterious as you think."

"And you're full of shit. You want this too, but it's easier to pretend I'm the problem."

Moving away from him, I frowned. "No, you're right. It's better if I give in so you can treat me like shit."

"Why the fuck would I?"

"Because that's how you treat all those other girls."

"You're not like them."

"How do you know? You fuck those girls then throw them away like used condoms. They might be exactly like me, but you wouldn't know. You never fucking talk to them. If I had fucked you that first night, you'd have tossed me aside without talking to me too."

"Bullshit. You wouldn't have fucked me the first night."

Stepping back, I glared at him. "I'm not pure. I'm not the good girl. Just like they're not whores. People are complicated, but you see what you want. You judge them worthy of your time then dismiss them. You'll do it with me and I'll be lucky to have gotten screwed by you."

"Fuck!" Cooper yelled, startling me a foot off the ground. "You won't let me show you. You think this shit about me and you won't let me do anything different. You won't let me do anything period."

"I don't want to go to dinner," I said, crossing my arms.

Hurrying towards the front of the house, I hoped Bailey was around. Somehow, I sensed she knew what was happening and decided to keep herself invisible.

When Cooper grabbed me around the waist and forced me to face him, I thought to struggle. Yet, I knew how men like him reacted to a challenge. Instead, I waited for him to make his move. If he pushed me too far, I would fight. I'd lose, but I'd hurt him a little too.

"Just let me show you," Cooper said.

"Show me what?"

"Those girls aren't you. Let me show you what I see when I look at you. Stop telling me who and what I am and just let me show you."

"You're not my type."

"I'm exactly your type. That's why you're shaking. You're afraid if you get a taste that you'll never want to let go."

"I'm shaking because you yelled at me and grabbed me. You're violent and I'm afraid of you."

Cooper let go and stepped back. "I hit assholes, not girls."

"I guess."

"You can keep running, but I'm not fucking kidding about chasing you. I won't give up until you give me a chance. A real chance to show you who I am and what I see happening between us. You can talk about used condoms and me being a scary slut or whatever, but until you give me a chance, I'm not letting you go. If you really think I'm that guy and I don't give a shit about you, go to dinner. What harm is there in that?"

"I don't want to encourage you."

"Every time you look at me... Hell, every fucking breath you take encourages me. Just knowing you exist encourages me because I can't get you out of my head and that doesn't happen with me. If I don't want to think about something, I just don't. I can't do that with you, so I'm not giving up until you let me show you who I am."

"If I go out with you tonight and want to leave, you'll let me?"

"I'm not keeping you chained up, if that's what you mean?"

"You know what I mean. I don't have a car. It's like the night after work when you had complete power over where we went and how long we stayed there. I want your word that if I want to go home, you won't play those games."

A frowning Cooper scratched at the angel tattoo on his left arm. "You have to give me a real chance though. No playing your hot and cold games. You want me. I can see it in your eyes and I know you're full of shit when you act like you want to be my friend. I know you want more and I want you to try tonight. If it doesn't work out, I'll back off. If you fuck around though, I'm not walking away."

Based on Cooper's expression, he wasn't kidding. When I nodded, the anger around his jaw eased and he stepped a little closer

"I know a nice place," he said softly. "Good food. Calm. It's where I should have taken you the first time."

"What should I wear?"

"It doesn't matter," he said, brushing his fingers against my cheek. "The place is casual, but nice. You'll like it."

With my arms wrapped around me, I nodded again. Frowning, Cooper focused his gaze on me and swallowed hard.

"I shouldn't have told you to fuck off on Sunday," he whispered. "I shouldn't have called you an uptight bitch either. You were just scared. I knew that, but I wanted you and didn't know the right thing to say. Tonight, I'll know the right thing."

Fighting the heat in my eyes, I didn't want to cry, but he was looking at me as if I had value. While I shouldn't care what he thought, Cooper was beautiful, smart, funny, and he wanted me. I had really hoped he wanted me, but now I was scared to get my wish.

"Tonight," I said because it was all I could think to say.

"It'll be calm. I promise no fights. No bullshit. Just you and me eating and talking like normal people."

"That sounds nice."

Cooper erased the space between us. "In case something fucked up happens and tonight doesn't work out, I want to kiss you now."

"Why would something fucked up happen?" I asked alarmed.

Cooper shrugged then leaned down to kiss me. I thought to step back, but lifted my lips instead. Remembering how good his kisses felt before, I wished he was the one for me. I wished things could be easy because I wanted to have someone look at me and see value. Yet, as Cooper kissed me, I knew I was fooling myself to think I would end up as anything more than a used condom.

Chapter Nine

I never heard Cooper's motorcycle before he knocked on the door. When I answered, he gave me a soft, maybe even nervous smile. I returned it, feeling anxious while shutting the door behind me.

Glancing over my jeans and pink tee, he swallowed hard. "You look beautiful."

"Thank you. You look really good too," I said, noticing how he wore all black from his boots to his shirt.

As we walked to the front of the complex, Cooper suddenly stopped. "This is for real, right?"

"What?"

"This date. You're really giving me a chance, right? I need for you to be open to things and not just playing along because I said I would keep chasing. I need a real chance because you've got me all messed up inside."

Staring up at Cooper, I held his gaze and forced a smile. "I like you a lot. I don't think we make any sense, but I wish we did."

"We could though," he said, taking my hand. "You're scared of all the surface stuff. The tats and the way I mouth off, but that's surface. On the inside, I know you're special. It's why I need a chance."

"I'm going on the date."

Sighing, Cooper frowned. "Because I said I would basically stalk you until you said yes."

"I don't expect anything from tonight. Good or bad. I just want to see what happens. I'm giving you a chance."

Cooper glanced around the muggy night. "This place has great pasta. Do you like Italian? If you don't, we can go somewhere else."

"I love Italian."

Giving me his cocky grin, Cooper opened the door of a big black truck. "There are rare moments when a Harley isn't the best form of transportation. This is one of those moments."

I climbed into the Ford F-350 and strapped myself in. Cooper joined me and his gaze was soft in a way that made me want him so much I nearly cried at the futility of even hoping. I didn't cry though. I planned to enjoy myself tonight. I also intended to be a different kind of Farah.

As he started the truck, I took off my seatbelt. Cooper immediately looked startled as if I might make a run for it. Instead, I leaned over and kissed him gently. He made no effort to deepen the kiss. Letting me lead, Cooper stared at me with those smoky eyes when I pulled away and returned to my side of the truck.

"Hell..." Cooper muttered full of heat as he drove from the apartment complex.

"How is school going?" I asked, acting casual.

"It's school. I go to make my parents happy. I don't care one way or the other."

"What would you do if you didn't attend college?"

"Travel around, I guess. My family goes on road trips in the summers. I love RVing around the country and up to Canada. There's a shitload of places to check out. We camp, hike, ski, explore. Some of my best memories are on the road."

When Cooper talked about his family, he seemed approachable and not so different than me. "If you could go anywhere right this minute, where would you go?"

Cooper glanced at me then focused on the road. "Do you want the happy answer or the real one?"

"Both, I guess."

"The happy answer is I'd go to the Grand Canyon. I love that place and can go there a million times and still notice new things."

When he stopped talking, I asked, "What's the real answer?"

"I'd go wherever your sister is and bring her here so you wouldn't be alone."

Turning away, I stared out of the window and fought the urge to cry. Cooper said nothing for the rest of the drive to the restaurant. When we arrived, he turned off the truck and sighed.

"Are you angry?"

"Angry that you said the nicest thing anyone's ever said to me?" I asked, glancing at him with slightly wet eyes. "I miss her so much and I mentioned that one time and you remembered. So no, I'm not angry."

Cooper gave me a slight smile. "Let's eat and you can tell me more about her."

"Really?"

"I want to know you and I sense you fake things to make yourself seem like everyone else. Your sister is real for you though and I want real."

When he moved to get out of the car, I touched his arm. His gaze met mine then our lips became acquainted again. It was a short soft kiss and I found myself wanting more, instead of waiting for it to be over.

Soon, we walked inside the small Italian restaurant on the outskirts of town. Seated quickly, we looked over the menu and I was excited to eat whatever I wanted because I'd always loved Italian food. My dad said it was too expensive though. Based on the prices, the food wasn't cheap, but I didn't think about it when I was with Cooper. I knew he was like Skye, using money as if it was mere paper to be tossed around.

"Tell me about Tawny," Cooper said, sitting across the table and watching me with such a warm gaze I felt nervous to ruin his mood.

"She's really perceptive. If I'm kinda book smart, she's common sense smart. Great at reading people. A hard worker too. She's shy though and hates school."

Cooper reached across the table and wiped away the tear from my cheek.

"I'm sorry, but I've never gone this long without seeing her. It's like a part of me is missing."

"Why can't she move here?"

"My dad won't let her. Mom doesn't want her here either. I'm saving up though and I'll get an apartment for us. Tawny can get a job and we'll be together, but it probably can't happen until she turns eighteen."

"Where is she now?"

"I'm not sure. My dad is in trouble with some people and he's laying low. They're somewhere in Texas."

"That's bullshit," Cooper said quietly as he tapped hard on the table. "Raising kids that way is crap. Some of my pop's friends are assholes like that and their kids turn out to be shit. You and your sister shouldn't have turned out great, but here you are."

"I don't like to think of my dad as an asshole."

"But you know he is and that's why you don't like thinking about it."

"He took care of me and Tawny. He has his good qualities."

"So did Hitler. So does everyone. No one is pure shit. Everyone can be great in little ways. I'm sorry, Farah, but the way you are about stuff tells me that your dad didn't do a great job."

Frowning, I felt embarrassed like he just called me a loser. Cooper reached across the table again and this time took my hand.

"You want to fit in so much. I see this need in your eyes to be like everyone else and you can't see how amazing you are just being you. Plus, there's the way you freaked out on Sunday when the fight broke out. Baby, that wasn't a normal chick move. You were terrified in a way few other girls would have been. I've had rich bitches around when a fight broke out. At the most, they scream and hide under a table. You took off like your life depended on it. You don't get that kind of fear response by growing up feeling safe."

"He did the best he could."

"Protect your own," he said, slowly pulling away his hand. "I get it. Look at Tucker. He's a turd in every way, but he's my little brother. I'd kill to protect him. Die too, but I know he's a loser. Knocking up Maddy was ridiculous. Well, actually knocking her up was pretty ingenious for him, but then he told everyone he did it. That's why he's a turd. The douche made himself and Maddy look stupid. They are stupid, but he could have kept it quiet."

"Ingenious?"

"Maddy is flaky and he thought she would ditch school and go home. He wanted her to stay and devised a plan. It was a stupid plan, but for him to think it out and put it in motion was pretty brilliant for Tuck. In reality, she would have stayed for the same reason she didn't admit to knowing those weren't her pills. She wants to keep him. Maddy's like you in a lot of ways. Poor and struggling to get ahead. She saw a chance to be with a guy with money and jumped at the chance. The weirdest shit is how she actually loves him. I can't imagine why anyone would love that idiot if they had a choice, but she thinks he's the funniest sweetest guy ever. It's pretty nauseating, but they're happy and I have to be happy for them."

"Did you have a good childhood?"

"Hell yeah," he said, grinning in a way that made me believe him. "My parents are cool. My mom was young when she had me so when we'd go hiking and rock climbing, she was right there with us like one of the kids. She's a badass too. It's why I don't move off the property. What's the point? I have my privacy and my neighbors are cool and they do my laundry and cook for me."

I smiled at him as our salads arrived. Cooper picked the tomatoes, croutons, and cucumbers out, but left the rest.

"When is Tawny's birthday?" Cooper asked.

"In November."

"And yours was in January?" Frowning at him, I didn't answer. Cooper finally grinned at my irritation. "I did my homework on you. Hoped your birthday was coming up so I could do something big and romantic. You chicks love that crap."

"Oh, we really do," I said, smiling now as I ate my salad. "When's your birthday?"

"Beginning of December. I'm a Sag," he said, as if I should be impressed. "What will you give me for my birthday?"

"Probably something with me naked. Well, assuming I haven't grown bored of you by then."

Leaning back in his chair, Cooper smiled. "I like the way you say naked. Makes me think of you naked."

"Big shock."

"I really want to see that."

"Well, let's see how dinner goes first."

Cooper laughed a little then adjusted in his seat like he was uncomfortable. I knew why he was uncomfortable, but there was no way I was acknowledging it. He grinned wider when I ignored his discomfort.

"Tell me about your childhood," he said a little too forcefully then took a breath. "Please."

"My mom was barely eighteen when she married my dad and had me. She was a poor girl and he was a charmer. They must have started out doing pretty well because when I was a baby we lived in a house. By the time of my first memories, we were in an apartment. By the time I was in school, we lived in motels."

Any hint of amusement left Cooper's face. "Who the fuck lives in a motel?"

"Poor people who can't afford a deposit on an apartment or have bad credit or can't be sure they can pay the rent from one month to the next. Basically, people like my family."

"So since you were, what, five?"

"Yeah. We had a few short periods when my grandma would pay for us to get into an apartment. It never lasted though and eventually she stopped helping us."

"How do you go to school when you live in a motel?"

"Just like when you live in an apartment or house. We registered at the local school then a bus picked us up. When we moved to a new motel, we sometimes started new schools."

"Hell, Farah. No wonder you're such a nerd."

Rolling my eyes, I grinned at him.

"You want to be a teacher, right?" he asked.

"Yes."

"How come?"

Without answering, I glanced around. I was a private person. No one except Tawny knew all my secrets. I was proud of this fact because I was raised to be secretive. Even if I hadn't felt a weird sense of pride in keeping everything hidden, I knew Cooper was my weakness. I wanted him in a way that was dangerous. Worse was how I really wanted him to want me too.

As long as we kept up all of our walls and talked about me naked and him being a scary beast, we had fun. Fun was temporary. As long as I thought of Cooper as short term, the less it would hurt when he dumped me and never looked back.

"Do you want the rest of my salad?" Cooper asked when I said nothing.

I did want his salad, but eating someone's leftovers was a poor chick move. While technically a poor chick, I wanted to pretend. Cooper though wanted the real me. I wasn't sure what to do.

Cooper took my empty bowl and set it aside before placing his in front of me. Leaning back in his chair, he shrugged. "I share with my sisters all the time. I can't help it that I'm a softie."

"Thank you. I am hungry."

"But you wouldn't have eaten it, right?" he asked, studying me again. "Because you think that's the right thing to do. Well, fuck the right thing. Just do what you want."

"Spoken like a rich hot guy who always gets what he wants."

"True, but it doesn't make what I said wrong."

Nodding, I ate the lettuce Cooper didn't want. "I didn't have lunch today."

"Why?" he asked, frowning darkly. "I thought you made enough money to at least feed yourself."

"What does that mean?"

"I don't want my girl starving."

"Do you really think I'm your girl?"

"Hell yeah."

Smiling again, I ate more lettuce. "I've been having lunch with Skye. She usually pays, so I didn't bring money. I normally would bring a backup sandwich, but she can't have peanuts around her."

"Why? I saw her eat a whole container of nuts one summer."

"She thinks she might be allergic."

"She's not allergic," Cooper muttered. "Why would she even say that?"

I thought back to the day Skye first took me to lunch. Her excuse was how I couldn't eat the sandwich. Once again, I realized how she hadn't stumbled upon me, but was likely assigned to be my friend. Watching me innocently, Cooper was oblivious to how Skye lied for his benefit.

"Who knows?" I said, shrugging. "Anyway, I didn't have anything to eat."

Cooper studied my face and I knew we were onto each other's lies. A weird moment passed then he gave me a knowing grin. "You didn't explain why you want to be a teacher."

"I just do."

"No, I sense a story behind it. Tell me and I'll share my dessert."

"What types of dessert do they serve?"

"Awesome cannolis." I just stared at Cooper who frowned. "Don't tell me you've never had a cannoli." When I shook my head, he sighed. "Man, we could have fun, Farah. I'd show you a million things. Not necessarily sophisticated things, but cool shit nonetheless. Hell, I bet you haven't even seen the Grand Canyon."

"We drove past it once."

Cooper smiled softly then reached across the table and caressed my bottom lip. As soon as he pulled away, I wiped my lips self-consciously.

"Did I have gunk on them?"

A smile spread across his lips and he shook his head. "You're gorgeous."

"My lips?"

"And those eyes. Hell, every inch of you makes my jeans too snug."

"I feel like a princess now."

Cooper laughed for a minute then sat up with a jerk. Snapping his fingers, he pointed at me. "You know what I forgot to ask?" When I shook my head, he continued, "Why did you want to be a teacher?"

Laughing, I finished the salad then tried to explain. "I had this teacher in third grade. Her name was Mrs. Prescott and she was the best. Lively and funny, smart and tough. The year I had her, she also had a daughter in third grade."

Feeling awkward continuing, I said nothing as Cooper crossed his arms. "You wanted to be that little girl."

"How can you know that?" I demanded, wondering what stalker shit he was pulling.

"You always want to be someone else."

Embarrassed for him to be correct, I also crossed my arms, hiding what I knew he wanted to get his hands on.

"Yeah, I wanted to be her. I'd see pictures of their Thanksgiving and Christmas and how they had a big happy family. I would see their tree and nice house. Not a rich type of house. Not a house like you grew up in, but middle class. For me, that seemed beyond my reach. I would see Emily in school and I'd wish I was her. Wished I had her parents and her house. Even her dog. I wanted to be her so badly because her life looked perfect." Pausing, I wiped my eyes and frowned at him. "Why do you want me to tell you things that'll upset me?"

"Because I need to know you."

"Why?"

"So I can better manipulate you into sleeping with me." Laughing, I shook my head as he grinned at me. "You and I aren't anything alike. I need to know you because I don't know you. Get it? I can't just guess everything. I need you to help me."

"To get into my pants? You know, that might happen just from the free dinner."

"Bullshit," he growled, giving me a little smile. "And screw you for the false hope. You can't know how bad I want in those pants."

"I can guess."

"As a girl, I seriously doubt it."

"Because girls don't get horny?"

"Not girls like you. I bet you've never been horny in your life."

"Shut up, jerk."

"Keep telling your story, nerd."

Sighing, I glanced around and hoped our food arrived. "Obviously, I would never be Emily because my family was never going to be like hers. I sometimes dreamed the state would take us away from my parents and send Tawny and me to a nice foster home. In reality, we would have ended up with our grandma who would have given us back to our parents. There was no escape, so I couldn't be Emily. I could be Mrs. Prescott though. I couldn't have a childhood like Emily's, but I could still have those nice Thanksgiving and Christmas pictures. I could have a pretty house and a nice husband like Mr. Prescott. He would bring in treats for class parties. He was nice like her. Funny too. I started imagining having my teacher's life instead of Emily's. I wanted it so much, but I was afraid I would always be poor."

The food was taking forever and a little part of me wondered if Cooper had them hold our order in the kitchen so I wouldn't stop talking.

"I asked Mrs. Prescott if someone like me could be a teacher? I remember that upset her. She actually cried a little. She told me that no matter where I was living or who my parents were or how little money I had, if I worked hard I could get into school. Any school, she said. Start at a community college and work into a four year degree. Do whatever I could manage, but if I believed in the dream, I could be a teacher."

Wiping my eyes, I was glad the restaurant wasn't very busy. Cooper watched me with an odd expression though. Somewhere between sad and angry.

"I stayed in her class the whole year and it was the best year of my life. I kept worrying we would move. We did a few times, but always stayed in the area. Every time my dad said we might move, I'd beg him and my mom to stay close so I could keep Mrs. Prescott. I don't know if they did it on purpose, but we stayed. One of the hardest things I ever did was say goodbye to Mrs. Prescott. She would sneak me treats and even gave me Emily's hand-me-downs. That last day of school, we were moving out of the state and I wouldn't see her again. I hugged Mrs. Prescott so tight because I wanted to stay with her. As long as I saw her every day, I had hope. She told me to keep in touch and I did. I still write to her every month and she tells me how she knows I'll be a great teacher."

Drying my face with a napkin, I shrugged. "That's why I want to be a teacher."

Cooper stared another minute then let out an unsteady breath. "Then, you'll be a teacher. I can read people and I know when they're bullshitting themselves. When you talk about it, I know it'll happen. People like you make it happen."

Smiling slightly, I watched him. "I've never told anyone that except for Tawny."

"Aren't you glad I bullied it out of you?"

Nodding, I smiled wider. "Yeah, actually. It felt liberating."

Cooper leaned forward and caressed my cheek. "You have a million walls up, baby. When I saw them the first time you walked into Spanish class, I told myself you were too much effort, but I was a fool. You're worth every ounce of trouble you give me."

"Oh, and I give you trouble as part of my devious plan?"

"No doubt about that. There's your finger. Here's me wrapped around it."

Laughing again because of his earnest expression, I felt lighter since sharing my story. Mostly, I felt like I had a stronger connection to Cooper. As if I showed him a never healing wound and he didn't poke at it. He wasn't what I expected and I liked how he surprised me.

The food arrived soon after I finished telling my story. Even with no proof, I knew Cooper kept them from serving us until he got what he wanted first. The food was hot though and I wondered if they had to remake it because people who came in after us were already eating.

No matter the timing, I didn't care once I took a bite. Moaning quietly, I smiled at him.

"Best Italian in the state," Cooper said. "Of course, it's Kentucky so maybe that doesn't mean much, but it's fucking good."

"It is very fucking good." Cooper's eyes locked on mine and he gave me his "jeans were too tight" look. "You have issues," I teased. "Like maybe you need to see a doctor?"

"It's been two weeks since I've had a release. You had to be so hot, didn't you?"

"Not even your hand?" I whispered.

"Well, that hardly counts."

"See, that's your problem right there. You're spoiled. Lower your standards and life will get easier."

Cooper laughed. "Is that your way of saying I won't get any help this evening?"

"I grant you permission to imagine me while alone with your hand. Is that the help you were looking for?"

"I've already done all kinds of things with you in my head. So no, that won't be enough help."

"I'm not having sex with you," I said then added, "Tonight."

Cooper leaned back and grinned brightly. "Ah, finally the disclaimer."

"I think about you when I'm alone," I whispered.

Cooper's expression sent me into hysterics. Everything from horny boy to shock to joyous relief got stuck into one weird facial expression. Even after I was laughing, he seemed unable to respond.

"You're a wicked little bitch, aren't you?" he finally said, adjusting in his chair.

"Stop calling me a bitch."

"I call everyone that. My sisters, my dogs even the male ones, my brother, my Harleys. I called a squirrel a bitch yesterday. To be fair, the little furry bitch had it coming."

Laughing behind my hand, I finally settled down and returned to eating. "I don't masturbate. What's it like?"

Cooper spit out his soda then glared at me. "You timed that."

"Yes, I did. It's not fun having someone mess with you, is it?"

"Oh, it's on. Since you asked, masturbating is a great stress releaser. You know what else is?"

"Is this going to make me vomit?"

"Probably," he said, laughing. "Yeah, I should wait until you finish eating. Dry heaves are the worst."

Chewing and laughing, I struggled not to choke. When I finally settled down, I took a sip of my soda.

"I'm glad you asked me out tonight."

Cooper's ornery expression faded into a soft smile. "I wanted it to be like this. Ever since the bullshit on Sunday, I wanted another chance and for it to be like this. It feels really good, doesn't it?"

There was genuine need in his question and I smiled. "It feels great, Cooper. Better than I've felt in a long time."

"And you haven't even enjoyed a canolli yet."

Grinning, we finished our pasta then sat back and waited for dessert.

"I know tonight will be no more than some very heavy petting," Cooper said full of sincerity. "I know my hand and I will have to finish the job without you. I know all that so don't freak out when I ask this question. Deal?"

"Ask first."

Cooper grinned. "This weekend, I'd like you to come to my house and hang out. We have the pool and a TV the size of this restaurant. Oh, a pool table too. It'll be fun and I'd like to spend time with you like we did tonight. You're pretty irresistible when you're relaxed."

"But I'm resistible when I'm tense? I've been tense since we met so why do you keep asking me out?"

"Fine, you're irresistible period, but you're especially sexy when you let yourself be you. Teasing me like that was pretty awesome, though I think I really might need medical attention now."

As I nearly spit out my drink, Cooper laughed. Suddenly, I wasn't Farah Smith. I had no past or future. I was just in this single moment with this beautiful funny man who wanted me. I didn't worry if he'd want me tomorrow or next week. At this moment, we were perfect and I embraced the feeling.

"I would like to come over this weekend."

Cooper's amusement faded and he studied me. "You feel it, right? It's not just me because I can't have it be just me."

"I feel it," I said softly.

"Thank God. I was going nuts thinking I'd suffered a brain injury without noticing."

"I don't have a swimsuit," I lied. "I'll need to get one."

My swimsuit was on its last thread, having been worn going on six years. I wondered if I could find a new one under twenty dollars.

"You could just wear one of Bailey's. She has a million and she'd share. She likes you."

"I like her too," I said then frowned. "Will your parents be there? Bailey said I couldn't come into the house without them there."

Cooper's lack of a reaction told me Bailey was blowing smoke up my ass to get me to talk to her brother. I sighed at how they played me so easily.

"Chicks lie," he said, shrugging. "What can I tell you?"

"If she'd let me borrow one, that would be great. There's no pool at our apartment complex and I'd hate to buy a suit if I'm not going to use it a lot."

"Stick with me, baby, and I'll have you running around half naked twelve hours out of the day. You'll be naked the other twelve."

"I was wondering where horny Cooper went?"

"Speaking of twenty four seven," he said, giving me a wink. "I hope the horniness will get easier after I've gotten a taste."

"You're kinda gross, you know?"

Cooper wiggled his eyebrows. "Haven't you heard? I'm very talented at that sort of thing."

"Who would I have heard that from?"

"Skye."

"You and Skye?"

"No, but she knows. Ask her."

"No way."

"You'll ask her," Cooper said, glancing over my shoulder at the arriving waiter. "You're curious now."

"Maybe."

The waiter set down our desserts and I took no time digging in. The food was so good that I had a physical reaction to it almost like when Cooper kissed me. My body softened and relaxed in a weird comforting way.

"Good, huh?" he said, eating half then leaving the rest for me to finish.

"Aren't you hungry?" I asked, wanting more.

"I'll have another dinner later."

My heart jumped and I spoke without thinking. "You're going on another date tonight?"

Cooper lost his smile and glanced around the restaurant. Twisting his lips, he finally settled on a grim frown. "I thought you said you felt it too. I thought you understood, but you think I'm going on another fucking date?"

Cooper's voice was no more than an angry whisper, but other customers glanced in our direction. Lowering my gaze, I didn't know how to answer.

"I'm sorry," I finally said. "Can I still have your dessert?"

Sighing, Cooper pushed the plate to my side of the table. "If it's just me, you should tell me. I don't want to be a fool."

"I told you I felt it too," I replied in a quiet voice, avoiding his gaze.

"Like I said, chicks lie."

"So do guys. I'm afraid I'll be a fool believing you like me so much."

Cooper eased back into his chair and the rigidness left his jaw. "I'll let it go because I know you have issues. I just don't want you pretending because it's real for me."

"I didn't mean to act like it wasn't for me. I'm just not used to attention from guys and you're not an average guy. I feel like it's a joke for you to like me."

Cooper's dark eyes studied me then a little more irritation left his face. "You have those walls up and that's why guys don't make a move. When you're too tired, the walls come down a little. Like the night at the party when guys were making moves. Even with you wearing that uniform, they wanted you. I think deep inside you know they do, but you like to pretend you're undesirable. It makes you feel safe."

"Safe from what?" I asked, fearing his answer.

"You're alone here. Vulnerable. You need to feel in control because you aren't in control. When Bailey feels out of her league, she gets loud and rude. You just shut down and put up all those walls. You can't know how hot you were when you let one of the walls come down and told me about your dream to be a teacher. I'd never seen anything more beautiful."

Swallowing hard, I couldn't respond. Wouldn't respond with a trite thank you or I like you too. I just remained silent and ate the cannoli and hoped we could kiss later. I couldn't believe I wanted to feel him against me, but I craved the closeness he promised. I also believed he wouldn't push too far. He was waiting now. No matter his talk of tight jeans and medical attention, Cooper would wait.

"I'm glad I couldn't go into your parents' house the other day," I said as a lame way to admit how much I enjoyed myself.

"Sometimes when Bailey lies, magic happens."

"I ate way too much."

"But it was good."

"It was great," I said then took a deep breath to build up my courage. "My mom won't be home for a while. We could sit and watch TV and do the heavy petting you mentioned."

Cooper stared at me expressionless. Finally, he shivered. "Took all of my self-control not to throw you over my shoulder and run back to your apartment. I'm good now though."

Smiling, I finished my drink. "Whenever you're ready, I am."

"Girl, you know just the right things to say."

Cooper paid the check and soon we were back into the hot evening. He wrapped an arm around me as we walked to his truck and I inched closer so I was right next to him. Even without looking, I knew he liked that gesture. His breathing came out unsteady like he was fighting for control. Once we were in the truck, he lost it.

I might have panicked at the suddenness of his kiss and how I was immediately wrapped in his strong arms. Despite his need, Cooper was gentle and I relaxed into the embrace. I understood him better now. At least, I hoped I did and wasn't lying to myself because he was so beautiful.

Cooper's strong hands were in my hair, pulling me closer. His passion should have overwhelmed me, but something changed in the restaurant. I felt like he knew me and this gave me power. Bravely, I wrapped my arms around him and pressed my body along his.

Moaning into my mouth, Cooper deepened his kisses. The hunger behind them intensified until my bravery felt insufficient. He wouldn't stop and I wasn't ready for him to take it all. He knew me and I had power, but it wasn't enough. I wasn't in the now with Cooper, but back to being Farah Smith.

Fear shot through me and I tried to break free. Cooper knew I wanted him to let go. He felt my hands wedged between us, pushing him off, but he didn't stop. Not right away. His kisses softened, but he didn't let me go for another few minutes until I was nearly clawing at him to stop.

There was a moment right then between us when I wanted to jump out of the truck and run away. His gaze challenging me, Cooper wasn't teasing or horny. He was claiming me and my desires weren't even on his radar. Now, we were on his timetable, not mine.

Instead of running away, I put on my seatbelt and stared out the window. Cooper started the car, turned up the radio, and let it sink in how he was in charge. I'd shown him how important he was to me so he wouldn't beg. Didn't have to beg when I needed him more than he needed me.

Fuck him!

His friends, money, and affection were shit next to my dreams. I didn't need him. I needed to be a teacher. I needed my sister. Being fucked by this asshole wasn't even on the top hundred things I needed.

Arriving at my apartment, Cooper looked for a spot to park, but I undid my seatbelt once we reached the entrance.

"I had fun tonight. I'll see you at school."

"Fuck," he said, grabbing my arm before I jumped out of the still moving car. "You're nuts."

"You're an asshole."

"Yeah, but I'd rather be an asshole than a crazy bitch."

Cooper was right. I did need him because the moment he called me a crazy bitch all of my confidence was gone. With those few words and his dismissive expression, I felt like nothing. Of course, he would hurt me. It was what guys like him did.

One of those silent moments passed where we just stared at each other. Cooper released my wrist and put the car into park. He didn't turn it off though.

"Tonight was fun. I'll pick you up tomorrow to go swimming."

Cooper offered a truce. A deal where I got out of the heavy petting with him, but I still had to come to his house and run around half naked. I assumed this would lead to heavy petting. He'd just have to wait a day for it.

"What time?" I said, feeling defeated and desperate to call Tawny.

"Is ten too early?"

Shaking my head, I opened the door. "Thank you for dinner."

"No goodbye kiss?" he muttered.

"You got it back in the parking lot," I said, slamming the door.

When I heard Cooper pummeling the steering wheel, I couldn't help smiling. I might need him, but I wouldn't give him whatever he wanted. Or maybe I would just fuck him and get him away from me? Why was I wasting so much time pretending like he and I would be together when his needs were all in his pants?

Once in my apartment, I decided I would sleep with Cooper that weekend. Get it over with then he could dump me and I'd move on with my life and focus on what mattered. Soon, I told my plan to Tawny.

"What if you're so good at it that he won't dump you?" Tawny asked as we watched Paula Deen on TV.

Laughing, I nearly dropped the phone. "Yeah, that'll happen."

"You never know."

"You should see this guy. He's the stud of the campus. He just needs to nail all of the freshman girls so he can say he's ruined them for everyone else. He thinks he's got mad skills."

"What kind of skills?"

"I don't know. I'm afraid to ask. I'm assuming just sex stuff."

"Ew. Yeah, I wouldn't ask either," Tawny teased. "So you got to eat Italian?"

"Yeah, it was delicious and not super expensive. Well, with salads and desserts it was. If we just ordered the pasta and water, we could afford it occasionally."

"Cool. I can't wait until I move there."

"Me either. Everything will be better once you're here."

"I know this guy and those fake friends make you feel weird, but you should enjoy it while it lasts. Soon, you won't need them, but right now, you're alone. Might as well hang out with people."

"True."

"Plus, we love swimming. Just think about that and not how Cooper is an ass."

"True again."

"Are you really going to have sex with him tomorrow?"

"I'm going to try. If he's too mean, I probably won't go through with it. If he's half decent, I will so he'll leave me alone."

"What's so bad about the free food and stuff?" When I didn't answer, Tawny sighed. "I know it'll hurt when he dumps you, but you're strong and beautiful. Other guys will like you and one of them won't dump you."

"This is why I miss you. No one else understands and you always say the right things."

"I'll work hard when I move there," Tawny said, sounding very young suddenly. "I'll work two jobs to help pay for things. We can get a one bedroom and I can sleep on the couch or the floor. I don't care. I won't complain."

"It's okay, Tawny," I said softly, trying to soothe her panic. "You're the most important person to me and I need you here. We'll make it work. Even if we end up living in a motel for a while, it'll be fine as long as we're together."

Tawny exhaled hard and I felt her calming herself. "I need to be with you. Hiding with Dad and not knowing what'll happen next was easier when you were here."

"Maybe you should come now?"

"What about Mom?"

"If you move here, I'll find a way to make things work."

"I don't know exactly where I am though. I don't know where to go to get to a bus, even if I had the money."

"Soon then."

"Soon," she whispered.

We watched another ten minutes of TV together then I had to hang up. Dealing with Cooper, school, fake friends, and my mother would be easier if I could talk to Tawny for more than fifteen minutes every few days. To settle my aching heart, I promised myself I would see her soon.

Chapter Ten

Before Cooper knocked, I opened the door and walked outside. He looked as edgy as I felt. Besides the edginess, Cooper looked hot. Wearing a wife beater over his strong chest plus faded jeans, he was hotter than I remembered. This was when I knew my mind was playing tricks on me.

"So are you bailing? Is that what this is?" he muttered, staring angrily at me.

"I have your number. If I wanted to bail, I would have called and told you to fuck off."

Cooper exhaled hard then looked around the courtyard. Returning his gaze to me, he shook his head. "Why is everything so difficult with you?"

"Because you're an asshole who makes me feel bad," I said then added, "On purpose."

"You wanted me to kiss you. We had a nice dinner and you wanted to be close. I tried to be close and you punished me for it."

"Fuck you," I whispered, stepping back against the door. "You knew what you were doing. You figured I liked you more than you liked me, so you could do whatever you wanted. I'm just trash."

"Fuck you back," he growled. "There is no way in hell you like me more than I like you. If you did, you wouldn't keep saying no."

"So fine, let's just fuck today and get it over with. That way, you can get on with your life."

"Shit!" he yelled, walking halfway down the path before turning around and hurrying back. When he reached me, I flinched at the ferocity of his movements.

"I want you so bad, but it's not just sex. If it was, I'd fuck someone else and pretend she was you then flip you off and move on with my life. I tease you, but it's not about sex. You fucking know that too."

"I don't know anything," I said, nervous now because I wondered if he might hurt me. Looking like he was ready to hit something, his hands flexed in and out of fists. "I was really happy after dinner. I wanted to bring you here and make out, but then you scared me. You did that on purpose to make me feel weak. Fine, I feel weak and I'm afraid of you."

Cooper glanced to his right at the sound of people talking. Looking back at me, he lost much of his irritation. "It's hard being patient, okay?" he said in a needy voice.

"Then, we'll get it over with today and you won't have to be patient anymore."

Cooper's expression softened into a panicked, almost pained look. "I want all of you. Not just sex. I want you to take down all of your walls for me. It felt so fucking beautiful to see you a little better after you told me about Mrs. Prescott. I felt relieved, but also desperate. I want you to look at me like you did after you told me that story, but I have to wait. I get that."

"Sex will be another wall."

"We're not having sex today," he said, sighing. "You're looking at me like I'm a piece of shit that'll hit you. You actually look afraid of me. No way do you want to have sex and I'm not doing it unless you're really giving yourself to me. No fake Farah shit. No walled up crap. I want the real you and the real you doesn't want to have sex with me," he muttered then added, "Today."

"Had to put in the disclaimer, huh?" I said, grinning slightly.

"It was too painful not to put it in."

"I do want to go swimming."

"And spend time with me?" he asked, nudging me with his knee. "Throw me a bone here."

"And spend time with you. Until you got pushy, I was really excited to spend time with you. I'd like to be excited again."

Cooper again glanced towards the voices. Sensing he was irritated by any interruption, I stepped closer and took his hand.

"Can we go?" I asked. "It's getting hot."

When his soft gaze focused on my face, he smiled. "I brought the bike. Is that okay?"

"No, now go home and get your truck and come back," I said, grinning as I tugged him away from the neighbors who were getting louder. "Did you ask Bailey if I could wear her swimsuit?"

Cooper nodded. "She's really excited to have a poor friend. It makes her feel better about herself. Now, she'll want to share shit all the time to give her life meaning."

"She's young."

"Yes, but she won't like how you'll fill out the top of the swimsuit better than her. Get ready for bitchiness."

Glancing down at my small C-cup breasts, I frowned. "We're around the same size."

"Not really. I've seen her go streaking before, so I know exactly what size she is. Bailey pads her bras."

"You shouldn't tell people that."

"I'm not telling people," he said, climbing onto his bike and grinning back at me. "I'm telling someone who is too nice to tell her what I said. If you were a bitch who'd make fun of her, I wouldn't have told you. I can read people, remember?"

Climbing on behind him, I smiled. "Read me now. What am I thinking?"

"You're thinking you hope we get hot and heavy today, but not too hot and heavy. You're also hoping my parents like you. I also sense a little worry over how you'll look in the swimsuit because you want me to think you're hot, but you don't want Bailey to think you're too hot."

Hiding my face against his back, I wrapped my arms around his waist. "Not even close, Coop. Not by a long shot."

"Even without seeing your face, I know you're lying. You're just that bad at it."

"Whatever. Let's go before I sweat through my clothes."

Cooper said nothing for so long that I twisted around his shoulder to see him. "What?"

"I'm just thinking of you all wet. I needed a minute to get myself under control."

"Perv."

"Dork."

"Dipshit."

"Beauty."

"Sexy bastard."

"Hell yeah."

With that comment, he started his Harley. Tightening my hold around his waist, I felt his breath catch and knew he was having another horny moment. At this rate, he really would need medical attention soon.

With the breeze cooling my skin, the drive to his house was relaxing. As we turned onto the road leading to his house, I realized I was genuinely happy. Despite his behavior the day before and even the way Cooper scared me earlier, I couldn't stop smiling because I would spend the day with him.

Pulling past the main house, Cooper parked next to the garage. His dogs watched him and waited for a signal. He didn't give it to them though. Instead, he waited for me to climb off the bike. Joining me, he told the dogs to go away and they did grudgingly.

"They want to slobber on you," Cooper said. "I understand their pain."

Grinning, I glanced around. "Where do you live exactly?"

"In the apartment above the garage. It's private. You can scream as loud as you want without my parents hearing," Cooper announced, giving me a naughty grin.

"Are you threatening me?" I asked, squinting hard as if suspicious.

"Bitch."

"Asshole."

"Hell, I want you naked so bad you can't possibly know how much."

"That didn't make much sense so I'm assuming too much blood left your brain for southern regions."

Cooper groaned, twisting around as if uncomfortable. "Should have worn looser jeans."

"Weirdo."

"Geek."

Laughing, I noticed a small blonde girl with wild wavy hair appear from the house. She wore a yellow summer dress and an AC/DC cap as she strutted towards us.

"Hey, Sawyer."

"Is this your newest whore?" the little girl asked.

Scooping Sawyer up, Cooper tossed her over his shoulder and spun around. The hat went flying and she screamed in horror and maybe a little joy. When Cooper lowered her onto his hip, she looked dizzy under her long hair.

"This is Farah," Cooper said, grinning. "She's my girl. Don't call her names."

"How come?"

"Because she's not a whore."

"How do you know? You test her out yet?"

"Holy hell!" Cooper said, dipping her upside down. "Who is teaching you that shit?"

"Fuckwad!" Sawyer screamed as Cooper set her on the ground gently. "He said good girls get rings and bad girls get STDs. I want a ring."

Rolling his eyes, Cooper sighed. "Tucker's too stupid to know better. You aren't so do yourself a favor and never listen to a word he says."

"She's pretty. I like blondes better," Sawyer said, eyeing me from head to toe.

"No one is better than my girl," Cooper said, giving me a quick kiss. "Is Mom around?"

Sawyer screamed, "Mom" until a curly haired blonde woman appeared from the house wearing shorts and a Harley tank top. Her bare skin displayed an assortment of tattoos from skulls to butterflies. Her blue eyes were bright as she looked up at her son then down at her still screaming daughter.

"Tucker is teaching her crap," Cooper said.

"You're the oldest. It's your job to kick his ass for me."

Cooper laughed. "Mom, this is her."

"Ah, her," his mom said, grinning. "The girl who's got my son wrapped around her finger."

Standing there awkwardly, I gave my best non-awkward smile as Cooper's mom gave me the once over.

"I'm Jodi and you must be a special girl for my boy to want you so bad."

Ignoring the special girl part, I forced my smile to grow. "Hello, Jodi."

"You hungry? We're getting ready to grill."

"I ate earlier. Thank you."

Cooper snorted. "She's lying. I felt her stomach growling on the way over."

Glaring at him, I felt my face flush in embarrassment. Jodi just laughed and took Sawyer by the hand.

"Come on in and get something to eat before you go swimming. Need to keep up your energy in this heat."

Still irritated, I glanced at Cooper. Instead of giving a shit about my anger, he grinned at me like his pants were still too snug.

"Yes," he said, nudging me towards the house, "we must keep up our energy. I have plans for today."

"Okay," I said, nervous about a lot of things now.

His mom was nice, but I'd never met a guy's parents. Also, Sawyer was a little like Bailey and I feared being embarrassed. Then, there was Cooper's horniness. I had woken up with the plan to have sex with him. When he said it wouldn't happen, I relaxed. Now, I didn't know what to think. His moods were all over the place. Sweet one minute. Terrifying the next.

Cooper kissed my neck before corralling me into the air conditioned house. I turned to look at him and his smile faded.

"What?" he whispered.

"Nothing."

Cooper stood behind me and wrapped his arms around my chest, pulling me to him. "You work at that job. You never miss school. You deserve a little fun and we're going to have fun. Soon, my pop will grill and you'll pig out and I'll lick barbeque sauce off your lips. Then, I'll take you home, safe and sound. Do you understand?" I nodded again, but Cooper sighed. "Why do you look ready to cry?"

"I'm nervous."

"Don't be. My family's a mess. We're sloppy. We eat too much. Talk too loud. Fart constantly. Next to us, you're a princess."

Grinning, I nuzzled my cheek against his bicep. This time when Cooper sighed, there was longing behind the sound. "Today, I'm kissing you like you've never been kissed before. Prepare to be ruined for all other men."

"Is that a threat?" I asked, squinting hard at him.

"Gorgeous."

"Sexy jerk."

"Let's get something to eat."

The inside of the house was even nicer than the outside. It wasn't chandelier fancy, but warm and countrified. Even with the animal heads on the walls, the place felt grand because of the two-story windows facing the river and woods.

Cooper wanted alone time with me, but Sawyer was busy monopolizing his time. I didn't mind the distraction as I worried about wearing a swimsuit around him and Bailey. This fear was soon realized when Bailey appeared and smiled in a fake way. Cooper glared at her until she punched his arm. Then, he chased his screaming sister out of the room. It could have gone better.

By the time I was alone with Bailey in her massive princess room, my empty stomach twisted with anxiety.

"I'm nervous about wearing a swimsuit in front of your brother," I told Bailey who was searching for the right one.

She glanced at me full of irritation then her brain caught up with what I said. The annoyance washed away and she smiled. "He's been with a lot of really hot girls. He's bound to compare you."

While I succeeded in making Bailey feel better, I'd managed to screw myself with her helpful honesty.

"He really wants to fuck you though," Bailey added when I just stared at her. "He's determined to fuck you, so it won't matter how bad you look."

"Okay."

Bailey settled on a faded blue, nearly shapeless one piece that wasn't nearly as cute as hers. Yet, at that point, I wanted to get the whole reveal and Cooper's reaction over.

Following Bailey back to the family room, I remembered what Tawny told me. Enjoy Cooper and his money. Don't take anything personal. Relax and make the best out of college life. Just chill.

Chilling as I returned to the kitchen, I immediately felt overheated. Cooper wore black swim trunks that hung loosely from his hips. His incredibly sexy hips. Staring at his chest, all of the hard muscles and golden skin, I could ignore the tattoos reminding me of things I didn't want to remember. As Cooper stared out of the back windows, I watched him for a full minute before he noticed me. Then, we were both drooling. It was pretty awkward.

Cooper walked to me and whispered, "She picked the ugliest suit she could find and you still look so hot that I need..."

Unable to finish, he just leaned down and cradled his head against my shoulder. Once he felt under control, he sighed and stood again.

"You're killing me. I'll likely die and it'll be all your fault."

"If it makes you feel any better," I whispered, staring at him with big frightened eyes, "I think my pants are snug now too."

With that comment, I placed my hand on his chest and Cooper lost all brain function for maybe a minute. He just stared like he might actually die. Finally, his gaze narrowed and he glared at me.

"You're mean."

Laughing at the sincerity behind his words, I let my fingers slide down his powerful chest and hard stomach. His skin felt warm and soft under my fingertips. I hadn't expected the soft part and I stroked him gently wanting more.

Horniness under control, Cooper watched me in a passive way. I wanted to touch him and he was letting me. Nothing else would happen especially not with the three Johansson ladies nearby. Soon, he touched my chin and lifted my lips to his.

The kiss was gentle and without heat. Just his soft lips against mine before he pulled back and smiled. "I see another wall falling for me," he whispered tenderly.

"You look really hot," I said, trying to distract him.

"Let's eat then we'll go down to the river and swim. It's too nice a day to stay at the pool."

"I've never swam in a river before."

"College is all about new experiences," he said, wiggling his eyebrows.

Ignoring his teasing, I asked, "What's for lunch?"

"Meat. Mom made a really great macaroni salad too. She's a hell of a cook. You should try her extra cheesy mac and cheese."

The way Cooper spoke of his mother made me smile. Not a fake nervous smile, but a genuine one. He was so sweet about his mom and I was happy he had such a good relationship with her. Jodi must have sensed she was being spoken about because she appeared and waved for us to head outside.

At the grill, a tall muscular man stood while Tucker sat nearby with Maddy on his lap. Cooper took my hand and led me towards his dad.

"Pop, this is Farah," Cooper said in a tone that nearly sent me into giggles.

He sounded excited like a little boy and I couldn't believe he was so happy to show me off. Never feeling as important, I realized my self-esteem now depended on Cooper's feelings for me.

The Kirk from Whiskey Kirk's was like an older rougher version of his son. None of the boyish charm. None of the softness in the dark eyes. Only grizzled badass. Without knowing what the Johansson family business involved, I couldn't imagine Kirk controlling anything legal. He had a scary violent edge to him even as he gave my hand a quick shake.

"She's a sweet one," Kirk said.

Cooper tightened his grip on my other hand and narrowed his gaze. Glaring at each other, dad and son had a little showdown until Kirk grinned.

"Go away while I cook," he muttered, grinning as he returned to grilling.

Cooper didn't walk away until his dad opened a beer. Finally, he pulled me along with him.

Nervous again, I stared up at Cooper. "Did I do something wrong?"

Cooper glanced at me. "Naw, we just have to play whose dick is bigger so he can feel like leaving the business to me is a safe move. He does that shit all the time. Sorry about the sweet thing comment. He's not sensitive like me."

Laughing at him, I reached up and pushed a lock of blond hair out of his eyes. Cooper immediately reverted to horny guy. There was a moment where our eyes met and I thought he might fuck me in front of everyone. I knew my eyes widened, but I didn't know about my mouth until Cooper glanced down at my lips and burst into laughter.

"A perfect 'O' every time. It's like a cartoon character," he said then added with too much intensity. "A really fucking sexy cartoon character."

"You make me happy," I said and his cocky grin faded into the softness I preferred. "Do I make you happy?"

"When you give me exactly what I want and don't piss me off, you make life perfect."

Glaring at him, I shook my head. "So never then, huh?"

Cooper leaned down and whispered so quietly I almost couldn't hear him. "I want you naked right now in my bed and I'd make your life perfect. I'm that good, baby."

"Sure, let's go."

Cooper sighed. "I want you to want it so bad that I'll have to pry you off me. We're just not there yet."

"I really can't see that ever happening. I'm not a girl who glues myself to people."

"You will with me. How can you not?"

"No comment."

Cooper gave me a very serious expression. "I'm going to do something. Do not freak out. Be casual. Can you do that?"

"No," I said in a panic.

Cooper reached behind me and I felt his fingers on my ass. Forcing myself to stay very still, I felt him fiddling around then he pulled his hand away.

"That suit is old and it's riding up," he explained, taking a beer from his brother who walked by. "I didn't want anyone seeing my girl's ass cheeks."

"I didn't notice," I said, reaching behind me awkwardly.

"It's too hot out to notice. You're fine now."

"You could have just told me," I said then rolled my eyes. "But why would you when you could touch my ass instead?"

"My girl is pretty fucking smart," he said, giving me a big bright smile.

"Did you have braces?" I asked, basking the imperfection of his teeth.

"Yeah."

"I have pictures!" Bailey screamed, suddenly in front of us.

As she ran into the house, Cooper sighed and frowned down at me.

"I'm dating this guy right here," I said, touching his chest and ending his brain power for a moment. "I don't care about the old dorky Cooper."

"Can I see pictures of you as a kid?" he asked with a genuine smile.

"No. Never. I'll burn them first."

A laughing Cooper sighed again when Bailey returned with a picture in her hand.

"Here's the loser with his braces."

"You had braces too, shit for brains."

Bailey ignored him and thrust a picture at me. Looking it over, I frowned. Basically, the picture was of a slightly shorter, slightly less muscular, still as tanned and gorgeous Cooper. Oh, and he had braces. Clear fucking braces. He didn't even look like a dork. I couldn't catch a break.

"Disappointed?" Cooper asked, grinning.

"He was so ugly back then," Bailey said. "Like a mutant." When Cooper squinted at his sister, she backed away. "He wet his bed too."

Bailey ran away screaming even though Cooper merely walked slowly behind her, taking his time to exact revenge. I stared at the picture of a teenage Cooper with his tattooless chest. I wished that chest still existed. The tattoos were his only physical flaw. Otherwise, he looked like absolute perfection to me. Even as he threw a tater tot at his sister, he was gorgeous. So busy staring at him in wonder, I didn't notice Sawyer grab the picture from me.

"Don't mock him!" she screamed then ran into the house.

Startled, I froze and remained very still as everything sped up around me. Cooper stopped hounding Bailey so he could wrestle with Tucker who must have whispered something to his brother. Now, they were shoving each other around on the deck while Maddy watched on. Bailey walked to the grill and whined to her father about something, but Kirk just shrugged.

With all of the fighting, the dogs got riled up below the deck. Sawyer ran back outside and pushed Bailey away from their father. Quickly, the sisters were screaming at each other while the brothers continued their sweaty battle.

Standing on the deck overlooking the amazing view, I ignored the chaos around me. Cooper and Tucker were beating on each other while Sawyer threw a pickle at Bailey who then made a lewd comment about pickles and dicks. Kirk laughed at her comment as he turned over the meat. Oh, and maybe a hundred dogs were attacking each other below the deck as if reenacting the siege at Helm's Deep in the Two Towers.

Soon, Jodi joined me and lit a cigarette. I glanced at her and smiled as she watched me with those bright blue eyes.

"You're eighteen, right?" she asked, exhaling a ring of smoke.

Nodding, I felt small under her gaze. Even knowing I had mother issues didn't prepare me for the stress of having a mom dissect me with her eyes.

"I was sixteen when I met Kirk. He was forty two. People told me it wouldn't last. People told me when I got pregnant with Cooper how I'd end up dumped in a trailer park and never see Kirk again. People don't know shit though. You'd be best to ignore them when they give you advice."

With the way the locals feared the Johansson family, I doubted I would ever get negative advice about the relationship. Yet, I nodded anyway.

"Boys like Cooper come in two sizes. One is like his pop. He probably fucked every woman in the state and couldn't find a single one who interested him. He just didn't have it in him yet to settle down. By the time he met me, he had a need no easy fuck could satisfy. Kirk grew into commitment. Some say he got too old to fuck, but trust me he hasn't slowed down any."

Jodi and I shared a smile.

"Then, there are guys like my boy. He isn't ready to be committed. He needs time and to fuck everything that walks past him. Instead, he found you. Now, he can't let that feeling go. Sometimes, a man grows into an ability to love. Sometimes, they just wake up one day in love whether they've grown enough or not. Cooper hasn't grown shit, but he's in love. He doesn't know it yet because he's an idiot. Men his age are all idiots, but Cooper's especially stupid. Mostly because he's the smart one in the family. It makes him think he doesn't have to think. He just assumes he has all the answers. With you, he doesn't because he's not ready for you. He thinks he is, so he's going to fuck up all over the place. You best prepare yourself for that."

"We just met," was my idiot reply.

"Every time you two butt heads, he comes whining to me. His pop tells him to fuck someone else and it'll be fine. I know though. I saw the stupid in Kirk's eyes when he realized he was in love and wasn't walking away. Cooper's got that stupid look now, but he's too stupid to understand. He just wants what he wants. When it ain't easy, he gets pissed. Then, he whines about how getting pissed didn't fix anything. Then, he wants to dump you and move on. Then, he realizes he can't because he needs you. Then, he figures he'll make things happen like he always does. When it doesn't work immediately, he's pissed again. The fucker is in a downward spiral, but he's a good boy and will eventually figure things out."

In those last few minutes, Jodi said more to me than my mother had in the last two weeks. I felt an odd need to impress this woman. Maybe not so odd since my need for a mom was why I grabbed onto Mrs. Prescott so tightly. She was everything Amy wasn't.

Now, Jodi was sharing with me. Before I could get too comfortable with the idea of bonding with her, she continued, "My boy deserves the best. I don't know that you're good enough, but you're what he wants. If he can't have the best, he deserves to have what his heart needs. You better be kind to my boy because I'd hate to go mama bear on you."

Jodi smiled like she was kidding, but I knew she wasn't. I didn't know much about the Johansson family, but I knew they caused scary people to get out of the way. Like those guys at the party who roofied Bailey and I never saw again. It was a small college and I'd seen one of them every day at school before the incident. Afterwards, he was just gone. People who could make that happen would have no problem disappearing me too.

"I understand," I said.

"You're a smart girl. Coop says you want to be a teacher. That's a nice job for a young woman. Then, when you give me grandbabies, you can stay home and teach them."

Nodding, I glanced at Cooper who had Tucker in a headlock. The brothers were both eating hot dogs, but Cooper wouldn't let Tucker go. Yet, his younger brother didn't even care. He was too busy flirting with Maddy who had a bad case of the giggles. I think she liked seeing him in the headlock, but would never admit that fact. I didn't blame her. The Johanssons were a scary family.

Once Jodi left to turn on a Heart CD before joining Kirk at the grill, Cooper finally dumped Tucker next to Maddy. He strolled to me with a hotdog covered in ketchup, mustard, and relish.

"Is someone hungry?" he teased, pressing the hot dog against my lips.

"Thank you."

Cooper stepped close enough for me to lean against and I did because his mom had scared the shit out of me. What happened if Cooper and I had a fight? What if I didn't put out? Anything could happen to me and who would even care?

"Did she threaten you?" Cooper whispered in my ear as his arms wrapped around me.

"No."

"Really?" he said, smiling. "I thought she loved me?"

"I'm doing my best."

Cooper's smile disappeared. "What does that mean?"

"I don't upset you on purpose," I lied.

"She's teasing you, Farah. Or maybe not, but she just wants me to get what I want."

"Maybe we should, you know?" I asked, biting into the hot dog even though my stomach churned full of anxiety.

"Should what?" Cooper asked, taking the burger Bailey handed him.

"You know?" I whispered. "Go to your apartment and be together."

"Oh, yeah, we're already doing that."

Frowning, I felt overwhelmed. I also felt lonely. Everyone knew their place and I was the outsider. Always the outsider.

Cooper leaned down and whispered, "Wait, did you mean sex?" Grinning at me, he shook his head. "Sorry, but I'm not emotionally in the right place for that. You'll have to fix your pants problem yourself."

Even on edge, I laughed because he could be so silly when in the right mood. Cooper took my hand and pulled me to the stairs where we sat on a step and ate our food. Twice, he left then returned with burgers and drinks. I was beyond stuffed by the time we finished eating.

Feeling comfortable enough to be a little daring, I leaned my head against Cooper's shoulder. He smiled at me then glanced back at his noisy family. When his gaze returned to my face, he leaned down and kissed my forehead.

We sat quietly for a while, watching the dogs. Soon, Cooper told me about each dog and how he learned to train them from his uncle Vic. He said he liked Rottweilers, but his favorite dog was a mutt named Rafe. When he wasn't being loud or horny, Cooper seemed just like any guy. Approachable and safe. Like Nick maybe, but Cooper was mine for now.

After the food settled, we walked hand and hand down the stairs of the deck and out towards the river. It wasn't a long walk, but we needed to take a winding staircase on the side of a hill. I didn't know how someone could have built it, but I'd never had an eye for those things. I just followed Cooper who paced his movements so I could keep up. When we arrived at a deck overlooking the river, Cooper let go of my hand and stretched.

"The river's current is slow as shit. No one gets pulled down stream. No one has ever drowned."

"I could be the first," I muttered.

"You're such a nerd," he said, caressing my hair. "A hot as hell nerd."

"So we walk down to the water and swim?" I asked, feeling uncertain about how to gracefully swim with living things floating around.

"No, you jump!" Bailey screamed from behind me. Shoving me forward, she started laughing. I staggered towards the edge and knew the momentum would take me over. Cooper caught me and pulled me back against him.

"Damn it, Bailey!" Cooper yelled. "You can't shove her in like that. She's scared."

"That's how you taught me to swim."

"If you want revenge, you push me, not her."

"Whatever," Bailey said, rolling her eyes as she ran off the end of the deck and disappeared into the water.

Cooper grunted. "She's feeling really fucking insecure today. I think Skye having a guy is making her into a bitch."

"Thanks for not letting me fall."

"You want to try jumping?" he asked, tugging me closer to the side. "It's not a long drop and the water is deep. You won't get hurt. Uncle Cylas is a huge guy and he jumps off all the time without a problem."

I stared down at the water where Bailey swam around casually. When she glanced up at me, I waved as if I wasn't irritated with her for being a competitive bitch. Frowning, she waved back. Then, her frown eased and she smiled.

"You're good with her," Cooper said, smacking a mosquito on his arm.

"She just wants to feel special. Most people do."

"Don't you?" he asked, kissing the top of my head.

"No, I just want to be average. Normal."

Cooper said nothing and I glanced up to find his expression cranky.

"Average is shit," he finally said. "Why be normal when you can be more?"

"I want to dream of something I can actually get."

"You're gorgeous, hard working, hot, smart, and sexy. You have a lot going for you. You're patient too."

Smiling at his compliments, I was still nervous. "Can I ask a stupid question without you making fun of me?"

"Sure."

"Does it hurt when you hit the water?" I asked, looking down at the river.

"No, baby, it doesn't," he said softly, taking my hand. "Want to jump together? I'll make sure nothing happens to you."

Smiling, I looked at the water again. "New things scare me. It's stupid, but I'm afraid to jump."

"I promise I'll keep you safe. Do you trust me?"

Nodding, I felt like I might cry. All the anxiety from the day rushed up at this exact moment. The part of me that wanted to be safe said not to jump. Don't take chances. I could get hurt. Depending on Cooper was a mistake and he might fail me. What if I drowned and no one was there to help Tawny get away from those shit motels in the middle of nowhere? Don't jump, my brain screamed.

Tightening my grip on his hand, I swallowed hard. "Don't let me drown."

"You've swam before, right?"

"In pools."

"I won't let go."

We walked to the very edge and I stared at the water. It felt too far down. The impact was bound to hurt. I was too scared. In the distance, I heard Tucker whooping it up and knew he was on his way down. If he got there and was too loud, I'd chicken out.

"I'm ready," I said, looking up at Cooper.

He smiled softly as his dark eyes studied my face. "Let's break down another wall, baby."

We stepped off and I panicked immediately. I even tried to brace my fall, but Cooper held my hand as we dropped into the warm dark water. The lack of light scared me again, but I felt Cooper pulling me back to the surface. Kicking my legs, I held onto him.

Cooper never let go. Not when we fell or when we kicked our way to the surface or even as we floated on the peaceful water. He held on and I was safe.

Smiling at him, I glanced up at the deck. It didn't seem like such a big deal now, but I would have bailed if not for Cooper.

"Thank you," I said as he grabbed the inner tube Tucker threw down.

"I'll never let you go," he told me.

Soon, as we floated, I leaned over to kiss him. Cooper wrapped an arm around my waist and tugged me closer. The kiss deepened and I nearly let go of the inner tube. Cooper kept me afloat though. When his lips left mine, we just watched each other while floating on the lazy waters. After a long few minutes passed, I faced away from him.

"I really like you," I said, leaning my head on the tube and still looking away.

"Why do you sound sad?"

"I didn't expect to meet anyone right away. I wasn't really ready."

Cooper tapped my shoulder so I would look at him. When I finally did, he frowned. "Why do you need to be ready?"

"I just need to prepare for things. It's how I stay comfortable with life."

Cooper leaned his forehead against mine as we floated into deeper water.

"There's no preparing for me," he said then grinned. "I don't even know what I'm doing from minute to minute. Could be worse though. I could be Tucker."

Smiling, I glanced up at his brother who was preparing to cannonball into the water. Maddy didn't want to jump though and they were having a minor tiff. When I looked back at Cooper, I found him watching me in a weird way.

"I forget how you had nothing growing up and every little good thing is a big deal. I need to remember that."

"Today is a really good thing," I said, blinking away the stupid tears. "It's unexpected is all. Moving here was so big for me then I met you and it's a lot."

"I'll be patient," he nearly whispered. "I really want you, Farah. I also really want you to want me. I'm starting to get the hang of being with you."

"Maybe I'm too much effort?"

"No fucking way. It's just I normally get what I want five seconds after I want it. This is new and I need to adjust. You're worth adjusting for."

I held onto the tube with one arm then reached out and caressed his face. Tracing his lips, I couldn't believe how beautiful he looked under the late summer sun.

"After we swim a little more," I said, smiling confidently, "can we go to your apartment?"

"To talk about school and study?" he asked like a smartass.

"Among other things."

Cooper's grin became tender. "You're even more beautiful when you relax. Like the most beautiful thing I've ever seen. Right now, you look very relaxed."

"I've never done anything like this. The way you live. The comfort of it..." I paused, unable to explain. "Yes, I'm very relaxed."

"Hell yeah, you are."

"Hell yeah, I am."

Wiggling around in the water, Cooper groaned. "And these are loose shorts too, but it just doesn't help."

"Won't going to your apartment only make that problem worse?"

"Maybe, but it'll be worth it. I'm going to ruin you for other guys, remember?"

"Oh, I remember."

"But do you believe?" he asked with complete sincerity.

"That you're talented in bed? Oh, I believe alright."

"Asked around, have you?"

"No," I muttered, frowning now.

"You really don't get curious about me? I was curious about you right off the bat."

"I'm curious, but that doesn't mean I'll stalk you or hit up people for dirt. I don't know anyone around here, remember?"

"True," he said before dunking himself underwater. When he reappeared wet, shiny, and pretty damn irresistible, I smiled like I wasn't uncomfortable with how attractive I found him. "You want me," he said, grinning.

"Of course."

"It's all over your face."

"I didn't know I was so easy to read."

"To me, you're an open book. Well, your face is. I sometimes can't see the rest of you behind all of those walls."

"I'm trying."

"Oh, I know," he whispered, sliding his body against mine in the water.

When Cooper pressed our bodies together, I felt how hard he was, but I wasn't sure what to do? Were we having sex in the water?

"Relax," he whispered, grinding softly against me. "I know you're turned on. We're just playing, okay?"

Looking into his eyes, I nodded. No sex. Just a little help for his pants problem. Everything was fine, I told myself. Of course, I worried about an audience.

Glancing up at the deck where Maddy argued with Tucker, I didn't know where Bailey had gone.

"They don't care about us. We're not even on their radar," Cooper said, nuzzling my neck with his lips.

Focusing on Cooper, I refused to freak out. We were just messing around, having a little fun. I wrapped my legs gently around his hips and he groaned into the crook of my neck. With a hand on my butt, Cooper moved me slowly up and down over his erection. I didn't like the feel of it, so I focused on his strong shoulders. Caressing his golden skin, I didn't think about anything waist down.

Instead, I ran my fingers through his wet hair, pressing a lock behind his ear. He was beautiful, so finely built like a model or fantasy man. Cooper was real though and I wanted him. Maybe I didn't want the sex part, but I wanted the man who wanted the sex part.

I needed him to want me too because I wasn't ready for us to be over. I wanted more time to enjoy his teasing and those hungry gazes he gave me. So I let him use me to feel good. I wanted Cooper enough to help a little by grinding against him. He liked that enough to find his relief.

When he looked at me, I knew Cooper worried I was angry. I liked the concern in his eyes and I wanted him to still care about impressing me. One day, he wouldn't and I wasn't ready for that to happen.

"You okay?" he asked, still concerned.

Smiling, I wrapped my arms around his neck. "You have a sickness," I teased. "Did the treatment help any?"

Cooper laughed. "I want you too much to be healthy. I've never been in a constant state of heat before."

"All part of my plan."

"I'm glad I can tell when you're lying. If I thought you were really messing with me, I'd take it personal."

"Stop threatening me," I said, giving his crotch a quick grind.

"Holy hell, you're making me crazy."

"I offered," I said, pulling away from him and dipping my hair into the water to cool my head. "You said no."

"You offered, but your heart wasn't in it."

Sensing Cooper's feelings were hurt by my ability to tell his hot bod no, I reached out and caressed the cross tattoo on his chest.

"I always get nervous the first time I'm with a guy."

"Have you been with a lot of guys?"

"Thousands," I said as my finger traced the perfect lines of the cross. "Too many to count."

Cooper watched me then glanced down at where my fingers slid over his nipple. "You're the devil, Farah. No way you really run this hot and cold."

"I'm not cold. Just nervous."

"Seriously," he said, tapping at my chin to have me look at him, "you've been with a guy before, right?"

"Yes," I said quickly then added, "Just not with you. It's different each time. For me anyway."

"Oh, but not for me because I'm a slut."

Pulling away, I frowned. "You did say you could fuck someone else and pretend she was me. I don't think sex means as much to you as it does to me."

His face a mask of hurt, he asked, "Do you like me at all?"

"Yes," I whispered, frightened by his tone.

"Why? My money? Because I'm hot."

"You make me laugh. You can also be gentle. When you are, I want you more than anything."

Cooper's expression softened. "If you like me and you're not a virgin, why are you so nervous?"

"My life was never predictable and I get startled and nervous easily. I just need to mentally prepare for certain things. Sharing my body is one of them. I'm not confident enough to do it without getting ready first."

Cooper studied me with those dark conflicted eyes. "I keep forgetting your shit childhood and how I need to adjust to that. I'm spoiled, I guess."

"Hell yeah, you're spoiled," I teased.

A grinning Cooper stroked my cheek then let his hand slide down my shoulder to my waist.

"I need to know you like me for real," he said, pressing me against him as the current gently tossed us. "That you feel what I do because I'm nervous now. Like if I fuck up, I'll lose something irreplaceable."

Staring at him, I had no idea how to respond. I kept worrying he was only conning me as a way to add another freshman to his list of bang and hang girls.

"I'm getting hot," I said and Cooper immediately grinned. "Like from the heat. Could we go see your apartment? It's air conditioned, right? I mean, a spoiled guy like you wouldn't expect anything less."

"You don't like it in the water?"

"I do, but the sun is making my head hurt. We can stay if you want."

"Screw the river. I've seen it before. You're all shiny and new and I'm going to figure you out and make you worship me."

"Good luck with that."

"See the steps up?" he asked, pointing towards where the riverbank was the steepest. "We'll swim over and walk up and then walk up some more and eventually we'll walk up the stairs to my place. By then, you'll be too tired to complain when I kiss all over you."

"Why would I complain?"

"We'll be alone near a bed. You're bound to get nervous."

"No sex though or will we? I need to plan in my head for it."

"Baby, I want you to ask me for sex, not the other way around. If you don't ask, it ain't happening."

"So no sex then," I said, kicking away and swimming towards the edge.

"Bitch," he muttered.

"Dickhead," I called over my shoulder.

"Temptress."

"Playboy."

Cooper said something else, but I didn't hear. When I glanced back, he was watching me with an odd expression. I decided not to worry and just swam the rest of the way to the edge. Soon, he joined me up the stairs where Cooper dropped the inner tube on the deck. Tucker had given up on Maddy jumping, so they were making out instead. I didn't see Bailey, not on the deck or as we walked up the stairs to the main house.

Cooper found me a towel and I had it wrapped tightly as we made our way to his place. Upon arriving, I wasn't sure what to expect for an apartment over the garage.

"It smells good," I said then covered my mouth.

Cooper pressed up behind me. "Why wouldn't it smell good?"

"Men are stinky," I said, grinning at him over my shoulder. "It smells good though. Like a model home."

Cooper started to speak then thought better of it. As we entered, there was a small modern kitchen on our left. Straight ahead was a little area with a huge leather couch, giant TV, and enough electronics and video games to keep a teenage boy happy.

Cooper stopped in the kitchen and found two drinks from the refrigerator. A beer for him and a soda for me.

"My girl doesn't drink alcohol because it's illegal," he said in a little girl voice. "What would the man say?"

"Shut up. Laws exist for a reason."

"Yeah, as a way to keep a boot on the neck of people. That and to give certain assholes a sense of power. Nothing more than that."

"Fine, then give me a beer."

"No way. You're too young," he said, taking my hand and leading me to the couch. "Now, we're pretty dry from the heat and the endless walk up here. We should be fine on the furniture, but if you'd like to strip down and go bare ass, I promise not to complain."

Sitting next to him, I cuddled against his chest. "If I was naked, there's no way you'd stop nagging for sex."

"You're that hot, huh?"

"Oh, yeah, irresistible."

"Don't I believe it? You're so hot in that ugly suit that I'm ready to do some begging right now. But I won't because of how you need to mentally prepare." Frowning, I thought he was making fun of me, but he just winked. "No pressure. I'm happy you're here and not looking for reasons to leave."

"I do need to study."

"Oh, lord," he grumbled to himself.

When I licked his jaw, he shut up. "Do you have anything to eat?"

Cooper grinned. "Let me go to the house and get something good. I'm sure there's a shitload of leftovers."

"You don't have to. I can eat anything."

Cooper jumped up. "I know, but you don't ask for much. When you ask, I'm at your command, baby. Watch TV if you want," he said, walking towards the door before coming back and kissing me hard. My tongue met his tongue halfway and I suddenly didn't want him to leave. Wrapping him into my arms, I kept him still and the kiss lingered until he finally let go.

"You're so frisky when wet," he teased, stepping back even as I tried to keep hold of him. "Feel free to snoop around my place while I'm gone. I have no secrets from my girl."

"I'll watch TV."

"Aren't you the least bit curious?"

"If I want to know something, I'll ask."

"Spoken like a true goody-two-shoes. I love it," he said, disappearing out the door.

Returning to the couch, I took the giant remote and pushed forty buttons before getting the damn TV to turn on. The next few minutes, I flipped through channels, completely disinterested in anything not Cooper related.

Finally, I ran to his bedroom just to see where so many girls shed their panties for Cooper. I would be one of those girls soon. A little part of me wanted it to happen as soon as he came back. Only part of that part was interested in the sex though. Mostly, I wanted to know.

Was Jodi right about him falling for me? Or was Cooper just horny for the girl who dared tell him no?

Staring at the bed, I thought it looked comfortable. Extra large and partially made as if he yanked up the covers in a halfhearted attempt to fix up the place. The image of us having sex terrified me, but the thought of lying there with him talking and cuddling made me smile.

Imagining the many girls who enjoyed their time on the bed, I wondered how many used Cooper as much as he used them. I wished I could be confident about sex like those girls because I really wanted Cooper. Mostly, I wanted to know if he would like me in a week or month.

Hearing him at the door, I ran back to the couch and acted casual while watching soccer. Cooper entered with a box full of food in his arms and a bag dangling from his hand.

"I brought your clothes, so you can change."

Standing up, I grinned at him. "Thank you."

"I'm getting the hang of this."

"Stop talking like I'm a grumpy person you need to maneuver," I muttered, giving him a grin so he knew I was teasing.

Ignoring my comment, Cooper licked his bottom lip and my gaze was immediately glued to the gesture.

"You can get naked in my room. I promise not to join you and..."

Rolling my eyes, I grinned. "You want to get yourself riled up."

"Maybe. Getting horny feels good." When I took the bag with my clothes and glanced inside, Cooper sighed. "I did look at your panties and bra. How could I not? I didn't sniff them or anything inappropriate like that."

"Sniff them?"

Cooper grinned. "Tucker sniffs Maddy's panties. He's very proud of this fact."

"I think it goes without saying that I'm not commenting on that."

"No need. The fucker sniffs panties and runs around telling people like he's discovered the cure for cancer. That shit speaks for itself."

Leaving Cooper to set out all of the food he brought over, I shut myself in his room then in his adjoining bathroom. It was clean, functional, and male. Upon smelling his cologne, a weird hot sensation grew in my stomach then moved south. I'd never gotten aroused from a smell before. Staring in the mirror, I realized I was screwed.

No more keeping Cooper at arm's length. No playing it cool, I had fallen hard and wanted to keep him. The thought of being tossed aside already stung, but it was coming one day. Maybe soon. Yet, I might be able to keep him interested for a while.

Again, I considered having sex and testing his interest. My nerves would prevent me from doing anything really sexy like actively participating. I still needed to know if I could keep Cooper after the wait for sex was over.

As soon as I changed into my shorts and tee, I returned to the living room and considered asking Cooper for sex. He was only interested in food though. Hamburgers, hot dogs, corn on the cob, coleslaw, and pounds of potato salad along with sticky buns his mom made after we left. Joining him on the couch, I took the plate he offered. Too nervous to ask, I dug into the food. Cooper sat at the other end of the couch with his feet propped up on the table. When I scooted sideways to face him better, he smiled.

"I can't believe how much food I'm eating," I said after a few minutes of pigging out.

"Why didn't you eat before you came?"

"I did. A piece of toast."

"Watching your weight, baby?" he asked. "Girls are always obsessing. Fucking Bailey thinks she's fat and she's a damn board."

"Watching the checkbook, stud. Gotta make every penny count if I want to pay for school and move Tawny here."

"I could help."

Avoiding his gaze, I shook my head. "You already think I want you for your money."

"Or my hot bod. They're both worthy of worship."

Grinning, I still refused to look at him. "I want to work my way through college. That way when I graduate, I'll know I earned it."

"Doesn't anyone help you?"

"I get a little financial aid and my grandma pays for some stuff. She's not a nice woman, but she doesn't want more losers in the family. Without her help, I wouldn't be here."

"I love her then," Cooper said, leaning forward and stretching so he could kiss my cheek. "She got my girl to New Hampton."

Once he sat back in his groove, I considered smooth ways of asking for sex. Instead, I chickened out again.

"Your mom is a great cook," I said, enjoying the macaroni salad.

"Yeah, self taught. Trial and error. Can you cook?"

"We usually didn't have a kitchen in the motel. I can warm stuff up, but that's it."

Cooper studied me then nodded. "I'd have my mom teach you, but she's pretty scary in the kitchen. Her way or the highway thing. They have evening classes at the college where they teach cooking. Maybe once you get settled in, you can take a class. I know how my girl loves to learn."

Swallowing hard, I blurted out, "After we eat, can we go to your bedroom?"

Cooper glanced at the television and sighed. "No fucking way."

"Why?"

"Your face is why. You look like you might puke."

"I'm nervous, but I want to."

"No fucking way times ten, baby," he said, glancing back at me. "Today is going too damn well. There's no way I'm ruining it by having sex when you're still not sure about me."

"When then?"

"When you look at me and I know you want it. When I know you're giving with your heart and not that big head of yours."

"My head isn't big."

"Figuratively."

"Oh, I still don't think it's big. I'm an average student. Steady like a tortoise."

"Don't talk shit about my girl," he said, gnawing at a corncob. "She's fucking brilliant. She likes me after all."

"Yes, she does," I said then added, "Very much."

Cooper watched me and an emotion flooded his handsome features then was gone.

"We're good together," he said, returning to eating. "Different but complimentary. Don't you think?"

"Yes," I lied.

"My parents are like that."

My stomach flipped. My heart raced. My mind screamed, "You're eighteen! Stop thinking forever! Think of now!" Then, my heart told my head to shut up.

"My parents are too similar," I said. "Maybe that's why they didn't last?"

"Probably. Can you imagine how difficult it is to argue with yourself?"

Smiling, I finished the food and set the plate on the table. After wiping my mouth, I wondered if I should brush my teeth first.

"I should get home soon," I said and Cooper's expression was what I expected. "Do you want to kiss more before I leave?"

As I hoped, this question distracted Cooper from his regret over my leaving. "Hell yeah," he murmured before his lips were on mine.

Shoving his plate on the table, Cooper leaned me back on the couch. He kissed my lips, lingering on the thicker bottom one, before kissing both of my cheeks.

"Why can't you stay later? It's not even dark."

"I didn't get a chance to study a lot during the week. I need to catch up."

"We could watch a movie," Cooper said, his left hand caressing my bare thigh. "Eat dinner and talk. We can talk about Tawny, school, whatever. I'm not ready for you to leave."

"What if we make out for a while then I leave?" I asked, tracing his pouty lips.

"Or we could make out then watch a movie?"

"How long is the movie?"

"Just long enough for you to stay for dinner."

"I just ate."

"We could go swimming in the pool and build up your appetite again."

Grinning at him, I sighed. "I should leave soon."

"No, you should relax. Let me help."

When Cooper's lips found my neck, I actually shuddered. My body sent all kinds of unwanted signals to my brain. The hot tingles were unhelpful hints screaming, "More!"

As my arms wrapped around his wide shoulders, I leaned my head to the left. His lips sucked softly, probably too softly to leave a mark. When his tongue slid up my neck to my mouth, I met him hungrily. Quickly, my legs wrapped around his hips, tugging him closer.

Cooper groaned into my mouth and I felt him tighten his grip around me. My body didn't care about anything except how good he felt and how he promised pleasure. I deserved pleasure, my body assured me. Did I deserve Cooper though? Was he too good for me? Wouldn't he use then forget me?

Ignoring those thoughts, I enjoyed every kiss from Cooper who even in the heat of his need didn't lose his stellar tongue work. Slow, teasing, thorough, he tasted me. So good, I wanted to go to his bed immediately before the fear returned.

"Cooper, please," I moaned when he nibbled at my ear.

"Stop?" he asked, looking at me. "What's wrong?"

"No, don't stop. I want to go to your room."

Cooper gave me his little boy lost expression while stroking my face with his fingers. "Why do you look like that then?"

"Like what?"

"Terrified."

"I'm nervous, but I want to go in your bedroom."

"Why?"

Frustrated, I grinded my hips against his. "That's why."

"You look upset though."

"I'm nervous. Please."

Cooper brushed my hair away from my face then kissed me softly. "You're not ready."

"It's not your place to say that," I muttered.

"It is my place because I'm the one who will look at your face when we're together and know you're not really giving. I'm not sure why you're offering, but you don't really want it," he said then added, "Yet."

"I do."

"I sense your body does," Cooper said, grinning at my hard nipples and flushed face. "You're not ready though. If we went into my room, I don't think things would turn out the way we want. Let's just play around then watch a movie."

Touching his face, my fingers enjoyed the prickles on his jaw. Cooper was so beautiful and I wanted to keep him. While I didn't know if sex would end our relationship or take it to a better level, I needed to know.

"Please," I whispered.

Cooper kissed my forehead then shook his head. "No fucking way. You're not ready. I don't care if you've been with thousands or millions or billions of guys, you're not ready to be with me today. Don't you think if I thought you were that I'd have you in my bed naked by now? Trust me that saying no is killing me, but I want you to be happy and I don't see a wall coming down when I look at your face. I see one going up. So no, Farah,"

Leaning down, he sucked at my throat then spoke quietly in my ear. "Now, if you're interested in some heavy petting with a hint of dry humping then, fuck yeah, we can do that."

Caressing his still slightly damp hair, I sighed. "Yes, please."

A grinning Cooper kissed me and we didn't stop for an hour. Finally, Cooper pried himself off of me and leaned back into the couch. Running his hands through his now dry hair, he gestured for me to come closer.

Cuddling up next to him, I rubbed my lips and smiled. It was rather sad how the human heart found so much self-worth from others, instead of from within. Cooper suddenly had complete control over whether I felt beautiful or ugly. Whether I was a winner or a loser. Whether I deserved to be happy or was kidding myself.

"What movie do you want to watch?" he asked, wrapping his arms around me.

"I don't care."

Cooper turned on The Avengers and we sat for another two hours cuddled up. When the sun was low in the sky, Cooper disappeared to find more food. Again we ate, but I pigged out less after eating so much earlier.

We didn't really talk about anything important. Cooper seemed nervous and very careful with his words. I knew how he felt. After a trip to the bathroom to clean up, I was ready to go.

"Sure you don't want to swim again? We can go to the pool."

"Maybe next time."

Cooper exhaled softly. "There will be a next time, right?"

"If it's up to me, yes."

Giving me his cocky grin, Cooper wrapped an arm around my shoulders as we walked out. Soon, I was on the back of his bike, my arms becoming familiar with the feel of him.

After arriving at my apartment, we stood in front of the door for a minute, saying nothing. I suspected he wanted me to invite him inside, but I knew Amy was home by the sound of the TV.

"Wanna come back over tomorrow?" he asked.

"I have to work and study."

"I thought you didn't work weekends?"

"A girl wanted to take the day off and I need to make extra money for..." I peeked back at the apartment door. When I turned back to Cooper, I whispered, "For Tawny to move here."

Sighing, Cooper glanced around all grumpy like and I waited for the bitching to begin. "What time are you working?" he asked, looking back at me. "I'll visit you."

"From ten to four."

"When will you have time to study?"

"Before and after."

"On Monday, I want you to sit next to me in the back. No front row crap."

"I like the front row."

"More than you like me?"

Frowning, I shrugged. "It's a toss up, but I'll give the back row a try. The view's better."

"Hell yeah, it is."

I stepped closer. "My mom is inside and I don't want to stay out here long. If you plan to kiss me goodbye and leave me wanting more, get to it."

Cooper stretched out his long leg, took one big step, and was against me. I stared up at him in fear and lust. As usual, Cooper looked beautiful, yet terrifying as if he were my salvation and doom wrapped into one tanned muscular body.

His strong hands cupped my face and pulled me closer. I might still worry Cooper was faking his long term interest in me, but I never worried if he was faking his attraction. Kissing me as if claiming me, Cooper was careful though. I felt him holding back and I appreciated this gesture. When I knew he was under control, I could let go and enjoy his affections.

Eventually, he pulled his lips away then kissed me once more softly. Stepping back, he let out an unsteady breath. "I'm not going to say anything about my pants."

"You just did," I muttered, fanning my cheeks.

"Man, that was hot. I'm kissing you like that tomorrow on your break. Prepare to get overheated again, baby."

Cooper was giving me such a cocky grin that I had to mess with him. Placing a hand on his chest, I stared up into his eyes with my most earnest gaze.

"I'll miss you."

Yep, that worked. Cooper's smile faded and he just stared full of longing. Less horny hunger, more all encompassing desire. The kind of need I worried would destroy me.

"Don't tease," he whispered.

"I'm not. Well, I was, but I will miss you. I had a lot of fun today. Even more than at dinner."

Cooper gave me a soft smile. "I'm leaving before I fuck up and scare you off again."

"I'll see you tomorrow."

Cooper's grin widened. "Make sure to wear that sexy uniform of yours, okay?"

Laughing, I rolled my eyes then reached for the doorknob. Yet, I didn't go inside right away. Instead, I watched him walk away, knowing he knew I was watching. Even if I wasn't certain based on what I knew about Cooper, it was confirmed when he reached the front gate and gave me a naughty wink.

Chapter Eleven

Sunday flew by faster than I anticipated. As soon as I got up, I called Tawny. She was still stuck in the motel, but Dad had returned for a few minutes to say they would be leaving soon. Even though I knew she was freaked out, my little sister mostly wanted to talk about Cooper and kissing. We had to keep the conversation short, but I gave her all of the juicy details.

Cramming a long list of required reading into the few hours before work, I didn't get very far. Amy wasn't around so I used the busses to travel to work. I hadn't worked a Sunday in Ellsberg before and it was completely different than the night shift. Table after table of customers and tons of tips, it was so busy I nearly missed when Cooper walked in with Maddy and Tucker.

Unlike his nightly visits to the restaurant, Cooper didn't stay for more than an hour. He did talk to the manager so I could get my break early. Those fifteen minutes consisted of Cooper taking me outside, pressing me against his truck, and kissing the living hell out of me. Trying to keep up, I even attempted to make my tongue do that slow methodical tasting thing he did. Instead, I just got excited and sucked at his tongue while grabbing him tighter. Though I didn't improve my kissing skills, I was getting a whole lot more confident.

As bummed as I was when Cooper left, I returned to a very busy shift. I even picked up a few extra hours when a girl needed to come in late. By the time I headed to bed, I was a little behind on my schoolwork. I also missed both Cooper and Tawny, but knew I would see him the next day. If I kept picking up extra shifts, it wouldn't be long before I saw my sister too.

On Monday, Skye was too busy to hang out. Eating alone, I saw Nick doing the same against a nearby tree. Thinking of how far behind I was with schoolwork, I joined him. We did the basic hellos and small talk then I got to my point.

"Do you think you'd have time to study together? I'm having trouble keeping up."

Nick patted the ground next to him. "They had me work double shifts at the store over the weekend, so I didn't have time to do anything either."

After finishing our lunch, we spent the last few minutes before our next class going over an assignment. Nick might have been falling behind, but I got the sense I was even farther behind than him. A lot of what he said didn't register like it should. Once in our English Lit, I copied his notes from past classes. Not only were his notes more extensive, his penmanship was excellent. I could imagine him making a great teacher.

When Nick smiled at me, it wasn't like how Cooper did. Nothing overtly sexual or teasing, he was just friendly. If he still liked me, he wasn't obvious about it. While I found Nick attractive, I was hooked on Cooper. My whole body hummed whenever I thought of the sexy jerk. If I thought about him for too long, I would smile randomly like an idiot for everyone to see.

By the time Spanish class arrived, I could barely wait to see Cooper. Yet, a little part of me worried he might be cold. What if he lost interest overnight or met someone else? Even knowing this was unlikely, I worried I'd lose Cooper now that I needed him so much.

Standing at the front of the class, I talked with Nick who sat in his seat. Cooper was usually one of the last people to arrive and I didn't want to sit in the back without him. The stoner and sleeping guy were grumpy and hated when anyone approached them. Cooper could because he was fucking scary.

When Nick dropped his pencil and managed to kick it halfway across the class, the look on his face sent me into hysterics. This was the moment Cooper chose to enter the room. This was also the moment I understood our honeymoon phase was over.

"What's so fucking funny?" he muttered.

It had been a great day. A great last few days, but all of my joy and confidence disappeared.

"He dropped his pencil."

Cooper rolled his eyes then took me by the back of the neck and pulled me closer for a really inappropriate kiss in front of the whole class. As a few girls giggled and a guy whistled, I just waited for it to be over.

After letting me go, Cooper pulled me to the back of the room and yanked a chair closer to his. Finally, he sat down and patted hard on it for me to sit down.

"Why are you always fucking hanging around him?" Cooper whispered loudly once I sat down.

"He's in a few of my classes and he's helping me study."

"I'll help you study. I'm a hell of a lot fucking smarter than that piece of shit."

Cooper spoke so loudly that people outside the room likely heard him. Wanting to disappear inside myself, I thought to distract him.

"I missed you," I said softly, giving him the best smile I could manage.

"Didn't seem like it when I arrived."

"Why do you care so much about Nick?" I whispered. "He's just a guy who wants to be a teacher. Besides being freshmen, that's all we have in common. I really like you, but you're scaring me."

Placing my hand on his forearm, I hoped to settle Cooper down and have him focus on me. Instead, he glared at Nick who did his best to ignore him. Unsure what to do, I lifted my hand to return it to my lap.

Cooper grabbed my hand and replaced it on his arm. Staring at him, I felt like nothing I remembered from the weekend was real. He might have even only liked me out of a weird competitiveness with Nick.

When Manuel entered the room, everyone breathed again except for Cooper and me. I sat with my head down and my hand stuck against his arm. Cooper dug his heels into the ground, making squeaking noises as his boots met the linoleum.

"Why him?" he growled in my ear.

There was nothing to say. Nick was a nice guy, but I'd fallen for Cooper. I even imagined a future for us, but I wasn't sure I wanted him anymore.

Cooper let go of my hand and crossed his arms angrily. He sat like that for the entire class while everyone ignored us. I didn't pay attention to the instructor. I could only fight the urge to bawl and run away. Why did Cooper have to ruin everything?

When class was almost over, Cooper leaned towards me and spoke quietly. His voice lacked much of the earlier heat, but his gaze was again on the back of Nick's head.

"Tell me you're my girl and I'll let this go."

"I was yours, but not anymore."

Cooper glared harder at Nick. "If he takes you from me, I'll kill him. I'm not kidding."

Leaning away from him, I packed my books. "Don't worry about it. I'm done dating for a long time. Men are assholes."

As soon as Manuel said we could leave, I bolted out of my chair and ran for the door. I needed away from Cooper. I didn't want to see Nick either because I felt guilty for drawing attention to him. Crying, I hoped to get to my bus, go home, and hide for a while before work.

Feeling his gaze on me, I knew Cooper was following and I couldn't outrun him. The people around me backed off and walked away, unwilling to get sucked into the upcoming drama. In that moment, I accepted how I was completely on my own in Ellsberg. Grown men, instructors, and even a security guard walked away, leaving me alone on the grassy quad with Cooper.

Turning towards him, I clenched my hands into fists. My fight or flight kicking in, I realized flight was no longer an option. Staring up at Cooper, I saw his expression shift from anger to surprise then he looked a little panicked.

"It's okay," he said softly. "Don't cry."

"Leave me alone."

"I just want to talk."

"Fuck you," I muttered through clenched teeth. "I made myself think you were this great guy and I missed you all day then you showed up and embarrassed me. You treated me like a piece of trash in front of everyone. You threatened Nick who's never been anything except nice to me. You're acting like a psycho."

Knowing the words were harsh, I'd likely sealed my fate. Yet, I expected to be hurt anyway. I could imagine a slow painful death after Cooper was done playing with me. People wouldn't care or mention I existed. Tawny would sit alone in a motel room, waiting day after day for me to call.

"Farah," Cooper began, his movements careful, "don't be scared."

"Leave me alone. I want to go home."

"Let me drive you."

Shaking my head, I backed away when he stepped forward. Cooper sighed and reached out to caress my wet cheeks.

"I'm so crazy about you," he whispered in a pained voice. "I hate how our schedules don't match up except for this fucking class. I waited all day to see you too then some asshole asked if you and I broke up because he saw you hanging out with another guy. I ignored his bullshit, but then I saw you with that piece of shit and I just freaked, okay?"

"Not okay. Nick is helping me get caught up because I'm falling behind in class. Even if he liked me, he knew I was dating you and he's scared of you like everyone else."

"Including you?" Cooper asked, reaching out to gently unclench my hands. "I acted like a jackass in class, but I'm not going to hurt you."

"You did," I said, yanking my hands away as more tears broke forward. "You embarrassed me. I don't want everyone looking at me and laughing. People think I'm just some slut you're fucking. Like I'm nothing."

Stepping closer, Cooper used his thumb to caress away a little of the wetness on my cheeks. "That's not what they think. They think I'm an asshole and you're my hot girlfriend."

"It's not funny."

"I'm not being funny. I'm an ass for acting like that. I looked insecure and stupid. They're judging me, not you."

Between his calm tone and gentle touch, I settled down a little. Did I even have a choice? Could I tell Cooper goodbye and he'd move on? I wasn't even sure I wanted to tell him goodbye. I'd spent all of Sunday and most of Monday thinking about how he might be mine. Now, I was confused.

"Let me drive you home," he said, trying to hug me, but I jerked away. "People are still around and I embarrassed you earlier. Let's talk in private."

"You're trying to manipulate me."

Staring up at the sky, Cooper sighed. "When I saw you with that douche, I lost track of what I wanted. I got so focused on keeping him away from you that I forgot to make sure you were happy." Returning his gaze to my face, he sighed again. "I'm floundering here, but I need you to give me another chance. I let my temper get away from me. I know that and I'm not someone who freaks out a lot. It won't happen again."

"Ever?"

Cooper grinned. "I'll be a perfect angel from this moment on."

"I feel like I should stay mad at you. Like I'd be encouraging bad behavior by forgiving you."

"You're thinking about this all wrong," Cooper said, turning me around to face the parking lot. We walked to his Harley then he smiled. "You did nothing wrong today. You were perfect. Why should you miss out on a ride home? Why not let the asshole get you a decent meal? Why not have the piece of shit kiss your neck when we both know you love that? Why not even have him help you study because he deserves to be really bored?"

Smiling despite my better judgment, I hitched up my backpack. "It's true I would benefit from forgiving you. I still think you should suffer for being such an asshole. You acted like Tucker back there."

"Hey, now that's a bit harsh, don't you think?" he muttered, faking like he was angry, but I saw through his bullshit. "I've never been jealous like that before. Apparently, I need to build up a little resistance so I don't lose my shit every time a guy enters my territory."

"I'm not territory."

"But you're mine," Cooper said, leaning down to kiss me.

I kept the kiss brief. My hands were still shaking from earlier and I knew my makeup had likely smeared from crying. I wasn't letting Cooper's psycho behavior in class fade away just because he wasn't pissed anymore.

"I guess a ride home would only be fair, but I want you to know I'm using you when I agree to this."

Cooper grinned then leaned down to kiss me again. I kept this kiss brief too, making him sigh.

"Wanna go for a ride first?" he asked, nuzzling my hair.

"I need to study."

"A short ride," he said, finally giving me a hug.

Like an idiot, I shuddered at the feel of him. Giving him all of the power again, I couldn't stay angry. At least, not when he was gentle, but now I knew he wouldn't always be gentle. Sometimes, he would scare the shit out of me, embarrass me, and treat me like a possession.

Looking up at him, I found his gaze soft like from the weekend. "I should go home."

"A short ride to relax you. Just imagine the wind in your hair on this hot damn day," he said, his fingers teasing my scalp. "We could stop and have a quick dinner. You've had a tough day. Why not enjoy a free dinner from the one who fucked things up?"

"I know what you're doing."

Cooper's dark eyes studied my face then he smiled. "I really am crazy about you. Let me make it up to you."

"What about Nick?" I asked, daring him to freak out again.

His jaw twitching, Cooper shrugged. "He's a guy. He gets it. In fact, I think he's hot for one of those giggly blondes in class. Shar, I think is the one. No need for me or anyone else to care about old Nick."

"So I can study with him?"

Cooper narrowed his eyes and exhaled hard. "Why him?"

"He's in a bunch of my classes and he takes great notes."

"Great notes? Is that code?"

"I waited all day to see you, Coop," I said, placing my hand on his chest where I knew the cross was hiding under his white tee. "I missed you then you ruined everything by focusing on him. Will you keep doing that? I need you to focus on me."

"You want me, right? Not him."

"I want you so much, but I think it's a mistake. You obviously don't trust me."

"Don't make it about trust. It's not even about you."

"What the hell does that mean?" I asked, removing my hand.

Cooper looked ready to grab my hand and return it to his chest. I saw him fight the urge then he forced a smile. A really fake smile that never reached his eyes.

"It's about me. It's about my feeling like someone is trying to take away what I need. You aren't doing anything. I just can't have a man sniffing around my girl."

"He's not sniffing around me."

"Don't be naïve."

"You said he liked Shar."

"Why do you care who he likes?"

Backing away, I sighed. "I'm taking the bus home."

"No, wait," he said, wrapping his arms around me as I retreated. "Look, I'm jealous. That's not a bad thing, is it? If you saw me with some chick, wouldn't you be jealous?"

"Yes, but I wouldn't freak out and scare everyone."

"That's because you're classy. I was raised to be a caveman though. I should get credit for not taking you by the hair and dragging you back to my cave. You know, after clubbing your boyfriend to death first."

"You're nuts."

"I'm teasing you."

"Not completely," I said, staring at him in horror.

"No, not completely. Well, I'm not kidding about clubbing him to death, but I'd never drag you back to my cave. Me want woman to want it bad."

Grinning, I shook my head and turned away. "I feel like encouraging you is wrong. If I don't punish you, how else will you learn?"

Wrapping me up in his arms again, he nuzzled my hair. "That's not how people learn, baby. Positive reinforcement works better. Lots of treats to reward good behavior."

"What good behavior?" I asked, leaning back against him.

"The good behavior of me driving you to a quiet place where we can eat and talk. Then, the good behavior of driving you home so you can study a little before work. Then, the very good behavior of me tipping you something crazy tonight at work."

"I do like tips," I said, grinning again.

"Oh, and I love giving them. I also love giving you rides and meals. I'm so generous that way. It's enough to offset my asshole behavior."

"Almost enough."

"Sure, whatever," he said, kissing me.

Pressing myself against Cooper, I tried to forget what happened mere minutes before, but I couldn't. I had grown up believing around every corner was a threat. Yet, Cooper wasn't around a corner. He was in my arms and had too much power over me. While I still wanted him to be mine, I was beginning to realize what I wanted wouldn't matter. Cooper got what he wanted and I'd just have to survive it.

Chapter Twelve

The next day in the middle of my Government class, Cooper appeared at the door and gestured for me to come outside. At first, I thought he looked nervous then realized he was in hurry.

"I need to leave town for a day or two to handle something," Cooper said, twirling my hair in his fingers. "I wanted to tell you before I left, so you wouldn't read too much into it."

"Is everything okay?" I asked, touching his chest.

Cooper only smiled. "I'm going to miss the hell out of you, Farah."

"Just a day or two?"

"Will you miss me?"

"Of course," I said as my heart raced. "Why are you leaving?"

"I need to handle something for my pop and Tucker's coming with me. It'll only be two days at the most."

"I'll miss you," I babbled, feeling uneasy with him leaving. "Be careful."

Cooper grinned. "It's nothing, baby. I went ahead and arranged to have Skye drive you home from school each day and to work. My buddy Aaron will pick you up from work and take you home."

"That's not ne…"

"Haven't you heard about the assholes harassing girls around here?" When I shook my head, Cooper sighed. "Every year when school starts, new assholes arrive and see what they can get away with. The assholes this year have grabbed a few girls and nearly raped another. Until we find out who they are, you're not safe to travel alone."

"I can…"

"This isn't up for discussion. If you want, I'll have Aaron tail your busses home. Whatever way it happens, I need to know you're safe. I'm making the same arrangements for Bailey and Skye. That's why she can't pick you up after work. I don't want you out at night without a guy or a group of girls around. These idiots will hit a few girls alone, but more than three and they pussy out. I don't blame them. A girl managed to mace one of the fuckers. Too bad he got away and is still out there."

Cooper grinned at the idea of a girl using mace. "Anyway, I can't leave town and worry about you. As long as you're at school and work, I know you're cool. It's traveling between that makes me nervous. Do this for me, okay? No bitching about me controlling shit. Just let my friend drive you home."

"Who is Aaron?"

"He and I own a tattoo place," Cooper said, wrapping me in his arms. "I shelled out the cash and he's the artist. Known him since middle school. Solid guy and he'll make sure you're safe."

I wasn't sure what my face did, but a smiling Cooper caressed my cheek.

"He's not scary. Yes, he's sporting a snake up his neck and a shaved head, but the guy's the real sensitive type. Probably writes poetry."

Grinning now, I sighed. "I'm sorry. New people freak me out."

"New tattooed people are the worst, aren't they?" he said, holding me tighter. "I will be back soon and we'll hang out. Oh, and don't take shifts for this weekend. I want to make up for lost time, kay?"

Nodding, I stared up at him, suddenly afraid he wouldn't be mine once he returned. Cooper likely sensed my fear because he kissed me as if making very clear how he wasn't done with me yet.

The rest of the afternoon sucked and I wasn't interested in hanging out with Skye. Her life revolved around Tyler and I doubted she was happy to give up time with him to follow Cooper's commands. No matter how she felt though, Skye showed up for lunch and talked the whole time about Tyler. Her enthusiasm was funny and distracting.

After class, she insisted I hang out at her dorm where we ordered a pizza and studied. This last part ended as soon as the food arrived.

"I wish Tyler was Jewish so my parents could meet him," Skye said as she picked toppings off the pizza and ate them. "I guess it's possible he'd give up the Jesus thing."

When I only smiled at her, Skye shrugged. "I hope we stay together for the rest of the year. I'm sick of hooking up. All through high school, I went to parties at the nearby college and hooked up. I wasn't interested in dating anyone. I had a lot of stuff going on and a boyfriend takes too much work. Now, I'd like to have the same guy for a while."

"Tyler smiles a lot when he's around you. That's a good sign."

Skye grinned. "I've been a crappy friend because I forgot how good a friend you are."

"I just don't want you to worry. Tyler seems really into you."

"Yeah, he's so hot though that a girl is bound to stress."

After a few minutes of eating toppings off the pizza and pretending to study, Skye nudged me with her foot.

"Have you and Cooper done it yet?" When I shook my head, Skye frowned. "Why not?"

"We've only been really dating for a week."

"So? My friend in Memphis fucked him within three hours of them meeting. It only took her that long because her little brother was around. Once they were alone, she and Cooper swapped fluids. What's your hold up? Oh, wait, are you a virgin?"

"No," I said, fiddling with a pencil. "I've been nervous about being with him though."

"He thinks you're hot, Farah. Cooper's too shallow to hang around a chick for this long if he didn't think you were really hot. Strip him down and get you some of that sexy bastard. My friend Kacey said he's really good at both redneck fucks and mama's boy fucks. He also has a very talented tongue. Super thorough." Skye sighed. "Tyler and I haven't done oral yet. Hopefully, we will this weekend. I'm a big fan of oral. Well, not giving, but receiving."

Skye watched me for a minute. "You do like sex, right?"

"Not really. I mean, it's never been that great."

"Oh, well, it will be with Cooper. This isn't me talking. That's Kacey and she wasn't a virgin so she had something to compare him to. Cooper's great in the sack."

"What do the redneck and mama's boy things mean?"

Leaning back on her fluffy white bed, Skye laughed. "You don't know anything. What did you talk about in high school?"

"We moved a lot so I didn't talk to many people."

"Oh, really?" Skye asked, suddenly concerned. "Didn't you have any good friends to bullshit with?"

"Just my younger sister."

"Bummer. I had a solid group of friends and I miss the shit out of them. Oh, well, the various fucks. Okay, so the redneck fuck is fast and hard. Some chicks dig that and all guys do. Most guys around here can only fuck fast and hard. They couldn't slow themselves down if their lives depended on it. Tyler's good though. Real mama's boy."

Sitting across from Skye, I mentally prepared for the fast and hard fuck from Cooper.

"Now, some guys love their mamas so much that they get real sensitive to a girl's needs, if you know what I mean?" When I just stared, Skye continued, "Thorough, you know? They take their time and really make the girl come apart. Cooper is known for being really good at fucking a girl until she can't walk and not like Tucker does. That boy will fuck a girl so hard she'll lose brain function afterwards from the head injury she gets from hitting the headboard so much. Cooper's got some moves. And Kacey said the fucker has the best tongue. I'm sure you've enjoyed more than a few major hot kisses by now."

As I nodded, Skye's gaze became distant. "Tyler kisses like heaven. I really wish I could keep him, but my dad wouldn't be cool with it. Even if I could convert Tyler, my mom would still be weird about having a science nerd in the family. She's so weird that way."

"Do you think Cooper is okay with this thing for his family?"

"Sure. He's inheriting the mantle from his dad so he'll need to handle a lot of shit soon."

"What exactly do the Johanssons do?"

Skye studied me in an odd way. "Cooper hasn't told you?"

"No."

"Maybe I shouldn't then."

"If you did tell me, I wouldn't tell him you did."

"Well," she began, sucking in a deep breath, "they're in management. Or sales, I guess. No management of sales."

"I don't get it."

Skye twisted her long blonde hair around a finger and shrugged. "Kirk worked in Memphis for a long time for a powerful business. When he met Jodi, she wanted to move somewhere quiet to raise their kids. She also wanted to be near a college so she could take courses. It was always her dream to do that, so Kirk found this place. Back then, another business managed the area, but Kirk talked to his bosses and they agreed to help him remove the businessmen. Kirk would take over and give a percentage back to his old bosses. That was obviously a few decades ago and since then the Johanssons have managed this area."

"Managed what exactly?"

"Do you really want to know?"

Everything about Cooper was something I wanted to know, even the bad stuff.

When I nodded, Skye squinted hard at me. "If you mouth off about his family business or blab to the cops, even Cooper can't protect you," Skye said, snapping her fingers. "Just like that you'd be gone and no one would even ask about you. You understand, right?"

Even with my heart pounding like crazy, I needed to know because I wanted Cooper to be mine.

"They manage everything," Skye said, holding a pillow on her lap as if for protection. "Drugs, whores, guns, gambling. Anything that doesn't fall under the banner of legal, they manage it. They allow people to work in their territory for a chunk of the profit. If someone doesn't pay or starts trouble, the family gets rid of the problem and installs someone new. If this area's criminal activity is a business, they are management. Soon, Cooper will be the new CEO."

"Oh."

"Don't fucking tell anyone," Skye hissed. "Don't think it's cute or cool and talk about it with anyone. Not your mom or anyone. If you do, Cooper will have to cut you loose. I don't think he'd have the stomach to get rid of you himself because he seems really into you, but Tucker would do you in a minute. That's what the idiot's good for. He doesn't care about that shit, so don't fucking talk."

"I won't," I promised, thinking of how I'd have no one to tell even if I wanted to blab. "I wouldn't hurt Cooper or his family."

Skye's angry expression eased and she sighed. "I just don't want you blabbing and anyone getting mad at me, okay? My dad is an accountant. He's not some badass. If we were in trouble, he wouldn't know how to hide like some other fuckers. Man, you better not tell."

"I promise I'll never tell. I just want to go to school and hang out with you and be with Cooper. I have no reason to start trouble for anyone."

As Skye nodded, I saw both fear and anger in her eyes. After a few minutes of sitting silently, she nodded again.

"You're cool, Farah. It's why I told you," Skye said, calming herself. "I have a good life though and my parents worked hard to do well. I don't want anything fucking that up."

"I'll never tell anyone what you said."

Skye looked around the room then back at me. "You need to fuck Cooper soon if you want to keep him. I'm not trying to be mean, but he doesn't go long without fucking. He shouldn't need to wait for anyone and no other girl would tease him. If you're teasing to make him like you, just stop. If you're scared or nervous or whatever, get over it. Guys like Cooper get what they want and he wants you. Either you'll give him what he wants or he'll stop wanting you. Again, I'm not trying to be mean, but if you want to keep him then you need to ditch your emotional shit and put out."

"I was thinking this weekend."

"Good. Anything longer and I don't think Cooper would want you anymore. I mean, he likes you for real, but he's got needs," Skye said, glancing towards the door where girls talked loudly. When her gaze returned to me, she smiled. "I know he likes you, so maybe he'd wait. Not wait for sex, but for you. He'll just fuck someone on the side until you're ready. I don't know about you, but I wouldn't want Tyler fucking someone on the side because I was too uptight to put out. Not that you're uptight. I mean, if you've had crappy fucks before then you're bound to not want to jump in bed. Still, Cooper's really good so just put out as soon as possible."

"This weekend," I said quietly, feeling anxious now.

"Look," Skye said, sitting closer and softening her expression. "I get how you're scared. A guy like Cooper can be overwhelming, but he can also be a great friend. Like even after he's done with you, he'd still help you out if you needed something. Like if you were short on cash or if someone's hassling you, Cooper would make things easier."

"I heard he acts like he doesn't know girls' names after he's done with them."

"Oh, yeah, sometimes, but only if they get clingy. Also, a few of those girls were bitches to Bailey. Cooper can't have anyone shitting on his sister. Still, with Kacey, he was always nice. When her ex was hounding her, Cooper busted the guy's head open. Problem solved. They weren't even fucking anymore, but Cooper helped her out. That's what you need to keep in mind. You have a tough life with being poor and having nothing, but Cooper can make it easier. Not just while you're together, but even afterwards. It's a long four years you'll spend here and why not have a friend like Cooper? So when you think about how maybe you're not ready or whatever, just think about how being a friend to Cooper is better than being the bitch that teased him and never put out. Don't be that bitch."

Swallowing hard, I nodded. "I won't."

"Of course, you won't because you're cool. That's why you're my best friend. Even better than Bailey who threw a beer at me because I have a boyfriend and she doesn't. You'd never do that, would you?"

Shaking my head, I smiled at Skye who smiled back at me.

"Bailey is like a cousin to me. That's how family is, you know? They suck sometimes, but you still love them. Well, I love Bailey, but she sucks a lot. You better be ready to duck if you go out with us this weekend. She's really pissed about not having a boyfriend."

"She's so pretty and fun. It seems weird that she can't find someone."

Skye frowned at me then reached for another pizza slice. "Would you want to date a chick like Bailey, knowing who her family was? Like what if you pissed her off and Tucker showed up at your place with a baseball bat? Not cool."

By the time Skye drove me home, I was ready to cry for the rest of the night. I felt stuck in a relationship with a scary guy from a criminal organization. A scary guy I couldn't get enough of either.

Arriving home, I found Amy at the kitchen table with a hippy-looking guy. While he was probably a decade younger than her, my mom screamed MILF. Cougars ran in my family too.

"Yo," the guy said. "I'm Tex."

"That's my oldest girl. I have two, remember?" Amy mumbled, sounding drunk.

"Oh, I remember," Tex said, giving her a grin. "I remember every sexy word you say."

Amy laughed while I tried not to roll my eyes. Walking to my room, I shut and locked the door before considering whether to shove a dresser against it. I wanted to call Tawny, but my thoughts were all jumbled up.

I needed to have sex with Cooper that weekend. It was all I could think about as I waited for Skye to pick me up for work. If I put off sex any longer, Cooper would punish me. Or cheat on me. I didn't like either consequence. If I made Cooper happy, he could be a good friend. I needed good friends.

Under all of the panic, I missed Cooper. Like when Skye scared the shit out of me during our friendly chat, I wanted Cooper to hold me. He made the ugliness in the world fade away. Yet, he was scarier than Tex or Skye. Cooper was the guy other scary guys were afraid of and I was planning to have sex with that uber scary guy. I just hoped I didn't do anything wrong to make him my enemy.

On the ride to work, Skye talked about Tyler's chest. How she liked to touch it with her fingers. How she liked to lick it. How she liked to rub her nipples against it. Skye was deeply in love with Tyler's chest. I also sensed she was getting me revved up for my sex weekend with Cooper. Instead, I felt worse because I doubted I would ever like Cooper's chest as much as she liked Tyler's. I just wasn't that horny of a person.

Work sucked. My only customers were rude college students who tipped me a dime then came back and asked for change. My normal older customers arrived during my break so they ended up with Piper. Overall, it was a crap shift until Aaron arrived an hour before I was ready to leave.

The cobra up the neck gave him away and I doubted he could do stealth well. Once Aaron was seated, he ordered coffee and a burrito then kept his head down. I glanced at his sketches when I delivered the food and he really was an artist. I suspected he was the one who did the beautiful black and gray angel on Cooper's arm that I loved so much.

Aaron wasn't at all what I was expecting. Quiet and clean cut, he looked like an average guy except for his tattoos. He also had a great smile as he walked me to his little Honda.

"You're not what I was expecting," Aaron said as we drove to my apartment.

"Why?"

"Cooper is in heat over you," he said then added quickly, "Not that you aren't hot. I just thought you'd be a wild harlot or something."

"Oh."

Aaron smiled. "Coop's a great guy. Loyal to a fault. He'll bail you out when you're in trouble. Do whatever necessary to help a friend in need. He's loyal with girls too. Not that I've seen him in a relationship that lasted more than a week, but he didn't mess around for that week."

Nodding again, I wasn't sure what to say so Aaron continued as we neared my apartment, "So Coop's great, but he's also an entitled ass. He was born thinking the world owed him shit. Things have always been so easy for him too. He's got money, a good family, looks, brains. Everything is just handed to him so he has no patience. He wants what he wants that very second or the world has screwed him."

Remaining quiet, I thought everything Aaron said was dead on.

"I know Cooper can be too much. He can be loud and rude. He can dominate those around him and see nothing wrong with it. I've been ready to tell him to fuck off plenty of times over the years. He just takes what he wants and only after people complain does he ever think about consequences. Yet, if you like him even a little bit and think you can endure the stupid shit that comes out of his mouth sometimes, I'd suggest you hold onto Cooper. He's pretty crazy about you and that doesn't happen with him. Who knows, maybe you can train his rude mouth so it doesn't spit out whatever insane shit he's thinking?"

"I don't know if I'm that good."

Aaron pulled to the curb and turned off the car. "Don't get offended by him sharing this with me, but I know you two haven't slept together yet. Cooper has a rule about waiting a week for a girl to put out. It's been longer than a week since he started talking about you. You haven't put out in that time, but he's still waiting. You have more power than you think so don't let his big mouth make you think otherwise."

"I really like Cooper, but he's a bit..." I said, unable to finish.

"Rough? A huge asshole? I know, but he's gotten away with that all of his life. If he needs to behave, he can though. I hope you'll give him a chance. He's my friend and I want him to be happy, but you're not what I thought you'd be. I prefer what you are because it makes me think he has good taste."

When I smiled, Aaron sighed. "I want to make it clear that I'm not kissing your ass or coming onto you. I should just point out how if Coop ends up with some loudmouth ballsy chick that he'd never shut the fuck up. He needs someone to keep him from turning into a fulltime asshole."

"Do you think he's okay? I don't really know what he's doing and his leaving happened so fast."

"He'll be fine. Coop gets what he wants, remember?"

Nodding, I still felt lonely with Cooper so far away. He was the person in Ellsberg I trusted the most. I knew it was foolish to become so attached, but he was mine and I needed to know he still wanted me. I'd have to wait two more days to find out.

Chapter Thirteen

One of the evening regulars was an older woman named Nancy. She came in nearly every night for dinner and every morning for breakfast. For her evening meals, she began requesting me. Piper hated me a little for this, only because I think Piper was homesick and was happiest when hating someone.

Nancy and I were talking about the weather when her gaze focused on the person waiting to be seated. Looking towards the front of the restaurant, I nearly giggled with relief at seeing Cooper. For whatever reason, I had started worrying he would never come back.

Excusing myself with Nancy, I tried to casually walk to Cooper, but nearly ran instead. Then, he gave me a cocky smile, knocking the wind out of me. As if I was the latest stupid girl to think she mattered.

"What now?" he asked, losing his smile. "You were happy then somehow the walk over here made you unhappy. I have a talent apparently."

"I missed you."

Cooper's smile returned, but this one was softer. His dark eyes studied me then he pulled me to the front door where there was more privacy.

"Hell yeah, you did," he whispered, kissing me as his arms wrapped me against him.

My fingers gripped his white tee and I wished everything I thought about him was true. Could he be mine forever? Forget his money and influence, Cooper's affections made me feel special. I had never felt that way before and it was addictive.

Pulling his lips away, Cooper kept me snuggled in his arms. "Never have I missed a girl like I missed my girl the last few days. You can't know how crazy bad I wanted to get to town."

"I missed you," I said again, unable to explain how much better I felt with him back.

Cooper studied me in a gentle way like maybe he did understand. His strong fingers twirled my ponytail. "Baby, let me hang out until you get off. Then, I'll drive you home and we'll stop missing each other."

Nodding, I thought of sex. Cooper used his ability to read my every facial expression to figure out what I was thinking.

"You look tired," he whispered in my ear. "I drove half the day and my ass is asleep. I'm not having our first time happen with a tired butt."

Laughing, I tugged at his shirt. "I really missed you and I didn't take any shifts for this weekend. Hopefully, your ass will feel better by then."

Cooper lifted a brow and gave me a little nod. "Oh, it'll be tiptop by then."

"I hope so," I said, squirming free of his warm embrace. "Will you have your usual?"

"When do you go on your break?"

"In an hour."

"I'll wait to eat until then so you can join me."

Smiling like an idiot, I missed him more than I should have. Even so, everything instantly felt better knowing Cooper was nearby.

Saying nothing specific about his trip, he mainly asked about Aaron and if anyone hassled me. I told him I was fine except for missing him. This comment sent Cooper's horniness into overdrive and he proved how much he missed me when we got to my place.

The next day, I hadn't seen him except in passing when he ran over, sucked on my lips a little, then told me that he was in a hurry. I spent the next few hours worrying he was in a rush to meet someone else. At some point, I'd become convinced he was losing interest.

On my way to the parking lot to wait for Skye, I heard a motorcycle approaching and turned to find Cooper pulling up. His gaze was dark and serious.

"Why don't you like sex?" he asked, a smile fighting at the corners of his lips.

Glancing around in horror at everyone who heard him, I muttered, "You've got to be kidding."

"Look, Farah," he said, finally grinning while climbing off his bike. "One bad lay shouldn't mean you give up all fucking forever."

"That was very charming. It should be quoted on romantic Hallmark cards."

"Yeah, I do have a way with words. Seriously though, sex is fun. Just because you fucked some limp dick who lasted only a minute or came in your eye or shoved it up the wrong hole or whatever the problem was doesn't mean you should give up on getting properly fucked."

"Stop talking," I said, still glancing around at the other students. "People can hear you."

"I don't give a shit about people. Besides, I'm sure they'd agree with me. Even if they didn't, my only concern is getting in your pants."

"Well, maybe this weekend."

"Don't tease. Seriously, my dick gets hard every time I see you."

"Stop saying stuff like that."

Cooper leaned down and nuzzled his lips against my hair. "Did limp dick talk to you like that and so it brings up bad memories of his shitty moves?"

"Yes, he was a pig, just like you."

"Fortunately, you love pork."

Walking away, I wanted to either laugh or cry. Embarrassed, I felt exposed and betrayed. Yeah, betrayed! I told Skye in confidence my views on sex because I wanted her to understand why I hadn't humped Cooper the moment I met him.

Cooper roared up behind me on his bike then reached over, grabbed my backpack, and pulled me to a stop. Turning to him, I tried not to cry right there. Yet, I hadn't been so embarrassed since I leaked on my period and no one said anything for half of the day. I didn't know why everyone was giggling until Tawny told me at lunch. While that was temporary high school crap, I'd enjoy this embarrassment for four years.

"Hey," he said softly, wrapping his arm around my waist. "Don't be sad. Bailey told me because she knows I like you. She wanted to warn me that you aren't playing cold because you're a bitch. You just have your issues. Don't cry."

Wiping my eyes, I refused to look at him. "I'm embarrassed."

"Because some guy gave you a bad fuck? Shit, half of the girls in school can claim that from the last month. You need to stop taking everything so personally. You don't like sex because you had sex with an asshole. They don't know what they're doing and don't want to learn. I'm a good student though."

Smiling slightly, I glanced at him and exhaled slowly. "I'm not a bitch."

"I know. You're sweet and I was just playing with you," he said, wiping a tear from my cheek. "Want a ride home?"

"Yes, please."

"Look at those manners. Like I said, sweet as sugar. Sweet like those pretty lips I'm going to suck on when we get to your place."

"Of course, there'd be a condition for the ride."

"Nothing's free," he said, giving me a wink.

"Just lip sucking?" I asked, staring hard at him.

"Oh, I want under your shirt too, but I'll build up to that."

"I have a lot of schoolwork."

"So do I, but I'm planning to make time for my hands and your tits to become acquainted."

Rolling my eyes, I climbed on behind him. "I told you how they don't like being called that."

"Well, if they want me to be sweet to them then they need to be sweet to me. As I pointed out, nothing's free in life."

Wiggling my breasts against his back, I waited for the groan. Cooper glanced back at me and frowned.

"I need to start wearing sweatpants or else you'll kill me."

"I don't understand," I said, batting my eyes innocently. "Are you talking about this?"

Wiggling my breasts against him again, I jumped when his hands went to my bare thighs. Stroking from my hips to knees, Cooper gave me a grin. "I'm getting you naked this weekend. Even if I have to lie, cheat, and steal, I'm hitting a homerun with you, baby."

"Sure, whatever. Can we leave now?"

"Temptress."

"Dickhead."

"Beauty."

"Stud."

"A stud that needs sweatpants."

"If it's such a hassle, maybe we shouldn't fool around at my place?"

Cooper just laughed while pulling away from school. He was laughing again when he parked at the curb next to my apartment building.

"What's so funny?"

"Nothing. When I don't get enough oxygen to my brain, it gives me the giggles."

Now, I was laughing as we walked to the front door. "My mom might be home."

"I'll be sure to feel you up silently then."

Grinning, I unlocked the door and pushed it open to find the air conditioner running high.

"My mom sometimes gets overheated."

"Lady issues. Check. No more info is necessary or desired."

Shutting the door, I turned down the air conditioner before finding two sodas in the refrigerator.

"I need a shower."

Cooper stared at me with a pained expression. "Sweatpants."

Laughing, I left him to my crappy cable. After a quick shower, I changed into a loose tank top and shorts. Feeling daring, I chose to wear panties, but no bra.

Returning to the living room, I found Cooper stretched out with his legs over the coffee table and his arms spread out along the back of the couch. He looked large and menacing then he glanced at me and grinned.

"Would now be a bad time to mention I'm horny?" he asked as I opened my soda and joined him on the couch.

"If I never again heard a single thing about you being horny, I'd still be well informed."

After a gulp of soda, I braced myself, took a deep breath, and willed a little courage. Straddling Cooper, I rested my hands on his chest and smiled.

"No sex," I said, waiting a beat before adding, "Today."

A grinning Cooper pulled me down for a kiss. Still feeling bold, I ran my fingers though his soft blond hair. He felt so perfect like he was mine.

Pulling away his lips, he gave me a questioning look. "No bra?"

"I don't have work tomorrow. I know everyone is going to that party and I thought afterwards we could solve your sweatpants problem."

Cooper caressed my lower lip with his thumb. "Earlier when I was teasing you, I realized you hadn't been treated well. That's why you don't like sex, right?"

Nodding slightly, I let my fingers drift over his jaw as he teased my lips.

"I promise you'll feel good with me," he said without bravado.

"I heard all about your skills."

"Finally asked around, huh?"

"Didn't have to. People come up to me on the street to share stories of your escapades."

Cooper laughed. "Hell yeah, they do." Running his fingers down my back, he studied me as his expression softened. "I've wanted you since that first day in Spanish class and it's killing me to wait. I know you're nervous, but I'll make you feel so good that you'll forget about the loser from before."

"I'm not really that good myself," I said, losing my courage.

"You can lay motionless through the whole thing and I'll still make you feel good."

Smiling slightly, I had already started worrying over disappointing him.

"I want you," he whispered, holding my face with both hands. "Fuck that. I need you, Farah. I need to help you knock down all of those walls. I promise it'll be great if you trust me."

"I do."

"You do," he said, his eyes locked on mine. "I feel you lowering another wall and nothing feels better."

Staring into his dark eyes, I believed everything would always be alright as long as he was with me. It was ridiculous and my brain screamed for me to get a grip, but I ignored it.

"I have to be at work soon," I said, leaning forward so my breasts were pressed against his chest. "Meaning, I'll need to put on a bra soon."

"Message received," he said, kissing me while his warm hands slid under my shirt and along my spine. When I pulled back to allow access, those fingers caressed my stomach then moved between my breasts as if teasing. Before I could complain, his thumbs grazed my nipples.

Panic and lust rushed over me in equal amounts of intensity. My nipples didn't react the way my panicked brain wanted. Instead, they hardened as Cooper teased them so gently. If he had been any greedier, I might have freaked out, but he was in his mama's boy fucking mode.

Moaning into his mouth, I pressed my hands flat on his chest and tried not to freak out. It felt so good, yet I wanted to yank his hands away and ask him to leave. My body was on one page while my brain was in a whole different place.

"Are you okay?" he whispered as his lips tasted my jaw.

"Nervous is all. Don't stop."

"No, I don't think I will."

Cooper moved a hand from my breast to my hip then guided me against his erection. Understanding what he wanted, I focused on this and not my panic or lust. I would help him. Yes, I could do that instead of freaking out.

Groaning deep in his chest, Cooper suddenly shifted us so I was back on the couch and he was over me with his lips at my throat. I couldn't think about helping him when my body was on fire. Even wanting more, I needed him to stop. Confused, I wished I could just relax and enjoy Cooper's amazing moves.

Sliding lower on the couch, Cooper lifted my shirt and gazed at my breasts. I had no time to feel self-conscious before I felt the tip of his tongue across my right nipple. I cried out, wanting him to stop, yet my hands were in his hair as if begging for it to never end.

Cooper used those sexy lips of his to suck at my nipple slowly, sending me into a nearly brain dead state of horniness. I couldn't think, could barely breath, and I thought I might lose consciousness. I'd never felt anything so hot before, never thought I could enjoy something so amazing, but here I was squirming in ecstasy as Cooper leisurely teased my nipple with his mouth. His fingers caressed the other nipple then he switched sides and I lost the ability to speak.

Knowing he was horny as hell, I didn't understand how Cooper moved so tenderly. As if in no hurry, he stroked my nipple with his tongue, sucked softly, and stroked again. If we weren't on the couch where my mom might walk in, I'd have asked for sex right then.

Suddenly, Cooper stopped and I opened my eyes to find him propped up over me. Frowning, he caressed my face.

"It's okay," he said softly.

"I know."

"Then, why are you whimpering like that? You sound like a scared puppy."

Having never realized I was making any noise, I lied, "I was worried my mom might come in."

"Then, why didn't you ask me to stop?"

"I didn't want you to stop."

Cooper nodded and sat back on the couch. Lowering my shirt, I felt awkward sitting next him.

"I know I said I was getting you naked tomorrow, but we don't have to do anything if you're not ready."

Tears stung my eyes as I moved closer. "I didn't mean to make those noises."

"You just sounded scared. I don't want you to be scared and think you can't ask me to stop. I'm not the shitty lay you had before. You can tell me what you like and don't like."

"I liked that."

"Why are you crying?" he asked, caressing my cheeks.

"It's embarrassing. Other girls don't make stupid noises. Now, you think I'm stupid."

"I think you're scared and so tightly wound you can't ask for what you want."

"I wanted that."

A scowling Cooper studied me. "But if you didn't, you'd tell me, right?"

Nodding, I knelt next to him on the couch and hoped he didn't dump me. "I'd never felt like that before. Like it was so much better than I expected and I got weird."

Cooper gave me a little smile. "You're so hot, Farah. I don't know how you haven't been fucked well before, but I'm going to be that guy."

Grinning, I wiped my cheeks. "Tomorrow, I'll be ready. Like I'll know how good it's going to feel and I won't make stupid noises."

"It wasn't stupid," he said, losing his grin. "You need to relax and stop saying crappy things about yourself. Sometimes, you just need to let go and enjoy stuff, but maybe you're not there yet. I can be patient."

"But you've been waiting since the first day in Spanish class," I whispered, giving him a grin. "How have you not died yet?"

Laughing, Cooper wrapped an arm around me until I was snuggled against him. "I've had a few close calls, but you're worth waiting for."

"You only have to wait until tomorrow."

Frowning slightly, Cooper again studied me as if searching for something. "Promise you'll ask for what you want."

"I promise."

"I can't make you feel good if you're not honest."

"That did feel good though."

"Hell yeah, it did," he said, grinning. "Your breasts and I became fast friends."

Laughing, I looked up at him. "You didn't call them tits."

"It's the least I can do after they were so sweet to me," he said, winking. "I did get carried away though."

"I'm really hot."

Cooper groaned. "You can't know how hot."

"You're really hot too."

"Yes, but I'm an arrogant prick so I know how hot I am. You have no clue how hot you are."

"Oh, I know. I'm just working the modest angle."

Cooper threw his head back and laughed so hard that his strong body jiggled me an inch off his lap.

"It's a con. I fucking knew it," he finally said.

"We can still fool around before I need to get ready for work."

Cooper eyed me and I saw everything in those eyes. The lust conflicted with the worry. He wanted me, but was holding back. I thought about how Skye said Cooper wouldn't wait forever and I didn't want him to hold back. If he got used to doing without, he might decide I wasn't worth it. Or my whimpers were lame or my crying was annoying. He might just find someone who knew how to make him feel good without being told.

"Let's try something," he said, pulling off his tee. "You sit here."

When I straddled him, he tugged off my shirt. His arms wrapped around me, holding me at my shoulders as I pressed my still excited nipples against the hard muscles and soft hairs on his chest.

"I want you to learn to trust me, baby," he whispered. "Learn to let go and know you're safe with me. Once you're comfortable, I bet you'll be a tiger in bed."

"Claw you up," I said, growling like a dork.

Laughing, Cooper caressed my thighs. "I'm kissing the hell out of you now."

"You better back up that threat."

For the next twenty minutes, Cooper did just that and I could feel him on my lips for the rest of the night. His lips and mine became attached again after the ride home. I felt so safe with Cooper that I even considered asking him to stay the night. Except Amy was in the next room with Tex and I didn't want my first time to be with them around. No, I was waiting until Friday night. I had the whole thing planned out and it would be perfect.

Chapter Fourteen

The party was at a large rundown white house where a dozen or more students rented. By the time we arrived, the place was already loud and crowded. Looking around at all of the girls dressed in barely there shorts and tank tops, I wondered if I was overdressed. My ass wasn't hanging out of my shorts, not that I had much of an ass to show off. When Bailey and Skye appeared as soon as I climbed off the Harley, I noticed how neither had their asses hanging out.

Cooper took my hand while surveying the place. "Fucking freshmen," he muttered then glanced down at me. "Very few of them are worth my time."

"I feel the same way about seniors."

Cooper grinned then wrapped an arm around me. "Stay close. I don't want you getting lost."

"Fuck that!" Bailey cried. "She's coming with me. Skye plans to hang with Tyler and I need a wing chick. You can go play with Aaron. I saw him talking up some stupid redheaded bitch who thinks she's tough shit."

Cooper frowned at his sister. "Did she fuck with you?"

"Couldn't remember my name. Can you believe that shit? Fuck her. I hope she dies."

"Sorry about the hit to your self-esteem, but I'm keeping Farah with me."

Bailey shoved Cooper then grabbed my hand and yanked me away. When Skye laughed at him, Cooper focused his irritated gaze on her. Pretending to be terrified, she ran away still laughing.

Entering the packed house, I was immediately overwhelmed by the heat, plus the smell of BO and way too much cologne. Bailey glanced back at me and dry heaved.

"No way are we finding hot guys in this stink pit."

"I already have a hot guy!" I yelled over Toby Keith.

"He likes when girls make him jealous. It's his favorite thing. Let's give Crapface what he needs."

Following Bailey, I wondered if Cooper was really angry. Probably not since he had a lot of patience when it came to his sister. Yet, I still hoped to see his handsome face in the sea of otherwise average ones. Not paying attention, I bumped into Bailey eyeing the two beers in her hands.

"Are these roofied?" she asked the guy who handed them to her.

"No."

"You sure? Cause if you roofie me and her, Cooper Johansson will cut off your dick and make you eat it. You looking to eat your cock, asshole?"

The guy stared in horror at Bailey who was a foot shorter, but looked ready to hit him with the bottles.

"No," he finally said.

"Well, alright then," Bailey replied, handing me a beer.

"I don't drink."

"Yeah, heard you were a nerd," she said, pulling me away from the guy who still looked like he might shit himself. "I also heard you don't like sex. I've been thinking about that."

Bailey downed half of her beer then burped. "I had a friend in high school with a small pussy. She was the only girl who fucked Cooper and didn't think it was the greatest shit ever. Do you have any idea how it feels to have all your friends telling you how great your brother's cock is? It's disgusting."

Bailey finished her beer then dropped the bottle and held out her hand until someone gave her a new one.

"Anyway, if you have a small pussy like my friend Billie and you try fitting Cooper's big cock in you, it'll probably hurt. But if you get drunk enough, you'll loosen up and that cock will slide in real easy. Billie learned that eventually. Now, she loves big cock."

Nodding, I had to admit I was nervous about sex. In fact, the thought of Cooper's big cock had me gulping down the beer. Bailey gave me a knowing smile then handed me another bottle.

"My family is full of drunks and addicts," I said.

"One night of boozing won't turn you into a fucking loser. Just drink up and get your pussy relaxed. I was drunk my first time and it was pretty fucking awesome. I recommend drunk cherry popping now. In fact, when Sawyer gets older, I'm giving her that advice. Not that the stuck-up bitch will listen."

Things got a little fuzzy after the second beer. Bailey started laughing over something that I didn't think actually happened then she had us do shots of tequila in the kitchen. Next to us, a guy and girl were essentially fucking. Once I focused on how her skirt was up and his pants were down a little, I realized there wasn't anything essentially about it. I was next to two fucking people fucking. This sent me into giggles and Bailey could barely stand she was laughing so hard.

A guy appeared to chat with Bailey who immediately tossed her hair off her shoulders and thrust out her boobs. The guy glanced down at her chest and grinned. Then, he pretended they were having a real conversation and she wasn't shitfaced.

When I just stood there staring and swaying, Bailey turned to me. "Go get my brother and his big cock," she said, shoving me out of the kitchen. "Wait, take one more shot first so your pussy will be relaxed."

As I downed another shot, we laughed then nodded at each other like we were sharing a secret message. As I stumbled out of the kitchen, Bailey thrust her boobs at the guy again, nearly knocking him to the ground.

The party was somehow louder and more crowded, making me wonder how long I had been drinking with Bailey. The sun was gone outside so I suspected it had been more than ten minutes. The still functioning part of my brain laughed at the wasted part that thought only ten minutes had passed. Giggling to myself, I stumbled upon Cooper in a hallway talking to a guy with a faux-hawk.

"Go away," Cooper said to the guy who literally ran down the hall and disappeared. Looking at me as I rubbed my hands over his strong chest, he grinned. "Are you drunk?"

"Hell yeah."

"What about the law and you being a dork?"

"I want you," I whispered, staring at him through my beer goggles and finding him not the least bit scary. "I'm saying yes. I'm not trying to get away. I'm giving you your shot."

Cooper didn't need to be told twice. He swept me up into his arms and my legs wrapped around his hips. Our lips met and I opened up for him without fear. Tequila had given me confidence and I now owned my sexuality.

Skin hot and sweaty in the overheated house, our bodies gyrated against each other. Hungry for his touch, I smiled when his lips found my throat. He sucked softly from my collarbone to my chin then back again until I was breathing in gasps. Cooper's lips met mine as he pressed me against a hallway nook and I felt his erection between my legs.

Forcing my lips free, I mumbled, "Not like this for our first time. People could see and I..."

Cooper returned his lips to mine then lifted me from the cove and walked us down the hallway. Soon, we were in a stranger's bedroom and I was pulling off my shirt. Cooper removed his black tee then leaned down and kissed me full of heat.

Maybe the tequila was wearing off because I wasn't feeling so confident anymore. Seeing Cooper hovering over me with his shirt off and all the flesh covered in tattoos, I wasn't really in the room with him anymore. Closing my eyes, I tried to think of something else. Schoolwork or waitressing or talking with Tawny. Anything to get through the sex.

"Farah," Cooper said in a rough voice, "look at me." Opening my eyes, I struggled to stay calm. "Stay here with me," he said, his gaze holding mine. "You know me. You want me. You don't need to be afraid."

Realizing I was crying, I wiped at the tears then forced my eyes to remain on him as he removed my jeans and underwear until I was as naked as him.

"I do want you," I whispered, breathing too quickly as he kissed my thighs. "Please, Cooper, don't wait."

I reached for him as he explored while unwrapping a condom. The feel of him terrified me, but I knew it was almost over. Cooper didn't move completely over me. Instead, he lingered at my nipples, licking at them then pulling gently with his lips. I remembered how Bailey said he was a boob man and smiled at the thought, but I just wanted it to be over.

"Tell me this is what you want," he said as he stroked me with his cock. "You're drunk and scared and I don't know if I should stop."

"I want you."

"Because you're drunk?" he asked, his hips no longer moving as he studied my face.

"I got drunk because I want you. Please, don't stop."

"Promise you won't hate me later."

"You're not taking, but I'm scared if you wait too long that I won't be brave enough to do it. Please, just keep going."

"Scared because of me?"

Holding his gaze, I shook my head and I think Cooper understood. He kissed me tenderly and I felt more tears as his erection opened me up. His hand reached back behind my knee and arched my leg slightly. I didn't understand, but suspected he wanted a better angle. Or maybe I was fighting him about opening my thighs enough. Either way, he moved slowly, entering me inch by inch.

Cooper looked both beautiful and terrifying as he hovered over me. I avoided focusing on the tattoos and the way his muscles moved while he worked himself slowly into me. Studying his face, I stared into those beautiful dark eyes. They were smoky with need, but his expression was soft. As he moved in and out of me, Cooper never took his eyes off my face. He was giving me a mama's boy fuck. I told myself he did this because I mattered to him and had value.

Watching me intently, he leaned down to kiss me gently every time I started crying again. When he was tender, I could focus on his handsome face and sexy lips. Concentrating on Cooper made everything a little better because he was like magic.

Yet, even with the heated make out session in the hallway where I'd gotten myself riled up nicely, I couldn't enjoy the feel of Cooper inside me. Hating the sensation of being full, I tensed and it hurt more. Even knowing I was making the pain worse, I couldn't control my body's reaction.

Tracing his lips and grazing the stubble over his jawline and cheeks, I focused on his face and not on what our bodies were doing. When I did that, it didn't hurt so much and I panicked less. I enjoyed the feel of his skin as I stroked his chest and arms. Even if I didn't like the actual sex, I wanted to be close to him. I also wanted to give him pleasure.

I fought my tears when Cooper's movements sped up and he came. My mind felt scrambled and I had trouble focusing on the now with Cooper. I didn't cry though until he was out of breath over me, kissing my face and soothing away my tears.

Hiding my face against his chest, I said his name again and again in my head. I was with Cooper Johansson in the college town of Ellsberg. I wanted this man and I was happy he wanted me back. This was a good thing. I said it again and again until Cooper pulled out of me and rested to my right side.

Opening my eyes, I found him studying me. My fingers stroked his lips and his frown eased away.

"Are you okay?" he whispered as music played loudly just outside the door.

"Yes."

"You drank too much," he said, caressing my stomach and breasts before settling his hand flat over my belly button. "You look ready to pass out."

"I feel fine," I lied as my head swam. "You're so beautiful."

Cooper gave me a half smile and kissed my face. Then, he was kissing my lips and I worried we would have sex again. I wasn't ready and the room wouldn't stay in one place. I also felt like my head had been kicked in. Lying very still, I tried to make the room stop spinning. Cooper watched me as his fingers explored softly.

Loud voices startled me and Cooper sighed. "I don't even know whose room this is?"

"I'm sorry," I mumbled, closing my eyes. "I feel weird."

"Yeah, I know," Cooper said as he moved around on the bed. Waiting for more sex, I flinched when he touched me. "I have your panties." Opening my eyes, I saw he was dressed and helping me put on my clothes. "Do you think you'll be sick?"

"No, I just feel like the room is spinning."

"Yeah, it'll do that with enough booze. What did you drink?"

"Tequila and beer. I think the tequila did it."

"Mixing alcohol isn't a nerd move, Farah," he teased, helping me put on my shirt even though I was missing my bra. "If you need to puke, let me know and I'll hold your hair back."

Laughing, I almost fell over, but Cooper scooped me up into his arms and picked up my sandals. As he carried me out of the room and down the hall, I nuzzled my face against his neck. While certain he would drop me, I soon rested inside a truck.

"Whose car is this?" I asked, confused and worried he might hand me off to the next guy.

"I'm borrowing it since I'm fairly sure you'd fall off the bike. Rest and I'll get you home."

"I'm sorry I ruined your fun," I babbled, leaning over against him. "I don't know what I'm doing. Do you?"

Even in the dark, I could see he was unhappy. Yet, Cooper gave me a little smile. "Just rest, baby."

"Don't dump me," I begged, clawing at his shirt. "I can do better. I won't cry and I'll be really good. I promise. Please, don't dump me."

Frowning darkly, Cooper glanced at me and I thought he wanted to dump me right there.

"Don't cry. It kills me when you cry," he whispered, giving a deep sigh.

I opened my mouth to say something really profound that would keep him interested in me. The next thing I knew, I woke up alone in my bed.

The room was dark and I felt too weak to get up. Falling back to sleep, I wondered if Cooper would remember my name in the morning.

Chapter Fifteen

Waking up to a sick stomach and dull headache, I figured it could be worse. My hand touched between my legs and found the area slightly tender. Closing my eyes, I fell asleep for a short time before knocking at my window got me up. Cooper stood outside with a cup in each hand. Hurrying around to the front room, I opened the door and inhaled the wonderful smell of coffee.

"How are you feeling?" he asked with a sweetly concerned look on his beautiful face.

"Okay," I said, taking the cup of coffee.

"Did you get sick last night?"

"No, I just crashed and woke up feeling kinda crappy."

Sitting on the couch, Cooper frowned. "You're not pissed at me, are you?"

"Why would I be?"

"You were drunk and we... You do know what we did, right?"

"I wanted to. I told you that."

"Yeah, but I thought you might wake up and figure it was a mistake and I'm an ass."

"I'm not mad at you. I am a little shocked you remember my name, but otherwise we're good."

Sighing, Cooper leaned back and draped his arm across the back of the couch. "I keep saying you're special and not like the other girls and you keep waiting for me to forget your name."

"I was teasing you."

"No, you weren't."

Easing into a chair, I sipped the coffee. "I'm sorry."

"Come to my house today."

Lifting my gaze to his face, I saw Cooper waiting for me to say no.

"I'm not feeling that great."

"I know and sitting in this tiny apartment won't make you feel better. When my mom gets hung over, she likes to sit in the sun. We've got the hot tub too. It's relaxing."

"That sounds nice," I said, standing up. "I'll get dressed."

"Don't worry about a swimsuit. You can borrow one of Bailey's again."

I started for my room then stopped next to the couch. "I'm sorry I cried last night. I know that's lame."

Cooper glanced at me and his gaze darkened. "We both know why you were crying and you should never apologize for that."

Nodding, I left to get dressed in shorts and a loose lavender shirt. Returning to the living room, I found Cooper looking out of the window.

"How did you get the coffees here?" I asked, making stupid chitchat.

"Brought my truck. Figured you might not feel up to riding the bike."

"Thanks."

As soon as I had my backpack on, Cooper reached for my hand. We walked quietly through the hot morning to his truck and I slid inside. Cooper joined me and reached for the air conditioning. I touched his hand while setting my coffee in the cup holder.

"Can we have the windows open? The fresh air will probably help."

Cooper nodded. "Sure, baby. Just rest."

The smell of late summer had an intoxicating effect on me and I dozed off. When the truck stopped, I figured we were at the Johansson place. Instead, I turned my head to find us parked on the side of the road and Cooper staring out the front window with an angry frown. I was just about to ask if he was okay when he pounded on the steering wheel. As the truck shook, I squirmed closer to the door, ready to run.

Cooper stopped pounding and stared out of the window again. "Last night was a mistake," he said in a rough voice.

"Why?"

"I keep saying you're special, but last night wasn't special. You were drunk and we were on some guy's bed and I should have stopped."

"I had to be drunk or else I'd have been too nervous, but I wanted to be with you."

Cooper glanced at me and I felt uneasy under his gaze. "You have this effect on my heart. When I think I'm losing you, my chest hurts like I'll die. It makes me crazy and I thought I'd lost you because of last night. Then, you were all cool with it, but you should be angry. Last night was shit. You were drunk and scared and I don't think you liked any of it. I should have stopped myself, but I felt weak and I wanted you so bad that I fucked up."

"Cooper, if you really think I'm special and want to be with me, we'll have other chances. The first time was probably going to be weird anyway, just because I'm weird about sex."

Glancing at me, he frowned. "Why did you tell me you weren't a virgin?"

"I'm not."

Cooper eyed me angrily. "How many guys have you said yes to?"

Shrugging, I looked out the window. "Who cares?"

"If some guy fucked my sister like I fucked you, I'd kick his ass. And if the asshole told me he loved my sister, I'd tell him he was full of shit. Last night, there was a moment when I knew you weren't ready and it was your first time and I thought to stop. I didn't though."

Cooper said a lot of important things, but like any girl I focused on the word we all wanted to hear from a guy. Instead of responding to the magical word though, I focused on calming his self-directed anger.

130

"If you had stopped, I probably would have cried anyway. I would have felt embarrassed and might not have given you another chance."

"Don't bullshit me. You had to get drunk to sleep with me. You actually fucking said those words and I just thought about how much I wanted you and it would all be fine."

"It is fine."

Sighing, Cooper started the truck. "You know what I said."

Realizing he was talking about his feelings for me, I nodded. "Things inside me are all jumbled up."

"I'm not asking you to say it back. I'm asking you to let me give you a better time. I don't want last night to be your first time."

"It wasn't."

Cooper smashed his fists on the steering wheel and exhaled angrily. "What happened before doesn't count! You fucking know that, right? It didn't count. You were a virgin last night and I fucked up."

"Okay!" I yelled, shaking from his rage. "You fucked up! Let it go and drive me to your house or take me home. Just stop scaring the shit out of me."

Glaring at me, Cooper didn't put the car into drive. "Why are you with me?"

"I don't know," I said, shrugging as I looked out the window. "I just like being with you. I like the way I feel when I'm with you."

"Even now?"

"Yeah, even now," I told him, finally meeting his gaze. "If you want to make things up to me, why are you yelling and acting scary? How does that make it better?"

"It doesn't, but you have to understand something," he said, holding my gaze. "I'm fucking perfect."

Despite my common sense, I laughed at the sincerity behind his words. Cooper gave me a tiny grin.

"I don't fuck up. I don't do stupid shit. I'm the smart one in my family. Tucker fucks up. Bailey acts emotionally. I don't do that. It's why I have to be the lawyer. Why my pop wants me to take over for him when he's ready to sit on his ass and pretend he's retired. I'm the perfect one, but there was nothing perfect about last night. I just wanted you and I lied about the rest. I knew I'd fallen hard for you and I figured that meant I could keep going and it would be fine. The perfect part of me knew I had it backwards. You were special and I needed to stop. I hate that I let myself be so stupid. I don't want to be Tucker."

"Who would?" I said, grinning.

Cooper laughed. "I know, right?"

Even with the urge to take my chances walking home rather than remain tied to this complicated man, I unbuckled my seatbelt and leaned over to kiss him.

"You make me stupid too, Coop," I said, grazing his lips with mine. "You make me crazy and scared, but I like you so much that it feels worth it. I wish I knew if my feelings were love. I wish I could make a declaration, but I'm not used to having nice things. No matter how much you scare me, you are a very nice thing and I never dreamed I'd have a shot at keeping you interested. I'm glad I was wrong."

Cooper pulled me closer and kissed me hard and deep. I realized he hadn't given me a real kiss since arriving that morning. I also realized he truly believed I would dump him and it was making him miserable. As horrible as it was, this fact made me happy. Cooper possessed so much power over me that it was a relief knowing I had power too.

"How do I make it up to you?" he asked, holding me on his lap.

"Is that a sex question?" I asked, kissing his neck.

"It could be. Baby, I need to do something special for you because last night wasn't special."

"There's one thing I want, but it's not sex and I don't think you'll want to do it."

"It's not lame, is it?"

Lifting my head from the crook of his neck, I frowned at him. "Never mind."

"No, tell me. Even if I'll hate doing it, I want to prove I'm not Tucker."

"You're not Tucker."

"Tell me," he said, leaning his forehead against mine. "Pretty please."

Laughing, I sighed. "The first night you came to my apartment, you did something that felt really good."

Cooper scowled as he replayed that evening. "I don't remember making any especially hot moves on you."

"I said it wasn't sex."

"Well, we didn't have sex that night so I knew it wasn't sex."

"You won't want to do it. Forget it. A nice day at your house will be my reward for you not being perfect."

"Nope," he said, holding me still on his lap. "Tell me."

"I want a foot massage."

"Bull."

"No, really."

Cooper grinned. "Why wouldn't I want to massage you? I want you to feel good like you make me feel."

"My feet are killing me from working and walking so much and you have talented fingers."

"Hell yeah, I do," he said, kissing me as his fingers explored my waist.

Cooper's naughty fingers merely teased as I squirmed in his lap, causing him to groan.

"Let's get to the house so you can soak up the sun and relax."

Sliding back into my seat, I grinned while he shifted the truck into drive. As I watched him, Cooper glanced my way and smiled like he had plans for me. When I saw the wicked gleam in his eyes, I never in my life wished more to be someone else. Someone who could see that look and meet it with vigor.

Cooper parked next to his apartment. "It's parents' weekend as you likely know. Skye's parents are in town and they'll be with my parents for the day. Tucker is with Maddy and her parents. No employees around to spy on us either. We have the whole place to ourselves."

"Cool."

"Hungry?"

"A little."

"Let's go hang out in the house. We'll eat, find you a swimsuit, and I'll take you out to the hot tub for a nice relaxing foot massage."

"I get really relaxed when you massage my feet," I said, trying to be sexy.

Cooper opened the front door for me. "Yeah, I remember how you fell asleep that night."

"I meant a different kind of relaxed."

Heading into the kitchen, he glanced back at me and grinned. "Oh, I know what you meant, minx."

"I'm not doing that right now. I want you too much to say mean words."

"I take jackass as a compliment."

"Oh, then you're a giant sexy jackass."

"Hell yeah," he said, before leaning into the refrigerator to search for food. "Fuck. We have hit the motherload. Ribs and potato salad."

"That sounds great." My stomach responded with a loud growl and Cooper peeked up from the fridge and grinned. "I've never had ribs for breakfast."

"Stick with me and you'll eat like a queen."

Cooper proved this fact by feeding me until I could barely move. The meat on the ribs fell off the bone and the potato salad tasted like nothing I'd ever had before.

"How do you stay so hot when you eat like this?" I asked him.

Cooper grinned. "I work out with weights. I swim a lot. I beat up a lot of stupid people. Burns a lot of calories."

Imagining the other way he burned calories, I didn't want to think of all the girls Cooper slept with over the years.

"If I keep coming here, I'll need to find a way to burn calories too."

"Oh, I'm sure I can think of a fun way to do that."

Staring at him blankly, I pretended like I didn't understand. Cooper only grinned wider.

"I'm going to pick out a suit for you."

A few minutes later, Cooper strolled down the stairs with a naughty grin on his face and his hands hidden behind his back.

"I found the perfect one. Though I doubt my parents have any idea Bailey owns it. They certainly wouldn't let her wear it around here."

"Oh, crap."

"Hell yeah," he said, grinning from ear to ear as he held up the tiny leopard printed bikini.

"I don't think I'll fit in it."

"I promise not to complain if you fall out."

Laughing, I took the bikini. "Why even wear it? It hides nothing."

"If you want, we can go nude?"

"Naw," I said, standing up and dropping the suit on the couch. "I feel like you need to work for it a little."

Cooper gave me a smile that faded as soon as I pulled off my shirt. His breathing shifted as I stripped down in front of him then wiggled into the bikini. Once I was dressed, I smiled casually as if I was someone comfortable with her sexuality.

"I want my foot massage, slave."

"Hell yeah," he whispered as if breathless. "You can't know."

"Oh, I know. I feel the same way when you strut around shirtless."

Cooper smiled again and his shirt came off seconds later. "Hot tub time."

Taking his hand, I walked with Cooper out the back door over the deck and past the pool. Cooper leaned over and turned on the spa before stripping out of his shorts, leaving only his skull and bones boxers.

"My mom," he explained when I smiled at them. After Cooper found us a few cold sodas, we settled into the hot water. "Give me those feet," he said, sitting across from me. "I'm going to relax the shit out of you."

"Stop threatening me."

"You look so fucking hot in that suit that I'm having trouble concentrating."

I fiddled with the bikini top barely covering my areolas, let alone the rest of my breasts. Lifting my gaze to meet his, I smiled. "Thank you for bringing me here today."

Cooper sighed. "Last night sucked. I need another chance."

"You have another chance and last night wasn't that bad."

"You didn't see your face," he whispered as his strong fingers worked at my arches.

"I'm sorry," I moaned, leaning farther into the water and resting my head on the back of the hot tub. "I can do better."

"Don't think about that. Just let me serve you."

Grinning, I moaned again as he rubbed at my heel. For the next few minutes, we watched each other and I knew we were thinking the same thing. Relaxed under the late summer sun and soaking in the hot water, I really felt like I could do it sober. Cooper needed to be mine. He said he loved me. Despite what I said in the truck, I knew I loved him too. I needed to let go and embrace this opportunity.

Tugging my feet away gently, I sat up then reached for him. Cooper exhaled in a way that made me think he was waiting for this moment since we stepped into the hot tub. I straddled him and was a little surprised to find him already hard between my legs.

"Been that way since you stripped down for me in the house," he said as I frowned. "Your face is so expressive that it's like every thought is there for me to see."

Rolling my eyes, I held onto his shoulders then stood and lowered my bikini bottom. Cooper hooked a finger in the material and tugged it off. Looking up between my legs, Cooper just sighed.

"Every inch of you is perfect."

"Doubtful."

"Shut up," he spat, squirming out of his boxers until they were floating nearby. "You see things all wrong when it comes to you. It's like you're blind."

"Or stupid."

Cooper wrapped his arms around me as I settled over his erection. "Never stupid. My girl can't see what I see about her. That's a good thing though. I don't want her getting stuck up and dumping me."

Rolling my hips so I caressed his stiff cock between our bodies, I whispered, "Today is a perfect day." I lifted my hips as Cooper guided himself inside me. "Perfect."

Once full, I tried to find a rhythm, but it felt wrong. I met Cooper's gaze and he frowned.

"What's wrong?"

"I don't know how..."

When I lowered my gaze, Cooper took me by the chin and forced me to look at him. "Know how to what?"

"Like how, you know, the rhythm."

"Oh, I have a simple technique that will help you."

Expecting his hands to move to my hips, they instead removed my bikini top and settled on my breasts.

"Just follow my lead," he said, giving me a sexy little grin.

"Wha...?"

I gasped as his thumbs stroked up over my nipples to tell me to lift my hips. Then, his thumbs stroked down and my hips followed. I never would have guessed I'd love having my nipples teased, but it felt like heaven. While I would have told Cooper this fact, I'd lost the ability to speak as we worked ourselves into a nice rhythm.

Holding onto his shoulders, I lifted and fell at his direction until Cooper was at the brink. One hand curled around my neck and pulled me down to kiss him. The other hand took my left hip and guided me. Soon, both hands were on my hips as he helped me bring him closer and closer. Finally, he groaned in this wonderful way that made me feel like I accomplished something great. It was stupid, but I felt proud to see him come apart because of me.

As Cooper wrapped me in his arms, I felt completely safe. Even though I smiled at him, he stared at me with a hurt expression. "Why are you crying?"

Wiping my eyes, I hadn't even realized. "I don't know."

"Did I hurt you?"

I shook my head. "It was so good."

"You didn't come."

"It was still really good."

Cooper wiped my cheeks. "I really thought you were ready to come. I'm usually good at reading girls, but you started crying instead."

"I'm just weird. Broken or something. It's not personal."

I looked down into the water where we were still together. Cooper lifted me gently off him then pulled me closer onto his lap.

"I'm sorry," I whispered. "I can get better."

"Stop saying that," he whispered back at me.

"I don't want you to dump me."

Cooper shook his head. "Those days out of town were fucked up. I missed you way too much to be normal and I knew then. I just knew you really were my girl. It wasn't some crush on a hot chick who teased me. You were the one and I loved you. That's the fucked up part. I love you and you're mine and I can't get you to feel good. Hell, forget feeling good. I can't even keep you from crying while I feel good."

"It's not you."

"I'm not helping matters."

"By complaining?" I asked, looking up at him. "No, you're really not helping."

Cooper grinned. "You're such a little bitch."

"And you're a raging asshole."

"I love you, Farah. I'm not messing around when I say that. I'm not someone who spouts off about feelings and shit. I don't lie to keep girls. I lie to get rid of them, but I plan to keep you."

Studying his handsome face, I leaned my head against his strong shoulder. "When I said I was all jumbled up about my feelings, that wasn't true. I knew I loved you when you were gone because I felt like nothing mattered until you came back. It was so dumb to feel that way. I have school and my dreams and Tawny. I have good stuff to care about, but I still felt like I needed you to make those good things mean something."

"Say it straight and simple."

"I love you."

"Say you're my girl."

"I'm your girl."

"And you know I love you, right?" When I only nodded, Cooper frowned. "I need to make you feel good, baby. It's not an ego thing. It's who I am. I take care of the people important to me. I protect my friends. I help out my family. It's what I do to feel like my life has meaning. I need to make you happy, but instead I make you cry."

"It's not you," I whispered.

"You really weren't with anyone else before? No one who counted?"

Shaking my head, I cuddled closer, afraid to have him ask a question I couldn't answer.

"So you don't know if this is just how you are or if it's me making you cry?"

"I know it's me because I was happy and didn't even realize I was crying."

Cooper wrapped me tighter against him and we rested this way as the water bubbled around us. The day wasn't as hot as some of the recent ones, but my skin felt baked after a few minutes of silence.

"Tell me what to do," Cooper said, caressing my hair.

"What do you mean?"

"I need to make you happy, but having my girl buck naked on my lap is tricky. Tell me what to do."

Sliding my hand into the water, I caressed him. "I didn't cry because it hurt. I didn't cry because I didn't want you. I just think I'm overwhelmed by how intense everything is. I've never been close to someone like I am with you and it makes me a little crazy. That doesn't mean I don't want you to want me like this."

Cooper lowered his lips to mine and kissed me softly. Even after it deepened, he moved slowly, taking his time until the kiss alone had my nipples hard and my skin on fire.

"Are you sure?" he whispered, lifting me off his lap and turning me away gently.

"Yes," I said, unsure what he was doing.

Cooper guided my hands to the edge of the hot tub then he maneuvered my knees on the seat. Glancing back at him, I smiled even though I was nervous. Cooper touched my cheek, holding my gaze as he searched for something.

"Tell me."

"I love you."

"You want this."

"I want you."

"That's not the same thing."

"Help me get comfortable," I whispered, hoping he would relax because he was making me tense.

Cooper kissed me softly then slipped my hair off my throat. As he moved behind me, his lips sucked at my neck and I tilted my head to give him better access. His right hand teased my breast while his free hand moved between my legs. I jerked slightly when a finger slid over my clit.

"I want you to feel good," he whispered in my ear then sucked at the lobe.

"I do," I moaned as the head of his cock opened me. "I really do."

Cooper teased me just right while he worked himself in and out. Much like his best kisses, his rhythm was aching slow. I knew he wanted me to come. I wanted to come too, but I didn't know how to make it happen. I just held onto the side of the hot tub and stared out at the amazing view.

The pleasure built inside me as I got the hang of moving with him. His fingers were gentle, teasing more than pushing me. Cooper was trying something different and I thought it would work. I wanted it to work so badly.

Instead, I started crying as I felt the orgasm building. A wall shot up and the pleasure wasn't real anymore. Even trying to hide my tears, I

137

knew Cooper wasn't stupid. Hearing the difference in my breathing, he sagged against my back.

"I love you," I whispered, hoping he wouldn't be upset.

"I can't get enough of you saying that."

Glancing over my shoulder at him, I smiled. Cooper smiled back, but his dark eyes were conflicted. Sex was fun for him. He wanted to let go and enjoyed every stroke and thrust. He loved me though and refused to be selfish when I couldn't enjoy it the way he did. I decided to answer the question in his eyes.

Pressing back against him, I met his hips and Cooper groaned. "Show me," I said, glancing at him again.

"Maybe if we go slow enough…"

"It won't help. I don't know why, but I can't get back to that moment."

"Was I…"

"You weren't anything except the hottest fucker I've ever seen."

Cooper gave me a cocky grin. "Hell yeah."

"Please, don't stop," I said, caressing his arms wrapped around me. "It can't be healthy to stop in the middle like that. Or at the end or whenever you stopped."

Cooper laughed. "You have the hottest sex talk ever."

"Oh, yeah," I moaned dramatically. "Oh, hell yeah."

Kissing my shoulder, Cooper moved slowly, building the momentum he lost when I started crying. He seemed a little tentative, so I kept saying, "hell yeah" like it felt wonderful. At that point though, my body had shut down and wasn't feeling much of anything.

Yet emotionally, I felt safe in Cooper's arms. Pushing himself closer, he was gentle, maybe hoping I might come along with him. As soon as he finished, Cooper turned me to look at him. Sliding his fingers into my hair, he searched my face for something.

"Spend the night with me," he whispered, still studying my expression.

I said nothing as my mind ran through a million reasons to say no.

"You want to. I can see that on your face. Why aren't you saying yes?"

"I don't have anything for an overnight stay."

Cooper blew his breath up, tossing his bangs out of his eyes. "Dork."

"Hey, I need stuff. I'm a girl and we're high maintenance."

"Whatever you need, I have here."

"Okay then."

"You sound excited," he said, sitting back against the side of the hot tub and stretching out his arms along the edge. "Thrilled."

Wanting to cross my arms over my chest, I felt like an idiot standing naked before him. Cooper watched me with a hurt expression then another emotion lit up his eyes.

"Fuck, Farah," he muttered. "Don't look at me like that."

He lifted an arm and gestured for me to sit with him. I did immediately, feeling relieved as if I was lost without his approval. I hated the feeling, but it wasn't something I had power over anymore.

"I was with this girl once," he said softly as his arm wrapped around me and we slid a little farther into the water. "She was nervous and maybe a virgin. Anyway, she was so tense the first time that she didn't come. Didn't seem to do anything except stare at me. It was weird, but then she got drunk and we did it again. The second time, she loved it because she was relaxed. Do you know why I'm telling you about a chick I fucked years ago?"

"To make me feel special?" I teased.

Cooper laughed. "Hell yeah. How could you not?"

Placing a hand on his chest, I smiled up at him. "I feel like maybe your giant brain needs to dumb things down so I can understand."

Still grinning, Cooper gave me a nod. "That girl was the only time I didn't win a chick over in the sack. I might irritate girls when our clothes are on, but I'm a stud for a reason. Yet, three times we've been together and you didn't enjoy any of it."

"I did enjoy it. You weren't paying attention."

"I need you to enjoy it more."

"I'm sorry, but you need to stop being such a giant fucking baby."

Cooper burst out laughing so hard that he nearly knocked me into the water. Fortunately, he wrapped his arm tighter around my waist and kept from dunking me.

Still grinning, he said, "I want my girl to feel good. Isn't that a worthy cause to whine about?"

"Yeah, sure, but you ignore all of the good stuff. Like how I'm running around naked in front of you. That's not me. I'm modest and afraid of being judged and embarrassed. Yet, I'm naked outside because I feel comfortable enough with you. Plus, I'm not letting you have sex with me to be nice. I want to be with you. It's obvious how I'm messed up and stuff. You should be impressed that I love you enough to want sex even though I get weird about it."

"Yeah, I'm pretty amazing."

"Very."

"You'll stay tonight, right?" he asked, kissing my neck. "I missed the shit out of you when I left town. Leaving you last night killed me and I stayed for an hour, just willing you to wake up and ask me to spend the night."

"I'm sorry."

"Don't be. It probably would have freaked you out to wake up drunk with me staring at you."

"Sexy stalker."

"Hot bitch."

"I'll stay, but I'm not going to lie and say I'm super comfortable with that."

"Why?"

"Bad breath and other embarrassing stuff."

"Baby, you're mine and nothing is going to change that."

I planned to say something really sexy or profound or likely dumb, but my stomach growled loudly enough to be heard over the hot tub.

Cooper glanced down and frowned. "You need to eat more."

"It's all of the food from earlier. It made my body think more was coming."

"Oh, and it is. Hey, let's grill. I'll get a few steaks going and we'll grill potatoes.

Studying Cooper, I felt a weird sadness rush over me. For a minute, I just watched him then blinked away tears. His smile faded and we stared at each other until I could speak.

"The way you live is pretty amazing to someone like me."

Nodding, Cooper glanced back at the hills nearby. "See over there," he asked, pointing to dense woods. When I nodded, he continued, "One day, I'm building my dream house out there. It might seem creepy living that close to my parents, but I figure they can babysit while me and my girl have fun."

"I'm glad you have your family."

"You have them too. My mom..." Cooper leaned back and scratched at his stubbled cheek. "I told her about last night. About how you reacted and how I thought you might hate me today. Mom gets how you're mine and she doesn't blow it off. You're mine and that means you're theirs too."

Smiling, I nuzzled my lips against the cross on his chest. "It's not the money," I said, without looking at him. "You know that, right?"

"I know, baby. You never ask for anything."

Fortunately, my stomach made a weird noise and drew his attention away from the awkward silence.

"I'll be back," Cooper said, standing up in all of his naked glory.

Dumbfounded, I stared wide-eyed. When Cooper noticed my approval, he gave me a wink while walking his fine ass past the pool and into the house.

With him gone, I suddenly felt very naked. Glancing around, I got it into my head that someone could be watching and taking pictures. What if they spread those photos around school and everyone called me a whore? I was nearly ready to panic until I remembered what Skye said about the Johanssons. Would anyone be stupid enough to take pictures of Cooper and me on the Johansson property? Not even stupid. Who would be that suicidal?

I was wondering if Cooper ever killed anyone when he reappeared with a towel wrapped around his waist and a shirt hanging over his arm as he carried out a tray of food and beer.

"Get modest on me?" I asked.

"I figured you might have trouble eating if you were busy drooling."

"Good point," I said, stepping out of the hot tub and feeling really really naked.

"You can wear this."

I slipped Cooper's tee over my head and it came down far enough to hide my butt. Smiling, I joined him at the patio table where we spread out the food.

"We'll snack for now. I have the steaks thawing. Is that okay?"

"Perfect," I said, diving into the plate of pasta salad. "Everything today has been perfect."

Noticing Cooper watching me, I paused mid-chew.

"You really are happy, aren't you, baby?"

"Yes," I said, stroking his shirt and feeling giddy. I'd never imagined I would share anything like this day with anyone, let alone someone as beautiful as Cooper. "Are you happy?"

"If you're happy, I'm happy. That's how men are. They like when their women are content."

"Did your dad tell you that?"

"Oh, yeah. Pop hasn't stayed married all these years by being a fool."

Wrapping my arms around my body, I thought back to a girl in high school who wore her boyfriend's jersey. Seeing her look so proud, Tawny and I never understood what the big deal was, but now I knew. I understood the power of wearing my guy's shirt and smelling him on me.

"Why do you look sad?" Cooper asked, sitting across from me with a chicken leg in his hand.

"I was thinking about Tawny," I said, giving him an awkward smile. "I can't wait to tell her about all this."

"Wanna call her now?"

"It's long distance and my phone is at home."

Cooper gave me a weird frown then glanced around. "Who gives a shit about long distance?"

"I do."

"Last I checked, you don't pay my phone bill. Here," he said, handing over his phone.

"Later. I need to get my thoughts straight first."

"Must be a girl thing."

"It is," I said, setting the phone on the table. "Can we go swimming after we eat?"

"Only if we don't wait thirty minutes first."

"Because the thirty minute rule is the man keeping a boot on the back of your neck?"

Cooper grinned. "You can never be too safe."

Sharing his smile, I finished eating then leaned back and let the food settle.

"Not thirty minutes, but how about like twenty nine?"

"How about ten minutes while I finish off this chicken and admire you in my shirt. It fits you really well."

When Cooper's gaze locked on my breasts, I fought the urge to cross my arms and hide them from his hot stare.

"Where were you born?" he asked, still eyeing the part of me now responding to his gaze.

"Near Charlotte. How about you?"

"In the local hospital. Do you have an ideal place you want to live once you're done with school?"

Grinning at the thought of Cooper ever being a tiny baby, I barely heard his question. "Somewhere quiet would be nice."

"By quiet, do you mean safe?" When I nodded, Cooper grinned. "For a college town, Ellsberg is very safe. For a Johansson, it's nearly crime free."

Smiling, I stood and walked towards the pool. "Is the water cold?"

"Shouldn't be. Pool's heated and it's hot as hell out."

"Not as hot as earlier in the week. Autumn might finally show up.

Cooper walked up behind me and wrapped me in his arms. "It's really fucking beautiful around here in the autumn."

"I look forward to seeing it," I said dumbly because Cooper had removed his towel and was now descending into the water.

Once he was waist high in the water, Cooper hooked a finger and gestured for me to join him.

"It's not really been ten minutes."

"If you cramp or start drowning, I'll save you."

Grinning, I pulled off his shirt and walked quickly into the water, finally diving forward and swimming to Cooper. The view underwater was a bit too much to handle and I emerged wide-eyed.

"Already?" I asked, pushing my wet hair back.

Cooper just grinned. "I was a little hard the minute you put on my shirt. Once you took it off, I was done for."

Shaking my head, I swam past him and to the deep end. As Cooper watched me swim back and forth, he wore the intense gaze like when he first visited Denny's. I both loved and feared that gaze. Finally, I swam up to him.

"You're so needy," I teased.

"And you're everything."

Startled by the intensity behind the words, I remained silent. Running my fingers over his chest, I caressed his nipples and Cooper exhaled hard.

"Not even an option now," he said, wrapping me in his arms. "If you say no, I'll fucking cry."

"Yes, I often horny up guys I plan to reject."

Cooper smiled before kissing me hungrily. I felt nearly swallowed up by his need then he reached out and grabbed an inner tube floating by. It was the kind where a person leaned back into it and relaxed under an umbrella while the rest of them remained underwater. Except Cooper had plans for the rest of me.

Lifting my legs gently, he caressed my knees then leaned down and kissed where his fingers had been. The soft lingering kisses making me squirm, his lips moved upward and I panicked a little. Trying to close my legs, I noticed Cooper stop and frown as his lips found my inner right thigh. I avoided his confused gaze, instead staring up at the clear sky.

Cooper took the hint and moved his affection to my stomach, giving my belly button a lick. "An outie," he said, grinning.

Smiling too, I was relieved he wasn't forcing the issue. Relaxing my legs around him, I watched Cooper explore. At first, I thought he was just amazingly thorough then I realized he was testing me. So he was amazing and perceptive.

Cooper soon learned what I had discovered an hour earlier. I had very sensitive nipples. They and Cooper shared a long make out session. By the end, they were his slaves. Grinning as if knowing he'd won them over, Cooper kissed me tenderly.

I wrapped my legs around his hips and waited for the pressure of him filling my body. Once he was inside, I smiled. "I can't believe I'm running around naked like this," I nearly whispered, so relaxed as the upper part of my body floated and the lower part rested in the confident hands of a man in no hurry.

"I can't believe how calm you are," he said tenderly, his tone matching mine. "When we met, you were a ball of nerves. Now, look at how relaxed you are."

"It's all because of you."

Cooper smiled, but I knew he was thinking of how he messed up in the past. I wasn't thinking of anything besides the delicious pressure of Cooper moving in and out of me. As he held me in position with one hand, his free hand explored. Teasing my nipples then setting between my legs, they tried to coax an orgasm out of me.

As I stared up into the cloudless day, a hawk flew high over the massive trees. I watched the bird as my body inched closer and closer to an orgasm. My breathing sped up and I felt every nerve on fire. It was ready to happen when something just clicked and my eyes burned. As the moment passed, I refused to look at Cooper.

"I'm paying attention," he whispered. "My girl is relaxed and doesn't look afraid. Even with the tears, you look calm."

Finally, I met his gaze. "I was so close."

"It'll happen," he said, thrusting a little faster now, yet without any real intensity. "It's my mission in life to make it happen and I never fail."

I watched him return to exploring. His fingers grazed my lips then slid down my chin, just learning every groove of my body. By the time Cooper held my hips with both hands and worked towards an orgasm, I had my legs wrapped tightly around him. Loving to watch his face when he came, I found it extremely gratifying to see him so unguarded.

I floated there for a while longer with him inside me and his hands again exploring. We were so calm with each other that I couldn't believe we'd slept together for the first time only the night before. While that time hadn't been amazing, this day was perfect in too many ways to count.

Eventually, Cooper slid out of me then pulled me into his arms. "You look tired."

"So do you," I mumbled.

"We could take a nap in a guest room then grill our dinner. Maybe even swim again. The house is pretty much ours for the evening."

"A nap?" I asked, grinning. "Who takes a nap?"

"I do all the time. I'm up at night and you don't want to know how grumpy I get without enough sleep."

"You, grumpy? I don't believe it."

"That there," he said, gesturing towards a small stall, "has a shower. We could wash off the chlorine then head inside. My girl needs more rest than she's getting with her crap job."

Even thinking to defend my crap job, I was actually really tired. A nap sounded nice, though I doubted I would sleep. We left the warm water of the pool and hurried to wash off before the slight breeze clung to our wet bodies.

After the shower, Cooper wrapped me in a towel while he remained nude. Taking my hand, he led me to a guest room where he lowered the shades and found an extra blanket.

"I always get cold during naps," Cooper explained. "Plus, we're naked."

"We are so naked," I said, licking my bottom lip.

"Stop making me hard."

I undid the towel then dropped it on a chair before sliding under the covers.

"I'm cold. Do you think you could warm me up?"

Cooper grinned. "You had me at the lip lick."

Soon overheated from his tongue's affections at my stomach and chest, I still wouldn't let him lick lower. When Cooper pressed open my legs, he didn't struggle with me like the night before. I really felt in the moment until the pleasure grew too intense and I shut down. Cooper watched my face as he moved slowly in and out of me. If he thought it would make any difference, I think he might have held on for another hour.

When I ran my nails along his chest, Cooper gave up and just let go. Those last few thrusts were so deep that the sensations sent me somewhere between abject terror and intense pleasure. I was always so close to coming, but couldn't get past the wall.

Cooper said nothing after we finished. Cuddled with me, he made sure we were snug under the blankets. I didn't think I could sleep in a strange bed with a man wrapped against the back of me especially with the slightly painful tingles between my legs. While certain that I'd stare at the wall until Cooper woke up, I was instead asleep within minutes.

Waking to a murky room, I wondered how much time passed while I napped. I turned to find Cooper lying on his side watching me. He smiled when our gazes met.

"Have you been up long?" I asked.

"Twenty minutes top."

I reached for his face and let my fingers slide across the stubble on his cheek. Lifting my head to kiss him, I felt him press something against my lips.

Cooper grinned. "A mint so you won't have to worry about your breath."

Opening my mouth, I took the mint before smiling so widely my face hurt. "You're too perfect."

"Yeah, I know," he said, leaning down to kiss me. "Man, you're hot when you sleep."

I had no time for a response because his lips were on mine and the kiss stretched into us wrapped together. Our bodies were so warm under the blankets and I knew what Cooper wanted. Well, more like needed. I felt a little sore, but when he touched me just right, I opened my legs for him.

There was something extremely comforting about being in that room with Cooper. The house smelled like peaches from a nearby air freshener. It was quiet and warm and I felt safe with Cooper as if he alone could hold back all of the ugliness in my life.

Chapter Sixteen

Tawny answered on the first ring like her hand was hovering over the phone. While I thought maybe she sensed I would call, her voice sounded panicked for her to be expecting me.

"Tawny, what's wrong?" I asked.

"We're somewhere else now."

"Is Dad around?" I asked, sitting in the guest room while Cooper readied our dinner.

"He's got a con going and thinks he could have the money to pay off those people. I still don't know what he'll do about the cops, but he says he's close to fixing one problem. Then, maybe we can move somewhere else and I can get a job."

Tawny sounded like she was reciting Dad. I hated when she did that because it meant she was on autopilot. I remembered how when things were really bad my little sister would pull deep within herself and go through the motions. Sometimes, it was difficult to reassure Tawny enough for her to come out of hiding and I feared she'd lock herself away forever.

"Are you okay?" I asked gently, feeling guilty to have spent such a wonderful day while Tawny was trapped somewhere.

"Yes, I'm glad you called. Did you sleep with that rich guy?"

"Last night."

"Was it good?" she asked, sounding more like Tawny now and I could see the little grin on her face.

"It was okay."

"Was he mean?" she asked, the humor gone.

"It was just weird and..." I glanced around like someone might be listening even though I knew I was alone. "I cried last night and again today at Cooper's house."

"Why? You said he wasn't mean."

"He wasn't. He's really hot too and I want him, but then I started crying. It's weird."

Tawny said nothing for nearly a minute. "You need practice. It's like when I would get nervous at new schools. Every time I had a new class, I would cry. Then, I got practice and it wasn't scary. Yeah, you just need more practice."

Smiling, I felt like Tawny was in the room with me. I really wished she was and my eyes burned at how much I missed her.

"He's been so great today. Like taking care of me and saying really nice things. He makes me feel like I'm important."

"You are important."

"I guess, but most people don't think that. Cooper has all his money and he's really hot and I know other girls don't cry and act weird. I know he can do better so I'm excited by how he likes me so much."

"You have a calming thing," Tawny said, again sounding confident like she just knew stuff. "You make people feel relaxed and people like that. I always felt better when you were around even if everything was shitty. You did that and maybe he needs that calming thing too. Maybe that's what you have that those other girls don't have? You're beautiful, smart, and funny too, but a lot of people have those things. A lot of people aren't calming though."

"You'd make a great therapist."

"Why would anyone listen to me?"

"Because you make things sound good. That's your talent. You make a person see things they don't see on their own."

Tawny said nothing and I felt her pulling away a little. "I can't go back to high school. I hate the classes."

"I'm not asking you to go to school. I'm just saying you're good with people. You can be good with them without going to school."

"Oh."

"I'm going to get you here, Tawny."

"What about Cooper? What if he wants to keep you around?"

"So?"

"So he might not want me around. Like we were going to get a place, but what if he really likes you and wants to keep you and you can't get a place with me?"

Tawny was crying. I couldn't hear it, but I knew her voice and she was scared.

"He loves me," I said softly. "He wants me to be happy and he knows you're my best friend. He knows I miss you and he wouldn't take you away from me. He even asks about you. Cooper won't stop me from bringing you here."

"He said he loved you?"

"Yes, and I love him too."

"I know. I could tell when you kept trying to talk yourself out of dating him. Why else would you want to stop seeing a rich hot guy unless you were worried you felt more for him than he did for you? Yeah, I knew you were in love."

Laughing, I wished I could give her a hug through the phone. "See, you're smart. School just isn't for everyone."

"Yeah, I'll find a job when I get there and I'll help pay for stuff. I'll pull my weight."

"Even if you don't, I want you here. I miss you."

"I miss you too," Tawny said then sighed. "I'm sorry you cried."

Swallowing hard, I forced out the words. "I felt a little like I was back there."

"It's the tattoos. You said he has them and that's why. You'll get used to those tats and you won't feel that way. Like I said, you need practice."

"It's been a great day and I can't wait until you meet him."

"I won't embarrass you," Tawny said full of sincerity. "I won't ruin things for you when I get there."

In that moment, I saw Tawny and me the way others did. How we were always the dirty outsiders who didn't belong. I had forgotten some of that living in Ellsberg. While I felt like I belonged, Tawny was in a motel, feeling like trash. I wept at the thought of her seeing herself that way.

Tawny and I didn't really say anything for the rest of the call. We just cried and tried to think about the future, but instead wallowed in our past. We needed to get away from all of the ugliness and be new people. I was trying so hard, but she was still stuck in the crap life our parents built for us.

After I hung up, I washed my face then went looking for Cooper. I found him outside on the deck, grilling the steaks. He looked a little ominous in only jeans. His size and those tattoos still scared me, but then he glanced in my direction and smiled. Suddenly, he wasn't the scary guy from the first day of school. He was my Coop who gave foot massages and kissed like he had nowhere important to go. He loved me. I just had to hold onto this fact so I didn't ruin things.

"Is everything okay?" he asked, frowning now.

Nodding, I knew my face was red from crying. "She's alone in a highway shithole and I wish she was here."

"I could bring her here."

My heart leapt, but I didn't agree. My mind recalled how suddenly Cooper had fallen for me and imagined how suddenly he could lose interest. If I started hoping for Cooper to save me and Tawny, I'd stop working to save us. Then when he dumped me, it would hurt more.

"You think about it," Cooper finally said, studying my face. "Want to help me grill?"

"Isn't that man work?" I asked, eyeing him through my narrowed eyes. "Fire is a guy thing, right?"

"I'm a caveman who likes a strong cavewoman."

Cooper handed me the giant grill fork and had me turn over the steaks. While I worked, he stood behind me and kissed my neck.

"I can't think when you do that," I moaned.

"I can't think period when you're around."

"How are you going to be the perfect one if I'm around all the time?"

Cooper stopped kissing my neck and I think he finally figured out what my early thought process had been. He stood very still for a few beats then kissed my neck again.

"I'm just perfect enough to wing it."

Cooper sucked hard at my throat and I melted against him. "I don't want to cook. You do it and also do that. I just want to worship those lips."

Cooper laughed against my throat then returned to sucking at my skin. Somehow, he also flipped over the potatoes while never leaving my body unloved.

Dinner consisted of eating way too much, followed by swimming until I thought I'd puke, and finally we fooled around on the deep end of the pool. I didn't know if Cooper was showing off by having me hold onto him while he gripped the sides and did all of the hip work, but I was impressed. Wrapping myself around him, I tried not to ruin the moment.

Cooper's parents and sisters remained in town overnight at a hotel with Skye's family. To celebrate having the house to ourselves, we had sex a lot. Cooper swore no one would know. I swore they could tell. Cooper swore if they noticed anything that they wouldn't care. I swore they would be horrified to know we befouled their family room, living room, music room, and gym. Cooper acted offended by my referring to our lovemaking as befouling things. I acted shocked at him referring to our fucking as lovemaking. He then shut me up with a kiss that led to more sex. Cooper won the argument and the house was thoroughly marked.

Eventually, we stumbled up the stairs to his apartment for a roll around his bed. The whole last effort involved me giggling because he was half asleep and still trying to score. Cooper refused to relent until he nearly dozed off inside me.

"I'm officially done," he muttered, falling asleep as I cuddled next to him.

After my nap, I was certain I wouldn't sleep even when I checked the clock and found it after one. Lying in the dark with my head resting on his chest, I listened to his heartbeat and was out within minutes.

Dissolving into sleep while wrapped safely in Cooper's arms, I awoke in a dream that was less fantasy and more memory. Tawny was crying nearby and I heard her murmuring my name as if waiting for me to save her. I stretched out my hand to her, but she was in the next room. Saying her name, I felt a hand cover my mouth.

"If you miss your sister so much, we can go watch," Travis whispered with humor to his voice.

Awaking with a cry, I scrambled away from the warm body in the dark room. The man moved towards me and I screamed again. Throwing out my hands, I wasn't awake enough to fight him off, but I hoped to keep him away.

"It's me, baby," Cooper soothed, but I wasn't with him really.

"Leave me alone," I whimpered. "Don't touch me."

Cooper turned on a lamp and my wet eyes adjusted slowly to the dull light.

"Hell, you're shaking," Cooper said, attempting to comfort me, but his touch sent me halfway off the bed.

"I need to leave. I need to go home. It's not safe here."

"It's safer here than anywhere in town," Cooper muttered, sounding angry. Yet, when he spoke again, his voice was softer. "You just had a bad dream."

My hand touched between my legs and I knew it wasn't a dream. Somehow, it felt too real now as if it happened last night and not five years earlier.

"I need to leave."

Cooper stared at me in the dimly lit room and I saw pain in his eyes. "I'm not driving you home in the middle of the night."

"I don't want you to touch me."

Cooper's lips twitched and he blinked a few times. His gaze moved around the room as if he was thinking. When his focus returned to me, Cooper nodded.

"Here," he said, taking a pillow and laying it in the middle of the bed. "I'll stay on my side and you'll stay on your side. I won't touch you, but I'm not driving you home. You're scared and there's no way you'll feel better alone in that apartment with your mom."

The thought of seeing my mother after the dream sent a chill up my spine. I just wanted to be safe and feel the way I had the day before.

"If that's not enough," Cooper continued, "I'll sleep in the living room."

I glanced towards the door leading to the rest of the apartment. While I couldn't deal with Cooper touching me, I didn't want him out of the room either.

"I like the pillow idea," I whispered in a squeaky voice. Swallowing hard, I tried to find moisture, but my fear sucked me dry.

Cooper left the bed, walked to the bathroom, and returned with a coffee cup full of water. I drank it then gave him the best smile I could manage.

"I'm sorry."

Taking the cup, Cooper just shook his head. "Everyone has bad dreams."

Nodding, I watched him set the cup on the table behind him then he rested on his side with the pillow separating us. After a few minutes of looking around as if someone might be waiting to jump out, I rested on my side and stared at Cooper.

"Do you want to leave the light on?" he asked.

"For a little while please."

His gaze unreadable in the murky light, Cooper nodded. We stared at each other for a while and I worried he was angry. What if in the morning, he drove me home then pretended I didn't exist? I knew he could do that and I would have no choice other than accept how he was done with me.

"Do you still love me?" I asked.

Cooper inhaled harshly. When he spoke, his voice broke. "So much it hurts."

"I love you too. I'm sorry."

"Stop apologizing."

"I heard something like gunshots," I said, glancing back at the window.

"It's fireworks. A lot of people party when parents are in town. Shows you what kind of students we have that their parents are wild."

Smiling slightly, I pulled the covers over me. When I had trouble yanking up his heavy comforter, Cooper reached out to help. Without thinking, I flinched and nearly fell off the bed again. His expression wasn't unreadable anymore. He looked like a hurt boy who lost his best friend.

"I..."

"Don't say you're sorry."

"I want to hold your hand."

Once Cooper laid his hand palm down on the pillow in between us, I rested mine on top of it.

"The dream felt so real," I said, trying to explain.

"Was it about me?"

Shaking my head, I frowned. "Why would I dream anything bad about you?"

The corner of Cooper's mouth twitched like he wanted to smile, but his mood was too miserable. "You're still shaking," he said after a minute.

"I'm glad you're here. I would have been so scared in my apartment."

Cooper finally smiled just a hint, but I knew he was bothered by my inability to find comfort from his touch. He rested on his side and watched me until I fell asleep.

When I woke up, Cooper was staring hard at the ceiling. He looked so angry that I was afraid for him to notice my eyes were open. Eventually, I slid out of bed and walked to the bathroom. After cleaning up, I returned to bed where Cooper still glared at the ceiling.

Unsure why he was upset, I felt a panic deep in my gut over losing him. I didn't have any words to fix his anger so I used something I figured he would enjoy more.

Kissing his chest as I slid in next to him, I licked the outline of the cross on his chest. Cooper's breathing shifted, but I didn't dare look at him and ruin the possibility of improving his mood.

I tried to channel the sexy part of me that knew what to do to make him feel good. Cooper's hands were behind his head as I climbed over him to tease his chest. Then, I moved lower to his hard stomach and softly kissed the flesh the way he always did to me. In no hurry, I imitated Cooper and his leisurely way of making me squirm.

Cooper's breathing sped up as I slid down past his belly button. Finally, I lifted my gaze to his face where he watched me with an odd expression. It was somewhere between horny as hell and examining an alien life form.

The horny as hell part made it an easy transition from his stomach to his hard cock. As it thickened even more in my mouth, I might not feel confident, but I could fake it. I'd gone to school sick before. I'd smiled on bad days. I could fake a lot of things and I could fake like I was a pro at blowjobs.

No matter my plans, Cooper stopped me. I tried to keep going, but he sat up and pulled me off him. "Just stop," he said, wiping my wet cheeks. "It's awful. You know that, right?"

"I can get better."

Cooper shook his head and leaned back on the bed. He was still so hard and I wasn't giving up. Either I needed to be more confident or fake it better. Straddling him, I tried to guide him inside, but couldn't. Suddenly, I was too small or he was too big or I was just aiming wrong. Again, Cooper stopped me.

"Knock it off," he growled, his dark eyes irritated. "You're going to hurt yourself."

"I want this," I whimpered, full of frustration and panic. "Please."

Cooper lifted me off his hips and I started to cry until he leaned over and kissed me. Soon, he was angled between my legs as his fingers stroked my nipples and his lips sucked hard on my tongue. Pulling his mouth away, he nuzzled his face in my hair.

"Tell me you love me," he murmured in my ear. "Make me believe you want me."

"I do. I love you so much, Cooper. More than anything. Please."

Somehow, when he thrust inside me, he fit perfectly and I didn't know how the hell I messed it up minutes earlier. I decided to concentrate on him, but I still felt that panic in my gut. Fear growing in waves, I had trouble relaxing enough to even take a good breath.

My hands stroked his chest, wanting him to know I loved him. Wanting Cooper to ignore my tears and the look on my face. The same look that forced him to close his eyes as if he couldn't finish if he saw me.

Afterwards, I rested against him as he again stared at the ceiling. Cooper was silent for nearly a half hour. A braver girl would have asked already, but I wasn't brave. The last week was tougher than the first and I didn't want to fight with Cooper. So I laid next to him with my hand on his arm, just over the patriotic eagle. By the time Cooper spoke, I had memorized the tattoo, down to every feather.

"Something has to change," he said softly as his gaze remained focused on the ceiling. "I don't know how you can mouth off about the smallest shit, but then lay there and let me fuck you when you hate it."

"I don't hate it."

Cooper sighed angrily. "You're not much of an actress, Farah. Your every damn emotion is written across your face. When you're pissed. When you're happy. When you're miserable with me fucking you, it's all right there for me to see."

What could I say? Sorry my face does things I can't control? Sorry I don't like sex and applaud like every other girl? In the end, I just went with sorry and Cooper sighed again.

"Sorry you don't want sex or sorry that I know you don't want sex? Or maybe you're sorry for not being able to get away from me? What exactly are you sorry for?"

"I'm sorry you're upset."

"Liar."

"I don't know what you want."

"That's the problem, isn't it?" he said, turning over to glare at me. "You don't know what you want, so how the hell can you know what anyone else wants?"

"I know what I want."

"To go to school. To be a teacher. You want shit you filled your head with when you were a kid. Now, you're an adult wanting that crap. Do you really want it though? Do you want me? Do you even like guys?"

"I'm not a lesbian," I said, getting out of bed and reaching for my clothes. "That's such a cliché guys go to when a girl doesn't react the way they want about sex."

"No," Cooper muttered, yanking on his jeans. "You might actually be a lesbian and not know it. I'm not sure you do much thinking about stuff outside your kiddie dreams."

"I am attracted to you. You are not a girl. I am not a lesbian. If I was, I would have told you to fuck off right away."

"Maybe not. It's a small town. People act stupid. Maybe you figured you'd play along. I do tip well and you get friends and rides and shit by pretending to like me except you can't pretend. Your fucking face won't let you lie."

"Lesbians don't have sex with guys so they can get tips."

"How would you know?"

"Fuck you. You don't get your way and your immediate response is to accuse me of using you. I couldn't just be young and unsure. No, I'm a bitch mooching off the rich guy. Fuck you, Coop."

Once dressed, I wanted to leave, but needed a ride from the asshole behind me. Turning to him, I found Cooper so pissed I was surprised steam wasn't pulsing out of his ears.

"I'm leaving," I said, crossing my arms.

"We need to fucking talk."

"About what? All the ways I use you and how you're an innocent victim of my lesbian trickery? You're an idiot and I want to go home."

Walking to the door, I wasn't surprised when Cooper stepped in my way and blocked the exit.

"I said we need to talk."

"And I said about what?"

"About how you cry every time we're together. Even out in the hot tub where for five seconds you seemed to enjoy yourself, you ended up bawling. Why do you keep doing shit you hate? Hell, when you went down on me, I thought you might puke you were crying so hard."

Wrapping my arms tightly around my body, I tried to disappear. Even if Cooper wasn't looming over me looking scary as shit, I wasn't discussing my sex issues with him again.

"Fuck!" he hollered, punching a hole in the wall two inches from my face. "You just shut down whenever you don't get your way. You won't talk to me about anything. I get that you have a shit family, but that's no reason to spend the rest of your life making shitty decisions."

Trembling at how close he came to punching me, I whispered, "I'm going home."

"I'm not taking you home. If you want to leave, fucking walk."

Staring into Cooper's angry eyes, I realized he expected me to back down. He expected wrong.

While I might have issues with sex and talking about my every farting feeling, I had no problem walking long distances. My family was routinely without transportation when I was growing up. Either the car didn't work or we didn't have money for gas.

Leaving Cooper's apartment, I walked down the stairs and pulled on my backpack. If I walked steadily, I could make it home in an hour. Two at the most. Screw him for thinking I would give a shit about a little exercise. Screw him for being so pampered that he didn't realize others survived without having their asses wiped every day.

Once I had been walking for nearly fifteen minutes, the realization of Cooper and I being over suddenly hit me. Tears burned my eyes as I felt all that loss. The more I considered my feelings for Cooper, the more I accepted how I had hoped he would grow into a man I could trust completely. He was rough and sometimes the things he said hurt my feelings or made me want to run in the opposite direction. Yet, when we were together in bed, he could be so tender. It was the main reason I wanted to have sex. If I ignored the actual sex part, I enjoyed being so close to him. Now, it was over and he wouldn't even remember my name when he saw me at school.

In the end, some part of me always knew it would be over because Cooper had no reason to change into someone less intense. Mister Perfect would take five seconds to find a new girlfriend who wouldn't want him to change. Most of the girls loved how rough he was, laughed at his rude mouth, and moaned over his every caress. They would do everything right and make him happy. He had no reason to change, but unless he did, I would never feel comfortable with him. Deep inside, he scared the shit out of me and I figured he always would.

Even depressed, I was resigned to the upside of breaking up with Cooper. He and I were always going to break up, but now he would find someone who could handle him. I could find someone like Nick who was soft and calm. Dull in a sexy way, instead of gorgeous in a wild scary way. Even accepting how right I was to end things with Cooper, I still sobbed because he was my first love. He had been mine, but now he wasn't. It was the reality of life in a nutshell.

The first two times I heard motorcycles, I thought Cooper had changed his mind about giving me a ride home. Dozens of motorcycles roared past me on my walk. Some headed to town, others out to the countryside. I ignored them after realizing they weren't Cooper. One guy stopped and offered me a ride, but I told him I was waiting for someone. It wasn't a complete lie, yet I didn't think he believed me especially because I was crying so hard.

When another motorcycle stopped, I shouldn't have known it was Cooper. I should have zoned out the possibility, but I felt him and stopped walking. Lifting my gaze to where the Harley idled, I hurried forward. Cooper didn't look at me or speak when I climbed on. Keeping up the silence, I wrapped my arms around him as he roared back onto the road and towards my apartment.

Resting my face against his warm back, I wished things were different, but they never would be. Cooper was from his world where he was fucking perfect. I was from another world where he was fucking scary. Besides, Cooper thought I should just stop being damaged like it was a choice. Like I wanted to cry during sex, instead of enjoying his hot body.

I felt like I did the best I could when I was essentially alone in a new place without the only person I truly trusted. Maybe I would be less moody or more vocal if Tawny was living with me, but she wasn't and I couldn't give Cooper more than I already had. Nothing would change either of us. No matter how good he felt or how much I loved him, I had to let him go.

Cooper pulled up to the front of the apartment complex and turned off his Harley. Sliding off the back, I wasn't sure what to say. I hadn't even been sure if he wanted me to say anything because he hadn't spoken on the drive. With the bike silent, I suspected he wanted to talk. Nervous, I weaseled out of a conversation.

"Thanks for the ride. I'll see you at school."

Grabbing my wrist, Cooper stared at me almost as if in shock. "That's it? You're just done with me?"

"We're too different. We'll just make each other miserable."

Frowning darkly, Cooper glanced around then back at me. "Fuck."

Cooper released my wrist and soon the bike roared to life and down the street. I watched him go and stood a few minutes longer, just thinking about how wrong the day turned. Walking to the apartment, I told myself my unhappiness was from Cooper's potential revenge towards me. In reality, I missed the safety I felt in his arms. A safety defying the rest of Cooper's personality.

Chapter Seventeen

Despite my depression that evening, I didn't call Tawny. Mostly, I was embarrassed I hadn't been able to keep Cooper. How would I explain to my sister stranded in a shit motel that I had a chance with a rich hot guy that loved me, but I was too awful at sex to keep him from thinking I was a lesbian? Tawny wouldn't judge outwardly, but I knew she would think I messed up. Girls like us had few chances at anything great in our lives and Cooper was great in many ways.

He wasn't perfect though. Despite what he thought about himself, Cooper had nearly punched me in the face. Thinking back to that moment, I should have been warier of my next move. I had chosen to leave without considering how he might hurt me. Maybe I hadn't taken it seriously enough or maybe I had been too upset to care, but I was reckless.

If I talked to Tawny, I would likely tell her how Cooper almost hit me. She would say it was good we broke up. She would judge Cooper and I didn't want her to think poorly of him. I shouldn't protect the asshole, but I loved him. Somehow, when I got up the nerve to call her in a day or two, I would figure out a lie to answer why Cooper and I weren't together. I wasn't great at lying to Tawny, but the truth was too embarrassing.

Crying in my room, I turned on the cheap clock radio to muffle my sobs. Amy and Tex were in the living room watching TV and laughing it up. While they partied, I replayed the morning with Cooper.

Finally falling asleep just after dark, I was exhausted, depressed, and dreading the next day. I woke up with the same worries. Would Cooper take away my friends? Would he show up with a new girl and rub it in my face? Would he embarrass me by acting like I didn't exist?

By the time I saw Skye, I was prepared for the worst. Upon seeing me, she shook her head.

"Guy troubles, huh?"

"How do you know?"

"Honestly? You look like shit. Like you cried all night. Also, I heard from someone that Cooper was raging through town last night. He's been pretty mellow lately. I figured he was freaking out because you two had a fight. The guy has temper issues."

"We broke up."

"Broke up?" Skye yelled then looked around and lowered her voice. "He dumped you? Man, that's harsh. You guys just hooked up on Friday night. Everyone was talking about how he carried you out of the house. You seemed wasted or something. I don't really know because I was all into Tyler. I met his parents, you know?"

"How did it go?" I asked, relieved to have the subject off of me and Cooper.

"Great. I'm awesome with parents. They were nice too, but my parents didn't like Tyler. I tried to guilt them into liking him by saying they were racists if they didn't, but they just don't like how he's into Jesus. It would really help if he didn't wear the giant crucifix, but his mom bought it for him and he's sweet on his mom."

"I'm sure it'll work out. You wanted to keep him for the year at least. Your parents not liking him won't change that, will it?"

"No, but I don't need my mom nagging at me. My little adopted brother started first grade so she's lonely during the day. Nagging me is a fun hobby of hers."

I forced a smile. "Screen your calls, I guess."

Skye laughed. "Yeah, I should. That would drive her crazy."

Once in class, I tried to pay attention to the instructor, but my mind was on seeing Cooper. Afterwards, Skye was back to talking about Tyler and how his abs were hotter than any in the universe. So busy nodding at everything she said, I didn't see Bailey storming towards us.

"Hey, bitch!" Bailey announced, cornering me against a wall.

The thing with Bailey was her friendly banter wasn't all that different from her raging. I wasn't sure she was angry until she looked me up and down then did her little lip pucker "something stinks in here" expression.

"Because of you, my brother shaved off his head last night."

"His head?" Skye said, laughing.

"Fuck off, bitch!" After Skye's laughter stopped mid-giggle, Bailey glared at me. "You hurt him because you're a bitch and mentally deficient."

"He shaved his head off?" I asked confused.

"Yeah, dumbass!" Bailey yelled, shoving me against the wall hard enough for my head to bounce off the bricks. Then, she paused and her eyes focused upward. "Oh, his hair, I mean. He shaved off his hair. Not his head. Anyway, because you suck, Coop and Tuck got wasted and shaved their heads. Now, my mom is pissed because she doesn't like their hair that short. She said it makes them look like skinheads and she doesn't like suspenders."

I doubted Bailey was really certain what her mom didn't like. Either way, I wasn't explaining anything to Bailey who punched girls over minor infractions. My head already hurt and I hated getting punched in the face.

"I'm sorry Cooper is upset."

"Are you?" Bailey said, eyeballing me. "What's your problem anyway? Don't you want nice things? Are you stupid? Cooper has money and one day he'll take over for my pop and have more money. He's hot and smart and the responsible one. Hell, if he wasn't my brother, I'd date Crapface in a minute. Every girl in school would like him to go all hearts and flowers over them, but not you. You think you're too good. Like you could do better. Is that what you think, Farah? That you can win over someone better than Coop when you dress like a trailer trash reject?"

Glancing down at my clothes, I thought they looked just like everyone else's. Jeans and a tee, nothing special, but not trashy.

"Let's be honest, bitch," Bailey said, really hitting her groove. "The only reason any guy likes you is cause of those lips. You have dead eyes, shitty hair, a weird round head, and small tits. You're nothing special except that they look at you and think of blowjobs. You might want to keep that in mind when you think of discarding my brother."

"I make Cooper mad a lot," I said, hoping to give her an excuse that wouldn't lead to her punching me in the face. "I thought he'd be happier if I gave him space."

"You're so dense. So stupid and poor. You have a rich guy interested and you want away from him. Look at Maddy. You think she couldn't tell the difference between her birth control pills and fucking Tic Tacs? She figured out what Fuckwad was up to and saw a lifetime of money and security. She let him knock her up because even if they break up, their kid will tie Maddy to Tuck forever. His kid won't want for nothing so neither will she. Maddy might be a poor turd like you, but she's not stupid. Maybe you need to pull your head out of your ass and start thinking about how to make things right with Cooper? Like how many blowjobs will make him forgive you for being such a bitch?"

"Okay," I said quietly.

"Okay," Bailey mocked before walking away.

Skye watched her go then sighed loudly. "I guess you need to get back together with Cooper."

"I don't think he wants to get back together," I said quietly, walking with my head down and hoping people weren't staring now that Bailey was gone and it was safe to stare.

"If Bailey says you need to make things right, Coop wants you back. Explains why he trashed that frat house with Tucker last night. He's pissed and probably horny. You fuck him a few times and it'll be fine. Coop's not that complicated."

I wasn't explaining how the fucking was what made Cooper dislike me. Skye was great at many things and fun to be around, but insightful she was not.

By the time I started my shift at work, the little lump on the back of my head throbbed. I was also thinking about whether to call Tawny that night when Cooper walked into the restaurant. Even after skipping his classes, Cooper came into Denny's and walked to his spot in the corner. He hooked up his laptop, pulled out papers, books, and pens, and waited with his hands clasped.

Walking to his table, I saw how Bailey wasn't kidding about him shaving off his hair. With it buzzed short against his head, Cooper looked edgier. Okay, he looked scary. His intense gaze was no longer softened by his blond hair. Now, when he stared at me, I only saw those eyes swirling with anger, resentment, and maybe a little longing.

"What would you like tonight?" I asked.

"No, hello?" he muttered. "We're just strangers now?"

"Sorry," I said, taking a deep breath. "Hi, Cooper. How are you tonight?"

"Didn't you hear, random Denny's waitress? My girlfriend dumped me because I love her too much. Real shame too because we had a great thing going until she blew a gasket over nothing."

"Girls can be such bitches that way. Would you like to order a burger to help deal with the pain of being screwed over by some psycho?"

Cooper didn't smile. Well, his lips didn't, but I saw a gleam of humor in his eyes.

"Unless I can fuck the burger, it won't help much, but pigging out might soothe my broken heart."

"Seasoned fries?"

"Yeah, and bring me the appetizer thing with chicken strips. I'm really going to pig out so when I get wasted tonight, my stomach won't care."

"I'll get this in for you."

When I turned away, Cooper reached for me. "Don't you miss me at all?" he whispered roughly. "You said you loved me and yet you look at me like I'm nothing. How cold are you?"

My eyes burned. "I miss you."

"Bullshit."

"You and I don't work. I make you angry."

"Everything makes me angry. When my team doesn't win a ballgame, I get pissed, but I don't stop watching football. Why would you walk away if you really loved me?"

Glancing around, I saw the place was dead as usual. When I turned back to Cooper, I forced out the words.

"You think I'm a lesbian using you for money. And that day at your place when you got so mad, I thought you were going to hit me."

Cooper flinched then let go of my wrist. "I don't hit girls."

Nodding, I felt awkward under his gaze. "Some men can love a woman and still hit her when they get angry."

"Some men. Like who? Like Daddy? Or do you have a secret ex who smacked you around?"

Stepping back, I wanted to find Cooper another waitress. He reached for my hand before I moved too far away.

"When my sister and I fight, I never lay a hand on her. When I had a girlfriend who keyed my truck and slashed my tires, I didn't hit her. Even when she tried to cut me, I didn't hit her. Look at me," he said, tugging me closer. "Look at me, Farah." When I finally met his gaze, he exhaled hard. "I don't hit women. I'm not an out of control freak who hits people because I can't stop myself. Everyone I hit, I hit on purpose and I would never hit you on purpose. I would never hurt you or any woman, but especially not you."

"Okay."

"Okay what?"

"Okay, you would never hit me."

"Damn it," he grumbled when I tugged my hand free. "Why won't you talk to me?"

"I am."

"No, you're humoring me because you're at work. Just talk to me please. I miss you and it's killing me pretending otherwise."

Glancing around, I wished someone needed me, but I was alone in the dining room with Cooper. When I looked back at him, I was startled by the pain in his expression. I hadn't really thought about how much our breakup would affect him. Mostly because I figured he could find someone else. A pretty fun girl who laughed at his jokes like I did and who enjoyed sex with him like I didn't.

"I'll be on break in a little bit. I could come back and talk then."

"Why not now? There's no one here."

"I'm not on break though."

"No one cares."

"I do. I like rules. Without rules, people do whatever they want."

"So you think I need rules, is that what you're saying?"

"No, I'm saying some people can get away with doing whatever they want like you do. Some people are like me and breaking the rules will ruin them."

Cooper inhaled hard then let it all out. His tight shoulders eased as did the stiffness in his jaw. Nodding, he laid his hands palms down on the table.

"Fine. When you have your break, I want you to bring a drink for yourself and something to eat too. I want you to sit down and act like we're friendly and not like you have no choice. Can you do that?"

"Yes," I said, turning away. "I like your haircut."

Unable to see Cooper's reaction, I didn't dare look back. Instead, I put in his order then brought his drink. He watched me walk to his table and he watched me walk away. I wasn't sure what to do so I hid in the bathroom for a few minutes while his food cooked.

Cooper was everything bad for me. He was violent in such a casual way as if hurting someone was like breathing. While he was beautiful, his tattoos reminded me of my greatest fear. He was wealthy, but that just gave him a sense of entitlement. I had nothing and maybe I was nothing, but I wanted to be someone. I wanted to have the life I had dreamed of since I was a kid. A teacher who lived in the suburbs and lived a safe calm life. Could I really have that with Cooper? Not only did he mock my dreams, he would hate living in the suburbs. He already had to be a lawyer for his family so the last thing he needed was to create a dull life with me.

Yet, why did it have to be about forever? Couldn't we just spend time together now in college then go our separate ways when we were older? If I could keep Cooper for a while and know it was short term, I wouldn't feel so suffocated. Not only by the intensity of our relationship, but also by the idea that anything I did wrong could cause him to leave me.

If I stopped thinking love meant forever, I could enjoy all of Cooper's good qualities. No one made me laugh like Cooper except for Tawny. Since my sister was out of my life for now, I deserved a taste of happiness and I wanted Cooper.

When I brought his food to the table, I included a drink for myself. Watching me full of need, he exhaled softly when I joined him.

"You didn't get anything to eat."

"I'm not hungry."

"Eat a fry."

Frowning, I didn't take the fry he offered. "You can't boss me around so much."

"You need to take better care of yourself."

"I don't want a father especially a bossy one like my actual father."

"Your dad is bossy?" he asked, eating the fry I wouldn't take.

"He sometimes drank and got edgy and bossed me and my sister around."

Cooper studied me. "Did he hit you?"

"I really missed you," I said, changing the subject to one I was certain he would like.

"Hell, Farah, I feel like I can't breathe since yesterday."

"I love you, but..."

"No, buts."

"Yes, buts. You scare me. You nearly punched me in the face."

"I was never going to hit you."

Eyeing Cooper, I refused to turn to mush just because I missed him so much. "How was punching a hole in the wall next to my face a good thing? You wanted to scare me."

"I was angry. I want you so much and you hate being with me. You hate when I touch you and it was making me nuts, but hitting the wall was a mistake. I do that shit with Bailey and she laughs it off because she knows I'd never hit her. I thought you knew that too. I mean, I was pissed because you were forcing yourself to do things with me that you didn't want to do. I was angry because I wasn't a better man for you, so why would I turn around and hit you?"

"I don't really know you and you don't know me. You shouldn't assume I'll take things the way you mean them. I have no experience with having a boyfriend," I said then added quietly, "I'd never even been on a date before you."

Cooper rubbed at his head and sighed. "You love me though, right? I need you to love me because I'm drowning in how much I love you."

"It's too fast. We just met and I just moved here. It's a lot to deal with and I feel cornered."

Cooper's expression darkened. "Damn, is there anything I'm doing right?"

"I said I liked your haircut."

Fighting a grin, Cooper leaned back in the booth and flipped me off. "I got drunk and shaved it off as a form of protest."

"Against what?"

"My fucking heart."

"You're an idiot."

"Yeah, probably."

"If we could be more casual, I think I could learn to be with you and not feel so cornered. Like maybe it's not only you that's to blame for our fights," I said then watched him raise a cocky eyebrow. "Well, it's mostly you, but I'll take like ten percent of the blame."

"Twenty five percent and we have a deal."

"Whatever you need to tell yourself, but if we spend time together, we'd need to keep it more casual."

"I have no idea what you're fucking saying. Spend time together? Does that mean you'll give me another chance and we're together? And what is more casual? That usually involves fucking other people. I'm not fucking anyone else and I certainly don't want you fucking anyone else."

Squinting at him, I had to wonder if all of the booze had made him stupid. "After all the trouble I have being with you, do you really think I'd want another dick around me?"

Cooper grinned. "Is it wrong that my dick responded when you called its name?"

"Very wrong, perv," I said, laughing. "So do we have a deal?"

"No because I don't know what you're asking for?"

"We date and have fun and don't make it mean anything more."

"I love you and I'm not pretending otherwise. Screw casual."

"You're too intense."

"You need someone to take care of you."

"I need my freedom and to find my own way."

"Nope."

Leaning back, I drank my soda. Cooper studied a fry then reached out and pushed it against my lips.

"Someone's hungry."

"Fuck off," I nearly yelled then covered my mouth while Cooper laughed his ass off.

"Someone's going to get fired and need her rich boyfriend to pay for shit."

"I didn't say we were back together."

"You said you loved and missed me. Close enough."

"I did miss you," I muttered, ignoring the fry still caressing my lips. "I'm not eating that."

"Need a ride home?"

"Maybe."

"Yes, it is. Now, open up for the fry."

Staring at him, I managed to launch Cooper into a staring match. "I'm going back to work."

"Your break isn't over," he said, finally shoving the fry into his mouth. "You look tired. Did you sleep okay last night?"

"Yes."

"Want me to sleep over and give you a foot massage?"

Rolling my eyes, I couldn't fight my smile. "We'll see."

"Yes, it is. Man, you're very agreeable tonight."

Cooper looked full of life, just floating on a cloud as he devoured his burger with one hand and tapped to the overhead music with the other. I reached for the free hand and caressed his bruised knuckles.

"Get in any fights?"

Frowning, Cooper stopped mid-chew and sighed. Once he swallowed, he looked down at where my hand still held his.

"No one you know."

"Your hands scare me," I said, running my thin fingers over his strong ones. "When they touch me though, they seem so gentle. I guess that makes you complicated." Lifting my gaze away from his hand and meeting his intense stare, I sighed. "What?"

Cooper wanted to say something that I suspected wasn't light and casual. He finally shrugged. "The fair is this weekend. Go with me."

"I can't. I'm picking up extra shifts on the weekend."

Cooper frowned as he took my hand into his. "You need to work less, not more."

"I need the money for new clothes. Someone said I look like trailer trash. Maybe they were full of shit, but I feel insecure now and want to buy new clothes."

"Who said that?" he asked in a hard low voice.

"It was a girl so you can't hit her."

"What girl? I'll send Bailey after her." When I smiled softly at him, he rolled his eyes. "I'll push her into the pool for you."

"No, it's fine," I said, choosing not to mention the lump. "She was protecting you, but I want to make sure I look like everyone else."

"You look gorgeous just being you."

"I'm not like you, Coop. I don't want to be different. Average is my goal."

"You aren't average. You're special because you're the only girl who's ever made my heart hurt. You're mine and I'll buy you new clothes so you don't have to work this weekend." When I started to protest, he shushed me. "If you don't want to shop with me, I'll give you cash and you can go with Skye."

"I don't want you for your money. I'm not using you."

"I know," he said, giving me a nod, "but I don't care if you use me. I want you so much I don't care why you want me."

"That's crap," I whispered. "You care. As much as your money seems like an easy way out for me, I won't use you. Not only because you matter to me and I want you to know my feelings are real. I also want to survive as a grownup on my own."

"A grownup?"

"Don't make fun. I have dreams and they involve hard work."

"Work hard during the week then blow off the weekends. The fair is awesome and my family will be there and I want you to go. I want to share that with you because you work hard here and at school and you look tired. You look like you need to relax and working all weekend while everyone else plays isn't relaxing."

"I already told Arnie I'd work so the other girls could have time off."

"I'll talk to him."

Sighing, I scooted down in the booth and pulled away my hand. "You can't control everything. It's like you're a finished product and I'm a brand new idea. You're making all the decisions about who I can be and what I can do, but I can't make any decisions about who you are."

"Well, for one thing, I'm not eighteen. For another, you have control over how I feel and that's still power. Finally, maybe you grew up with a boot on the back of your neck so you need all of this independence to feel like you've accomplished shit, but you need to get over that. I take care of the people I love. My money can make your life easier and that makes my life easier. I'm not molding you and I don't think you need molding anyway. The only difference between us is that I know I'm a finished product and you think you still need to change. You don't and working this weekend so you can buy new clothes you don't need won't make you better. It won't make you stronger or smarter. It'll wear you down and give you a false sense of accomplishment. In the long run, your grades will suffer and you'll hate your job and school and, God forbid, me."

"I've dreamed of this life for a long time and I want it to be like my dream."

"Dream bigger, baby."

"You mean dream of you."

"A dream with me in it, yes, but I know you want to be a teacher. I see on your face what that means to you. I'm not saying give up everything for me and be my bitch. I'm saying live your dream along with being my bitch."

"Fuck you," I hissed, grinning.

Cooper shared my smile. "I have to protect you. I have to feel like I'm doing right by you because my heart hurts when you aren't happy. The last day sucked worse than any time in my life. I just couldn't give two shits about anything because I'd lost you."

"I don't know. I still feel like I should work this weekend."

Cooper sighed for nearly a minute then shook his head. "Healthy relationships are about compromise. Don't work this weekend and go to the fair with me and I'll buy you new clothes. See, compromise?"

"You get everything you want. How is that compromise?"

"I'm buying you new clothes that I don't think you need," he said, grinning. "I'm wasting money on your delusion. You're welcome."

Laughing, I finished my soda then stood up. "I'll think about it."

"And say yes when I take you home later."

Two hours later, I did say yes, only because I was tired as hell. Schoolwork was piling up quickly and I needed time to study. As we reached the parking lot, Cooper was humming with happiness when I slid on behind him. Literally humming like a happy child who received good news from Santa. He was humming the whole drive to my apartment. After a private shower even though I knew Cooper wanted to join me, I returned to my bedroom to find him exploring my dresser drawers.

"What are you doing?" I asked as casually as I could muster.

"Looking to see if you're on the pill."

"I told you I get those shots."

"Yeah, but I was hoping you were lying so I could find your pills, switch them out with Tic Tacs, and keep you with me forever."

"First of all, Coop, I'd know they were Tic Tacs. Secondly, if you want to keep me forever, just treat me well and I'll stay with you. Wouldn't that be better than having a baby we're not ready for?"

Cooper grinned. "My girl is so smart and rational."

"You weren't really looking for my birth control, were you?" I asked, sitting on the bed.

"Yeah. The last day was the worst of my life and don't you dare point out how I've had an easy life."

"I'll just think it then."

Cooper glanced out of the curtains then back at me. "You need a TV in your room."

"I'm saving up for one."

Cooper grinned. "Foot massage time."

"We could go into the living room and watch TV while you service me."

"I was thinking maybe I'd stay the night and a relaxing foot massage might put you in the mood for makeup loving."

Looking around, I wasn't sure I wanted to feel him inside me. On the other hand, I really wanted to kiss and hold him and that would lead to sex.

"Okay."

"Are you sure?"

"Yes."

"I want you to be honest," Cooper said, looking rather grumpy.

"I am."

"It breaks my fucking heart when you cry while I'm enjoying myself. Do you understand?"

"I can't promise I won't cry. It's a reflex."

"I'm not the guy who hurt you."

"I know."

"Maybe we should just hang out and mess around and keep it casual."

Frowning, I rested back on the bed and wiggled my feet at him. "I want to do what you said earlier."

"You can't even say it."

Crossing my arms, I frowned harder. "I heard these girls in class talking about how great sex was and I felt jealous. I want to be like everyone else and enjoy stuff like they do. I can't do that if I don't practice. It's like everything else. I just need to learn how to do it."

"So you want me to climb on you and fuck you while you cry?" he said and I felt my eyes burning. "You can't know how it feels to watch you cry like that."

"No, but if you want me to ever learn to enjoy it, you'll have to keep trying. If you want to give up, that's fine, but I can't learn to like it if I don't practice."

Cooper sat at the end of the bed and took a foot in his strong hands. "Is it that you think I'm going to hurt you like that guy did?"

Lifting myself up onto my elbows, I stared hard at him. "We don't talk about those things in my family. We don't say the words and I'm not talking about that."

"I just want to understand how to make you feel good too. I hate taking from you and watching you cry and waiting for it to be over."

"I told you. It's a reflex. My body reacts and I cry. I know it's you and I love you and I want you, but my body reacts. Talking about this is making me tense."

"We don't have to talk about it then. I need you to be comfortable with us being together though."

"Be close with me then. The more you are, the better it feels. Like when we first tried, even when I was drunk, it hurt because I tensed up. It got easier last weekend at your house. I still cried and got scared, but it didn't hurt. I want to have sex like everyone else. I want to learn, but there's only one way and that's through practice."

Cooper nodded as his thumbs pressed deep against my aching arch. I cried out, sounding somewhere between horny and in pain. Cooper just smiled and kept working at my feet as I watched him. After a few minutes, I was incredibly relaxed. I was also missing the feel of him against me.

I whispered, "I love you."

Cooper lifted my foot and kissed it as his warm gaze held mine. Smiling at him, I opened my robe to show nothing underneath.

"Hell," Cooper muttered.

"Your sister said my only good feature is my lips. Is that true and don't lie because you want sex? We're having sex no matter what you say."

Cooper didn't even look at me as he moved his kisses from my foot to my calf. He only paused to pull off his tee and toss it on the floor.

"You're so gorgeous I have to beat up guys constantly to keep them away from you."

"Is that true?"

"Uh-huh," he murmured as he kissed my inner thigh.

"You shouldn't beat up anyone over me."

"Sure, whatever," he said, kissing higher on my thigh.

"I don't like that," I yelped as his lips moved between my legs. "I don't want that."

"It'll feel good," he said, looking at me with a gentle gaze. "It'll relax you too. Girls really like it. Trust me."

"I don't want that," I said again, fighting the urge to close my robe and have him leave.

"Fair enough," he said, crawling up to kiss my stomach.

Realizing he stopped and wasn't angry, I let out a long sigh. Glancing up at me, Cooper licked at my belly button then left a trail of affection all the way to the soft underside of my breast. A breath caught in my throat as I waited for the fun stuff. A grinning Cooper sucked my nipple into his mouth.

"I like this," I announced like a dork, but I wanted him to know it wasn't all bad and I could loosen up eventually.

"We can make each other happy, Farah," Cooper said, lying between my legs and swinging his feet like a kid. His expression was tender as he teased my nipples. "I know you're mine. If you let me start over, we can be so fucking happy that all the shit that came before will be no more than a bad dream."

"I'm afraid to love you too much."

"It's normal to be scared when you grew up in a shitty way. I bet you spent most of your life worrying that anything nice might get stolen away. With me, with what we have, it's probably scary. For me though, losing you is the only thing that scares the shit out of me. I need to make you happy so you'll stay and I can be happy."

As my fingers caressed the soft prickles of his shaved hair, I thought about how much Cooper needed me. How he hadn't forgotten I existed or moved on the second I wasn't there. He really seemed to love me. I hadn't believed it, but there was no other reason he would have freaked out.

"Have you ever been dumped before?" I asked as Cooper snuggled his face between my breasts.

"What do you mean by dumped?" he mumbled, glancing up at me.

"Like what you did yesterday?"

"I guess."

"Maybe. When chicks blow me off, I don't usually care. I'm just about nailing them. Once I have, whatever happens happens." Cooper paused and his gaze met mine. "How many fucking times do I have to tell you that you're special?"

"A million? Possibly more."

Cooper grinned at my tone. "Fair enough. Now, stop interrupting my reunion with the girls."

Starting to laugh until his tongue lathered love on my right nipple, I groaned instead. Cooper smiled, taking his time at getting reacquainted with my body. By the time he was inside me, I was as relaxed as I could be after a long stressful day. Even later when the neighbors were loud and I was startled awake, everything felt better because I had Cooper with me. He was still mine and I needed to find a way to keep him.

Chapter Eighteen

The next few days, Cooper and I fell into an easy routine. I was usually at his house where we'd eat breakfast with the family before heading to school. Our schedules didn't mesh well so I barely saw him during the day. Cooper typically ran by and kissed the shit out of me during his lunch time. My lunch period was later so I was actually missing part of class to make out with Cooper. The instructor acted as if this behavior was all very natural even though another student was grilled after he walked out of class one day. Life was good for a Johansson in Ellsberg.

Cooper was so relaxed those next few days. I tried to relax too, but life taught me to treasure every moment because the good ones never lasted. When I was at work, Cooper hung around, talking to me and doing his schoolwork. Every night, we returned to his place where I received a much appreciated foot massage, followed by all of the sexual need he built up over the day. We sometimes didn't sleep until after midnight.

Thursday night, Cooper was especially horny. He couldn't get enough and we would barely finish before he was ready to go again. I didn't know him well enough to gage if this was a normal thing for him or if something in particular set him off? I did sense he was clingier than usual. Territorial too, so likely something irritated him, but he wouldn't tell me what?

By the time we fell asleep sweaty and exhausted, the clock read after two. I wasn't sure how I would get through the next day with so little rest, but the exhaustion would be worth it. Cooper fell asleep with a smile on his face like he had finally worked out his issues with enough naked time.

I rarely dreamt of the ugly incident. Most nightmares were about embarrassing myself at school like when I walked around with a blood stain on my butt. Occasionally, I dreamed of my parents hitting me or Tawny and me running from something. Those dreams were upsetting, but they weren't detailed. This nightmare though was a vivid memory.

By the time I woke screaming with Cooper shaking me, I wasn't eighteen and in Kentucky. I was back in that dirty trailer and Cooper wasn't my love. He was a threat.

Throwing myself away from him and off the bed, I crawled to the bedroom door, but didn't know where to go next. Cooper climbed out of bed, looking large and intimidating. I put my hands up to stop him, but my words made no sense.

"Who's Travis?" he asked, frowning.

"Why?" I cried. "Do you know him? Is he your friend? Are you going to give me to him?"

Grabbing a shoe, I threw it at Cooper who easily batted it away.

"Stop!" he yelled so loudly I fell backwards in terror. "Calm the fuck down!"

Staring up at him, I knew he would hurt me and give me to Travis. It was why he fucked me so much the night before. He was saying goodbye and finishing with me before handing me off to his buddy.

Cooper stared at me full of anger then he took a few deep breaths and stepped back. Swinging his arms, he settled himself down while I crawled to the corner behind a chair. Naked and cold, I knew something bad was coming as if trouble had followed me out of the dream. Eventually, Cooper dressed in a pair of boxers and sat on the ground nearby.

"You said his name when you were dreaming," he explained quietly. "He's the guy who hurt you, right?"

"Do you know him?"

"Farah, why would I know him?"

"He...I just don't want to go back."

"You're not going anywhere, baby. You're staying here with me."

"He could come. He could take me."

Gaze darkening, Cooper whispered in a hard voice. "If he tried, he'd be dead before he put a hand on you."

Nodding, I tried to tell myself how Travis didn't care about me. He hadn't come for me all these years and he never would. Wanting to be rational, I still felt his rough hands on me. I hurt between my legs like I did when he was done. He had marked me again in the dream and I would never be free.

After a short time, Cooper stood up and walked to the next room. Hating to be alone, I still flinched when he returned. He seemed bigger now. His shoulders wider, his face harsher, his whole demeanor reeked of potential violence.

Instead of hitting me, Cooper lowered a blanket behind the chair so I could cover myself. I stared at him as he sat back down. We studied each other for a long time as I waited for something bad to happen or the fear to fade. Neither occurred, leaving me stuck behind the chair for hours.

Cooper tried twice to caress my face and both times I jerked back and away from his touch. After the second attempt, he stood up and left the room. I heard the front door open and assumed he was leaving. Then, his big ugly dog Rafe waltzed into the room with Cooper following behind.

In his hand, Cooper held a gun and I pushed farther back into the corner. "No one," he said, kneeling down by the chair, "will come here and take you. If they do, Rafe will wake us up and I'll kill the fucker. No one is hurting you or taking you away from me. Do you understand?"

Staring into his dark eyes, I did understand. I craned my neck so I could see Rafe comfortable in the corner. When I looked back at Cooper, he sighed.

"Baby, it's nearly six in the morning. The sun is coming up and you need to sleep. I need rest too, so let's go to bed and I'll keep you safe. I won't even touch you, but I need you to go to bed."

"You love me," I said in a rough, exhausted voice.

"More than anything else. I will never let that piece of shit or anyone else come here and hurt you. You are mine and that makes you untouchable. Do you understand?"

Nodding again, I crawled out from behind the chair and Cooper helped me stand. He stepped back, willing to keep his distance to avoid scaring me. Reaching for him, I knew he would keep me safe. If I couldn't shake the fear of the dream, I could at least know Cooper was someone Travis wouldn't screw with. Rationally, I knew Travis likely forgot I existed, but I wasn't rational. I was primal and the monster was always waiting to ruin me again. With Cooper though, I was safe.

We walked to bed where Cooper's body warmed me until I could sleep. I dozed off, praying not to dream. When I woke up hours later, it was like I was in heaven. I literally had a smile on my face while opening my eyes, refreshed after a horrible night. The sun was out, but hidden by Cooper's dark shades. I could see a hint of light around the edges of the window as I glanced at the clock.

"Eleven o'clock!" I cried as if yelling might turn back time.

Before I could freak out more, and I was already freaking out pretty badly, Cooper appeared at the door then rushed to the bed.

"Don't freak."

"I overslept. Why didn't you wake me up?"

"You're kidding, right?" When I started crying, Cooper realized I wasn't kidding. "Baby," he said, wrapping his arms around me, "I woke up just before the alarm went off and there was no way I was waking you up after two hours of sleep. Not after the night you had."

"I'm missing school."

"It's okay. I called a woman in administration and she's having someone in each of your classes take notes. You won't miss anything."

"I'm going to get in trouble," I mumbled against his chest.

"It's college, not high school. No one takes attendance at New Hampton."

Staring up at him, I tried to stop crying, but I felt like I would be punished for missing a day of school.

"Since you're already upset, I'm dumping this on you too. I called in sick at your job."

Breathing too quickly, I shrugged him off. "You don't care."

Cooper wanted to be angry. His jaw set and his lips pressed together in a grim frown. Then, he cracked his neck. "Explain how I don't care about my baby needing time off?"

"I need money to pay for things."

"I'll pay for your lost wages."

"I don't want your money."

"My money. Denny's money. What difference does it make?"

I was angry. Outraged really, but I'd quickly become accustomed to seeking comfort from Cooper. So I snuggled against him then glared into his irritated eyes.

"You can't just do whatever you want."

"Yes, I should have woken you up to ask if you wanted to sleep. That makes sense."

"Don't make fun of me."

"Don't be a dipshit."

Pulling away, I found myself in his grip. His arms refused to relent and I gave up.

"Let's try this again," he said after a minute. "You had a tough night. So did I. In fact, it was the worst night of my life to be honest. You needed rest. I needed it too, so I made a decision. I did what you couldn't and I'm not sorry. You need to relax or you'll burn out."

Saying nothing, I listened to his heartbeat. When I didn't complain, he began stroking my hair.

"I want to have my dream," I whispered, relaxed now. "I need to prove to my family that I'm not a loser."

"You're not a loser. Everyone in your family either knows that or can't admit it because then they might be a loser. You need to stop worrying about what other people think."

"Except you, right?"

"Hell yeah," he whispered, grinning down at me.

Smiling, I kissed his chest. "I don't know what happened last night."

Cooper said nothing and I forced myself to look up at him. He watched me with the same pained expression as the night before.

"You had a bad dream," he finally said.

Wanting to apologize, I sensed he would be bothered by it. Instead, I sighed. "You took care of me."

Just as I hoped, Cooper gave me a little grin. He was like a kid sometimes, needing reassurance. The guy who asked his mom for relationship advice wasn't always the scary beast he showed to the world.

"So we'll study later?"

"Sure, but I was thinking we could clean up and go to lunch at the Italian place we had our first real date at. Or we can go somewhere else. I want you to have a good lunch since you skipped breakfast."

"That would be really nice," I said, smiling up at him.

"Then, maybe we could go to the movies."

While I wanted to hide how excited I was by this idea, Cooper was no fool.

"Tell me you've been to the movies before."

"Once when I was little, my grandma took me and Tawny."

"Who doesn't go to the fucking movies? I see poor people at them all the time. Trailer trash with their loud kids at the ten o'clock showing."

"It's not something we could waste money on."

"Well, we're definitely going then. So lunch, movies, we'll pick up your notes, do a little studying before a nice dinner. Finally, back here for swimming and hopefully you'll be up for a little loving."

"Why not now?" I asked, kissing his jaw.

"We should wait."

"Are you not in the mood?" I asked, nuzzling his neck. Cooper took my hand and set it on the erection in his shorts. "Then, why wait?"

"It's the sex, right?" he asked, frowning back at me. "Whenever we do it a lot, you have these nightmares. When we keep it to once or twice, you sleep fine. I figure we'll wait."

"Is it healthy for you to walk around like that?"

"I'm wearing my loose jeans, if that's what you're asking."

"I wouldn't mind being close before we go."

Cooper said nothing for a moment then sighed. "Last night was really bad."

"It's not only the sex. It's the walls. You wanted them to come down and they are. Not everything you'll see will be pretty."

"I know," he said softly. "It just breaks my heart to see all that terror in your eyes and know a little part of you is afraid of me."

"It's not you."

Cooper said nothing for a few minutes and I started worrying. Finally, he ran his hand down the back of my hair as he spoke. After a false start, he forced out the words.

"There was this chick I knew from my freshman year. She was ra...sexually assaulted at a party." When I immediately tensed in his arms, Cooper caressed my head again. "The guy was dealt with, but she was still messed up from what happened. She felt guilt and shame, but then she saw a therapist. Months after it happened, she seemed better. She was able to move past it enough to be happy. I'm not really into all that feelings crap, but maybe a therapist would help you?"

"Help me how? Get me to stop crying during sex?" I asked, angry to have him pushing me on something he knew nothing about.

Cooper suddenly loosened his grip and stared at me. The hurt in his eyes would have bothered me if I wasn't so edgy already.

"Fuck you," he muttered, nearly looking ready to cry. "How cold are you to say that?"

"Why are you asking me to see a therapist? I said we don't talk about stuff in my family. I told you, but you want to fix me. First, you wanted the walls down then you don't like what you see so you want to fix me. It's all about you."

"I love you," he said in something between a growl and a whimper. "I love you and you look at me like I'm going to hurt you. Like I'm a monster. I see that fear and I want to fix things. I want you to be okay because you're not. You're damaged and not talking about it won't fix anything. You think being a teacher and getting good grades will fix all this shit messed up inside you, but those are Band-Aids like not talking about it. You deserve to be happy."

Pulling free, I moved to the other side of the bed and stared at him. He was right in some ways. Maybe in all of the ways, but I felt cornered, attacked even. He was judging me, calling me damaged. True or not, I wanted away from him.

Cooper watched me for a minute then something changed on his face. The pained and slightly angry expression was gone. I could almost see his big brain churning as the hardness on his face eased away.

"You're mine, baby. No matter what you'll always be mine. I just need you to be really happy. Not going through the motions or happy for anything you can get happy. I want you to be joyously fucking happy and you can't be that way because you have all this pain you're holding behind those walls. Hell yeah, I want them down. I want every part of you open to me, but that pain isn't going anywhere."

"My dad is a gambler," I said, eyes on the wall and away from him. I just said the words without any thought behind them. Cooper needed something from me. To understand, I guess. He needed that and I needed him.

"A grifter too. He's always stealing money to pay off his debts, but sometimes his cons don't pay off in time. When that happened one time, he left town to find someone who owned him money. He told Mom if the people came around she should convince them that he was coming back with their money. If they wanted something to tide them over, she should give them her ring. My great-grandmother gave Mom the ring and she loved it. I didn't think she wanted to give it up, but Dad told her she might have to because the people were dangerous."

Pausing, I pretended Cooper wasn't there. Also, pretended I wasn't saying the words out loud. They were all in my head, safe from my heart. Just a bad dream to be forgotten when I woke up.

"The men showed up and they didn't care about Mom's excuses. Tawny was always so smart about people and I think she understood. She begged Mom to give them the ring. I remember thinking someone was attacking my mom because she started screaming and ran away. She ran down the hall to our room and locked the door. Even with her freaking out, I still didn't understand what was happening. We were always owing someone money and hiding from people. It always worked out though."

Looking at the light seeping in around the shades, I didn't think as I continued, "Tawny understood. She was twelve, but she knew we were in trouble. She took out twenty dollars..." Pausing, I bit back tears. "She had worked around the motel and the manager gave her twenty dollars. She was so excited because we were going to Dairy Queen to eat dinner for my birthday. She had worked so hard for that money, cleaning up nasty stuff in the pool. She earned the money, but she offered the biker guys her twenty for collateral. That's when I understood."

Inching away from Cooper reflexively, I wasn't even sure if he had moved towards me.

"Travis said what the fuck were they going to do with twenty dollars? Then, he said they needed real collateral. Even though he said that, the bastard still took her money. She worked so hard for those twenty dollars."

Wiping the tears falling down my cheeks, I moved away from Cooper even more, leaving me pressed against the headboard.

"Dad came for us a week later," I said, hearing Cooper exhale hard in response. "He paid the men and he took us back to the motel, but he didn't have us come inside. He just grabbed our stuff and packed up the car and we left. We didn't speak of my mom for years as if she never existed. Only when Dad started relying on my grandma's money did he acknowledge how he was once married to her daughter. Otherwise, Mom was just a memory."

After a long quiet minute, Cooper whispered angrily, "Why did you come here to live with that bitch?"

Finally, I looked at Cooper who stared at me with so much pain in those beautiful dark eyes. "They made it seem like it was the only way I could go to school. I needed my dream to come true so I came here. Maybe I also wanted my mom to know what she did hadn't ruined me. How I had worked hard and turned out better than her."

Cooper tried to touch me, but I flinched.

"Once, I tried talking about that week. Me and Tawny watched an Oprah episode and thought we could talk about it and be healthier or something. It was awful," I said, my voice cracking. "It was like being back there again. As if all the showers couldn't scrub away the smell. I never want to talk about it again. I don't want to sit in an office with a stranger and make myself remember the way it felt."

"Farah," he whispered softly now, "you don't have to do anything. I just wanted to help you and everyone was saying how Becky was helped by seeing a therapist."

I wished I could go see someone, tell them what happened, and make all of the bad stuff disappear. Life didn't work like that though.

After watching me for a few minutes, Cooper sighed. "I hate when you cry. I hate the look on your face when we're together because I know you're not with me really. You're back there and scared and waiting for it to be over. I hate knowing I make you feel that way."

"You make me feel other things too though. You make me feel like my body can feel things besides what it felt back then. You make me feel like I have a right to feel pleasure. Because of you, I feel like my body belongs to me more now. I know that makes no sense, but by choosing to give my body to you, I feel I'm not a ruined thing. I feel like I'm beautiful because that's how you see me. You look at me like I'm special and that's why I don't cry as much, but I do get scared. No matter how much I know I'm with you, some little part isn't. Some little part is always back there, but that part isn't as scared. Maybe therapy would help or maybe it would make me feel ruined again. I can't take the chance when I'm starting to feel like a woman with power. Sometimes, when you touch me, it feels so good and I feel like I'm rejecting all the ugly stuff. Like I'm saying I have a right to feel good and not go back there. I feel that way because of you."

Cooper's scowl eased. "I might be a pig towards girls, but I always made them feel good too. It's like a tradeoff. I'm a shitty boyfriend, but I'm a great lover. I'll give them pleasure then toss them aside. Maybe that's not a decent tradeoff, but it's what I do. With you though, I love you more than anything and I can't make you feel good."

"You do."

"Maybe, but it's hard to know that when I see the fear on your face. You look at me like I'm hurting you and I feel like I should stop, but you want me to keep going. I feel guilty for enjoying your body."

"I wish I could stop crying. I don't know why it happens some times and not others. I don't know how to control it. I just know I want to be with you."

Cooper watched me as his fingers tapped at the bed. Finally, he said what was on his mind. "Tell me you don't really think I want to fix you so I can have more sex."

"I don't," I said, feeling guilty. "The only person I've ever trusted is Tawny and she knows not to push certain things. I know you want to help, but I can't go back there. It seems like I already am, but it's only in small doses. I can make myself forget most of it. I'm sorry I hurt you and I don't really think that's why you want me to get better. If it was, I wouldn't have told you what I did. I never would have trusted you with even that much."

"Can I sit closer?" Cooper asked and I loved him for being so careful.

"I feel dirty now, but once I have a nice shower then I can feel normal. Does that make sense?"

Cooper shook his head. "I don't get it. I know I should, but I look at you and it's so clear how you shouldn't feel bad. Those fuckers should feel bad. Instead, you feel dirty. I don't get it, but I'm trying."

"Do you see me differently now?" I asked, lowering my gaze. "I want you to be honest."

"I still want you, if that's what you're asking. I wanted you the moment I saw you. It was just lust then. When you messed with me that first night at Denny's, I wanted you so fucking bad. Eventually, I needed you though. I know you're damaged and I've fucked up, but we belong together. Nothing you say or do or anything that was done to you changes how you're mine."

Smiling, I glanced at the shower. "I'll clean up and we can have lunch."

Cooper shared my smile, looking relieved. "I'll make you forget all about missing school and work. You'll be too happy to feel guilty for blowing off that shit."

Sliding off the bed, I walked to the bathroom with the plan of ridding myself of the dirtiness on my skin. I used the hottest water I could endure while scrubbing my body with Cooper's body wash. Leaving the bathroom, I found Cooper staring at his hands. When he looked up at me, he searched my face for something then smiled.

"You are so hot wet."

"We could still…"

"No," he interrupted, standing up. "I'm hungry and we're having a great day then I'm slobbering all over you. It'll be amazing."

"It sounds amazing," I teased, kissing him before he disappeared into the bathroom.

"I'll leave the door open so you can enjoy the view."

Laughing, I dressed then took him up on his offer. I rested on the toilet seat and watched him lather up behind the clear shower door. Cooper grinned when he saw me smiling.

"You can't know how difficult it is to be rational around you," he said, still grinning.

Glancing down at his erection pressed against his belly, I sighed. "I think I do know. I should join you."

"Don't. If you cried right now, I'd feel like shit. Let's just be happy for a while."

Frowning, I crossed my arms. "Well, I'm not leaving the bathroom. Nothing out there is as sexy as in here."

"Hell yeah," he groaned. "Don't tease though. I'm this close to turning the water to cold."

"Or you could fix your problem."

Cooper squinted at me. "Really?"

Pulling off my shirt, I lowered my bra. Standing closer to the shower door, I stretched. "Here's your visual inspiration. I could lick my lips a lot if you think it'd help?"

"Fucking A," he said, stroking himself. "Say my name."

"Cooper," I moaned softly, rolling my nipples between my thumbs and index fingers like he always did. "Oh, Cooper, I'm yours. I need you. I wish you were inside me, Cooper."

His gaze held mine as I teased myself and he stroked his cock. I eventually just looked at where he worked himself closer to relief. Soon, I licked my lips while thinking about making him feel good using my hand.

While I didn't know how long Cooper had been in a state of heat, it didn't take him long to find relief. I doubted it would take him long to need more relief. To prolong his comfort, I immediately dressed and left the bathroom.

Cooper appeared buck naked a few minutes later and I wondered if lunch should wait. Somehow, I'd gotten myself into a state of heat.

"Some of it's genetics," he teased, retrieving boxers from his dresser. "The rest is hard work."

"I have a response, but I don't want you getting worked up again."

"Give it five minutes and the memory of you touching yourself and… Fuck it, I didn't need five minutes."

We both laughed as he finished dressing in a white tee and faded jeans. His hands went absently to his short hair before he remembered he had nothing to fix up there. Shrugging, he shoved his wallet into his back pocket then reached his hand out for me. After we grabbed bottles of water, we headed down to his truck.

"Do you know how to drive?" he asked.

"Yes, but I don't have my license."

"Laws are for pussies. Here," he said, handing me the keys. "I know what you're thinking and a few dents won't mean shit."

Cooper got into the truck, leaned over to help me adjust the seat, and used his new proximity to kiss me like we had forever. With his directions, we arrived at the Italian restaurant's rather packed parking lot. I wasn't sure how to angle the large truck into a spot without wiping out a few smaller cars in the process.

"Scoot," Cooper said, before disappearing out of the passenger door.

Unbuckling my seatbelt, I slid over as he sat in the driver's seat. Cooper threw the truck into reverse, angled the truck without paying much attention, and slid it neatly into an open spot.

"My hero," I said, batting my eyes at him.

"Man, I love when you're easy to please."

"With the day we have planned, I think I'll be very easy to please this evening."

Cooper stared at me then let out an unsteady breath. "Too hot."

Leaning over, he kissed me hungrily then started to pull away. Soon, his lips were back on mine as I wrapped my arms around his neck. When Cooper's hand slid up my shirt and cupped my breast, I groaned so loudly nearby people likely heard.

"You're actually horny," he murmured, kissing my cheeks.

"Hell yeah."

"Let's eat before I have trouble walking," he said, finally dislodging his hand from my shirt.

Grinning, I followed him out of the truck and we walked into the restaurant. Even busy, they found us a booth in the back. After we ordered, I inched closer to him.

"Why do you look upset?" I asked.

Cooper stared at the bread. "Last night, I thought I had lost you. I can't shake that feeling."

"I'm right here," I said, cuddled against him as he wrapped an arm around my shoulders. "I had a bad dream and it wasn't about you."

"The way you looked at me though. I sat there with you staring at me in fear and I thought how could you ever love me again when you're so afraid of me?" When I said nothing, Cooper sighed. "I lived my whole life without you and I was fine. I was happy even. Then, I meet you and it's like an addiction. Like I can't imagine you not being there every day with me. Just the thought of you leaving is fucking awful and I feel like nothing is worth shit. I need you in a way that you can't understand."

"I do understand," I said, running my hand over his hard chest. "It's just that I'm used to doing without so I'm better at hiding it. When I think of losing you, I feel like my life will be shit too."

"You need me."

"More than you can understand. I've only had one person who ever loved me in such a great way and she wasn't able to give me everything. You have the power to make things beautiful for me and you love me enough to do that. I feel safer with you than ever in my life."

Cooper smiled. "You deserve everything and I'd give it to you, if you let me."

"Why would I stop you?"

"After losing you last weekend, I feel insecure. I'm not used to the feeling and it's fucking annoying."

"It'll pass. We've only known each other a few weeks. In a month, we'll have gotten over some of the early hiccups."

"Hiccups? Last night..."

"Stop talking about it," I said, sitting up and away from him. "I know it upset you, but I want to have a good day. I want to be here with you, not back in the panic of last night. I really don't want to be back five years ago."

"I'm sorry."

Caressing his lips, I smiled. "You look so hot when you pout."

"It's why I do it, Farah. The whole thing is a con to reel you in," he said, wiggling his eyebrows.

"It so fucking worked."

"I know, right?"

Laughing, we cuddled up and waited for our food.

"What's your middle name?" I asked when our lunches arrived.

"I don't have one. Pop doesn't believe in them. Thinks they're the man's way of tracking people easier."

Even though I could tell Cooper was serious, I laughed. "Makes sense."

"What's yours?" he asked, grinning.

"Delta, after my grandma."

"The one who helped you get to New Hampton?" Once I nodded, Cooper leaned back and studied me. "When we have a girl, we should give her that middle name in honor of the woman who brought us together."

Gazes meeting, we shared this weird moment where we imagined a future beyond the next month. I realized Cooper needed reassurance that I saw him in my future.

"I like the name Lily. Does that go with Delta?"

Cooper gave me a cocky grin that said he had me hooked. "Lily Delta Johansson sounds perfect. Even if it didn't, who the hell would complain? Our girl could be named something stupid like Apple and people would tell her it was awesome."

"But you'd prefer a boy, right? I mean to carry on the family business."

"Sure, but who says my sons would be smart enough? Tucker's a fucking idiot, but Sawyer's smart. Maybe Lily will be my heir? Maybe she'll make men cry when she enters the room and not just because she's hot like her mom."

"A real shitkicker, huh?"

"Hell yeah."

Grinning, I took his hand. "I like the name Colton for a boy."

"That's a man's name for sure."

We smiled and something clicked. We weren't Farah and Cooper dating. We were something else now. Feeling the change, I was suddenly more connected to this day instead of my ugly past. Cooper's anxiety also faded.

The rest of lunch was casual with Cooper telling me stories about his summers and all of the times he smacked Tucker upside the head. By the time we drove to the movie theater, I was beginning to wonder if Tucker's stupidity was genetic or simply from Cooper's roughhousing over the years?

The moment we entered the theater and I smelled popcorn, I was in a state of euphoria. For so many years, Tawny and I talked about movies we wanted to see. First as kids then as teens, we would dream of saving up enough to go. Yet, our money always went into our parents' pockets until I talked my dad into letting me keep my tips. Then, everything went into my nest egg. Plenty of times, I thought to take out a little money to splurge on my sister. Instead, I panicked at how I might waste too much and lose my chance at college. Now, I wished I had used the money to give Tawny more joy in her otherwise crap life.

Cooper kept smiling at me and I finally realized I was grinning like a mad woman. I remembered how big and amazing everything felt when my grandma took me and Tawny. We had even gotten snacks and Tawny drowned our popcorn in butter. Giddy about how great this day was and at remembering the one with Tawny, I drowned a huge bucket of popcorn in the runny butter. When someone complained I was taking too long, Cooper gave the guy a look that shut him up. Soon, I finished and walked with Cooper to the theater showing an action film.

Based on the time we arrived, our choices were a depressing drama or an action film with no plot and lots of explosions. It was a no brainer. Waiting for the film to begin, I kept laughing. Seeing me smiling so much, Cooper laughed too.

"My girl is so fucking hot when she's happy."

"Then, I must be super fucking hot right now."

"Hell yeah," he said, kissing me so the buttery flavor in my mouth mixed with his Milk Duds.

"Yum," I mumbled when he let go.

"You're like a little kid."

"You can't know how much this means to me."

"I'm getting a pretty good idea from the look on your face."

Leaning my head against his shoulder, I smiled at Cooper who watched me like I was amazing and could do no wrong. I felt the same way about him.

The movie was stupid, yet really great. I was startled by how loud and bright everything seemed compared to when I was a kid. By the end, I would have been sad to leave except I could enjoy this kind of thing now. I was no longer under the thumb of my parents who always had other uses for our money. Even if I didn't have the money, Cooper clearly planned to make the movie thing a habit. He was even talking about what to see the next weekend as we walked out of the theater.

After a quick stop at Whiskey Kirk's to pick up my notes from Tucker, we drove to my apartment. Amy was inside with Tex and they were clearly fooling around when we entered. Like two kids caught by their parents, they played it cool, but kept giggling.

Amy had made it obvious over the last few weeks how she wasn't interested in knowing me. She certainly didn't want me asking questions about her life. Questions like why was there always beer in the refrigerator if she in AA? Or where did she stay until late at night, only to stagger in for a few hours of sleep before stumbling to work the next day? Those were questions for her life and I wasn't part of it. I was simply the reason she had a nicer apartment. Oh, and I might be the reason she was drinking again because as she told Tex one night while I was trying to sleep, "Kids make life harder."

While Cooper waited in the living room, I packed up more clothes and necessities. I thought I heard his voice, but when I returned, everyone was silent. Yet, I knew he'd said something.

"Your boyfriend is a real prize," Amy muttered, disappearing into her bedroom with Tex following close behind.

Tex didn't even glance at me and I suspected he would never get caught looking at me. Not unless he wanted Cooper's fist colliding with his face. With the drama kept to a minimum, I took Cooper's hand and left the apartment.

When we arrived at the steakhouse, neither of us was really hungry after pigging out at the theater. Instead, we sat quietly in a nice booth by a window for decent lighting. For nearly an hour, we both focused on our required reading while people ate and talked around us. I loved how oblivious we were to everyone else. Yet, when a few rough looking men arrived, Cooper switched positions with me without speaking. Soon, I was snuggly in the corner of the booth with him blocking me. Smiling, I kissed him softly then returned to my reading.

After an amazing steak dinner where we ate so much that I was afraid to see the bill, Cooper watched me with a grin.

"It's been a great day, right?"

"The best. I'm starting to get used to have amazing days with you."

"The fair is here. The whole family is going and we're meeting Skye."

"I've never been to a fair."

"Fuck," he said, shaking his head. "I'm going to spend the rest of my life making sure you've checked off a list of fun shit to do."

"I really do love you, Coop. It's not fake or because you chase me or any of that. It's real and I never want to let you go."

Cooper smiled wider. "That was hard to admit, wasn't it, baby?"

"Yep. What if you suddenly changed your mind and ditched me?"

"Still here and I always will be."

Cuddling against him, I wanted to go back to his apartment. The one bedroom tiny space felt like home now. A place where Cooper and I belonged and no one could interfere, not even bad memories.

"I really want you," I said, caressing his leg and making him sigh. "I feel a little logy from the huge dinner though, so I might lay there and let you do all the work."

"After watching you touch yourself, I think I can merely close my eyes, think of that, and instantly come. I doubt you'll need to do much."

"If you do feel like you need more help, I could touch myself again."

"Shit," he groaned, grabbing the bill. "We're leaving."

Grinning, I packed my school supplies while he hurried the waitress to charge his card. Once the bill was paid, I followed him out the door.

Teasing Cooper the whole way home, I nearly climbed into his lap at one point. He loved it, but regretted not wearing sweatpants. Even though he was so horny that he nearly ripped off his clothes Hulk-style as soon as we were in his apartment, Cooper was careful. After our redneck fuck where he released hours of pent-up need, he slowed down and teased me until I was again seconds from an orgasm.

While I never pushed past the wall, I also didn't have bad dreams. We fooled around for a solid hour with another half hour of cuddling. Finally, there was one last round after I made the mistake of grazing Cooper's cock with my hand. Then, we were asleep and I dreamed of building a house in the river. I dreamed of pigging out at a trough. I dreamed of all kinds of silly things, but my mind never returned to Travis and the week with his friends.

Chapter Nineteen

The Westfield County Fair was a big deal in Ellsberg. Students and faculty talked about it all week and everyone I knew planned to enjoy the rides, food, music, and atmosphere. Even though I had agreed to pick up shifts over the weekend, Cooper had a conversation with Arnie who miraculously remembered how someone with more seniority asked for the shifts. Now, I was able to attend the fair.

Irritation felt like the right response to someone controlling my choices, but I really wanted to go to the fair. Plus, Cooper gave me a great Friday and I knew he would be bummed if I refused to go to the fair with him. He was like a kid wanting to show me everything he loved. His favorite corndog. His favorite chili. His favorite rides. The band he heard when he was a kid, now consisting of senior citizens. He told me how he sat on his dad's shoulders, eating cotton candy while they played. Cooper shared it all with me and I loved every moment.

As we sat on the top of the Ferris wheel, Cooper suddenly laughed.

"What?" I asked.

"You look like a little kid. The expression on your face is killing me."

"I was just thinking how you were so excited like a boy, instead of a man."

To prove he was all man, Cooper's gaze locked on my chest. "The girls jiggle in the best way every time the car jerks to a stop."

"You're so horny."

"You can't know how much."

Laughing, I glanced around, realized we were high up enough for no one to see, and caressed his crotch. I found him as hard as I expected.

"One day, when I'm super normal about sex," I whispered, "I'm going to do very wicked things with you up here. Then, more wicked things down there and over there. I'm going to sex you up all over the fair. Unfortunately, I'm not normal yet so you'll have to live with snug pants."

"Bitch," he said, grinning.

"Jackass."

"God, you're fucking hot," he muttered, removing my hand. "I'm going to jizz my pants at this rate and my mom is probably watching. Don't tease me and ruin the lie I tell her about being a virgin."

The very idea of him being a virgin sent us into hysterics. Laughing so hard that we still hadn't gotten ourselves under control when it was our turn to get off, we stumbled from the ride.

"Virgin," I whispered, rolling my eyes.

"I don't remember a girl before you."

"Bullshit."

Cooper paid for a pink heart-shaped balloon then handed it to me. "Fine, I have vague memories, but they fade every day I spend with you."

"More bullshit."

Pulling me to a stop, Cooper caressed my cheek. "When we broke up for that day, I saw this girl who has great tits. I never knew what the rest of her looked like, but the chick has banging tits. When I saw her that day, I didn't even notice her tits and trust me they were probably right out there for me to notice. It was the first time I noticed she was a redhead. That's how much I love you. I'm noticing girls' hair colors and personalities and shit."

"I find this confession oddly romantic."

Cooper's grin widened then he saw someone and his smile was gone. I tried to turn to look the direction he was staring, but he held me in place.

"Do you think about other guys?" he asked, holding me still.

"No. Who are you looking at?"

By the time Cooper let me turn, whoever he was irritated at had disappeared into the crowd. I glanced at him and frowned.

"Who?"

"You love me so it doesn't matter."

"I do love you."

Cooper's smile was back. "I have a surprise for you later, but first I need to ditch you with Bailey and the girls."

"Ditch me?" I asked full of disappointment.

Cooper wrapped an arm around my shoulders. "Just for lunch then I'll meet back up with you and we'll have more fun."

"Where are you going?"

"You know I'm not telling so why ask?"

"Because I don't want you to leave and I'm hoping that if I seem clingy enough you'll stay."

"Not working, but it's really sexy how you're trying."

Rolling my eyes, I saw how we were nearing one of the food tents. Skye stood next to Bailey who was counting out a wad of cash without any concern for someone stealing from her. Maddy sat at a picnic table nearby, looking lonely without Tucker. I knew how she felt.

"How long will you be gone?" I asked just to make very clear how I didn't enjoy getting ditched.

"As long as it takes. When I get back, I'll kiss you until you can't stand."

"Stop with the threats. I'll miss you even if you're a jerk."

Cooper laughed then gave me a long sloppy kiss until his sister heckled him from the tent. When his lips left mine, he smiled then walked backwards for a few steps before disappearing into the crowd.

I joined the girls who were arguing over what to eat. Tacos made them fart. Burgers made them fat. Chili made them fart. Hot dogs made them fat. It dragged on like that for a while before fattening won over farting.

Eating our burgers at the picnic table, we could hear a band playing from the other side of the food tents. At first, we didn't speak, just enjoying the music. The whole time, Maddy held a piece of paper in her left hand while eating with her right. Bailey finally snagged the note away.

"Don't," Maddy muttered, but she didn't put up much of a fight. No one ever did with Bailey. "It's from Tucker."

"A Dear Joan letter?" Bailey asked, barking with laughter. "Oh, gross, it's a poem."

Skye leaned over, took a second to read it, and laughed. "It's a really bad poem."

"He was drunk when he wrote it," Maddy said, crossing her arms tightly. "I think it's sweet. He calls me his flower."

"Original," Skye said, sitting back in her seat and playing with a fry.

Bailey rolled her eyes and returned the paper to Maddy. "Tucker doing his drunken poetry shit is as expected as Cooper and his singing during sex. Man, it's nasty how much I know about my brothers' love lives. Of course, between them, they've fucked everyone I know. Cooper alone has fucked every girl I've been friends with except for you two," she said, motioning towards Skye and Maddy.

"Sings?" I asked, ignoring the part where every girl I met was someone who had spent time with Cooper inside them.

Maddy smiled. "Hair of the Dog."

"I don't know that song."

"Don't go messing..." Bailey began.

"With a son of a bitch," Skye finished then they high fived.

"Oh."

"He doesn't sing it with you?" Bailey asked like maybe I would be dumped any minute and she should start saying goodbye.

"No. Not yet anyway. Why would he sing though?"

"It's like a countdown," Skye said, laughing.

Even smiling, I felt weird now. Why hadn't Cooper sung to me like he'd sung to the billions of girls he'd nailed before?

"You two have had sex, right?" Skye asked, suspicious now, though still laughing.

"Oh, they have," Bailey announced. "When they weren't, Cooper worked out with weights so much I thought his arms would fall off. Now, he's calm. Though he could be calmer."

Again, I smiled awkwardly because there was nothing like having your friend encouraging you to fuck her brother more.

"Maybe you're special," Maddy said, rubbing her tiny baby bump. "Tucker treats me different than the other girls."

"Doesn't come in your face then?" Bailey asked, causing Maddy to glare at her.

"Whatever," Maddy said, ignoring Bailey now. "The point is when Cooper sang to those other girls, he was telling them their time in the sun was almost over. Maybe he doesn't want you to leave?"

Bailey and Skye watched me like they figured I was on my way out. I sensed they might be sad about this fact, meaning they really liked me and weren't enduring me on Cooper's orders.

"Tucker and I started talking names," Maddy said, breaking up the awkward silence. "We went shopping for baby stuff, just looking mostly, and he got super psyched. Now, we're big time looking for baby names."

"If I have a boy, I'm naming him Steele," Bailey explained. "For a girl, it'll be something tough like Ryan or Logan. I don't want my girls having sissy names."

"Fuck that," Skye muttered, slurping her drink. "If I could get a guy to agree, I'd name my girls Princess and Precious. For a boy, I'd name him something cute like Axe."

"Axe can play with Steele," Bailey said, grinning. "They'll grow up nailing chicks together."

"What about you?" Maddy asked me. "You ever think baby names?"

"Sure, but I've never really settled on any," I lied, feeling protective of my names.

"I'm thinking a flower name for a girl," Maddy said and I nearly sighed with exasperation. "Tucker wants something like Scarlett or Delilah."

"Those all sound good," I mumbled awkwardly, just hoping no one stole Lily or Colton.

"Having a baby young is cool," Maddy said, watching me as Skye and Bailey checked out a few passing guys. "I'm still going to finish school eventually. That way my kids will take education seriously. I don't really want a job though. Not one out of the house anyway. I like babies." When I said nothing, Maddy squinted at me. "Don't you like babies?"

"I guess. I don't really know that many babies."

"Oh. I babysat a lot growing up so I love babies. I'm really good with them and I could teach you."

Suddenly, I understood Maddy's interest in me and babies. I had always thought she was embarrassed to get pregnant the way she had or at having people judge her. Instead, she saw it as a way to keep a wealthy guy she actually loved. Now, she looked at me with my similar poor background and figured I could ensure Cooper stayed interested.

"I would appreciate the help," I said, keeping my words vague. "No one in my family is very good with kids."

Thinking I planned to ditch my birth control, Maddy smiled. "It's not so weird being pregnant. Like I puked a lot in the beginning, but it was just certain smells that did it. Now, I feel fine. I'll probably finish out the semester then go back to school in a year or two."

"Unless," Bailey interrupted, interested in us again, "Fuckwad keeps you barefoot and pregnant permanently."

"Why would he do that though? If I was forever pregnant, he'd always have to drink alone. Don't be dumb."

"Don't call me dumb, bitch!"

A standoff occurred and I had the urge to take off running from the food tent. It was stupid, but I remained very still until Bailey shrugged.

"Can't hit a chick who's all preggers. Wouldn't be classy."

Skye laughed. "I don't want kids until I'm almost forty. I want to have plenty of time to party. Once I'm too old to have fun, I'll have kids and they'll be fun. Got it all planned out."

"I have nothing planned out," Bailey said, looking bored and ready to leave. "Why plan your life when you can just let it happen naturally?"

Both Maddy and I nodded like Bailey was onto something profound. Then, Maddy looked at me and smiled. I hadn't really thought about her as a real friend because she and I never talked before. I didn't even think she wanted to be my friend, but put up with me because she was with one brother and I was with the other. Yet, we weren't so different. Maddy was alone in Ellsberg except for Tucker. Her friends were people aligned to Tucker. Her life was completely tied to the guy she loved.

As we returned to silently listening to the band play, I planned to make more of an effort with Maddy. Talk baby stuff since no one seemed interested in the subject except her. Maybe she was lonely and I was too self-absorbed to notice until now. I even wondered if she had a Tawny back home.

By the time Cooper returned with Tucker, I felt closer to Maddy even though we hadn't spoken for the rest of lunch. I just saw her differently and suddenly I didn't feel so alone in Ellsberg.

Cooper took my hand and we walked over to where Aaron listened to another band play. Sitting on the other side of the picnic table, I leaned against Cooper as Aaron sketched in his book.

"Anything?" Aaron asked Cooper.

"Not a peep."

Frowning, I glanced between them. "What?"

"Patience," Cooper said, grinning.

Aaron smiled too then returned to sketching. "Maddy wants her tribal fixed."

"Of fucking course she does. No one wants a tribal anymore. It's poser shit."

When Cooper glanced at me, I nodded like I knew what the hell he was talking about.

Still smiling, Aaron sighed. "Can't fix it while she's preggers. Scratch that. Won't fix it. If she gets freaked or something goes down, Tuck will kill me."

His gaze still on me, Cooper nodded. "For my next one, I'm leaning towards something badass. Black and gray, maybe religious."

"If you can give me the gist, I'll draw it and we'll start working."

Cooper refused to look away from my face. Even when I glanced around like I was checking out the passing people, his gaze remained on me. Finally, I looked into his eyes and gave him what he wanted. A hint of a smile played at a corner of his lips then he ran a hand down the back of my hair. When I frowned because he was acting weird, Cooper glanced at Aaron who grinned. "She's not very perceptive."

"To be young," Aaron replied.

"I got a new tattoo," Cooper told me, giving his friend a nod of appreciation. "Take a look."

On his wrist was my name in cursive. Staring at it, I wasn't sure what to say. Love could be temporary, but tattoos were forever.

"Lord," Cooper grumbled, "there's no pleasing you."

Lifting my gaze to meet his, I knew he was angry. No doubt when Maddy saw her name on Tucker's wrist, she lost her mind and blew out a few eardrums with her squealing. I wasn't Maddy though.

"Um, is that for me?"

"It's your fucking name, so yeah."

"It's just that I just assumed that," I babbled, struggling for a way around his irritation, "if you got a tattoo in my honor that it would be like a big replicate of my face on your back or something. You know, complete with my giant lips."

Puckering up for him, I waited to see if Cooper's feelings were soothed. Just as I hoped, he laughed and high fived Aaron.

"Hell yeah. Screw a religious tat. Let's get her face on my back."

Laughing too, I ran a finger over the fresh tattoo. "Can you imagine how weird my face would look blown up like that?"

"I'll do it," Cooper said, staring hard at me. "You think I won't, but you're wrong."

"Please, don't."

"Why?" he asked, a hint of irritation still around the edges of his expression.

"Because if we have sex near a mirror and I saw my face looking back at me, I might freak out. Or at the very least, lose my loving feeling."

Grinning, Cooper gave me a soft kiss. "You lie like shit."

"I never had any complaints before I met you."

"People are either stupid or humoring you. Likely both."

"Um, I'm not getting your name tattooed on me."

Really?" Cooper said, pulling me closer. "I was thinking something like the words 'Property of Cooper Johansson' on your forehead. Unless you think that's too subtle?"

"And if we break up, I could just get bangs."

"We're never breaking up," Cooper murmured, resting his lips on my shoulder. "If you die, I'm dating your corpse."

"I'm being cremated."

"I'll date your urn."

"My urn already has a boyfriend. They're really serious too."

Cooper laughed against my neck then wrapped himself around my waist, swallowing me up with his warm embrace.

"My pop has my mom's name on his wrist," Cooper whispered against my cheek. "Underneath, he has my name along with the lesser crap kids he got stuck with."

"I'm in college," I blurted out.

"Yeah, I remember you mentioning that."

"Tattoos. Kids. Dating my corpse. Seems serious."

Leaning back, Cooper adjusted me so I rested against his chest. "I always planned to settle down when I was an old fart like my pop. Meet some cute piece of jailbait and make a few bad seeds plus one decent kid I could trust with the family business. Instead, here I am not even done with college with a tattoo of my girl's name on my wrist."

"You could change your mind."

"I won't. You're a keeper."

"I could change my mind," I said, wiggling my brows at him.

"Who would you replace me with? Seriously, look around and see what shit pickings you have to choose from. I'm the best you'll ever do, baby."

"You are pretty sexy. Tall too. Yeah, I can see keeping you around."

A grinning Cooper glanced at Aaron. "I'm so whipped."

"It's pretty nauseating, yeah."

Ignoring them as they discussed more tattoo stuff I didn't care about, I ran my finger over Cooper's wrist. I traced the letters of my name and tried to be rational. Cooper could turn on me at any time. Ditch me and forget my name. Except now it was on his flesh and I couldn't be rational. A man I hungered for despite my best judgment had marked his body with my name. He also expected to add more names when we had children.

A part of me never thought I'd be loved for the real me. Instead, I'd always pretend for my dull husband. It wasn't that he would judge me, but I would always worry he might. Dull husband wouldn't push my buttons and force the truth out like Cooper had. I would hide and dull husband would never know the real me.

Of course, I was assuming a nice guy would want someone who cried during sex. I had been assuming a lot when I built those dreams, but I never knew how messed up I really was until meeting Cooper. Bosses liked me. Coworkers liked me. Teachers liked me. I was likable. Safe and normal. Now, I realized I might hide my damage well, but it was still there.

Yet, Cooper loved me.

Lifting my gaze to his face, I found him watching me silently. I hadn't even noticed the conversation dying down. Aaron was flipping through papers and Cooper stared at me in the needy way he did sometimes.

"You got my name tattooed on you," I whispered.

"I'd like to leave now," he whispered back as his gaze grew needier. "Would you be okay with that?"

"Only if we're going somewhere to be alone."

Cooper's eyes searched my face then he swallowed hard. As I stood and Cooper followed, Aaron just grinned.

"Later, Coop."

"You'll know one day."

Still grinning, Aaron returned to sketching. Cooper took my hand and we made great time back to his truck. I was so excited to be alone with him that I nearly sat on the balloon I had tied to the loop on my jeans. Cooper laughed then punched the balloon out of his way so he could kiss me.

"I'd do you right here," he mumbled against my lips.

"No fucking way," I said, knowing there were a hundred people in the parking lot.

Cooper let me go so he could start the truck. "You're naked as soon as we hit my apartment."

"I'll start unbuttoning things now to prepare," I said, laughing as I undid my jeans and pulled the laces on my shoes.

Cooper forced himself to focus so we could leave the parking lot without running over anyone. Soon, we hauled ass down the highway to his house. By then, I had my shoes and socks off. My bra was unsnapped. I even leaned over and unbuttoned his jeans. Cooper gave me a cocky smile and I knew what that look meant. Hell yeah, we were having fun tonight.

Two hours later, we sat naked in his living room. I ate weird little taco things his mom made while Cooper downed BBQ chicken like a man starving. I had finished my first beer by the time the sun was setting. I was on my fourth when I decided dancing for Cooper was the sexiest thing ever.

He found a song on the satellite music channel and I shook my scrawny ass to Single Ladies (Put A Ring On It). It wasn't even Beyonce, but the Chipettes's version. Cooper alternated between laughing hysterically and getting so horny I was shocked when he didn't lunge across the coffee table and fuck me right there.

Sober enough to remain in control, Cooper waited to fuck me until we were in his bedroom. I was still wiggling around in my attempt to dance sexy. I'd never make a living as a stripper that was for sure.

"I love when you get all mellow," he whispered as we kneeled on the bed and teased all the naked flesh we had to work with. When he saw my face, Cooper sighed. "No, what?"

Unable to control the tears, I was drunk off my ass and everything felt too powerful and important. Nothing could be restrained.

"I'm sorry I get pissy and high strung. I just want to work hard and do better so I won't be trash," I said, my voice failing on the final word. "I come from a long line of trash on both sides of my family. I want my kids to have a home like I never did and to feel special. I want so much more than I have, but it's hard to dig my way out."

"Baby, you're not trash," he said, his eyes searching my face. "How can you even think that about yourself? You work hard. You follow the rules."

"I'm drunk. That's against the rules."

"Yeah, I'm a bad influence."

"You're not trash though. You're special while I just hope to be average."

"You ever see that show Storage Wars?" Cooper asked and I shook my head. "These guys bid on abandoned storage lockers. Lots of times, these lockers are full of trash. Sometimes though, they have hidden treasures. That's what you are. The hidden treasure in the trash of your crap family. You have value and I don't want you to think otherwise."

"That's how you see me?" I said, smiling up at him. "As treasure?"

"Of course. You're irreplaceable. It's why you make me so crazy."

I smiled in sloppy drunk way. "I'm giving you a hickey to mark you as mine."

Cooper burst out laughing, yet tilted his head to expose his neck to my loving. I licked at the skin then sucked softly. He tasted warm and beautiful.

"You have to suck harder, baby," he moaned, leaning back against the headboard.

"I'm afraid to hurt you."

"I can handle it."

Nodding, I sucked harder then felt him adjusting my body in his arms. When he pressed inside me, I let go of his throat.

"You're so horny."

"Hell yeah. Man, you're hot."

"I feel hot."

We both laughed as he moved in and out of me. Leaning me on my back, Cooper worked himself into a fast and hard rhythm.

"Feels so good," I moaned and I wasn't lying. Relaxed like this, I could imagine what other girls felt. Cooper was thinking about the difference too.

"Do you think you'll come?"

"No, but maybe it'd help if I sang? Don't go messing with a son of a bitch."

Thrusting harder, Cooper laughed even as he neared the finish line. Just thinking of it as a finish line made me laugh harder.

"How come you don't sing to me?" I asked, giggling.

"You're too classy for that shit."

Not knowing if he was serious or teasing me, I laughed so hard I snorted.

"Fucking adorable," Cooper said, kissing me before returning to his redneck fucking rhythm.

Without knowing the lyrics to Hair of the Dog, I only hummed while Cooper thrust deeper into me. He moved just right and I groaned in a weird way.

"Was that a good noise or a bad one?" he asked, slowing.

"So good."

"Do you think you'll come?" he asked again. "Should I slow down?"

"No, I'm fine. Go to it, champ."

Cooper rolled his eyes while I laughed and returned to humming. Maybe the song aroused him because he was thrusting wildly. Even holding onto his forearms, each thrust pushed me a tiny bit closer to the edge of the bed. Would I fall off? Would he fall with me? Would it even disrupt his rhythm if we went tumbling?

I never found out because Cooper came hard long before I fell off the bed. He was out of breath over me and I grinned at his flushed cheeks.

"You want me so bad," I teased.

Resting his body on mine, still deep inside, Cooper grinned as he wiped sweat from my face.

"I wished you liked it half as much as I do."

"I do."

"No, you don't."

"You don't know what I feel. I'm too mysterious."

Cooper laughed. "A femme fatale."

"I like when you're inside me."

Cooper smiled softly. "If you let me go down on you for like two minutes and hated it, I'd stop. I bet after two minutes though, you'd beg me to stay down there forever."

"No."

"It feels so good."

"How do you know?"

"Girls freak the hell out when I do it. You can't beat the response."

"No."

Tracing my face, he sighed. "Baby, you let me do other stuff those guys did. Why not let me help you feel good?"

Grinding my teeth, I wished he would get off me. Instead, he watched me with a light frown.

"He bit me," I whispered, breathing too fast. "It was the only time any of it felt good then he bit me. I don't want that. What if I freak out? What if...?"

Cooper kissed my cheeks. "It's okay. I'll never make you do something you don't want."

"I'm afraid I'll have a panic attack. Just thinking about it makes me feel like I'll have one."

"Don't be scared. I love you and I'll never hurt you."

"I love you too, but I'm messed up and I can't fix it."

"You don't cry as much anymore," he said, leaning on his side next to me. "You seemed to like it a few minutes ago. You're fixing yourself. Be patient."

Cooper sat up and reached for the beers. He handed me one then leaned against the headboard. When he lifted an arm for me to cuddle under, I crawled over and wrapped myself around him.

"There's no hickey." I said, looking at his throat.

"You didn't suck hard enough," he mumbled, finishing his beer. "Are you hungry?"

"I'm going to suck you until I make a hickey. I want to mark you."

Cooper laughed. "You're so goofy drunk. It's fucking perfect."

Straddling him, I licked his throat. "I'm going to suck on you like a crazed vacuum cleaner so prepare yourself."

Cooper was still laughing when I latched on. I didn't know if I sucked soft or hard. I wasn't really sure what happened next because everything got fuzzy fast. Waking up the next morning, I thought we had sex again and maybe ate. Otherwise, most of the night was a blank. Looking over my shoulder, I found Cooper asleep on his stomach.

After a quick trip the bathroom to clean up, I returned to bed where Cooper was still dead to the world. The morning light created a golden hue to his muscular back, so I tugged down the sheet to see the skull tattoo on the lower part of his back. Soon, the sheet rested at the curve just above his butt. Feeling daring, I tugged it down a bit more to admire his beautiful ass. I'd never thought I'd be a butt girl, but Cooper sported one hell of an ass.

The second the sheet reached his thighs, I was in a state of hysterics. Even covering my mouth, I woke Cooper who watched me through half opened lids.

"What?"

Wiping my eyes, I couldn't stop laughing. I reached over to rub his head then gave him a kiss on the cheek before enjoying my handiwork again.

"No, really, what are you laughing at?" he asked, propping himself up on his elbows.

"I figured out how to give you a hickey. At least, I hope it was me who gave you all those butt hickeys."

As I counted my love bites, Cooper twisted around to see as I poked each one. Giggling, I noticed his gaze was dark and hungry.

"What?" I asked, suddenly nervous.

"You're happy, right? I want you to be happy."

"I am," I said, patting his ass. "I learned a new skill."

Laughing, Cooper rolled off the bed. Walking his stellar ass to the bathroom, he moved around for a while then laughed again.

"I don't know when you did all that," he said, returning. "I could have sworn you passed out first."

Cooper studied me then pointed and twirled his finger. "Butt in the air. I'm getting even."

I turned over, resting on my knees and elbows. "Be gentle."

Cooper acted as if he would slap my butt then his hand stopped and he merely caressed me. Climbing onto the bed, he licked his lips.

"You branded me good, girl," he said, kissing my left butt cheek. "I wish I'd been sober for that."

"Me too," I said, smiling as he kissed me on the butt again.

Resting my head on my hands, I felt him moving around on the bed, getting comfy. Then, I felt the heat of his breath between my legs. Before I could speak, his tongue tasted me and I exhaled hard.

Cooper paused, waiting for me to complain. I turned my head and met his gaze. When I said nothing, he licked again and I shivered. Sensing the smile on his face, I knew he wanted me to feel good. What he was doing, softly, carefully, did feel incredible, but I knew I would panic. I would hit a point when I returned to the smelly trailer and wouldn't be with Cooper anymore.

Until the moment arrived, I soaked in every hint of bliss. He was so gentle and I felt the pleasure building. Cooper ran his tongue deeply from my clit to my anus then back. It felt amazing and I moaned into my hand. Yet, I felt the panic rising up in me as the pleasure intensified.

Inhaling harshly, I tightened my grip on the sheets and prayed he would stop. Without delay, Cooper crawled closer then pulled me up to kneel like him.

"It's me," he said, lifting my chin so I would look at him. "It'll never be anyone else. With me, you'll always be safe."

Placing my hands on his chest, I nodded. "I love you."

Cooper glared full of rage. "If I could find those bastards, I'd kill every one of them so you'd know they were gone from the world. No," he said, sliding his hands into my hair and pulling me closer for a kiss. Once his lips left mine, he gave me an angry smile. "I'd hunt them down and let you kill them. Let you kill them slow and make them suffer like they made you suffer."

The smile on my face confused me because I never once thought of revenge. While I always said I would kill them if they came back, I didn't really believe I would. Yet, when Cooper put the image in my mind of slowly killing those bastards, I liked the thought.

"You're mine," I said and Cooper smiled so sweetly. "It's why I marked your butt."

Cooper's soft smile shifted into a horny grin. "I still haven't retaliated for all those love bites."

"What will my punishment be?"

"I want to kiss all over you."

Knowing what he meant, I asked, "If I get scared, you'll stop?"

"Yes," he whispered, teasing my nipples with his thumbs. "I need you to come. I need to watch you lose control and know you feel even a tiny bit as good as I do every time we're together. I need you to let me give you this, Farah."

"Can I lie on my back so I can see you? I like watching you when we're together."

"Oh, do you?" he asked, grinning as I rested on my back.

"Yes, so much," I murmured, stroking my nipples and wiping the arrogant look right off Cooper's face. "You like when I do this."

"Once I figure out how to make you come, I'll teach you to make yourself come so I can watch. You look so hot when you touch yourself. Your lips do this sexy thing," he said, imitating my open mouthed stare.

"That looks stupid."

"Maybe on me. On you, it's fucking hot."

Wiggling on the bed, I spread my legs. "You have great lips too, Coop."

"Fuck," he moaned, clearly wanting to skip my part so he could find relief for his erection.

"We'll give it a few minutes. If it doesn't happen, you can climb up here and we try a different way."

Cooper grinned then kissed my inner thigh. "You're letting those walls come down for me," he whispered. "Every wall you remove makes you more beautiful."

Smiling until his fingers spread me open and he kissed my clit, I soon sighed long and loud. Cooper might be horny, but he was tender and slow with his every caress. His lips sucked and kissed me so patiently. Every time the panic struck, I looked at him and remembered where I was.

The pleasure built with waves of heat and I thought I might finally orgasm. Cooper thought it too by how he was careful not to push too hard. Even so close, I couldn't let go completely and I never came. The pleasure still felt better than anything I'd experienced before. Reaching for him, I was relieved when he was in my arms.

"One day, I'm making you come," Cooper whispered against my ear as he entered me, "and it'll be a day we mark on the calendar and celebrate each year like the Fourth of July."

Aroused from earlier, I wasn't interested in talking. Clinging to Cooper, I enjoyed his every thrust. Our lips met and I kissed him so hard I might have left a bruise.

"You're mine," I whispered as he propped himself over me and thrust in a hard frenzy.

Holding onto his forearms while he moved deeper and harder, I couldn't take my eyes off of Cooper. His muscles flexing with every movement, I remembered when his size scared me. Now, all of his power provided me a sense of security. Cooper loved me and I was safe with him.

Knowing he was close, I teased his nipples like he did to mine. While his weren't nearly as sensitive, it was all the help he needed as his need intensified.

"No one else," he gasped, finally coming hard inside me. "Never anyone else again."

"Never," I whispered, stroking his face as his movements slowed.

Once resting together, we said nothing. What was there to say anyway? We were where we belonged and nothing could tear us apart. As if proving me wrong, the sound of approaching motorcycles tensed me out of Cooper's arms.

"Shit," he muttered, getting up to look outside. "It's my pop's friends. I forgot they come in for the fair."

"Should I go?"

Cooper glanced back at me with a frown and looked ready to bitch before changing his mind. His frown eased as he walked towards the dresser.

"Let's take a quick shower and get breakfast."

Forcing myself to go to the window, I looked outside where thirty Harleys were parked in the massive driveway. Some of the bikers were women, most weren't.

"Do you recognize any of them?" Cooper asked, throwing clothes onto his bed.

"A few from your dad's bar."

"But none from before?"

Turning to him, I shook my head. Cooper nodded then reached for my hand.

"There are a lot of fucking bikers in this country so I probably don't know them. If you ever see one of those fuckers though, you tell me and I'll make him wish for death. Do you understand?"

Nodding, I walked with him to the shower. We soaped off without any fooling around. Nervous now, I tried to hide this fact, but didn't succeed. To avoid making my tension worse, Cooper never once got anything sexy going even though he was hard again. Seeing me wet had that effect on him.

Out of the shower, Cooper handed me his shirt to wear and I finally calmed down. I was impressed by how he thought to comfort me in such a way. In fact, he knew how to calm me better than I could calm myself now. Somewhere along the way, Cooper Johansson had become the Farah whisperer. When I told him this as we walked downstairs, he laughed so hard I thought he would fall.

"Hell yeah, I am," he said as we joined the others.

Chapter Twenty

The big Exam Day arrived and New Hampton fell into an eerie silence. Walking to my first class, I was shocked by the tension in the air. The first big college wide tests sobered the usually wild student body. The exams were scheduled on a single day to ensure everyone showed up. They were also scheduled on a Tuesday because students like Cooper didn't attend school on Fridays. I was still amazed by how much the administration kowtowed to certain whims.

Sitting in my first class, I wasn't overly nervous about the exams. I only missed one day of classes and I had always been good at tests. While I didn't necessarily expect to ace them all, I figured I should easily pass. Then, I looked at the first question and realized I might be in trouble.

By the third class, I knew I was in trouble. I would barely skate by because I really didn't know most of the answers. How had I forgotten so much of the lessons? I took good notes and studied each day. Maybe not as much as I should have since I had work and Cooper, but I did study. Yet, I figured I'd get low C's on the exams when I was accustomed to solid B's.

Waiting for the last exam of the day, I wished Cooper would arrive and cheer me up. My mind raced with all of the questions from all of the exams. I had also begun second guessing my answers. Instead of Cooper, Nick appeared.

"It's not that bad," he said, grinning. "The tests don't even count for much of our final grades. It's just a thing the school does to force students to stop partying and take classes seriously. A wakeup call."

"I sure got one," I said softly. "Are you feeling good about your tests?"

Nick ran a hand through his dark hair and sighed loudly. "Good? No. Okay? Yeah, I guess. I'm not great at tests, but I think I remembered most things."

"Do you think we could maybe study again like we did before? I don't really know anyone else in most of my classes and I'm pretty sure I did bad on the tests."

"Sure. I only have my roommate Tad to study with and the guy is drunk most days."

I felt like being proactive helped settle my anxiety. By the time Cooper arrived looking grumpy, I wasn't nearly as worried about the tests.

"Did your big brain let you down?" I asked as we sat in the back.

"What?" he muttered, still grumpy.

"Should I not talk to you?"

"Do you want to talk to me?" When his tone shut me up and I stared at my desk, Cooper leaned over and whispered, "Why are you always fucking talking to him?"

"Nick? He's in most of my classes. He's nice and he helped me study."

"I said I would help you. I'm smarter than him. I'm also your man, unless you want that to change?"

"You're breaking up with me on test day?" I whispered, starting to cry.

"Damn it," he said, pulling me out of the classroom. Once again, the other students became scarce to avoid Cooper. "I'm not breaking up anything."

"Why are you so angry?"

"I can't turn around without you and Nick getting cozy."

"That's bullshit."

"Whatever. Look, we need to take this test so we can get out of here. I need you to calm down."

"Are you going to calm down?" I asked, wiping my eyes.

"Say it," he demanded in a quiet voice. "Say it and I'll calm the fuck down."

"That I love you or that you're mine?"

"I know I'm yours. I need to know you're mine."

"Who the fuck else's would I be?" I growled at him.

Cooper grinned at my tone. "You're so fucking hot when you get pissed. I wish we could leave right now."

"I'm not getting naked with you until you stop acting like a douche."

"Even if I do this?" he asked, kissing my neck before returning to class.

Lowering my gaze, I avoided the looky-loos as I followed Cooper back into class where the instructor waited. Soon, Manuel handed out our tests and my panic returned. Half of the questions were in Spanish and I understood none of them. Was I supposed to know how to read this? Why hadn't I learned? Was the panic making me dumber or was I stupid and so I was panicking?

I spent so much time freaking out about freaking out that I had to hurry to finish the test in time. Handing the packet back to Manuel as I walked out with Cooper, I had a bad feeling that no matter who I studied with I might be in over my head.

Cooper remained grumpy for the rest of the afternoon. He even frowned during sex, watching me like he was searching for something on my face. By the time he dropped me off at work, I was ready for a little space. Even so, I worried the last few weeks with me had distracted him and he'd done poorly on his tests too.

Despite the wonky day, the first few hours at work were great. Test day put everyone on edge so they hadn't eaten much. After the exams were over, students showed up at Denny's and ordered most of the menu.

Super busy, I loved every minute of the rush. In fact, by the time Cooper arrived, I was rolling in cash and ready to celebrate. Maybe I'd treat him to something special?

Usually when Cooper arrived, he'd kiss me in a completely inappropriate way before sitting down where he spent the next few hours making lewd comments to get me to laugh. This time though, Cooper walked straight to the restroom and I assumed even Cooper Johansson got sick.

When he emerged, his sleeves were pulled down past his hands, making him look like a kid in an oversized shirt. His expression made me worry more.

"What's wrong?"

Cooper shook his head as he took my face into his hands still hidden in the shirt sleeves. "Tell me you love me," he whispered.

"I love you so much and you're scaring me."

"I had a shit day, but I need you to need me like I need you."

"I do," I said, sitting next to him in the booth. "You look sick."

"Just stressed. I have a lot of pressure on me to take over shit and I'm not even done with college. My pop is in a hurry to take a backseat in the business and it's all on me and I only have you to help me relax. Everyone else just takes. Well, Aaron is cool, but no one relaxes me like you do, baby."

Cooper turned to look at me and I saw such fear in his eyes. "You can't live without me, right?" he asked in a pleading voice. "If I fucked up, you'd give me another chance, right?"

"Fucked up? Like if you were with another girl?"

His expression full of pain, Cooper shook his head. "If I'm scared I'll lose you, why would I cheat?"

"I don't know, but you seem freaked out. I can't imagine what would be so bad that you'd be this way?"

Cooper studied my face in a way that made me think he wanted to confess. Was it really another girl? Was an ex pregnant? I couldn't imagine every girl was on birth control and Cooper wasn't great about using condoms. I waited for him to explain, but he only tightened his lips into a grim frown.

"You're coming to my place tonight, right?"

"Of course."

Cooper nodded, taking my hand. "I was thinking we should blow off school and work. Just take off for a few days. A little vacation."

"I want to find out how I did on the tests and they'll tell us tomorrow. Friday at the latest."

"I'll have someone email them to you."

"Why do you want to leave so badly? Are you in trouble?"

Cooper shook his head, but I knew he was lying. He'd done something bad enough to scare him. When he kissed me, I realized Cooper was shaking.

He said I relaxed him. Even without knowing what he did, I needed to soothe away his tension. Squirming around in the booth until I was on my knees, I had him lean against my chest while I caressed his head. His hair wasn't as short and it felt soft against my fingertips. Cooper wrapped his arms around my waist and exhaled softly against me.

"Whatever happened, it'll be okay."

"Do you promise?" he asked, sounding like a kid.

"Yes," I said, unable to say anything else.

Cooper looked up at me, his dark eyes overflowing with emotion. "Don't leave me," he whispered, fighting for control. "Fuck, Farah. We're perfect together so you need to stay."

Kissing him, I tried not to show my concern, but he had me worried. If it wasn't about a girl, what could he have done to cause me to leave? Did he kill someone? I knew his family business was violent. I knew Tucker likely dealt with those bastards harassing girls after Maddy made a toast to her hero who made it safe to walk the streets again. I understood Cooper would take over the family business and deal with his dad's old biker contacts. I just didn't think the violence would affect Cooper so strongly.

Later at his place, he never quite calmed down. When we were together, he held me too tightly like I might run away if he loosened his grip. As we dozed, I thought I heard him apologizing and saying he needed me to stay.

The next day, Cooper did everything he could to convince me to ditch school. He turned off the alarm, but I woke up on my own. He distracted me with sex and food. I still wanted to go to school and find out my grades. It was making me nuts not knowing and Cooper's secret wasn't helping me settle down. I promised him everything would be alright and he finally drove us to school.

Kissing me like he was saying goodbye, Cooper looked so young and vulnerable when I walked to my first class. I glanced back and waved, but he just stared. The mood in class wasn't any better. Apparently, everyone thought they failed every test. A lot of students didn't even show up to class, rather than learn their fates. I was nervous too, but then I heard how the counselors were calling in the people with really bad test results. When I arrived in my third class without an invite to the Admin building, I felt pretty confident. Then, Skye found me.

"I should have warned you that Cooper is the jealous type," she said, sitting next to me in class and checking her appearance in a little compact. "I think I just got distracted by Tyler's abs. Have you seen them? They're pretty fucking spectacular. Oh, and he aced everything yesterday. Didn't even break a sweat. Hot and smart, I've hit the motherload."

As usual, I had to wait until Skye finished before I could return to the first thing she said. "What about Cooper?"

"You didn't really like Nick, did you? He's cute, but not really hot. Not rich or smart. He's not Tyler and he certainly isn't Cooper."

"What about Nick?"

Shrugging, Skye focused on a crying girl who entered the room. The girl's friends descended upon her with promises to study more.

"I did fine," Skye said. "I mean, how could I not? I showed up. I took notes. I stayed awake. How hard is it to pass these tests? Fucking hillbillies."

Shaking my head, I wanted Skye to focus. "What happened to Nick? He hasn't been in class, but a lot of people ditched today."

"Oh, he's in the hospital. Cooper fucked him up. How could you not know that when it's your boyfriend and your whatever Nick is to you?"

As a cold dread settled into my stomach, I thought I might vomit. "Will Nick be okay?"

"You should stop worrying about Nick," Skye muttered, glaring at me. "Guys like Cooper don't want their girlfriends talking up losers. You need to keep your eye on the ball, Farah, or you'll lose him."

Normally when Skye got bitchy with me, I pulled within myself and avoided conflict. This time though, I walked out of the room just as the instructor entered. I didn't care about anything except finding Cooper and making him explain what the fuck he thought he was doing?

Cooper was in his Analytic Geometry and Calculus class when I found him, but he wasn't listening. His gaze was on the chair in front of him and he looked either pissed or depressed. Standing at the doorway, I waited for him to notice. The minute our eyes met, Cooper knew I knew and I saw his gaze harden.

Once we were alone on the grassy quad and away from the nearby classrooms, I waited for him to explain. Instead, he stared at me until I cried.

"Why him?" Cooper asked, leaning down to speak near my ear. "Why is always fucking him?"

"He's nice. That's all he's ever been to me. He helped me study. He talked to me about teaching. It was never anything more."

"Fuck that. I see the way he looks at you. I see how you two are always together. He wants you. Why do you think it got out of hand last night? I told him to stay away from you and he mouthed off. He didn't back down because he wants you. He said you're too good for me. What the fuck? He doesn't know me or you. He's an asshole and he brought the beating on himself."

Stepping away from Cooper, I remembered when he punched the wall next to my face. How he used his size, strength, and threats of violence to intimidate others into doing whatever he wanted. Usually he saw nothing wrong with it, but he had been freaked out the night before. Even now, I saw fear in his eyes.

"Do you think I'm a whore?" I asked.

Cooper stepped back and shook his head. "This isn't about you."

"You think I'd cheat on you? That I'm not loyal?"

"I said it's not about you."

"If Nick wants me and I don't want him, why would you care? You said lots of guys think I'm hot. Are you going to beat them all up even though I only want you?"

"Look," Cooper said, breathing too fast, "things got out of hand. He mouthed off then he didn't just take the punch and stay down. He had to prove some shit, but there was no way he could win. He should have fucking stayed down, but he didn't. He challenged me like he was saying he was taking you away."

"But I don't want him," I said between clenched teeth. "I did in the beginning because he was nice and you were scary. Now, I love you and I shared those private things with you, but you act like I'm a slut who isn't loyal. Like I'll spread for someone else when I have you. That's how you see me."

"No," he pleaded, taking my hands. "I saw him with you yesterday and he's always looking at you. I'd see him on campus with his friends. If we'd walk by, he looked at you. He's always staring. Even at the fucking fair, it's like he's stalking you. I wanted him to back off."

"He's not stalking me," I said, rolling my eyes. "He barely talks to me. I usually talk to him first and he never makes any moves. He might think I'm hot, but so what? Every girl thinks you're hot. They always check you out, but I don't hunt them down and put them in the hospital for looking at my guy. I'm not a psycho, but maybe you are."

"Farah, please. I messed up, but he made it worse."

"You started it. You went after him then things got out of hand. You had no reason to even talk to him though. I love you and I'm loyal. I would never cheat so you shouldn't have cared about Nick. You're weird about him."

Cooper ran his hands over his short hair and looked at me with mournful eyes. "That night at the party, you looked at him one way and me another. You felt something for him and you didn't feel it for me. I know he means something to you, so don't act innocent."

"So now I am a whore you have to worry about?"

"No, but I know he's not just any guy."

"He's nice and I wanted nice. You're not nice."

"Fuck that. I take care of you. I love you and he doesn't do shit."

"What is it that you thought would happen if you didn't threaten him?"

"I thought he'd find a way to take you from me."

"How?"

"I don't know. I guess, he'd be nice," Cooper sneered, trying to be angry, but looking as panicked as the night before. "You belong with me."

"You hurt an innocent person, just for being nice to me. I've shared so much with you and taken down all those walls and it wasn't enough. You still don't trust me."

"It's him I don't trust."

"But he couldn't fuck me unless I let him!" I yelled, losing my temper as we talked in circles.

"Fine, I'm sorry if it seems like I didn't trust you, but it wasn't about you. It was about him."

"You're still an asshole," I said, walking away.

Cooper followed behind me. "Yes, but I'm your asshole. You need me like I need you. I wasn't kidding last night about that. I can't breathe without you, Farah."

I kept walking even though I had no idea where I was going. My class was the other direction. My apartment was the other direction too. I was just walking to walk. Cooper followed me silently for a few minutes then placed his hand on my shoulder.

"I'll apologize to him," he said, forcing me to stop and look at him. "I'll pay his hospital bills and fix things. Is that what you want?"

"I want you to trust me so people like Nick don't get hurt."

"I do trust you."

"Not really."

Cooper flexed his hands and I saw how raw and bruised his knuckles were. The thought of them pounding on Nick broke my heart. Those same hands could be so gentle with me that I'd let myself forget what Cooper was capable of when pushed. Even if he was the one who pushed himself into feeling like violence was necessary.

"I need space," I said quietly.

"What the fuck does that mean?"

"You know what it means. I need time to think."

"I'll fix shit with Nick."

"Good, but you can't just fuck up people then apologize and act like it's cool. Maybe you need to hurt bad people for the business, but not someone who never did anything except want what you have. I hate to break it to you, Coop, but lots of people want what you have. Your money, your looks, your long list of pussy, your family, me, the Harleys. You can't pound on people for being envious."

The anger in Cooper's expression faded until he just looked tired. "How much space? Like for how long?"

"I don't know. There's no rule book for how long to punish a guy for putting another guy in the hospital."

"I didn't plan to fuck him up like that. I didn't even hit him that hard, but his head bounced off the curb and I knew it was bad."

"Did you leave him there?" I whispered, imagining Nick lying on the ground.

Cooper sighed. "There were people around. His idiot friends jumped in... Shit, I fucked up, but you promised you wouldn't leave me."

"I thought you did something bad like hurt an asshole or even fucked another girl. I wasn't sure I'd be okay with those things, but I told you what you needed to hear. It wasn't those things though. It was you hurting a nice guy who helped me out a few times when I was struggling with schoolwork. He didn't have it coming."

202

Cooper frowned at any positive mention of Nick. He still held a grudge and I knew forgiving him wasn't really my call. Nick was the one who suffered and he was the one who needed to forgive Cooper. I just needed time to figure out if Cooper would pound on every guy I talked to for the rest of our lives.

Leaving him standing on the quad, I returned to class. Skye said nothing when I joined her. When she spoke after class, it was about Tyler and his ability to bench press her. Admittedly, Skye's descriptions of Tyler's amazing strength did make me laugh. Yet, a hard ball of tension remained in my gut as I headed to my last class.

Cooper wasn't in Spanish, so I sat in the front. Manuel mainly reviewed old lessons because so many students in his classes had done "mucho crapido." Everyone laughed at this comment and the fifty minutes flew by. I was still thinking about the two empty seats in the room though. As I walked towards the door, I even looked back at Cooper's regular spot and wondered what to do.

"Farah," Manuel said, calling me back into the now empty room. When I was standing in front of him, he smiled and I knew I was in trouble. "Normally, a counselor would handle this, but it was felt because of your situation that requesting you go to the Admin building might be too...stressful."

Assuming he meant my dating situation, I waited for the bad news. "Am I in trouble?" I asked when he didn't continue.

"I want to assure you how many students are in the same boat as you. These tests are meant as a wakeup call for the lazier, more disorganized students. They can also reveal problems with students who really put effort into their studies."

"Did I do badly on your test?" I asked, knowing the answer.

As Manuel glanced around then smiled softly, I felt my eyes burning. "Technically, you didn't pass any of your exams," he said and I immediately felt lightheaded. "Yet, the administration allows instructors to bump a grade into the passing range when we feel the student is struggling, but not for a lack of effort. In your case, all of your instructors know you are a good student. You attend class, participate, and actively learn, but clearly the first month hasn't been easy and you'll likely need tutoring."

"Am I suspended or expelled?" I said, crying now. "Am I in trouble?"

Manuel reached out to comfort me then thought better of it. "No, Farah, it's fine. This was why we didn't want to call you into the Admin building. It's sort of like the walk of shame for those students who aren't putting in the effort."

Breathing deeply, I tried to calm myself. It had proven to be a long day though and it wasn't even four.

"Your exam scores were all bumped to D's. I know that sounds bad, but you're not on academic probation," he said. "We just want you to get a tutor or two to help you catch up."

"I study," I babbled, feeling ashamed to have sat in his class every day and learned so little. "I don't know why I did so bad."

"Many students have trouble with tests especially the first ones," he said, but I knew he was full of shit. My scores were bad enough that it wasn't test anxiety. It was a lack of knowledge. I just didn't know what I should have at this point. How had I fallen so far behind?

"Can I leave now?" I asked, needing to get home and cry for a while before work.

"Yes, of course. It really will be okay. These first exams are always a pain, but you'll catch up."

Thanking him, I hurried out the door and walked as fast as I could to the bus stop. Cooper wasn't around to drive me and I didn't notice Skye either. Maybe she was waiting for me somewhere, but I couldn't see through my tears. No one bothered me on the ride home, ignoring my quiet crying. I hurried into my apartment and past Amy and Tex watching TV and drinking beers. Once in my room, I turned on the radio and cried into a pillow.

All those years working to get to college, it never occurred to me that I would fail. I felt such shame at knowing my dream would never happen because I was too stupid. I really thought I was better than everyone in my family including Tawny. I always told myself how good I was at school, but clearly I was just getting by in the shitty schools I attended growing up. Now, at a school not known for being academically rigorous, I crashed and burned.

Though desperate to talk to Cooper, he was one reason I failed. I had blown off too many hours of reading and studying just so I could be with him. Now, I'd lost Cooper and failed.

Eyeing my phone, I considered calling Tawny, but was too embarrassed. How could I tell her I only stayed off academic suspension because I was dating a Johansson? She wouldn't judge me in her words, but I knew she would be disappointed. I had promised our dreams could come true and we'd be more than our parents. I was so certain I could be Mrs. Prescott. Now, I realized my teacher likely knew the truth. She just couldn't bear to tell a child that life only provided opportunities for people better than me.

By the time I arrived at work, I was depressed and just going through the motions. I didn't even check the ketchup bottles. Yet figuring I might spend the rest of my life as a waitress, I should at least take pride in the job.

When Cooper arrived, he rushed over to where I wiped a very clean table. "I apologized to Nick. He accepted my apology. I'm paying his hospital bills. The rest of his year at school too. We're best buddies now. He's even under my protection. It's all better."

"I'm glad."

"That's it? You're glad."

"I can't talk about things when I'm working."

"When do you have your break?"

"In an hour."

"We'll talk then."

Despite the urge to say no, I missed Cooper so much I felt like nothing else mattered. The feeling was a lie though. My dream mattered, but I'd pissed it away. Or maybe I was always going to fail despite how hard I worked. Was I too stupid to succeed?

When I gave him a noncommittal nod, Cooper studied my face. I knew he wanted more than the nod. Apologizing to Nick wasn't a Cooper move. He didn't really think he was wrong. While regretting Nick was really hurt and worrying over me leaving him, Cooper didn't genuinely feel guilty. He viewed me as his and anyone who interfered was an obstacle to be eliminated. Cooper's ferocity might be terrifying, but at least he succeeded when he put his mind to things. I couldn't claim the same about myself.

After I fed Cooper, I waited for break time when I would tell him how no amount of apologies could fix what was broken. I was the problem. Cooper was merely the symptom.

We stepped outside because I sensed he might not take things well and would get loud. Cooper reached for me immediately like he was dying without my touch. Even wanting to be in his arms, I stepped back.

"How much do you plan to punish me before we're okay again?" he asked with a needy gaze.

"It's been less than a day. Besides, I'm not punishing you. We just can't be together."

"What the hell is it now?" he asked. While his words were angry, his tone was more desperate.

"I need to focus on school," I muttered, avoiding his gaze. "I can't get distracted."

Cooper erased the space between us and lifted my chin to force me to look at him. "I want to spend my life with you and I'm a fucking distraction?"

"I failed all of my tests, Coop. If I was anyone else, I'd be on academic probation," I whispered, feeling ashamed. "I've always been a good student and I could get kicked out if I don't pull up my grades."

"Fuck that. I'll get it fixed."

"No," I said, stepping back. "Being a good student was the only thing I ever did well. I couldn't protect my sister. I wasn't popular or stylish. I never had any great skills, but I kept my grades steady. I was the good average student in every class. Now, I'm failing."

"I'll help you study. I'll hire tutors. I'll make it better."

"I want to make it better myself. I want to succeed on my own."

"You're not on your own," he said, cupping my face with his battered hands. "You have me. You have my family. You're not alone anymore." Stepping back, I hated to see his dark eyes filled with pain and even tears. "So you just throw me away like I'm shit?"

"It's better this way."

"How do you figure?"

"I don't know. It just seems like a thing to say."

"Am I supposed to wait around while you get your crap together and decide you have time for me?

"No."

"So you're fine with me fucking someone else?"

Biting back tears, I shook my head. "I can't be with you, but that doesn't mean I don't love you."

"Yes, it does. You're making a damn choice."

"I'm trying to accomplish the one thing I've wanted all my life," I whimpered, pleading with him to understand. "The one thing that gives me value."

"Why can't I give you value?"

"Because you're the one with value. I'm just your girlfriend."

Cooper looked at the passing cars then up at the half hidden moon. Suddenly, he turned and punched the brick wall. Once, twice, again and again, until I pulled him away. His hands were bleeding as he cupped my face.

"Fuck you, Farah," he hissed. "I hate you for this, but I'm waiting until you realize how you aren't alone because you and me are in this together. We'll always be in it together because you and I are real in a way your silly childhood dreams aren't. You are my treasure and I'm not letting you go because you got a few shit grades. Love doesn't work like that."

As easy as it might be to soothe Cooper and hope I could handle his love and my schoolwork, I knew easy choices were often mistakes. I needed to do well at school to have any value. Cooper couldn't understand because he always had value. He had a life where one failure didn't mean the end of the world. I had a life where one failure meant I was becoming my mom.

After using my apron to wipe his bloody hands, I inched back until I let him go. "I need to get back inside."

"Can I drive you home?"

His gaze reeked of need and his breathing was rough. He was a man barely holding onto his control, but I couldn't give him what he wanted. I couldn't even give myself what I needed.

"No thank you."

Cooper's shoulders sagged and he finally understood. He walked past me, yet stopped at the curb and sighed. "You're still my girl."

"Okay."

Without looking back, Cooper climbed on his Harley and left. I didn't know how to fix everything I had ruined. It wasn't as simple as going to a guy, paying his bills, playing buddy, and making things right. I needed to bring my sister to Ellsberg, but had no idea where she was. I needed to be a teacher, but couldn't even pass my first tests. I needed Cooper, but had brought out the worst in him. Everything I needed was out of reach, so I returned to wiping clean tables and filling already full ketchup bottles.

Chapter Twenty One

Thursday sucked from the moment I woke up to the sounds of my mom's horny cries to the walk to bus stop in the rain. I tried to pay attention in class, but my mind was everywhere else. At lunch, Skye talked non-stop about her vagina. It started with her concerns about natural childbirth and just dragged to her wondering if she smelled weird. I was relieved she didn't ask me to take a whiff and give her my opinion.

Walking into Spanish class, I saw Cooper, but avoided his gaze. I was tired and he looked so handsome in all black. I remembered how we planned to see a movie that weekend and go swimming if the weather was decent. Instead, I planned to study and try to catch up when I was completely lost. Scheduled to work with a tutor on Monday, I wanted to cram ahead of time so I wouldn't look stupid. It reminded me of how people cleaned their houses before the maid arrived.

As I left class, Cooper blocked my exit and I finally looked up at his beautiful face. I knew that face, every curve, every feature. I missed that face, but was too tired to argue again.

"I'm going to help you study and get your grades up."

"Coop, please..."

"Please, help you? Yes, I will."

Tears pricked at my eyes and I glanced around. "I'm really failing."

"And I'm going to help you."

"So we can date again?"

Cooper's expression darkened. "What we did wasn't dating. What we did was fall in love and I want you back. If you can't be with me until your grades are solid, we're making them solid."

"I can't be with you."

"Farah," he whispered in a harsh tone that startled me. "You're not listening. I can see you're tired and stressed, but listen. You're failing this class, but I'm not. You need my help. I want to help you because I love you and want you back, but those aren't the only reasons. I also know you deserve to do well. You worked too hard to get to this fucking school just to get distracted."

Cooper was right about a million things. Mostly that I was tired and stressed. I never slept well when away from him. I didn't eat well either. Cooper had provided too many missing needs from a lifetime without. Now, I'd lost him because I failed.

"What grade did you get on the Spanish test?" I asked as he took my books into his arms.

"An A."

Staring at him, I couldn't believe he did so well when I did shit. He must have seen the horror in my eyes. Not only the shock, but the disgust in myself for doing so poorly when my excuse for failing had done well.

"I'm older," he said, nudging me out the door and towards the quad. "I'm used to college. And in case you forgot, I don't have a job to go to after school. Every night, when I sit there with you serving me dinner, I'm studying. Now, I'm going to get you caught up."

Cooper stopped at a picnic table and set down the books. "We'll study outside where it's nice. Later, I'll get Tuck to bring us food. We'll get all of your work done so you can start your shift feeling good."

"Thank you," I mumbled, taking his hand while fighting the urge to sob in front of everyone. "I'm really behind. Like I didn't know what we were doing today in class. I used to be good at keeping up, but I'm lost."

"So we'll start from the beginning of the semester and get you caught up."

Sighing, I wiped my wet eyes and stared at the laughing students nearby. When Cooper leaned in, I realized how much I missed the feel of his breath on my skin.

"It took me a month to push you off course and it'll take more than a day to get you caught up. Soon, you'll be where you need to be and you'll forgive me and we'll be together." His voice sounded so desperate and his gaze looked so dejected then he faked a smile. "I'm going to make sure once we're back together that you have time to study. I want you to be a teacher like you dreamed."

"It's not your fault. You know that, right?" I said, feeling like I might drop from exhaustion. "I made bad choices."

"I'm not a bad choice," he muttered. "But I didn't make sure you were okay. I just wanted you to have fun, but I left you no time for school."

"It's really not your fault."

"It's not your fault either."

"How can it not be my fault?" I asked, frowning at him.

"It just can't. I say it's not, so it's not. You're too serious and you dump too much blame on yourself. You didn't protect your sister. You don't work hard enough. You didn't do this or that. You aren't perfect, but you're perfect for me. I'm going to be perfect for you too and I'll do that by being the best fucking tutor the world's ever seen."

Laughing, I looked at the books. "I can say and write hello and goodbye. That's it."

Cooper gave me a weird look for the slightest second and I knew he was shocked by how little I had picked up over the last month.

"I understood everything in class," I explained. "Then later, it got all jumbled in my head."

Giving me a nod, Cooper sat down. I joined him on the bench, careful to avoid touching, yet wanting to be in his arms so badly. Cooper missed me too. It was written all over his face.

"We'll start at the beginning and get you caught up. It'll be fine."

This time when I nodded, I actually felt like I would improve my grades. Cooper kept his word about staying focused and, hell, if he wasn't a great tutor. He spoke softly, taking his time to go over his notes from the first week. By the time Tucker and Maddy arrived with burgers, I felt like I was getting some of the early stuff. The four of us ate dinner before Cooper worked with me for another half hour. Finally, he drove me home where he waited as I dressed for work.

"I'm going to drive you each night like before," he said as if it wasn't up for discussion even though his gaze was worried.

"I'd like that."

Cooper gave me a small smile then we walked out to his bike. During my break, I sat with him and he quizzed me on what we had worked on earlier.

This was our new relationship.

During the weekend, we studied at my apartment while Amy went with Tex to a casino. We talked and ate, but no fooling around. Cooper did more than help me with Spanish. He basically re-taught me everything I hadn't picked up the first time. By the end of the weekend, I thought he was the one who would be an amazing teacher.

Once the school week started, Cooper picked me up every morning. We hung out in Spanish class and studied afterwards. We ate dinner while studying then he drove me to work. Also on Monday, a still bruised Nick returned to school and acted like nothing ever happened. He was friendly, but not too friendly. While Cooper faked like he and Nick were buddies, I knew he would find it easier to pretend if we were back together. Feeling insecure, Cooper still stood a little too close to me whenever Nick was in the vicinity.

By Wednesday, I was feeling pretty confident. As we sat on the quad studying like usual, my arm touched Cooper's and his gaze met mine. His eyes pleaded with me for a crumb of hope.

"I have a quiz in most of my classes on Friday. I think they want to see who used last week's wakeup call to study."

His arm still against mine, Cooper only nodded.

"I was thinking we could see a movie on Saturday. I could pay and everything." When Cooper reached for my face, I let him caress my cheek as I continued, "I was thinking I could spend the weekend with you too."

"But only if you do well on the quizzes, right?"

"No," I said, holding his gaze. "If I do badly on them, it's just me fucking up by not being smart enough. It's not like I haven't studied or you haven't helped me. Whatever happens, I still want to spend the weekend with you."

When Cooper kissed my forehead, I scooted a little closer so my hip pressed against his.

"I need you, baby," he whispered. "I need you to let me back in."

"Waiting isn't about punishing you. It's about punishing me."

"You have to fucking stop that," he said, frowning at me. "Hasn't life punished you enough with your shit parents and growing up like you did? Why do you have to keep hurting yourself? If anyone should be on your side, it should be you."

"I guess, but I'm afraid to slack off. After all, look at what happened."

"You didn't slack off. You studied, but you needed more help than you thought. It's your first fucking month at school. You think I aced everything on my first tests?"

"Yes."

Smiling slightly, Cooper rolled his eyes. "Yes, but I'm perfect."

I rubbed my cheek against his shoulder. "Soon, Coop. You just have to wait a little longer. I promise."

Cooper didn't perk up completely, but his mood did improve. Mine did too. No matter what happened on the quizzes, I knew I worked hard. While I might still be struggling, I wasn't slacking off. This counted for something. Besides, failed quizzes or not, I was spending the weekend with Cooper.

On Thursday, I called Tawny who answered in a whisper.

"Are you okay?" I asked.

Tawny said nothing and I asked again.

"I'm scared," she whimpered. "There are these weirdoes at the motel and one of them saw me at the window. I thought Dad might be back, but he wasn't and the weirdo winked at me. Now, I have the dresser against the door and I'm afraid to leave."

"Tawny," I babbled, freaking out at how she was too far away and I didn't know how to help her. "I have to get you here."

"I can't live with Mom. I can't pretend."

"Fuck her. She's just like you said. I was lying to myself remembering those few good times. I wanted her to be a real mom, but she doesn't care. She has some stupid smelly boyfriend and she's drinking again. Fuck her and this apartment. I'm using my nest egg to bring you here and get us a new place."

"What about college?"

"I'll still have enough to get through the year and next year probably," I said, thinking of how I might fail and have to redo classes. "I'll work extra shifts during holidays and the summer. I just want you out of that place."

"I don't know where exactly I am though or how to get to a bus station. I'm stuck here and there's like one convenience store then nothing. The only chance I have to get away is hitchhiking. What if someone bad picks me up?" she whispered, her voice breaking.

Tawny sounded like a little girl and I wanted to climb through the phone and hug her. I wanted to fix everything, but I had made a mess of my life and wasn't sure how to find Tawny.

"You're in Texas?" I asked, calming myself.

"Yes. I asked the lady at the convenience store what part of Texas and she acted like I was stupid. She said the southern part then said I had to leave if I wasn't going to buy anything. I looked in the motel room and there's no telephone book. I haven't seen a manager or maid to ask. The only people I see are the weirdoes staying in the next room."

"What's the name of the convenience store? Oh, and the motel. I'm going to see if Cooper can find you."

"I thought you broke up."

"We did," I said, losing a little of my confidence, "but if he can bring you here, I'll spend the rest of my life paying him back."

Tawny said nothing, but I heard her moving around.

"What's wrong?"

"I hear voices. Sometimes, those guys come around the door and look in the window. I'm hiding in the bathroom. I don't want them to come in here. Dad says they won't. He says they're just fooling around when they knock."

"Dad's an idiot. You need to find a weapon and keep it with you. I'm asking Cooper for help. He's smart and he knows people and he'll find and save you." Again, Tawny said nothing so I did. "When was the last time Dad was around?"

"Yesterday. He didn't get the money he needed and he can't pay for the room much longer," Tawny said then I heard her crying. "He said I'm lazy and I need to get a job. I told him I asked at the convenience store, but they're not hiring. He said I need to walk my fat ass to town then he threw a beer bottle at me. He's freaking out, Farah. He's mad that you left and we don't have money and he says I eat too much. I'm only eating once a day and it's junk food. I haven't eaten anything warm in two weeks, but he's still mad. Now, he's gone and I don't know if he'll come back?"

Crying now, I imagined my father the way he really was and not how I pretended. While he was nicer and more reliable than my mom, he was still a raging asshole. Mom might have left us with those bastards that day, but Dad was the one who put a target on our family. He was the one who brought trouble to our door. My parents could both fucking die for all I cared. I just wanted Tawny safe.

After reassuring Tawny, I called Cooper. God bless him for understanding anything I said over my sobbing. He listened then said he'd handle it. No ifs, no maybes. He was handling the problem and I instantly felt like it would be okay. Cooper Johansson was on the job and the damsel trapped in a shithole in Texas would be saved.

Before I hung up with him to call Tawny back, I told Cooper I loved him. Unlike his reaction to my panicked plea, he sounded so fragile when saying he loved me too. I knew he needed as much reassurance as Tawny so I ended the call with, "this weekend," and he exhaled like it was all he had to hear.

Friday flew by, but I felt Cooper's absence. I had plans to call Cooper after a trip to the grocery store. When the phone rang, I hoped it might be him. Once I hung up the phone, I stared at the wall and tried to process what the woman from the bank told me. While I wished it to be a bad dream, my nightmares weren't like this.

My nest egg was gone. When I bought a book for class earlier, I used my card. The payment went through, pushing me five dollars over what was left in the account. Somehow, in the last few weeks, the money I saved for three years dropped from nearly eight thousand to a measly thirty dollars. I'd used up the rest and the only reason the charge cleared was because the overture was transferred to my credit card. A card I never intended to use unless for an emergency. I would never need the card, I told myself when signing for it. I would never be stupid enough to waste all of my money. Maybe I wouldn't, but I knew who would.

If my mother had come home later, things might have turned out differently. Had she gone out to dinner with Tex instead of arriving home at that moment, I might have never confronted her. I wasn't sure if fate was on my side or out to get me, but a few minutes after I hung up, the door opened and my laughing mother entered.

Amy saw me and showed not a hint of concern for what she did to me or what I might do when I learned she stole my money. In fact, she ignored me like usual and walked to the kitchen.

"I'm moving out," I said quietly, instead of screaming like I wanted. "I won't have the rent."

My mother reacted like I expected. "That's not acceptable. I can't pay for this fucking place by myself."

"Didn't you save any of the money you stole from my account?"

"Wait now," Tex said, standing between us. "Stole is such a legal word. Borrowed is more like it. No one stole nothing."

"Like the bitch plans to pay me back. Like she could with her shitty job."

"Fuck you!" Mom screamed, storming from the kitchen. "Ungrateful little cunt!"

"Ungrateful? You fucked over me and Tawny years ago and you're doing it again. You stole my money!"

"Let's just calm down," Tex said, blocking Amy who looked ready to tear me apart. I truly hoped she made a move so I could claim self-defense. Meanwhile, Tex tried to play the voice of reason. "See, your mom had some bills to pay and she planned to give back the money."

"Bullshit! You used it to go to the fucking casino! You wasted all my school money so you could party, you fucking losers!"

"I wasn't giving it back," Mom sneered. "You think you're special because you attend some shit school? Or because you got some rich guy interested in you? He's probably just impressed by all the skills you learned from those bikers."

Five years of rage erupted as I ran at her, but Amy ducked and Tex shoved me to the ground.

"I don't give a shit what you think Amy's done," he said, hands out as if to reason with me. "You never hit your mom. That just ain't right."

"You selfish bitch!" I screamed, jumping back up. "You let them take us to save your fucking ring!"

"Like you cared! I saw you licking your lips, getting ready for them! Where do you think they got the idea to take you? From you giving off all your whore signals!"

When I ran for her again, Tex grabbed me around the waist and held me back.

"You're trash!" I screamed. "You're a loser! It's why Grandma hates you! You embarrass her!"

"You're no better! You were always a fuckup! Whining about wanting this or that! Feeling sorry for yourself! What about me? I lost your dad because you played up the victim bullshit, but we both know you loved every moment with those dirty bikers! You were born to be a whore! Both you and Tawny! Why do you think you like that Johansson boy so much?"

Yanking free of Tex, I fixed my hair and held up my head. "I'm moving out. When Grandma asks why, I'll tell her you stole my money. Let's see whose side she takes."

Knowing Amy was forever seeking her mother's approval, I also knew how much it hurt to realize your parents would never really love you. Now, she could explain to my grandmother how she fucked up once again.

Walking to my bedroom, I shoved my clothes into the suitcase I brought with me only a month earlier. My hands were shaking so badly I kept dropping things, but I couldn't stop moving. I needed to get out of the apartment and away from the bitch.

My mind was on reporting the theft when Amy stepped into the doorway. Glancing at her, I knew what she planned before she even moved. Instead of backing away, I met her halfway and landed a punch just as she did. We both staggered then I ran at her and shoved her against the wall.

"What?" I screamed in her face. "You can't stop yourself from fucking up, can you? It's in your blood to screw up everything you touch!"

"Fat bitch!"

Every time my mother pushed off the wall to attack me, I shoved her again. I wanted to tear her apart, but something held me back. What if I hurt her seriously and went to jail? What if she continued to ruin my life forever by giving me a record? I needed to follow the rules so I didn't beat on her like she deserved.

Ready to break up our struggle, Tex appeared and I assumed he would take his bitch and leave. Instead, he punched me square in the face. Falling against the wall, I saw stars and my nose gushed blood. Once Tex nailed me, Amy hooted in triumph. Jumping around excitedly, she kicked me in the gut as I tried to stand.

Fuck the rules, I thought, lunging for her. Before we hit the ground, I started punching wildly. My moves were frantic, but I made the bitch bleed before Tex yanked me back by my hair and threw me against the dresser. Smashing into the mirror, I toppled onto the floor as he stood large over me. Tex wasn't Cooper, but he had a solid six inches and maybe sixty pounds on me. Yet, I had a shard of broken mirror in my hand.

Waving it at him, I screamed as loudly as I could without blowing out my lungs. Tex actually covered his fucking ears like a sissy kid. Amy rolled onto her knees, finally getting to her feet. She threw the alarm clock at me, but her aim was off and it smashed into the wall.

Once my scream ended, I moved towards the door. "Someone's called the cops by now. If you don't move out of my way, the police will find your corpses when they get here."

"I'm going to kill you, Farah," Amy said with complete sincerity.

"No, bitch, you're going to run and hope you're faster than Cooper. Knowing your tendency to fuck up, you won't get very far. Now, back off."

The banging on the front door startled Tex who looked ready to grab the mirror shard. The bastard still thought he could fix things, but it was too late. My face was a mess and I had bled all over my clothes. There was no way Tex could sell this was an accident or misunderstanding.

"I've called the cops!" a booming voice said through the door as I passed by Tex and Amy. Grabbing my backpack, I opened the door to find a neighbor looking freaked out. "What the hell?" he said, likely worrying someone other than me had a weapon.

"Did you really call the cops?" I asked, slamming the door and hurrying towards the parking lot. "Shit, I don't have my phone."

Going back wasn't an option then the guy said the only thing I wanted to hear. "I called Johansson. He's on his way."

Thanking him, I suggested he return to his apartment just in case Amy and Tex decided to do something stupid. Stumbling to the front of the complex, I found a spot to hide.

From the very first day, no matter how much Cooper scared me or pissed me off, I knew he was mine. Please let him come for me, I begged while waiting between two cars and cradling my face in my lap.

The sound of an approaching motorcycle electrified my whole body, but I didn't look up. There were plenty of bikers around here. No need to get excited or disappointed. Just wait for Cooper and he'll come. When the bike stopped a few feet from me, I ran to him because the world was ugly everywhere except in his arms. Cooper was my home.

"Fuck," he growled, getting off his bike to look at my face.

"She stole my money," I sobbed, knowing he would understand. "She stole my nest egg."

So angry he was shaking, Cooper started pulling away. "Her boyfriend did that to your face? I'm going to fucking kill him."

"Coop!" I yelled, yanking at his shirt. "I need you. Kill the piece of shit later. Right now, I need to get away from here. I hate that bitch and I need to leave."

As Cooper's gaze focused on the complex, I felt his rage. He wanted retribution, but he finally looked at me as I tugged him back towards the bike.

"I love you and I need to get out of here."

I love you. Cooper heard those words and his anger shifted into the needy gaze I saw from him too often lately.

"That piece of shit will bleed," he growled, climbing on the Harley. "Where do you want to go?"

"I don't care. I just want to get away from here and keep going until..." Wrapping my arms around him, I sighed. "I needed you and you came."

When Cooper looked back at me, the raw pain and rage in his eyes made me shiver. "Hold on, baby."

Nuzzling my bloody face against his back, I closed my eyes and soaked in the heat of his body. With Cooper, I was safe and loved and my future still had meaning.

We rode for a long time, but I just held on and listened to his heart beating over the katydids singing in the woods. The snap of thunder awoke me from the dreamy state I fell into after too long on the road. By the time the droplets splashed down on us, I was ready to pull over somewhere and rest. Cooper found a Denny's at a roadside stop with a few nearby hotels and a store or two.

Cooper's face was a mask of anger, hard and unyielding, as he helped me off the bike. Hurrying under the awning, I saw a crack in the rage while he examined my face.

"You should be untouchable," he whispered, more to himself than me. "This shouldn't have happened."

"They're stupid people and you can't fix stupid."

Cooper didn't smile. Just stared out at the pouring rain.

"Can we eat?" I asked, trying to distract him.

"Yeah, baby," he muttered, more interested in revenge than food.

We walked into the restaurant and were seated by a young waitress who avoided looking at my face. The waitress who came to take our order wasn't as squeamish.

"Are you okay, hon?" she asked while refusing to look at Cooper.

"My mom's boyfriend hit me," I said, hoping she believed me.

The waitress nodded. "Want me to get you some ice for your face?"

"That would be great."

After she walked away, I looked at Cooper who stared out the window at the rain-soaked parking lot.

"I am going to lay waste to that asshole," he whispered. "Don't try to stop me either."

Climbing out of my side of the booth, I noticed Cooper's expression change to panic as if I might leave. Instead, I scooted in next to him.

"I saved for three years for my nest egg," I told him, my hand on his chest. "No movies. No snacks after school with Tawny. No new clothes so I could fit in with other kids. I saved every penny I made in tips so I would have a safety net when I got to school. So many times Tawny wanted to do something fun. Something not even expensive, but I told my little sister no every time so I could keep my nest egg. Three years of doing without, just so my mom and her loser boyfriend could piss it away on a weekend at the casinos." I paused to wipe my eyes. "I don't care what you do to either of them. If they disappeared off the face of the earth, I wouldn't care. I earned that money and I made my sister go without and it meant shit to my mom. Fuck her and that turd she spreads for."

Cooper held my gaze. "We're bringing Tawny here."

"I love you," I said, believing his words. "I missed you so much and I don't want to miss you anymore."

Cooper nodded then glanced at the restrooms. "Why don't you clean up before our food comes?"

Giving him a quick kiss on the cheek, I figured I looked like crap and he was having trouble calming down with me bleeding. After washing my face in the bathroom, I surveyed the damage. I'd have two black eyes for sure. My nose looked swollen, but not broken. My teeth were intact. My face throbbed, but I'd gotten lucky. No major damage. Not even the worst beating I'd suffered that year.

Returning to the booth, I sat next to Cooper, needing to be close. When he handed me his phone, I saw my bank account information was pulled up. Before I could ask how he accessed my account, I noticed my nest egg was back.

"Did the lady get it wrong?" I asked, feeling in bizarroland.

"You deserve that money," Cooper said, staring outside again. "You earned it."

"Coop..."

"No, listen," he said, looking back at me. "I need you, Farah. I want you to say yes to me, but if you don't have that money, I'll never be sure if you said yes because you want me or because you need me."

"I do need you. No one makes me feel like you do."

Cooper nodded. "I want you back, but I need you to promise me something."

Frowning, I realized he wasn't taking me back and his condition made me nervous.

"I'll probably mess up again," he said, rolling a napkin hard in his fist. "I love you and I'm perfect about most things, but I mess up with you. I get too loud or rude or angry and I scare you. I mess up and you always run. I want you to promise you won't run anymore. If I make you mad or scare you, punish me. Ignore me, cold shoulder, withhold sex, call me names, whatever, but don't run away. Don't leave me and make my heart hurt like it does when I've lost you. Can you promise me that?"

"Promise I'll never leave you, no matter what you do?"

"I won't cheat. I won't hit you. I won't hit some guy because you're talking to him. But, yeah, I talk out my ass sometimes and I don't think about how it sounds to you. When I act like a jerk, you need to deal with me, but don't run. I can't chase you anymore because every time I get you back, I feel nervous like I'll lose you again. I need to feel secure in us. I seem to have all of the power, but you give me a lot too. Without you, I feel like things make no sense. Like they don't fit anymore and I can't live like that. You have the power to rip me apart and I need you to promise you won't hurt me even though I accidentally hurt you. I promise I'll never do it on purpose, but I need you to promise too."

Twisting around in the booth, I sat on my knees and took his face into my hands.

"The whole reason I wanted Nick was because I had this fantasy in my head about who I am and what kind of life would make me happy. A nice guy wouldn't have known what to do with me when I cried during sex. He wouldn't have pushed my buttons or helped me break down my walls. I was in love with a fantasy for so long, but what I feel for you is real. I wanted a normal guy, but I'm not normal. You make everything wrong with me feel right. Like my crazy is okay. Like my damage doesn't ruin me. I wanted safe and you seemed dangerous, but with you, I feel safer than I have my whole life. You do that for me in a way no other guy could."

After kissing him softly on the lips, I pulled back and smiled.

"And you're a jerk sometimes. You act like a beast with no rules and I need to accept you the way you accept me. I do most of the time, but sometimes I run because I think away from you is safer. Today, I knew I could only feel safe when I was with you. Not because you kick ass or have money. I just knew you would understand what that money meant to me because you understand me. Besides Tawny, you're the only person who's ever loved me like I needed to be loved. I promise I won't run anymore, Cooper."

The smile he gave me set my heart thumping hard and I could barely breathe when he kissed me softly. Expecting more heat from his embrace, I frowned at his tenderness. Was he angry with me? When his gaze lingered over my face, I knew he was studying the swelling and bruising.

"You love me," I said. "I make you nuts."

"Hell yeah, you do," he replied then added softer, "You're my girl and we're making one hell of a life together."

Cuddling closer, I felt like the crap of the day was gone. I was starting over right this moment. I was no longer the Farah always wanting what she couldn't have. Or the Farah who came to college pretending she was the person she hoped to be, instead of the person she truly was. I was just Farah Smith. The daughter of losers, I loved Cooper, missed my little sister, dreamed of being a teacher, and would fuck the rules when necessary. I was still a nerd in some ways, but I'd be that nerd on my own terms. Not to please anyone else. Not to be anyone else. I was me and fuck anyone who didn't like it.

I knew Cooper liked it as he grinned down at me. "I texted Tucker," he said after our food arrived. "Told him to find that bastard who hurt you and make sure he didn't run. Also, told him to move out all your stuff. You're not going back to that place."

"Good. I never want to see the apartment or my mom again."

Cooper grinned. "I love when you get feisty."

"Will we drive home in the rain?" I asked, glancing outside.

"There's a hotel next door. We could stay overnight after picking up a few things at the convenience store. You'll need pain meds soon and we'll hang out here until the storm passes. Then, we'll drive home."

"I'm living in your apartment?"

"Unless you want to live somewhere else?"

Thinking about it, I really didn't want to be anywhere without Cooper.

"I belong with you, but what about Tawny?" I asked, finally pulling myself away from him so I could eat my burger.

"She'll stay with us once she gets here."

"At your parents' house because there's no real space at the apartment?"

"We'll need to get a new place together. A fresh start somewhere with space for Tawny."

"Really?" I asked, staring in an overly excited way.

Giving me a gentle smile, he kissed my forehead. "Really, baby. I want to start over in a nice comfortable way. I want you to feel safe. I want your sister to feel that way too. As long as you feel good about stuff, I'll feel good too."

"I'm not going to leave you. I promise."

Still smiling, Cooper nodded. "I didn't want to get your hopes up just yet, but my guy thinks he might have a handle on Tawny's whereabouts. He's tracking her down now."

"What happens when he finds her though? My dad won't let her leave when she's seventeen and can still bring in money."

Cooper gave me an angry frown. "How did someone so amazing come from such shit stock? Man, your parents are evil fucks." Sighing, he cracked his neck. "My guy can handle your dad. He'll grab Tawny when she's alone and bring her here. Your dad can come looking for her if he wants, but that would be a mistake on his part. I'm not in the mood to put up with anyone messing with you."

Leaning against him, I smiled. "You are nice. The nicest boy ever."

Cooper laughed. "I've got many talents."

Soon, we ate in silence, though Cooper did give the waitress a hundred dollars to run to the pharmacy up the road and buy me pain medicine. By the time we finished eating, she had returned and I downed four Tylenols as my face really started to hurt.

The hotel next door was pretty high scale and we had a room with a king sized bed. Once we entered, I peeled off my wet shirt and headed for the shower. I expected Cooper to follow, but he stood at the door, staring at the ground.

"What's wrong?" I asked, returning to him.

"I pride myself on protecting those I love, but look at what happened to you."

Caressing his damp arm, I sighed. "You can't control what everyone does. Amy and her dick are reckless people. You being scary wasn't enough for them to care. They're the kind of people who think they'll always make it out fine. They'll win at the casinos. They'll pay off the loan shark. They'll just squeeze by all the trouble they bring on themselves. You can't reason with them."

Cooper gave me a weak smile. "I thought you were so prissy when we met and I wondered how you could ever fit into my life, but you understand a loser's bullshit in a way maybe I can't because I've had it too easy," he said, pulling off his shirt. "I'm not alone at the top after all. I have you."

"You'll always have me."

Kissing me gently but thoroughly, Cooper claimed me before stripping down. Both cold from sitting wet through dinner, we warmed inside the hot shower and were soon goofing around in bed. As Cooper sat against the headboard, I inched down until I had his cock in my hand.

When I licked the head, he inhaled hard and frowned. "If you think you'll cry, just stop. Don't push yourself."

"Roger that," I said, giving him a wink.

Relaxing, Cooper watched me leisurely explore him with my tongue. Just like he did, I tested what he liked. While I expected him to like it, I never imagined I'd feel so empowered by making him moan. As he grew thicker in my hand, I felt a nearly violent urge rush through me. All the tension was gone and I just knew suddenly.

Crawling up, I kissed him and wiggled my butt. So horny he didn't ask questions, Cooper eased himself inside me. My hands on his strong shoulders, I closed my eyes while my hips lifted and fell quickly. I didn't know where all the desperation came from, but I couldn't stop.

Cooper might have understood or maybe he was just his usual thorough self, but he caressed my clit gently as I moved faster. The orgasm building, I waited for a wall to take away the pleasure. Holding Cooper's gaze, I felt at peace in his embrace. Safer than ever before, stronger than I could have imagined, I felt the pleasure just keep building. The past faded and my dreams were no longer out of reach. All of the pain and fear disappeared until I was in this very moment with the man I loved with all of my heart. Finally moving past where the panic usually took over, I broke though the wall.

Never did I realize how badly I wanted to orgasm until it happened. More than waves of hot bliss, it was like tasting freedom. As the pleasure overwhelmed me, I closed my eyes and held onto Cooper. My face cradled against his neck, I soon settled my breathing before opening my eyes to find him smiling.

"One big ass wall just fell, baby," Cooper said, wrapping me tighter into his embrace. "You should have seen your face."

"I was with you, Coop, the whole time. Nowhere else and it felt perfect."

Wiping the tears from my cheeks, he stared into my eyes and I knew then we would never be apart again.

"More please," I whispered.

"Hell yeah," he said as I started moving again. "You lead. Show me what you want."

Grinning, I had all kinds of ideas for Cooper. My face might hurt, but the rest of me felt better than ever. As soon as I helped Cooper find relief, I wiggled free of his embrace and rested on my back.

"We're trying this again," I said, spreading my legs.

"You'll never want me to stop. It's addictive. Sure you can handle it?"

"No, but I'm feeling fearless tonight."

Cooper crawled towards me with that arrogant expression on his face. "You'll be my slave after this."

"Then, we'll be equal."

Laughing, Cooper let his gaze roll over my naked body. I knew he saw the bruise forming on my stomach where Amy kicked me. For a moment, I thought he might be more angry than horny. I shouldn't have worried.

Chapter Twenty Two

The next morning, we returned to the Johansson property. When Kirk and Jodi appeared, the look on his face upon seeing my black eyes made me worry Cooper would one day seem so cold and unyielding. Then, I figured Kirk likely hid his soft side for his wife and kids. He didn't know me yet and I wouldn't get a glimpse of the other Kirk. Still, I knew he was pissed and he and his boys would take care of things.

Jodi hugged me and told me it didn't look so bad. She also said her mother was a bitch, but we couldn't choose our birth family. We did have the power to build a new and better one though. When she hugged me for a second time, I melted into her embrace. My mother was gone from my life, but I had a new mom. One who saw my value in a way Amy never could. After lunch, Bailey and Sawyer insisted we play beauty salon where they braided my hair to make me feel pretty. I was a Johansson now. Finally, Cooper pulled me away from his family and we retreated to his apartment where I found all of my stuff boxed up. This was my new home.

The rest of the weekend was spent making up for lost time. Cooper clung to me and I was relieved to have him always nearby. While happy to be away from my mom and even happier to be with Cooper, I always felt uneasy with change. I also awaited word about Tawny who was still barricaded in the motel room. Dad hadn't returned and she was nearly out of food, but too scared to leave with the weirdoes hanging around. She was also penniless and couldn't buy anything even if she dared go out. I just prayed Cooper's guy found her soon.

Feeling guilty for enjoying my life with Cooper while my sister suffered, I could only focus on building something good in Ellsberg. Something Tawny would soon share. At Cooper's urging, I quit my job at Denny's. I should have been terrified to give up my only income, but I trusted Cooper and I were long term. He also reminded me about my nest egg. It was the security net I would never need, but would always have.

One afternoon when we left school in his truck, Cooper took a different route home. I didn't think much about it because I was too relieved by my latest quiz results. As we drove into a part of town full of subdivisions with big houses and parks, Cooper glanced at me and smiled.

"I want a kid."

"You're too competitive with Tucker."

"Maybe, but look at the deal I have with the family business. It's just me. Tucker can do manual, no brainer shit, but I'm stuck doing all of the heavy lifting. Bailey seems to get dumber every day and Sawyer is more than a decade from helping and that's assuming she wants to. Except for you, I'm alone. One day, when my kid takes over, I'd like to think he or she will have a few decent siblings to help out so they won't be alone on the top."

"That doesn't mean we need to start having them now."

"I was thinking about RVing with the kids like I did growing up and I imagined how we'd go during your breaks from teaching. I saw us young and I liked that better."

"How soon?"

Cooper laughed. "It's not like a trip to the store, Farah. I figure we'll get settled in. You'll finish the year and feel good about that then we'll let nature take its course."

"I come from fertile stock. Once I go off my birth control, it could happen fast."

"So it happens fast. Or it doesn't. We know what we must do and that's being together. We also must finish school and live in Ellsberg. Those are nonnegotiable. The rest are hopes. Like I hope to have a bunch of kids with at least a few non-morons in the bunch so they can help each other run the business. I hope they'll take over when you and I are young so we can travel. That's my hope, but who knows if it'll happen."

Sighing, I wouldn't mind starting a family as long as I knew I would finish school. Even if I never taught a single class, I wanted the accomplishment of gaining a degree.

"I don't know how good of a mother I'd be," I admitted. "I've never even held a baby and I wasn't exactly raised well."

Cooper pulled into a wooded cul-de-sac then parked in one of the driveways.

"If you take care of our kids the way you took care of your tables at work, they'll always be clean and well stocked."

Laughing, I rolled my eyes. "I take pride in my work."

"Yes, and you'll take pride in being a mother. Just because you came from shit doesn't mean you're shit. You're so much better than what you've known and I bet you'll be a fucking awesome mom."

"And you'll be an amazing dad."

"Hell yeah. I'm great with kids. I have this talent where I listen to them babble, but not too closely so I don't lose my mind."

Laughing again, I looked around. "Where are we?"

Grinning, Cooper opened his door then waited for me to walk around and join him.

"The guy who owns this house is looking to ditch it quick. Pop said it's a solid house. It just needs character. Basically, the whole inside is a beige turd. Plus, it'll need new floors and stuff. Let's go inside."

Holding Cooper's hand, I followed him up to the front door. Big and beautiful, the house felt empty and unloved. The lawn was overgrown with as much weeds as grass. Still, the large window above the front door was stunning.

"So your dad wants this house?" I asked, following him into the two-story foyer.

"Baby, what's my pop going to do with a little house like this?"

"Little? It's huge."

"For suburbia, but my parents wouldn't live here. It's for us."

"You want to live here?" I asked, breathing too fast.

"Now, I know it's bare bones and beige up the ass, but use your imagination."

Cooper tugged me towards double doors leading into a room. For some reason, one of the doors was painted red.

"This would be our office. Imagine two desks and all of your school stuff in here. You can shut the door and study when you get home from school."

Smiling full of panicked excitement, I stumbled along as Cooper led me to a nearby room with a missing light and torn up carpet.

"This is supposed to be the dining room. I don't see the point of a dining room, but I guess if we have a lot of people over, we can stick them in here."

Next, Cooper showed me the small guest bathroom then a room adjacent to the two-story family room.

"I wasn't sure what to do with this room when I looked around earlier. Then, I was thinking about how the basement can be fixed up and made into a game room. A man cave is what guys call it. So if I get a man cave, you need a chick cave so I thought we could make this room for you. A quiet spot where you can watch TV or read or do whatever you want."

Saying nothing, I just smiled like crazy while trying to imagine myself in this big house. Cooper directed me to the family room where more carpet was torn up.

"This guy and his friends trashed the place, but we can paint and put in new floors. The kitchen is a decent size and we'll make that nice too. Clean the whole place up and make it just like we want."

"You want to live in the suburbs?" I asked, standing in the kitchen with my hands on the island.

"No, but I want to live with you in the suburbs. My girl has a dream and I want it to come true. One day, we'll build that big house in the woods. For now, we can live here. It's not far from the college and stores. It's big enough for us, Tawny, and a kid or two. I can't bring all of my dogs, but a few will fit. It'll be comfortable. Unless you don't like it?"

"Coop, when Tawny and I daydreamed about living somewhere nice, we never dreamed of something this nice."

Grinning, he sighed. "I wasn't sure you could see past all the fucked up carpet and shit. It's a solid house though. Pop's right about that. It's in a nice quiet area with families. You could feel safe here. Now, let me show you upstairs."

We walked up one of the two staircases to a walkway. "The first thing we'd have to do," Cooper said, frowning, "is paint this fucking place. I can't stand beige. It looks like old dog shit."

"I don't care what color the walls are. This house is amazing."

Cooper stopped walking and crossed his arms. "It might not be the right house though. Standing up here, I'm not sure I like it as much as I thought."

Panic struck me because I was already imagining this as our house. I pictured a life with Cooper and our family here, but now he was changing his mind.

"Why are you crying, baby?" he asked, wiping my cheeks. "We'll find another house."

"Okay."

"But you like this one."

"I really do, but if you don't like it, we'll find something else."

Cooper kissed me softly. "I was just fucking with you. I love the house too."

Wiping away the tears, I glared at him. "Why would you fuck with me like that?"

"To make sure you were telling the truth. I don't want you being happy because you think it's your job to agree. I want you to tell me the truth. You just did so let's look at the bedrooms."

Irritated, I followed him down the walkway to two small bedrooms with a bathroom in between.

"Here's what I was thinking," he said, ignoring my anger. "Tawny will stay with us for as long as she wants, but these aren't big rooms. What if one room is her bedroom and the other is like her hangout space?"

"Two rooms?" I asked, losing my irritation. "She's never even had a bedroom to herself."

"Well, I take care of my family and my sister-in-law can't be shoved into a tiny bedroom." Grinning big at him, I stared until Cooper rolled his eyes. "I'm not proposing. Not for real until Tawny is here. I want you to get all squealy and you can't be truly happy until your sister is safe. Once she's here though, I'm going all out on the romance stuff. I'll propose the shit out of you."

Laughing, I wiped my eyes. "You love me."

"More than you can know. Speaking of loving," he said, giving me a wink, "let's check out the master bedroom where I plan to spend a lot of time inside you."

"Hmm...sounds nice."

Cooper tugged me down the walkway to the other end of the hall and a small bedroom.

"This can be the baby's room. We could stick a few kids in here. That way they're close to us and away from Tawny."

"This is nice, but I want to see where we'll make those babies."

Cooper gave me his horny expression then nudged me to the next room. "Imagine it with new floors, paint, less trash on the floor."

"I'm imagining the bed right here," I said, grinning. "Us on top of it...Hey, where are you going?"

Cooper disappeared into a closet then returned with a box. "We're trying out the house tonight to make sure we like it. Food and drink are in the kitchen. We'll sleep on this inflatable bed. I'm not interested in sleeping right now though."

"I haven't seen the whole house," I said as he tugged off his tee.

"There's a basement, a big yard, a few toilets. It's awesome. Here, let me help you with your pants."

Laughing, I tried to look at the master bathroom, but Cooper had my jeans around my thighs and I couldn't move.

"The bed, Coop," I teased, causing him to sigh.

As the bed inflated, Cooper removed the rest of our clothes. Then, he plugged the bed before walking on his knees towards me. He looked so silly buck naked and I was ready to tease him until his lips found my nipple.

Arms around him, I glanced around at a bedroom in need of attention. The house was like me in many ways. Having great potential, it just needed a little tender care. As Cooper rested me on my back and went about exploring from my neck to between my legs, I realized I was home. I also realized Cooper was right about oral sex. Now that I was used to it, I never wanted him to stop.

Chapter Twenty Three

Within hours of buying the house, Cooper had guys working on it. The whole process flew by because Kirk paid cash and the guy who owned it was in a hurry to leave town. I didn't ask why. Just like I didn't ask what happened to Amy and Tex. Certain things didn't interest me.

New floors, paint, and furnishings quickly turned the rundown house into a palace. Our first night with everything completed, Cooper and I christened each room including Tawny's.

Cooper's guy had retrieved Tawny from a shithole in nowhere Texas, but they couldn't fly to Kentucky because she was too scared. On the phone, she sounded terrified of Cooper's guy, Dad finding her, everything. I think those last weeks stuck in the motel had eaten away at what was left of her youth. She sounded hollowed out, but I promised I would see her soon. I told her about the house and her rooms, but she didn't understand. Along the way, Tawny had shut down and pulled so deeply into herself that I wasn't sure how to get her back.

The day she was expected to arrive, Cooper was in a weird mood. I think he worried I wouldn't pay attention to him once Tawny lived with us. I reassured him with sex against the kitchen counter. That usually helped.

Later, I was tense because the sun was setting and Tawny hadn't arrived. Cooper calmed me with sex on the couch then in the chair when the first try didn't do the trick. I was pretty relaxed physically when Cooper got the call that they were coming up the street. Mentally, I was wired and my heart hurt at the idea of something bad happening before I could see Tawny again.

Running out to the porch, I waited for the car and prayed nothing ruined the happiness I had found in Ellsberg. Cooper stood next to me and took my hand.

"You saved her," I said, out of breath and teary-eyed. "She would have died out there, but you saved her. You gave me back my sister."

"It's okay, baby."

Even nodding, I needed to see Tawny. Building this amazing life, I lived in a beautiful house with my beautiful Cooper. I enjoyed my dream of college. I had a new car so I didn't have to walk everywhere or bum rides. I would soon be married to a man who loved me so much that it hurt him when I was unhappy. I had everything except my best friend.

When the SUV pulled into the driveway, I took off running towards it, panicked something could still go wrong. Life might still shit on the Smith sisters. Inside the Suburban, Tawny fought to remove her seatbelt. By the time I reached her door though, she opened it and lunged into my arms.

Time stood still while we cried against each other on the driveway. Nearby, Cooper spoke with a tall dark haired guy. He had saved Tawny, but I could see why she had been anxious about him. The guy was at least a decade older than Cooper and those extra years made him harder than my sweet beast. While the men spoke, it was all background noise because life had given me everything I needed.

Tawny felt too thin and her face looked sickly, but I knew she would bounce back. Here with me and Cooper, she would be safe and happy. She would heal like I did with Cooper's help. One day, she would be whole again.

Finally, I stood and lifted Tawny to her feet. She walked nervously towards Cooper who admittedly looked pretty intimidating standing with his arms crossed. Even with all those muscles and tattoos, I saw the softness underneath his dark expression. My gentle Cooper was underneath the beast and soon Tawny would love him too.

Epilogue

I officially stopped dreaming of being Mrs. Prescott and embraced being me on the day my first child was born. While I still admired Mrs. Prescott and wanted her better qualities, I realized there was power in simply being Farah Delta Johansson.

Our baby was born in the same hospital as Cooper with his family sitting in the waiting room well past visiting hours. Rules were for pussies, Kirk announced. With Tawny and Cooper at my side, I felt ready to give birth even though my therapist warned it might trigger certain memories.

Having started seeing her months earlier, I mostly talked about easy things like growing up poor and moving around a lot. Eventually, we might talk about the uglier stuff, but I wasn't ready. The one advice my therapist gave me was to get an epidural. The less pain, the less likely memories would be triggered. So I sat comfortably for most of the ten hours I was in labor. We watched television and Cooper sang Hair of the Dog to the baby bump as a form of encouragement.

Later, after family and friends were gone, only Cooper, the baby, and I remained. He sat up against the headboard with me cuddled next to him. Our baby was awake, looking undaunted by the new experience.

Cooper couldn't stop staring at his daughter. As he held her out in front of him, I'd never seen him prouder. He also didn't seem the least bit nervous about being a dad.

As we admired Lily Delta Johansson, Cooper sighed. "With those lips, our girl will be a heartbreaker like her mom."

Grinning, I studied my baby. "With those dark eyes, I bet our girl will be a ballbuster like her daddy."

Cooper looked at me with the most amazing expression on his handsome face. If I hadn't been sure he loved me, this moment sealed the deal. He glanced at Lily then back at me and smiled.

"Hell yeah, she will."

Made in the USA
Charleston, SC
18 July 2015